'Do you want something to eat?'

'No thanks, I've just had something.'

'Are you sure?'

'Yes. I distinctly remember eating it.'

The donkey ambled across to the fire and stood watching the chickens on the spit.

'You know,' said Tarl, 'there's a secret to good chicken.'

'Oh, what's that?'

Tarl looked sadly at the birds, which were still cold and raw on one side, and were beginning to blacken on the other.

'Buggered if I know,' he replied.

'It might help if you turned the spits round.'

'That's a thought.'

The donkey shook its head.

'I've heard of cordon bleu,' it said, 'but your cooking should be cordoned off.'

'Oh, very funny.' Tarl picked up the big wooden spoon, scooped up some of the melted fat that had collected in the tray in front of the fire, and poured it over the birds. This was a tactic he'd only recently been told about. Before that, when he had heard people talking about basted chickens he had just assumed they didn't like chickens very much.

James Bibby has contributed to 'Not the Nine O'Clock News', 'Three of a Kind', 'OTT', 'The Lenny Henry Show' and countless other TV comedy shows. *Ronan's Rescue* is his second novel and throws up even more chuckles than the first. He lives on Merseyside, where he divides his time between writing scripts and looking after his rapidly expanding family. And he knows what it is to suffer – he's a Tranmere Rovers supporter.

By the same author

Ronan the Barbarian

RONAN'S RESCUE

Further translations
from the original Gibberish by

James Bibby

MILLENNIUM

Orion Paperbacks
A Millennium Book
First published in Great Britain by Millennium in 1996
This paperback edition published in 1997 by Orion Books Ltd,
Orion House, 5 Upper St Martin's Lane, London WC2H 9EA

A CIP catalogue record for this book is available from the
British Library.

ISBN: 0 75280 876 1

Printed and bound in Great Britain by
Clays Ltd, St Ives plc

For Collette

Acknowledgements

Grateful thanks are due to Charon Wood and Caroline Oakley for their expertise and guidance in editing the first two Ronan books. And once again I have to thank Richard S. Ball for copious help and hang-overs. (I don't know what the 'S' stands for, but it sure isn't snooker . . .)

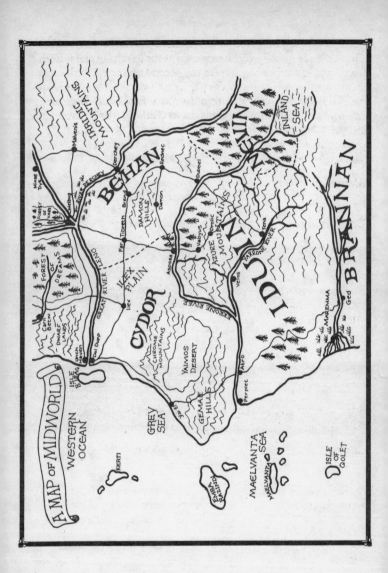

Readers who have previously experienced the first volume of the Chronicles of Ronan may be surprised at the paeans of praise with which the publisher has greeted the second volume. For the less credulous, here are some of the publisher's quotes, together with translations taken from *Rangvald's Plain English – Publishing Salespeak Dictionary* (available from Tarltrad Press (Welbug) Ltd, price 8 *tablons*).

'Epic . . .'	700 pages of turgid dross.
'Meticulously crafted . . .'	Written very slowly with a large quill pen.
'Confrontational . . .'	Lots of swearing.
'. . . hard-hitting . . .'	The author gets violent when drunk.
'. . . a writer unafraid to push back the boundaries of language . . .'	He can't spell, and as for his punctuation . . .
'. . . scholarly . . .'	Desperately dull.
'Still available from good bookshops everywhere.'	No one's bought it.
'A remarkable step forward in publishing . . .'	We've dropped a right bollock with this one.
'Critically acclaimed . . .'	There goes our Christmas bonus.
'. . . this eagerly awaited second volume . . .'	. . . of a two-book contract. We've been waiting to get rid of the untalented little get . . .
'You won't be disappointed . . .'	. . . unless you buy the book, that is.

You have been warned.

ISOLATED

The climate in the city of Atro is hot. Very hot. And so is everything else – especially the food. Atro is renowned for dishes such as Mulampos, *a highly-spiced and semi-lethal meat stew famous throughout Midworld. Its unfortunate side-effects have given rise to many jokes, such as 'What's the difference between your girlfriend leaving you and eating a plate of* Mulampos? *With one, the bottom falls out of your world. With the other, the world falls out of your bottom.'*

But be warned. Some Atrovian restaurants serve dishes that are even more dangerous. Guajillo's, a café-bar in the Street of Knives, is renowned for its Caheros, *a spicy soup so caustic that armourers use it as a cleansing agent. It will dissolve and remove dirt, rust, verdigris and even dead bodies from inside a suit of armour in seconds. And Satan's Grill at the Inn-Cubus on Riverside serves a* Matsikas *so hot that it is rumoured to have caused severe throat and mouth burns in full-grown dragons. In fact, the Great Fire of Atro is thought to have been started by a stray plate of* Matsikas *coming into contact with the restaurant curtains . . .*

The Rough Chronicle to . . . Iduin

Nuddo the Talkative thrust the tip of his sword deep into the burning-hot sand. Wiping his dripping brow with the leather sweat-band that was wrapped about one muscular forearm, he leant on the sword and surveyed the baying mass of humanity that packed the vast stadium of the Cumanceum. Above him the sun beat down with the force of a blacksmith's hammer, and the white marble walls of the podium that enclosed the arena shimmered in the heat haze.

'Good crowd in today,' he said conversationally. 'For a Thursday.'

The mortally wounded gladiator who lay stretched out at his feet moaned gently, and then summoning the last vestiges of his rapidly ebbing strength he began to drag himself painfully towards the distant iron-barred gate that was the arena's only entrance. The blood flowing from the massive wound in his abdomen left a red trail behind him, a trail that steamed in the vicious heat of the sun. As he crawled onwards, inch by inch, his breath came in ragged gasps.

Nuddo watched him dispassionately for a while, and then pulling his sword free of the ground he examined its red-stained tip. Bending, he picked up a handful of sand and wiped the blade clean, and then he began to stroll alongside his victim.

'Listen to them!' he continued, gesturing towards the howling spectators. 'Kill, kill, kill! That's all they ever think about. No interest in the finer points of combat. All they want is blood. I sometimes wonder why we bother. All that practice, all the fancy sword-work. And for what? Twenty *tablons* a day plus insurance. Not much of a living, is it? Well, not for you. Not for much longer, anyway.'

He paused, and looked at his panting victim with concern. 'You are insured, I hope? I'd hate to think of your wife and little ones being auctioned off into slavery, just because you've snuffed it and your insurance wasn't up to date. I'm with the Perplec, myself. The Perplec Regal Insurance (Contracted Killers Section). Love their adverts, don't you? "We're PRICKS and we're proud of it." Well, you have to laugh. That's what I always say.'

Unable to drag himself any farther, the wounded gladiator lay gasping on the sand. One hand fumbled in a small pouch at his waist and dragged out a ceramic pendant on which was a small portrait of a woman and three children. He lay there, his breath becoming more and more ragged, his clouding eyes fixed on the portrait, while around them the roar of the crowd grew louder.

Nuddo looked up to the section of podium where Myad the Long-winded, Leader of the Council and First Scapegoat of Atro, had just risen from his seat and was peering about myopically in an attempt to gauge the will of the crowd.

'Look at him, the pompous old git. We could be here all afternoon, waiting for him to make his mind up. Well, *I* could. Still, that's one good thing. At least you won't have to sit through any more of his interminable speeches. Always look on the bright side, hey?' Nuddo smiled down at the dying gladiator and scratched his armpit.

'Oh, well, look at that!' he continued as Myad, to the delight of the crowd, gave the thumbs-down signal. 'That *is* a shame, that is. I thought you deserved better than that. Oh, by the way. Sorry about the little trick with the fake limp, but as my old Dad used to say, all's fair in love and war. Randy old sod that he was. Well, see you in the next world.'

Reaching down, he pulled the man's head back, and with one swift sweep of his sword sliced it clean off. And then lifting the severed head by the hair he paraded it around the edge of the arena, calmly acknowledging the plaudits of the spectators.

Up on the podium, Myad the Long-winded viewed the ecstatic reaction of the crowd with relief. Next week was Retribution Week, and he badly needed to increase his standing with the general public. Otherwise, he and the rest of the Ruling Council were quite likely to end up facing Nuddo themselves the week afterwards.

Atro, one of the four Great Cities of Iduin, has a system of political representation that is the envy of most other cities. Quite simply, all elected representatives are bound by law to a strict code of morality. If a politician is caught telling a lie, his tongue is cut out. If he is caught accepting bribes or favours, his hand is cut off. (One result of all this is that Atrovian politicians have remarkably pure sex-lives.) And to renege on an election promise is a crime punishable by death.

The system dates back to the time of Adrian the Licentious, in whose dissolute reign the Cumanceum was constructed. He ordered it to be built in imitation of the Terrordrome[1] at Velos, hoping that regular sporting events and race meetings might have a pacifying effect on a population that was seething with discontent. However, it wasn't long before his own depraved tastes began to hold sway and athletics meetings and chariot races were replaced by gladiatorial contests, wild beast fights and public executions.

[1] For information on the Terrordrome, and other unfamiliar Midworldian items, see Appendix One.

The people, of course, loved all this bloodshed, but it didn't stop them from rising up in the Great Revolt of '71 and throwing Adrian and his advisers to his own wild animals. The spectacle of such a hated ruler being torn apart by half-starved *lenkats* was enjoyed so much by the people that, when the First Revolutionary Council was deposed a year later, the councillors were horrified to find themselves being frogmarched down to the Cumanceum by a populace that was looking forward to repeating the experience.

The Second Revolutionary Council was then elected, and they ruled Atro benignly but nervously for a year, after which they in their turn met painful deaths in the Cumanceum's torrid arena. The people were really beginning to get a taste for it by now. The Third Revolutionary Council had to be literally dragged along to the council building after the elections and were forcibly sworn into office. They spent the next year hiding under their desks and passing legislation such as the Free-Female-Slave-With-Every-Tax-Payment Act, and the Unlimited Sexual Favours For All Male Voters Bill, in a desperate attempt to curry favour with the electorate. They were very popular with the (mainly male) electorate, but after the Women's Revolt of '74 they too were thrown to the wild animals, along with quite a few fat old stand-up comedians, several philandering husbands, and a large number of single men who had never bothered to get in touch again afterwards.

The Council of Women then ruled for several years, during which time a number of interesting new laws found their way onto the statute book. Crimes punishable by imprisonment included Using the Latrine Without Due Care and Attention and Leaving Splashes All Over the Floor, Wilfully Leaving a Washbasin Littered with Hundreds of Tiny Beard Fragments after Shaving, and Leaving the Latrine Seat in an Upright Position when Specifically Asked a Hundred Times Not To Do So.

However, eventually it all settled down again and a truly integrated and democratic system of government emerged. But the conduct of the members of the Council of Atro is still bound by a rigorous code of laws, and as a result their rule is about as benevolent as it is possible to be without intimate physical contact.

*

4

In the Cumanceum, the day's events were gradually drawing to a close. Myad the Long-winded was slumped back in his seat, watching the laughing, cheering crowd with obvious relief. Down in the arena Nuddo had finished his lap of honour and was standing by the open gate, autographing programmes and throwing them up to the spectators. Behind him a beast-master was herding a puzzled and frightened flock of assorted sheep, goats and donkeys out through the gate onto the burning sand, ready for the final event. From the holding pens beneath ground level the excited snarls and growls of ferocious *lenkats* could be heard. They knew they were about to be fed.

Nuddo shook his head in exasperation. It really annoyed him that there was nothing a civilised crowd liked more to round off a day's entertainment than watching a group of small, terrified and defenceless creatures being ripped to pieces by savage predators. Somehow, he felt, it detracted from the grandeur and the prestige of the occasion. He loved the whole gladiator thing; the machismo of the weaponry and the armour, the adulation of the crowd, the burning sun on his back as he stalked his opponent, the thrill of his sword plunging home, the smell of freshly spilt blood in the afternoon . . .

He wrinkled his nose in distaste. There was a smell all right, but it wasn't blood. Someone should have hosed those *klatting* goats down. They stank worse than the Cumanceum slave-pits, deep underground. He glowered across to where two of the donkeys were simultaneously braying in fear and evacuating their bowels.

'Oh, wonderful!' he muttered to himself. 'How classy! What a tasteful way to round off the proceedings.'

Beside him, one of the donkeys was pensively watching the rest of the animals milling about in panic. It was small and brown and moth-eaten. It sighed sadly.

'I'm only guessing,' it said, 'but I reckon that if you were about to be ripped apart by a pack of starving *lenkats*, you might find that a bit of liquefaction of the bowels had set in.' Nuddo stared in amazement as it continued. 'But then it's all right for you humans. Oh yeah. You get a sword and one opponent at a time. You want to try going out there armed with just a few teeth and some hooves. You've no idea what us ungulates wouldn't give for opposable thumbs at a time like this.'

'You can talk!' gasped Nuddo. The donkey raised its head and stared at him.

'Well, that's not going to do me much good, is it?' it muttered. 'I mean, what are you suggesting? I should try distracting the *lenkats* with a few amusing anecdotes? I should bore them to death? Reason with them? Convert them to vegetarianism, perhaps?'

It put its head on one side and gazed at him like someone on a diet eyeing up a plateful of cream cakes. Nuddo felt a shiver run down his spine. He took an involuntary step backwards.

'By the way,' it continued, 'I wouldn't make any more smart-arse comments about my little mates over there. 'Cos you won't find it easy holding a sword with no fingers left. *Comprenez*?'

Then it turned and trotted briskly out into the arena. Nuddo the Talkative opened his mouth to reply, but nothing emerged. For the first time in his life, Nuddo couldn't think of a single thing to say.

Up in the stands, the hum of excitement reached a crescendo as the great metal gate closed behind the terrified animals and a massive iron cage slowly but smoothly rose up through a trap-door hidden in the sand at the opposite end of the arena. Inside the cage six large *lenkats* were hurling themselves at the bars in feverish excitement, their sleek oily fur bristling angrily and their razor-sharp teeth snapping with hunger. Each wore a narrow collar of a different colour.

Above them the spectators were betting feverishly on the outcome of the imminent slaughter. A week ago, the *lenkats* had set a new record, ripping apart and devouring every single prey animal inside three minutes. The smart money today was on this record to be beaten.

'Fifty *tablons*!' yelled someone. 'Fifty on the green collar to make the first kill!'

'A hundred!' shouted someone else. 'A hundred on the red to kill three!'

'Eighty says they beat the record!' called a frail old woman near the front. She was flushed with excitement and was frenziedly waving a bunch of five-*tablon* notes in the air.

'Two hundred!' said a fourth voice, and though it was slurred with alcohol and no louder than the rest it seemed to carry through the humid air, reaching every ear. 'Two hundred on that donkey to kill a *lenkat*!'

For a moment there was a stunned silence, and every head turned to peer at the small, seedy guy who had offered this ridiculous bet. He was sitting right at the front and was definitely the worse for drink, but he was clutching a very fat wad of notes indeed. As they stared he hiccuped, and an amiable but drunken smile spread slowly across his face like the tide coming in.

'Any takers?' he mumbled.

Two *klatting* hundred? thought the crowd, as one. On a donkey?? To kill a *LENKAT*?? Yeah, gimme some of that, ya mug!

Within seconds the man was surrounded by a densely packed mass of humanity who were waving money, yelling offers of odds, and jostling like a swarm of bees all trying to get at the same flower. And in their eagerness to take advantage, no one noticed that for a mug punter the little guy seemed to have a remarkable ability to calculate odds quickly.

Below them the small brown donkey was watching this with a vaguely satisfied air. It had trotted round to the rear of the *lenkat* cage, while the rest of the sheep, goats and donkeys were yammering with terror at the other end of the arena, as far away from the cage as they could get. Then, as the starting drum began to beat, it froze, blending in with the sand on which it stood.

The crowd surged forwards, suddenly silent with expectation, and then the drum-roll reached a crescendo and stopped dead, the cage door dropped, and the *lenkats* burst out as though spat and hit the ground running. They sped across the sand towards their prey, a sleek brown wave of destruction. One moment the far end of the arena was awash with terrified animals, the next it was littered with quivering chunks of glistening flesh, and five of the *lenkats*, their blood-lust sated, were gorging themselves.

The sixth and smallest, however, had been too slow off the mark to make a kill. It was prowling round snarling at the others, needing to hunt something down, to feel the kicking and hear the squealing as it ripped the life from some unfortunate creature before it would be willing to feed. And at that moment the small brown donkey at the far end of the arena trotted into view from behind the cage.

The *lenkat* took off as though someone had shoved a handful of *mulampos* up its rear end. It raced across the sand and flung itself in a great leap finely calculated to land it right on the little donkey's back . . . but at the last moment the donkey dropped to the ground and rolled over, and as the *lenkat* sailed past its head it lashed out. The *lenkat* hissed in pain as the donkey's razor-sharp teeth severed the tendons in its left hind leg, and it crashed to the ground in a fountain of sand and rolled over and over, coming to rest in a tangled furry heap at the foot of the podium. Roaring in pain and fury it struggled up and turned to attack again, only to be met by a sight that rooted it to the spot with surprise. The donkey was hammering towards it at a furious pace, its little hooves churning up the sand, and before the *lenkat* could move it struck again, teeth slashing, slicing through the thick fur and muscular flesh of the predator's neck to sever the arteries deep within. Yellow blood fountained in a huge arc and splashed against the white marble podium, then gradually died down, and the *lenkat* was merely a lifeless huddle of fur against the wall.

For a moment you could have heard a pin drop – and not a metal one either, but a plastic one dropping onto a bed of feathers in a padded cell several hundred yards away. And then ninety-nine percent of the Cumanceum erupted in absolute delight, cheering and yelling their hearts out. The rest stared in horror at the still-twitching body of the *lenkat* before switching their gaze to the small, seedy guy, who was leaping up and down and shouting delightedly to the victorious donkey. Rather suspiciously, they seemed to know each other.

'Yo, Puss! Way to go, kid!' he shouted, and waved a handful of currency in the air. 'Beautiful! Just look at all the dosh we've made! We've fleeced these suckers up here!'

The donkey was looking a touch nervously along the arena to where the other *lenkats* were voraciously cleaning up the remaining fragments of flesh.

'Er, Tarl . . . it might be an idea if we left,' it said. 'Like, now! If it's all the same to you, that is.'

'Yeah. Er . . . yeah. Right.' Tarl, the small seedy guy, was beginning to realise that some of the 'suckers' were looking a little aggrieved. A low murmur of annoyance was running around those nearby.

'It's a fix!' grumbled someone.

'We've been robbed!' muttered someone else. A squat but muscular warrior drew his sword and planted himself in front of Tarl.

'The bet's off,' he said. 'Give me my money back. Or else.'

Tarl stared at him a touch blearily, then stuffed the fistful of money inside his jerkin. Reaching down he picked up a half-empty bottle of red wine, took a long swig, and then grinned cockily at the warrior. '*Klat* off, snot-face,' he told him happily.

The warrior's face flushed dark red with fury. Snarling, he swung his sword back to deliver a scything blow. Tarl seemed to shimmer for a fraction of a second and then suddenly he was gone, and in his place stood a large and very solid iron anvil. The warrior's sword smashed into this with a reverberating 'clang', and then he was leaping about, swearing viciously and clutching a sword-arm that felt as though it had been kicked by a carthorse.

Down in the arena, the donkey had its eyes screwed tightly shut, as though waiting for something to happen. It opened one eye and looked around, and seemed a little perturbed to find that it was still in the Cumanceum.

'Oh, nice going, bollock-brain!' it muttered to itself. 'I might have known you'd screw up.'

At the far end the five remaining *lenkats* were squabbling over the last fragment of goat carcass. As this disappeared down the gaping maw of the largest the others stared about them, looking for something else to prey on. As one, they caught sight of the donkey, and with a series of blood-curdling roars and howls they raced down the arena towards it.

The donkey stood waiting stoically. It knew it might be a match for one *lenkat* at a time, but taking on all five was going to be like trying to stop a large, powerful blender by sticking your head inside it. However, it didn't have much option. Running was out – there was nowhere to run to. Flying its way to freedom or burrowing out through the sand might have been possible if it had had wings or large powerful paws, but once again the donkey was faced with the eternal fact that in normal, every-day life, hooves were bugger-all use, really. And so it stood there and waited.

The fastest of the *lenkats* hurled itself at the donkey, its deadly jaws spread wide . . . and the donkey vanished into thin air as though someone had turned it off at the switch. The *lenkat* hit the sand in a tangle of legs, teeth and fur, and came to rest against the podium beside the corpse of its fellow. The other four, robbed of their prey, howled in rage, and then for want of anything better to do, began ripping the corpse apart.

The crowd went wild. Watching a herd of inoffensive farm animals getting torn apart was all good fun, but for one of them to turn round and kill a *lenkat*, and then actually to get away afterwards! Wonderful! And so they stamped and cheered and applauded, and in his seat above the podium Myad the Long-winded smiled for the first time since election day. But behind the arena gate Nuddo the Talkative scowled furiously and swore at the beast-master. For the first time in years, he'd been completely upstaged, and not by some other warrior, either, but by a scruffy little donkey!

Nuddo the Talkative was not a happy bunny.

The customers of Ratcrap's Ale-house in Atro's East Side were very happy indeed, for it was Tuesday, and as the badly drawn and badly spelt notice above the bar proclaimed, 'Tuesday Nite's are Happy Nite's at Ratcrap's'.

Ratcrap, a half-orc with a nose for business and a face like a diseased lung, had come up with the idea of 'Happy Nite' in order to counteract the effect of a new wine-bar that had opened up just down the road. The basic idea was that you paid full price for your first drink, then for each subsequent one you paid ten per cent less than the previous one. So if the first round cost 100 bronze *tablons*, the second would cost 90, the third 81, the fourth 73, and so on. All Atrovians love a bargain, and so every Tuesday Ratcrap's would be full of people trying to drink enough to get down to single figure percentages of the usual price. And as a result, they all got so pissed that they totally failed to notice that Ratcrap was grossly short-changing them.

Ratcrap was making an absolute fortune.

The customers lining the bar were so intent on their drinking that no one noticed when Tarl suddenly materialised out of nowhere into a seat in the corner. He was still holding the bottle of wine and wearing the cocky grin he had used on the squat warrior, and he had a massive wad of banknotes protruding from his jerkin.

He looked around at the familiar surroundings, and inhaled deeply. The smell of stale beer, elf-weed and fresh vomit was oddly comforting, and he had clicked his shaking fingers at the barmaid for his usual pint before he realised that there was something lacking about the scene. There were plenty of humans lined up at the bar. There were a few half-elves and a couple of dwarves. There were tables and chairs and an awful lot of drinks. But the place was decidedly short of donkeys.

Tarl's jaw dropped open and a look of absolute horror crossed his face. Quickly he mouthed a spell, stumbling over the words, but nothing happened. He tried again, his eyes closed, his hands stretched out in front of him. The tendons in his skinny neck stretched taut with effort and the veins throbbed in his arms. A sheen of sweat stood out on his brow, and his hands clenched into claws.

Suddenly there was a small explosion of air and the donkey materialised in front of him, eyes screwed shut and every muscle in its small body braced. Tarl gave a huge sigh of relief and fell backwards against the rear of his seat, and the donkey opened one eye and peered round before throwing an accusing stare at Tarl.

'You cut that a bit fine,' it grumbled.

'I got the spell wrong,' muttered Tarl miserably. 'I couldn't . . . I mean, the words just wouldn't come.' His voice stumbled to a halt, and he held up one hand. It was still shaking visibly. 'I guess I may have had a drink too many or something. I dunno. My memory ain't what it . . . er . . .' He paused, and tried to remember exactly what his memory had been, but with no success. His hand slowly reached out for the wine-bottle as though acting independently from the rest of his body.

The barmaid swayed across and placed a foaming mug of Big Ollie's Patent Stomach Enlarger (a troll-brewed beer) in front of him. The donkey looked decidedly unimpressed.

'Wonderful,' it said. 'That speaks volumes, that does. Things to do, in order of importance. One, find a nice seat in the pub. Two, order a pint. Three, um, er, oh yes, let's see if we still have time to rescue any friends of ours who might be getting torn apart by wild animals in the Cumanceum.'

Tarl tried to think of something to say, but all that came out was, 'Can I get you a drink?'

The donkey looked even less impressed.

'You pranny!' it said. 'We're supposed to be trying to rescue our mate Ronan, but in the four weeks since we got to this hell-hole of a city you've turned into a complete piss-head, and you were bad enough before. I mean, I have seen creatures with a higher alcohol content than you, but they were all in big glass jars on a laboratory shelf. I nearly got killed this afternoon, and for what? For you to get enough money to be pissed for a month. Well, sorry, pal, but I've had enough. I'm off.'

It gave him one last angry look before turning and plodding to the door. It stopped briefly at a table to remove a large steak from the plate of someone who had just gone to the bar, and then pushed its way out into the street, chewing hungrily.

Tarl sadly watched it go. He felt he ought to do something, but he couldn't think what. His brain just wouldn't work any more. He looked down at the wine-bottle in his hand, which had suddenly emptied, and shook his head in perplexity. What the *klat* had happened to him?

For most of his adult life, Tarl had worked hard. Very hard. He had dedicated himself to doing what he did best – and that was having a seriously good time. As he liked to say, it isn't easy having fun. You have to work at it. And so he had. He'd been thrown out of every casino in the northern lands. He had conned his way into nearly every night-club. There was hardly a pub in which he hadn't managed to get a free drink.

And then one night he'd absconded from the place where he was working (the Blue Balrog night-club in Orcville) with the contents of the till in his pocket. Well, they were called the takings, weren't they? So that's what he'd done. Taken them. He had decided to head for the city of Welbug and have a few days in the casinos, and his path had led him through the wilderness of the Nevacom Plains. But here he'd fallen in with a half-starved and completely savage feral donkey, and with a young black warrior called Ronan who was on a quest to track down the man who had killed his father. And for some reason they had both taken a shine to him.

The next couple of weeks had been the strangest and most satisfying of his life. The three of them had discovered that Ronan's target was no simple every-day thug, but was a powerful warrior-mage called Nekros, who was at the heart of a plan to seize control of all the major cities of Baq d'Or. They had joined forces with Tyson, the Champion of Welbug, who was quite the most attractive female warrior Tarl had ever met, and for whom Ronan had fallen, hook, line and sinker. They had sought the help of Anthrax, an extremely laid-back but powerful wizard, and Tarl had discovered that he himself was one of the few people who had inherent magical powers. And they had met Nekros face to face and destroyed him[2].

But at the very moment of victory Ronan had been kidnapped by a sorceress called Shikara, who appeared to have lecherous designs on his body. Tyson, who was every bit as taken with Ronan as he was with her, had vowed to rescue him, Tarl had vowed to help her, and the donkey (which, thanks to the wizard, had acquired the ability to speak) had vowed that it might as well tag along just for the hell of it.

However, there was one major problem. They hadn't the faintest idea where Shikara had taken their comrade. Tarl, rather over-confident in his new-found ability with magic, had tried a *Locate Person* spell. This had been very embarrassing, as for best results it helps if you hold something belonging to that person in your hand, and the only thing they had which was in any way connected with Ronan was Tyson herself. And so one minute Tarl had been standing there clutching a highly suspicious female warrior, muttering the spell and going bright red, and the next minute this massively powerful counter-spell had come rocketing out of the blue and had nearly fried his brain. He had been lucky in that his hold over his own spell was tenuous, and also that his nervous system had become inured to sudden overload by years of substance abuse, but even so all the wax in his ears melted, and he was out cold for twelve hours.

When he finally came round, all he'd got for his trouble was a headache that lasted for two weeks and a vague impression that

[2] These exploits are chronicled in *Ronan the Barbarian*.

the counter-spell had come from somewhere hot. Disheartened, the three of them had set off on the long journey back to Welbug. Here they had conferred with Anthrax, who was currently staying at Tyson's establishment, The Dragon's Claw. The young wizard had seemed quite confident, and had dragged a strange metal object covered in dials and switches from out of his elegant leather suitcase.

'Well, we could easily trace him with a routine spell,' he had drawled in his well-modulated tones, 'but this does seem like rather a good opportunity to try out a little invention of mine. I call it a thaumatometer. You see, magic is just another form of kinetic energy, and as such is quantitative and measurable. This little machine is able to track down and evaluate areas of high kinetic energy, and to monitor sudden changes in electrostatic density. Thus we can locate and pinpoint any outbursts of acute sorcery with a fair degree of accuracy.'

Here the wizard had paused and stared resignedly at Tarl, who was gazing blankly at him with his mouth open.

'We do a spell with this magic box,' the wizard had added, and Tarl had nodded in comprehension. He had understood that bit.

And so Tarl, Tyson and Puss the donkey had watched as the wizard fiddled with dials and switches. The machine had started to hum, and the little needles in the various dials quivered. The wizard had been muttering to himself.

'Hm, yes, well it seems to be picking up signals . . . oh, now then, what have we —'

At this point the hum of the machine had suddenly turned into a penetrating scream, every needle had shot up to the top of its dial, there had been a loud explosion, several balls of smoking white light had exploded out of the wizard's body and narrowly missed the others, and he had been hurled backwards across the bed. A stench of singed hair had filled the room.

When the smoke had cleared, Anthrax was sitting against the wall with a stunned look on his face, holding the fused mass of metal that had been his thaumatometer. Wisps of acrid black smoke were curling up from his stylish and expensive suit, which had been charred to fragments, and most of his hair had fallen out.

'Well,' he'd muttered dazedly, 'I think we can take it that Shikara doesn't want to be found. And speaking personally, if that is an example of her ability then I for one don't want to find her.'

However, neither Tyson nor Tarl had been prepared to give up that easily. If using magic to find their friend was too dangerous, then they would just have to get out there and look for him on foot. And as Tarl had put it, someone with Shikara's looks and ability was going to get noticed. If they searched long enough, they'd find her.

Anthrax reckoned that his thaumatometer was picking up a reading a fair way south of Welbug when it was hit by the counter-spell, and this had tied in with Tarl's impression of somewhere hot. And so Tarl, Tyson and the donkey had headed south into Behan. By the time they got to the city of Far Tibreth, however, the magnitude of their task was beginning to hit home. The southlands were a pretty large place. Tyson suggested that they would cover the ground twice as fast if they split up, and she had set off alone on the East Road to Brend. Tarl and Puss had travelled south-west to Asposa, and thence down the river Errone to the city of Atro. And here it had all started to go wrong.

It hadn't really been Tarl's fault. It was the magic. He still hadn't got used to the fact that he could cast spells. In Tyson's company he had behaved himself, but letting Tarl loose with his magical powers was rather like leaving a child alone in a sweet-shop.

And he didn't know his own strength. The first spell he had tried was turning a large flagon of water into Cydorian brandy, and it had worked so well that when he woke up two days later in a bush in someone's back garden he couldn't remember how he got there or what his name was, and it had take him four hours to regain the use of the right-hand side of his face.

For a week or two after that he'd had a really good time. On occasions his conscience had managed to make itself noticed and he had tried sniffing around for traces of Shikara or Ronan, but nobody had heard anything, and he kept getting side-tracked by parties and card-games. He had told himself that he ought to move on, that his friend was depending on him, but Atro was a fun city, and he had kept putting it off.

And then he had started getting the magic wrong.

As with most things in Tarl's life, it had begun in a bar. He'd had a few drinks in the Red Gryphon and had got fed up with paying for his own, and so he'd decided to cast a *Spell of Benevolence* over a prosperous-looking merchant who had just come in. Unfortunately, being a little drunk he didn't get it quite right. Instead of smiling at Tarl and asking what he'd like to drink, the merchant had stalked across to him and had started violently smashing his head against the bar-top. Later, when he regained consciousness, Tarl had realised that he must have cast a *Spell of Malevolence* by mistake.

Again, like most things in his life, once he had started making mistakes he found it impossible to stop. He'd get a bit drunk, try a spell, slur his words, and it would come out all wrong. Sadly, it was always he who seemed to suffer as a result.

For example, one day he'd woken up with a foul hangover and had tried a *Cures Pain* spell. It had somehow got transmuted into a *Cause Pain*, and for the rest of the day it had felt as though he was back in the Red Gryphon, having his head smashed against the bar. Then there was the time someone had tried to mug him late at night outside the Black Nazgul Café. He had used a *Hurl Fireball*, one of the most basic magic spells, but as soon as he'd muttered the words he had felt this horrid tickling in his throat. For a few seconds he had stood there hawking and retching violently, and then he'd suddenly sicked up this foul mass of matted fur which had hurtled towards the horrified mugger and struck home with a sound like someone pulling a boot out of very deep mud. Tarl had to admit that it had been very effective, although he hadn't even known that there was such a spell as a *Hurl Fur-ball*.

But the worst time of all had been a few days back. He had been hitting the orcish brandy in some seedy little bar on the Vendai Strip. They had a guy playing the piano there, but he was playing it really badly and getting right on Tarl's nerves. He was a very big guy, however, and so Tarl (who only believed in picking fights with people who were *A*, much smaller than him, and *B*, unconscious) had surreptitiously cursed him. That had worked OK, but unfortunately he had also cursed the bar's owner. Never again, he had vowed the next day, would he try putting a curse on anyone who had a very large pianist. It had stung like buggery for hours.

And now he'd cocked up again, and his friend had nearly got

16

killed in the arena as a result. Unsurprisingly, Puss had had enough. Tarl was grateful and quite moved that the donkey had hung around as long as it had. It'd kept an eye on him whenever he'd passed out (and come to think of it, he'd passed out rather a lot recently), and had probably saved his life on a couple of occasions. Like that time a few nights ago when he'd fallen asleep in a little alley off the Street of Bones. He'd been woken up by an agonised scream to find Puss standing over him with a blood-soaked muzzle, and three half-orcs fleeing down the street. One of them had been screaming fit to burst. Beside Tarl on the ground had lain a bitten-off hand with a razor-sharp blade still clutched in its lifeless claws.

Tarl shook his head, and looked at the empty wine-bottle again. What the *klat* had happened to him? The drink and the gambling, that was what. After a life spent indulging himself, the first tiny fragment of responsibility that had come along had proved too much for him, and he'd taken refuge in having a good time.

Suddenly Tarl could feel a seed of resolution growing inside him. This was a turning-point. He could go after Puss and they could head off and search for Ronan until they found him, or he could stay here, drink himself into oblivion, and spend the rest of his (probably short) life using magic to keep himself in beer, food and fun. Let's face it, he thought, I'm drinking and gambling too much already. One more of each won't hurt.

'Hey,' he yelled to the barmaid. 'Bring me a beer.'

As she brought across another foaming tankard he fumbled in his pocket and dragged out a silver coin.

'OK,' he said. 'If you call it right I stay here and get drunk. Well, drunker. If you're wrong then I go look for my friends. So call it. Tits or bums[3].'

He flicked the coin in the air. The barmaid eyed him dubiously. 'Tit,' she said. Tarl wasn't sure whether this was a call or an opinion, but it didn't really matter. The coin had landed on the beer-soaked table-top and there, smiling up at him, was the image of a pair of buttocks.

The barmaid watched as, with a happy grin on his face, Tarl tossed her the coin and then weaved his way to the door.

[3] The rather tasteless images on Atrovian coins are another legacy of Adrian the Licentious, who decided that what the currency really needed was livening up a bit.

17

'What a happy little tosser,' she thought, and began to wipe down the table-top.

The donkey was standing in the shadows of the alley just off the Street of Bones. It had found out by trial and error that this was one of the best places in town for mugging pizza delivery-boys, and somewhere in the distance it could smell a Hot-spice Special. Its nostrils whiffled delicately as it sought to separate the appetising meaty pizza-smells from the countless other odours that mingled on the evening air. Then suddenly every single scent was completely swamped by the familiar smell of stale beer, wine, elf-weed smoke and human sweat. The donkey sighed.

'No,' it said, without looking round. 'Whatever stupid idea you've thought up for making some money, I'm not interested.'

Tarl crouched down beside it and laid one hand on its back.

'Look, I'm sorry, Puss,' he said. 'I went off my head for a bit. But I have this problem, see. Always have had. It's my legs. They just won't walk past taverns.'

'What a pity.'

'And I'm no good with responsibility. I just want to run and hide.'

'Shame.'

'I know I'm weak-willed and spineless –'

'And they're just your good points.'

'– but I can change.'

'Oh, yeah?'

Tarl stood up and scowled at Puss, but the donkey still refused to look back. Its nostrils whiffled again. It could hear the distant footsteps of the pizza delivery-boy approaching. Tarl tried once more.

'Listen, I feel really shitty about all this.'

'Ah, diddums,' answered Puss, in the sort of voice normally used by elderly madwomen when talking to three-month old babies.

'I realise I've been a crap friend, and I've let you all down –'

'Has he been a naughty boy? Has he?'

'– and I've been drinking too much –'

'Ah, wuzzum an ickle piss-head, den?'

'But if you'd just SHUT UP for a moment!'

18

There was a brief silence, punctuated only by the footsteps, which were now very close. The donkey tensed itself to spring, but before it could move Tarl had strode out from the alley and thrust the blade of his sword right up underneath the chin of the startled pizza delivery-boy. As the point of the blade pricked his neck the boy turned an unhealthy white colour, and with fumbling fingers undid the pouch of money at his belt and dropped it at Tarl's feet. With an exasperated sigh Tarl picked up the pouch and handed it back unopened, and then snatched the large cardboard box of pizza from the boy's other hand.

'This will do nicely,' he said. 'Now, get out of here. Go on, move it!'

The boy backed away, and then turning he ran off as fast as his shaking legs would allow. Tarl shook his head and opened the box. The smell of freshly-baked pizza hit them in the face like a garlic-and-tomato-soaked swing-ball bat.

'Mmm! If I'm not mistaken, a Hot-spice Special with extra *pasaroni*.' Tarl put the pizza on the ground right under the donkey's nose, and then grabbed its muzzle and fixed it with an unblinking stare.

'Right,' he continued, 'this one's on me. While you're eating, you can listen. And just for once, cut out the witty comments. Keep . . . your . . . *klatting* . . . muzzle . . . shut! OK?'

The donkey toyed briefly with the idea of enquiring how it was supposed to eat without opening its muzzle, but this was a new and more forceful Tarl, and it was a little intrigued. So it just nodded, and proceeded to wolf down the pizza.

'OK,' continued Tarl. 'We're trying to rescue Ronan, right? Now, we haven't heard from Tyson, so she can't have found him, or else she would have got in touch by using that spell I made for her.'

'Unless you cocked it up again,' muttered the donkey under its breath.

'And although Shikara is one dangerous mother – and I reckon that she's completely off her head – I think Ronan is still alive. If he was dead I think I'd know. I'd just sense it. So we have to keep looking. But we could spend years just wandering around the south without finding a trace of him. I mean, the world's a big place. We've already discovered that I can't use magic to trace him, or the bitch-queen from hell will fire off a counter-spell that will fuse my brain into a useless lump of charcoal.'

'It already –'

'Shut it.' Tarl paused for consideration. 'So. I reckon we need someone with magical powers who can tell us where we need to go without using a spell that's in any way connected with Ronan. Then we won't invoke the counter-spell.'

'Eh?'

'I'm definitely going to find him sooner or later, right? Law of averages. So we go to a fortune-teller and she tells us where I'm going to go in the future. Then we go there, and that's where Ronan will be. Clever, eh?'

'Clever isn't the word,' said the donkey, accurately. 'So, where are you going to find this fortune-teller, then?'

'As it happens, I woke up one morning a few days ago in the doorway of just the right sort of place . . .'

The doorway was in a dark, moss-covered courtyard behind the Vendai Strip. It was almost obscured by a mass of battered and rusting trash-cans which were full to overflowing with foul-smelling refuse. The flagstones were slippy with rotting vegetables and decayed fruit, and the only light came from a guttering smoky torch that was rammed into a mildewed wall-bracket beside the open door.

A couple of battered metal plates were screwed into the wall beneath the torch. On the first was etched the legend 'Griff Brothers, Private Diks. Confidenshal servis ashored'. The second one read 'Manya the Screw-loose. Sooths said, fortunes told, stains removed. First floor'. Fittingly, this one had nearly come off the wall.

Tarl and Puss walked into the gloomy hallway. It smelt in equal measures of dust, stale urine, and boiled fish. On the right was a single battered door with 'Griff Bros, nock and wate' written on it. Behind it someone appeared to be having very noisy sex.

At the end of the hall a set of rickety wooden stairs wound upwards into the darkness. Carefully they stumbled their way up, eventually emerging onto a bare landing that had more holes than floor-boards. A burning oil-lamp stood on a small table in the corner beside the solitary door, which was covered in peeling pink paint and had very badly drawn stars and moons sketched on it in black chalk. The word 'Soothsayer' had been stencilled in gold paint at eye level. Someone had scrawled 'and daft old bat' underneath in red crayon.

Tarl raised his fist to knock, but before he could a shrill voice yelled, 'Don't just stand there! Open the door and come in!'

Tarl's jaw dropped with an audible thump. 'Hey!' he mouthed in wonder. 'How about that? She knew we'd be coming! Impressive, or what!'

The donkey looked at him with raised eyebrows. 'Bollocks!' it snorted. 'Those stairs squeaked so much she'd have to be stone deaf not to hear us.'

Tarl threw it a dubious look and then opened the door, and the two of them walked into one of the strangest rooms they had ever seen.

It looked as though it had been decorated by Morticia Adams in one of her gloomier moods. Black walls were festooned with voluminous black muslin drapes, and black curtains covered the windows. Even the spider-webs that hung from the ceiling were black. Five high-backed blackwood chairs stood around a circular table which was covered with a black cloth. Ancient black leather books lined the shelves along one wall, and on sconces, wall-brackets and every available surface, dozens of jet-black candles flickered and gutted with a dull yellow flame, giving off the nauseating stench of burning toad-wax.

Sitting in one of the chairs was a bent old woman clad in a shapeless mass of robes that were, just for the hell of it, black. She was shuffling a pack of Cydorian tarot cards. As Tarl and Puss stared at her doubtfully she looked up and grinned at them. Tarl winced. Her teeth matched the room's decor perfectly.

'Come in, come in,' she cackled. 'I'm Manya. Manya of Port Raid. How can I help you?'

Tarl had seen some wizened old crones in his time, but Manya could have represented her country at being wizened. She had skin like a freeze-dried walnut, and arms that would have made any skeleton look porky. Her neck appeared to have been borrowed from a vulture that had fallen on very hard times indeed. She didn't so much have warts on her nose as a nose behind her warts, and each wart sprouted so much hair that it looked like a small shaving-brush. But the eyes peering out gleefully from under the black hood of her robe gave the impression of a fierce intelligence. It was a very good impression, but unfortunately it was a long, long way from reality.

The donkey nudged Tarl firmly in the small of the back, and he staggered forward into the room. The filthy black carpet was sticky and tacky underfoot, but he found that oddly comforting. It reminded him of some of his favourite night-clubs. He took a deep breath (nearly choking on the noxious toad-wax fumes), and launched into speech.

'Ah, hello, er, Manya. Of Port Raid, you say?'

'That's where I used to live, you see. But people always call me Manya the Screw-loose, for some reason. Yes, I used to have a thriving little business in a house on the market square. Very popular I was, except for some of the neighbours. Folk used to say they couldn't recommend me too highly. And they didn't.'

'So why did you move?'

'Fate, it was. It came to me in a dream one night. I seemed to hear a voice shouting to me from afar. "Why don't you move away to the south, you daft old biddy," it said. "Go on, clear off out of here!" It was Fate, speaking to me in a voice that sounded just like the man next door. And so I did. I cleared off down here. And since then I've never looked back. Well, it's my neck, you see. Terrible rheumatism. It plagues me. Plagues me. Still, I'm lucky to be alive. According to the cards I was going to die nine years ago. But I'm still here. And they still call me Manya the Screw-loose. Can't work it out.'

'Beats the hell out of me,' muttered the donkey.

'Anyway, what can I do for you?'

'Well, I've got this friend and he's gone missing and we want to trace him only we can't because we tried and we nearly did but it almost blew my head off, and I can't find any traces of him so we need to use magic, and I would if I could, but I can't so maybe you can, only I don't think . . .'

'He wants you to tell his fortune,' the donkey cut in sharply.

'Ah! Now you're talking!' Manya's hands suddenly seemed to blur as she shuffled the cards at a rate faster than anything Tarl had seen outside of an Orcville casino. Then she stopped abruptly. 'That will be two silver *tablons*. Sit down, sit down. I'll

22

use the cards in the horse-shoe spread. That always works best. Anyway, I'm buggered if I can remember any of the other spreads!'

She laughed, a high-pitched cackle that sounded like a chicken having an egg forcefully reinserted, and then held the cards out to Tarl.

'Cut the pack seven times,' she ordered. Tarl sat down at the table and followed her instructions. Taking the cards back she dealt out the first seven face-down on the black cloth in a horse-shoe pattern.

'Right, let's see what we can expect for you in the near future.'

She turned over the first card. It was a picture of several unfortunate people collapsing in a street. All had faces that were covered in red pustules, and were vomiting blood.

'Ah!' continued Manya. 'Pestilence! But the card is inverted, see, and so it indicates the advent of minor good fortune. Possibly a sign of nice weather. Tomorrow could be a good day to trim the hedge.'

She turned over the second card, a picture of a man and a woman. Both looked a little sulky. 'The Pair of People having a Bit of a Tiff,' she said. 'This is bad. It means disharmony and discord. You probably won't be able to sing in tune for a while. Keep away from pub sing-songs and karaoke evenings. Glycerine and lemon might help. All right? The next card is the Hanging Buttock. That's usually connected with nature. Off the top of my head, I'd say that a small brown eagle will fly past quite slowly one day soon. And the fourth card is . . . oh dear, oh dear! The Shrub struck by Hailstones! Bad. Very bad. Avoid green, whatever you do. Particularly pastels and light summery shades. Now, the fifth card is . . . the Breadshop. That reminds me, I must buy a loaf . . .'

Tarl watched apprehensively as Manya gazed at the tarot card with a frown on her face. She almost seemed to be staring through the card at something beyond.

'Terrible,' she muttered. 'Terrible.'

There was a long pause, and Tarl tried to imagine what foul horrors the old crone could see in his future. She shook her head tiredly and raised her eyes to meet his.

'You just can't get proper bread these days,' she muttered. 'It's scandalous, it really is . . . Now, where was I? Oh, yes! The tarot!' She turned over another card. 'Well, just look at that. The

Knacker's Yard, inverted. That's unmistakable, that is. No doubt about it. You're going to run out of glue quite shortly, so be warned. And the final card is . . . the Third Door on the Left. Hm, that's always a sign of travel. North-west, quite possibly, or upwards. Don't stay at home, dear, or you'll be asking for trouble. Well, there we are. I hope that's quite clear.'

Manya swept up the cards and shuffled them into the pack with a satisfied air. Behind him the bemused Tarl heard a stifled hiccup, and looking round he saw that Puss was backing out onto the landing, literally shaking with suppressed laughter. Tarl stood up, dropped two coins onto the table, and edged towards the door, nodding and smiling.

'Well, thank you. Thank you. That's, er, remarkable. Er . . . I'm most impressed. Really. Most impressed.'

Manya simpered revoltingly. It was like watching parchment shatter. 'Don't forget to spread the word,' she cooed. Tarl nodded even more vigorously.

'Yeah! Right! Er . . . I'll tell everyone that I can't recommend you too highly!' He slammed the door behind him and hurried down the stairs. From the courtyard below he could hear the demented braying of a donkey that is laughing so hard it is nearly wetting itself.

At the foot of the stairs Tarl paused and closed his eyes. Gradually his breathing slowed, and the scowl on his face faded and was replaced by a look of intense concentration. Suddenly his eyes shot open and he gasped with surprise.

'Wow!' he muttered to himself, and then he scampered out of the door into the gloomy courtyard.

He found the donkey standing in the archway that led to the street. It was leaning against the damp brickwork, chuckling gently to itself. Through the archway drifted the distant hubbub of the crowds of revellers on the Vendai Strip.

'You can laugh, fuzz-face!' said Tarl. 'But that Manya is the very same soothsayer who advised Ronan where to go on his search for revenge.'

'Yeah. And that took him over three years, right?'

'You can laugh –'

'Thanks. I will.'

'– you can laugh, but she's told us what we need to know.'

The donkey was about to scoff, but there was something about Tarl's manner that stopped it. For some reason he was exuding confidence. Intrigued, it kept its mouth shut and listened.

'Go north-west, she said, or upwards. So, if you travel north-west from here, across the Gemae Hills, where do you come to?'

The donkey thought for a moment. 'The sea?' it hazarded.

'Yeah. But what city do you find there, right on the sea? I'll tell you. Yai'El, that's what. The City of Canals. The oldest city in Cydor.'

'So?'

'So I've just done a little *Mindsweep* spell, looking for any signs of magic to the north-west. Oh, I was very careful, it was pretty non-specific, but it was enough. There are a lot of little tiny pockets of Power floating about, there always are. Conjurors, illusionists, village shamen, or unpractised prannies like me. But over Yai'El there's a massive blanket of magic, thick, dark, and impenetrable. I didn't dare go near it. But there must be a huge source of magic in that city. Something is going on there. And you and I are going to go and find out what . . .'

LONELY

. . . and there is, unfortunately, no getting away from it. Men are usually bigger and stronger than women. Thus the female warrior, when faced with a male opponent, needs to use guile and intelligence. True, the average male brain is physically larger than the female, but, sister, this doesn't matter a damn. Just about every man you'll ever meet thinks with his dick instead.

Tyson's Guide for Women Warriors

Tyson backed out through the door of the Bald Eagle tavern, letting it swing shut behind her, and a babble of voices broke out inside. She stood in the street poised and alert, sword in one hand and the Crow in the other, but no one followed her out, and gradually she relaxed.

In a sudden fit of anger she slashed at the inn-sign swinging above her head. Her sword carved through the wooden painting of a disgruntled eagle examining its receding hair-line in a mirror and smashed it into a hundred splinters. Feeling slightly better, she uncocked the Crow and slung it from her belt, and then with one last scowl at the tavern she turned and stomped off down the street.

Tyson had had enough. She was completely, thoroughly and utterly pissed off with Behan and all things Behanian. Particularly the ruling warrior caste, God rot them. Living in her home city of Welbug she had got so used to being treated with the respect which she had earned over the years that the attitude of the Behanian warriors had come as something of a shock.

The problem was that they were all male. There wasn't a single woman fighter in Behan outside of the illegal cellar-fights that took place in Rednec. So when confronted by someone who was five foot four, slim, and definitely female, virtually all the male warriors looked on her as either a joke or a challenge. And sometimes both.

She had walked unawares into trouble in the very first tavern she had visited in Brend. Used to taking her rightful place amongst warriors she had leant on the bar and ordered a beer, and when the half-drunk guy beside her had tried to stick his hand down her jerkin she had dislocated his finger for him. But instead of acting as a warning this had been taken as a challenge by the others present. A younger warrior had come at her, sword in hand, his face an open picture of scorn and lust. Ten seconds and one short rally later he had been sitting on the floor trying to staunch the flow of blood from a gaping wound in his shoulder and yelling fit to bust. And then the atmosphere had really changed. Six other warriors had drawn their swords ready to attack her, and she could have been in serious trouble if it hadn't been for the Crow.

She had had similar problems as a teenager learning her craft in Welbug some years ago. Her father, the town's champion, had consulted with an armourer friend of his, and the result had been the Crow, so called because it was simply an abbreviated crossbow. Nine inches long, it was a little miracle of engineering. She could load one of the tiny quarrels, fire it, and load again all inside two seconds. Within a range of twenty feet it was lethal. As soon as a warrior realised that she could put a bolt straight through his eyeball before he had got within slashing range he began to use his brain for once. With the Crow in one hand and her sword in the other she could hold off a roomful of men for as long as was needed to get the hell out of there. And it still worked. She had been able to walk out of the tavern in Brend unhurt.

Since then she had visited thirty-one taverns, the last of which was the Bald Eagle. In fourteen of them there had been trouble. In eight of these she had seriously damaged a couple of guys, two of whom had ended up dead. Every time she had walked into a tavern she had been either patronised or molested. Yes, she was heartily, thoroughly, totally pissed off with life in Behan.

It might not have felt as bad if she had come across any traces of Ronan or his abductress, Shikara. But she hadn't heard even the slightest rumour. And she'd been so confident. She'd really thought she'd found a fool-proof way of tracking them down.

It had been while travelling on the East Road to Brend, just after parting from Tarl and Puss, that she'd had her brain-wave. Shikara was a sorceress, and although she was remarkably

27

powerful, she would still need the ingredients of her craft. After all, you can't make charms and potions from nothing. She'd been out of circulation for five hundred years, and in that time a lot of her stock must have gone off. Tongue of dog, for example, was notoriously difficult to keep fresh. Even tinned dog-tongues only had a shelf-life of three years. So she'd need to restock. And you don't get hold of a supply of grated bull's pizzle by walking up to a live bull in a field armed with a cheese-grater. Not if you want to live, you don't. She'd have to go to a proper supplier, and there weren't that many around. If Tyson checked them all out, sooner or later she'd stumble across the one which supplied Shikara, and with any luck they would have a delivery address.

As soon as she had got to Brend, Tyson had bought herself a copy of *Witch Magazine* and had sat in a bar thumbing through the advertisements. There was at least one magical supplies retailer in every city in Behan. She had decided to check out the magic shops as soon as she came to a town, and if they drew a blank she would hang round the inns and taverns for a few days, talking to people and listening for rumours, before moving on.

So that was what she had been doing for the past few weeks. She'd visited just about every magical supplies outlet in Behan and questioned the staff. She had checked out Trans-4-mations and The Shaven Charm-pit in Brend, Sibyl Servants in Damon, Brew-ha-ha in Derchey, Voodoo-U-Do and The Specific Potion in Rednec, and El Dritch and The Cantripantry here in Dubbel. But not one of them had heard of Shikara, or had had any recent large orders from unknown clients. And she hadn't had any luck hanging round inns or taverns, either, just a load of trouble.

However, despite her lack of success and the hassle she had been getting, Tyson wasn't going to give up. The sales assistant in El Dritch had been very sympathetic and had advised her to head west into Iduin. According to him, the two largest suppliers in the south were The Sorcerer's A-Plentys in Tena, on the Yarrone river, and Shamen Corner in Drolic, up in the Azure Mountains. And Tyson couldn't wait to shake the dust of Behan off her feet. The problem was that it wasn't so easy to leave the *klatting* country.

Dubbel stood on the east bank of the Errone river, which ran wide and fast-flowing through the level plains of south Behan and east Iduin. The only way across the river was by an ancient chain-ferry known as the Dubbel Crossing, and to board this ferry you had to have an exit visa stamped by the Behanian Civil Transit Board. Getting this visa meant filling in forms, handing over money, and queuing in the Transit Board offices, a process that had been known to take weeks and could take even longer if the official involved was in a bad mood, disliked your face, or if you rejected his sexual advances.

But as the alternatives were trying to steal a boat, which was very risky, or heading south-east to the elven realm of Nevin, which was miles out of the way, Tyson had decided that she might as well try to get a visa. The barmaid in the Bald Eagle had warned her that all that would happen today was that she would hang around for hours just to be given a mountain of forms to fill in and another appointment in a week's time. But Tyson was no longer in any mood to be trifled with. Somehow she was going to get the officials to listen to her. Or someone would die in the attempt.

The Transit Board offices were situated in one of the squat, ugly red-stone buildings that were built along the four sides of Government Square. Tyson paused on the cracked marble steps and looked back across the wide, dusty piazza. The sun beat down on the rows of parched and dying lime-trees that lined the paths crossing from building to building, their twisted roots unable to extract sufficient water from the arid soil. Dead leaves blew along the pavements and collected in the empty bowls of the waterless ornamental fountains. Apparently, so Tyson had learned, the Clerk for Water Conservation had issued an edict the previous spring ordering all public fountains to be turned off except on public holidays (of which there were only two a year), and banning the watering of all plants except edible crops. Quite why Water Conservation was thought to be necessary in a city that was built beside a two-hundred-yard-wide river no one had yet explained.

Shaking her head Tyson pushed through the revolving doors and found herself in a massive stone-flagged lobby which appeared to have been decorated entirely in grey. A scrawny little officious-looking man was sat writing at a desk near the entrance.

He had one of those small square moustaches that dull, un-imaginative men think make them look important. Behind him a row of twelve interview booths lined the left-hand wall, but only two appeared to be in use. In front of them two queues of tired and fed-up people twisted motionless across the floor like snakes caught in a block of ice.

Tyson walked up to the man at the desk and, summoning up all the self-restraint she could muster, cleared her throat apologetic-ally.

'Excuse me, could you tell me who I see about exit visas, please?'

For a few seconds the man continued writing, then he paused long enough to give her the sort of look one would normally reserve for something unpleasant that one had just stepped in, muttered a couple of words, and went back to his writing. For a brief moment Tyson saw red, and her sword was half-way out of her scabbard before she realised that what he had actually said was 'far queue'.

Angrily she slammed the sword back and stalked across the floor to join the end of the indicated queue. And then she waited. And waited. And waited . . .

Three hours later there was just one person left in front of her, an overweight and heavily perspiring man who had spent the entire three hours talking at her. He was called Arvie, so he had told her, and he was a travelling salesman for Round World, a company of cartwheel manufacturers in Asposa. To prove it he had a leather bag full of his samples, twenty-three small models of the different wheels his company sold. He had shown every single one to Tyson, lovingly pointing out the finer points and dif-ferences, extolling the virtues of metal tires and ash-wood spokes until she had felt like screaming. ('You could say I'm a company spokes-man, ha-ha,' he had chortled, and Tyson had nearly hit him.)

Apparently this was his fourth visit to the Transit Board offices in six days, and he was due to receive an exit visa to travel on that afternoon's ferry. When Tyson had told him that it was her first visit and that she hoped to be on the same ferry he had laughed so much that for one brief, wonderful moment she had thought he was having a coronary. Wiping his eyes, he had sympathetically informed her that she had more chance of the river freezing solid so that she could walk across than of getting a visa first visit. Then, to cheer her up, he had started telling her jokes. When after half an hour she still hadn't even smiled, a little uncertainty seemed to set in and he'd paused and asked her a couple of questions about being a woman warrior, but before she'd said ten words he had interrupted her again.

'Do you know, I think it's quite remarkable,' he had told her fulsomely, 'the way some of you girls are having a go at doing men's jobs. And why shouldn't you? I'm all in favour, myself. In fact, I'm a bit of a feminist. I mean, if you haven't got yourself a man to look after you, you have to do something, don't you?'

Normally this was the point when Tyson would have gently explained with the aid of a dagger held touching his groin that if Arvie didn't shut up about himself and his 'feminist' beliefs she would help him to understand women more fully by turning him into one. But she was feeling so wretched that she just didn't have the heart, and so she let him jabber on. But she had to admit that she had learned something. After the man she loved had been kidnapped by a sorceress who had designs on his body, and she had spent weeks trekking through the hot, dusty southlands being harassed and provoked by macho male warriors with chips on their shoulders, she had thought that life couldn't get much worse. Three hours with Arvie had taught her that it could, in spades.

It didn't seem more than a couple of days before Arvie's name was called and he waddled across to the desk in the interview booth. Tyson watched tiredly as he shook hands with the Transit Board clerk and then surreptitiously handed over a little purse of coins. A few more forms were filled in and then Arvie was up and away with his visa clutched to his chest, and Tyson heard her name being called.

As she walked across to the booth she took a couple of deep breaths and tried to calm herself down. She knew that there was only one way she was going to get her visa today, and a polite and restrained appearance was an essential start.

The small dark-haired clerk who was seated on the other side of the desk appeared to have borrowed the moustache of the man by the entrance. He too was busily writing but there was a different feel to him, a sheen of corruption, a greasiness of the soul that seemed to permeate the air around him. It felt as if his whole aura had been well soaked in extremely cheap hair-oil.

The clerk finished his writing, adding a full-stop with an ostentatious flourish, and then his eyes flickered up and crawled over Tyson like a couple of slugs crawling over a rock. His mouth twitched into a slow smile of satisfaction as he dwelt on the slim lines of her body, the tanned and glowing skin, the smiling lips . . .

And then he met her eyes, and jerked back in his seat as if someone had thrown a bucket of cold water into his face. His smile vanished to be replaced by bureaucratic blankness as he rapidly reassessed. He could tell that he wasn't going to get anything out of this one. The look in those eyes was lethal! Nervously he glanced sideways to check that the three heavily armed guards were still leaning against the wall behind the interview booths. Their presence was often necessary to dissuade unhappy would-be travellers from making a scene, and the clerk had a feeling that it was a good job they were there today.

He looked down at his paperwork for a moment while pulling himself together. *Klatting* women warriors! Well, she wouldn't be looking so confident after kicking her heels in the queues of the Transit Offices for a couple of weeks. That would teach her who had the power around here. Anyway, from the determinedly polite look on her face it seemed as though she already knew just who pulled the strings. Excellent!

Contentedly he fixed his best superior smile in place and then looked up at her again.

'Good morning. What can I do for you?'

'I'd like an exit visa to travel across the Errone on the chain-ferry.'

'Certainly, certainly. Well, let's see. We'll need to fill in an initial application form.' He opened a drawer and slid out the form required, then ceremoniously dipped his pen into the ink-pot a couple of times. 'Name?'

'Tyson.'

'Tyson, Miss,' the clerk muttered, filling in the appropriate space. 'Forenames?'

'Just Tyson. And no Miss.'

'Oh. How unusual.'

Tyson shrugged. 'Why use forenames when one will do?'

The clerk stared at her, a little miffed. He was supposed to make the jokes around here. Time to rub her nose in it.

'And the date you wish to travel,' he asked, the epitome of smarmy politeness.

'Today. The ferry leaves in about an hour.'

'Today? Oh, dear. Oh, dear, dear!' He laid his pen down and gazed at her in mock surprise. 'I really don't think that will be possible. My dear lady, there are forms that must be filled in, channels that must be gone through, documents that must be checked. These processes take time. Even in severe emergencies, we have to . . .'

'This is an emergency. It could be a matter of life and death.'

'Ah, well now. In that case we might be able to speed things up slightly.'

Picking up his pen the clerk made a great show of searching through the form until he found the little box half-way down page five that had 'tick here in cases of emergency' written beside it. He ticked it with relish.

'Go to sub-section four, page eight,' he read out happily. Turning to the right page he continued reading. 'Please state clearly and concisely the exact nature of the emergency, attaching copies of any relevant documentation to the right-hand page.'

He looked up expectantly, pen at the ready. Tyson thought for a moment, and her left-hand fingers traced a delicate pattern on the stained wood of the desk-top.

'Hm,' she mused. 'Er, see below.'

'See . . . below . . .' he repeated, writing it down.

'No, I didn't mean see below on the form, I meant see below the desk. But I'd be careful, if I was you.'

The clerk stared at her, and then ever so carefully edged his chair slightly backwards and without moving more than a few inches squinted under the desk. Her right hand was resting on her thigh, and in it was the smallest crossbow he had ever seen. The needle-sharp three-inch quarrel that sat against the drawn-back wire was pointing directly at his groin. The clerk swallowed noisily, and the skin of his face whitened unhealthily until it appeared to have the colour and consistency of two-month-old milk.

'Considering how accurate I am with this thing,' she continued calmly, 'I would say that you definitely have a bit of an emergency here. The exact nature of the emergency being that unless I get my exit visa in one minute flat I am going to turn your love-onions into a mini-kebab. *Comprenez*?'

The clerk gazed at her, his mouth open. It felt as though someone had scooped his stomach out with a *klatting* great shovel. For a moment he thought he was going to pass out, and then he realised he'd stopped breathing and dragged in a passing lungful of air. His eyes flickered sideways to check out the guards, but they were all gazing unconcernedly into space. From their viewpoint there was no sign that anything was amiss.

His eyes strayed back to the little warning-bell that hung down the right-hand side of his desk. Tyson smiled sweetly at him.

'I wouldn't,' she said. 'Even if you feel like being a martyr, the guards would all be dead seconds later. Look.'

With her left hand she flicked back the cover on a leather pouch attached to her belt. In it he could see a little clutch of the quarrels. He tried to think, but the only thing that came into his mind was a vivid picture of one of those foul little darts stuck right through his . . .

'All right!' he hissed. 'You've got it!' Angrily he wrenched open another drawer, took out a visa, stamped it with the relevant stamps and signed it. Tyson reached across, took it from his hand and studied it.

'Thank you,' she smiled, and stood up. 'No little tricks now. Believe me, it's the best thing for both of us if I get the hell out of Behan and never come back.'

She turned and strode towards the door, the tiny crossbow all but hidden from casual glances in her hand. Furiously the clerk watched her go and then, as she neared the exit, he reached out to sound the alarm. But as he stretched out his hand there was a sudden whirring sound and a tiny quarrel smashed into the desk in the inch of space between his fingers and the bell. The clerk yelped with fright and snatched his hand back. It had been so close that the flights had brushed his fingertips. Bitch! He tore his eyes away from the still-quivering quarrel and stared across to the door, but the woman warrior had gone. Yet now that it was safe to

34

raise the alarm, somehow he just didn't feel like doing so.

Anyway, he had other priorities. Such as finding a dry pair of trousers.

The chain-ferry squatted in the dock like a vast wooden tea-tray. It looked as though it had started out once as a normal boat but that some vast almighty foot had long since trodden on it, squashing it into a misshapen oblong, and then kicked it about for a while. The once-white paint of the bulwarks was peeling and blackened, and the varnished decking was splintered and stained. Along the port side ran a raised deck with a tattered awning that stretched above rows of wooden benches and a scattering of tables, and here the first-class passengers found some relief from the burning afternoon sun. The starboard side, however, was bare, and in the well of the ferry the poorer passengers mingled with carts, baggage and livestock in a sweltering basin of heat.

But if the ferry had seen better days, the surrounding quayside looked as though it had never seen worse ones. The wooden piers were rotting and deserted, and weeds grew in the cracks of the stone jetties. Here and there a rotting skeleton of a boat was the only reminder that once this had been a thriving, bustling river port where trade and commerce flourished. The Ministry of Shipping, set up fifteen years before to regulate water traffic, levy taxes and collect tolls, had soon put a stop to all that thriving stuff.

Tyson strode down the wide gang-plank that led on to the ferry and pushed her way through the milling people and restless pack-animals towards the narrow stair that led up to the first-class deck. She had been ready for trouble, but it appeared that the clerk at the Transit Office had been sensible, and the officials and customs-guards checking papers on the quayside hadn't even given her a second glance once they had seen her visa. They were too busy dealing with a mob of irate, hot and visa-less travellers who were trying to bribe, beg or force their way on board.

She paused at the top of the stair and looked around the raised deck. Only a dozen or so of the passengers had paid the extortionate fee to travel up here in the shade. At the far end she saw Arvie sitting at a table tucking in to a plate of fried chicken with gusto[4]. When he saw her he nearly fell off his seat with surprise, and then beckoned her over.

'You made it! I can't believe it! One visit to the Transit Office? Just one? How did you do it?'

'I guess it must have been my happy smile.'

'Wonderful! Wonderful! Look, why don't you join me? Let me buy you something to eat.'

Tyson looked down at him suspiciously, but she could see that he was just desperate for company. There was something sad and lonely about him. Loneliness, she thought. Gee, tell me about it.

'Yeah, OK,' she answered, and sat down opposite him. 'You've been here before. What do you recommend?'

'Eating somewhere else, to be honest. The speciality of the chef is botulism. But as this is the last food-stop for thirty miles, we have little choice.'

Tyson studied the cardboard menu that was stuffed into a metal stand on the table-top, and then wrinkled her nose up and looked down into the well of the ferry.

'Someone must be taking a flock of goats across the river,' she muttered. 'Can you smell that?'

'Ah. That's not goats. That's the kitchen.' Arvie gestured with his thumb towards a wooden shack built at the front of the ferry. A metal chimney poking through the roof was belching forth smoke. Tyson grimaced and then beckoned to the half-orc attendant who was leaning against the wall of the shack, busily picking his cavernous nose with three fingers.

Five minutes later she was looking down apprehensively at a plate of 'chicken stew with seasonal vegetables'. The vegetables were almost unidentifiable and were tougher than the plate they came on. She prodded the pieces of chicken around with her fork. She'd eaten stew that had bones in it before, but this was the first time she'd ever come across a bit of beak.

At that moment a loud clanking sound began, and the ferry lurched forwards and began to inch out from between the sheltering pier walls on to the open river. In front of it the chain that connected it to the far bank was rising inch by dripping inch from the leaden water and disappearing into the bowels of the

[4] Gusto – an instant gravy made with a brown powder that smells suspiciously like cow-dung.

ferry, re-emerging from its rear to flop down into the water again like a long, thin, rusty turd. Slowly and painfully the old ship dragged itself across the river like a half-trapped fly dragging itself across a spider's web, and Tyson sat there with a faint breeze blowing into her face, staring at the distant Azure Mountains and thinking of Ronan.

Gods! She hoped he was still alive. Even if he'd had to give his body to that chubby bitch of a sorceress to stay that way. Well, he'd better be alive, because if he'd gone and let her down and died, she would *klatting* well kill him!

They had only had a few days together, and just two nights. She began thinking of the second night, the evening before Ronan had faced Nekros, when they had sat out under the stars beside a camp-fire in the wild with Tarl and Puss and had just talked and joked and laughed. Her whole adult life had been one long stream of endless responsibility, and it had been almost the first time that she had known such easy friendship, such fun. Now, as she sat here opposite a fat and boring sales-rep, with inedible food congealing on her plate and with a glass of white wine so sweet and cloying that they had needed to scoop it out of the bottle with a spoon, she desperately wanted to experience such good times again. She yearned to be sat outside some bar beside the sea, with a flagon of fine wine and food that you could eat, while Tarl told another of his dubious stories and Puss kept cutting in with his barbed little comments. She wanted Ronan sat beside her, his arm touching hers. More than anything she wanted to look at her man again, to run her hands over his skin, to smell and taste him. And she didn't even know if he was still alive . . .

Arvie paused in the middle of one of his favourite funny stories about cartwheels. 'Here,' he said, a little concerned, 'do you want to change seats? The smoke from that kitchen chimney is making your eyes water something shocking . . .'

The prisoner lay motionless on the straw palliasse, his back to the cold stone wall of the small cell. Only his eyes moved as he traced the patterns of the arched brick ceiling. No light penetrated through the heavy wooden door or the bricked-up window, no torch flickered in the rusting wall-bracket, and yet the cell was lit by an eerie luminescence that seemed to emanate from the walls.

It was cold and dank, but the prisoner felt happy. This was better. This was much better. He couldn't for the life of him remember who he was or why he was there, but he did know that being in this cell was one hell of an improvement. He couldn't remember much about the past few weeks, either, but some things did linger. Pink muslin drapes everywhere, and huge plump pillows covered in pink satin. In fact, now that he thought back, just about everything seemed to have been pink. The sheets and the furs on the vast bed, the impossibly deep carpets, even the little *yumble* which that woman had carried everywhere with her. All pink.

And that woman! The prisoner shuddered as he thought of her. She had fed him choice tidbits of food as they lay in the furs, had poured him sparkling wine into impossibly thin crystal glasses, and had run her hands all over him. But it hadn't been any good, any of it. It hadn't been what he wanted. He didn't know why, but she was the wrong one. It was the only thing that he had to cling on to, this knowledge that she was the wrong one. And she had got really pissed off when he hadn't responded, hadn't wanted to know. But she was pale-skinned and voluptuous, with cruel brown eyes and torrents of auburn hair, and he had a vision in his mind of a female warrior with a sword in her hand and a smile on her lips, a slim almost boyish figure with skin tanned to the same colour as the leather she wore, of dark brown hair cut short in elven fashion, and of a pair of green eyes so deep that a man could drown in them . . .

The prisoner sighed, and his eyes clouded over as his thoughts turned inwards. He couldn't understand why he could hardly move, why his legs felt so heavy, why his brain kept drifting so, but it didn't really matter. The only thing that did matter was to keep hold of the image of that face. For some reason, that was dreadfully important.

Shikara watched through the peephole in the door for a few seconds longer, and then slamming shut the metal cover she turned and stormed off along the passage. What a waste! What a *klatting* waste! She'd spent five hundred years under an enchantment, rotting in some barren cave under the mountains, and then this handsome, hunky black warrior comes along and releases her. As soon as she set eyes on him she'd known she just couldn't wait to show him how grateful she was, to thank him in the only way that a real woman can show a man. But had he been interested? Had he *klat*!

What was wrong with him? Shikara still had her looks. It hadn't been difficult to find a little coterie of handsome and well-muscled young warriors who were prepared to serve her in whatever way she required. She had established quite a nice little household here in the weeks since her release. But the one man she really fancied wasn't interested. It would have been easy enough to use her magic, to zap him into a more accommodating frame of mind, but that would have been like admitting defeat. She'd never had to persuade someone into her bed against their will in her life and she wasn't going to start now. It was just too degrading.

Shikara scowled as she swept up the cellar stairs. A few weeks living in the lap of luxury hadn't done the job, but maybe he'd be more amenable after a month or two in a cold stone cell. She knew what the problem was, of course. She could read his mind like an open parchment. It was that skinny bitch of a warrior, the one who had been with him when Shikara had been transformed back and Nekros had been killed. Well, he'd just have to forget her, if he knew what was good for him.

Angrily she pushed open the door to the lounge and strode in. Malkin, her pet *yumble*, was lying on the couch. It gazed up at her with huge dark eyes and began giving happy little yaps of welcome. She stared at it moodily. It was a sweet little thing, and only a total bastard would have been tempted to pick it up and drop-kick it into the waste-paper bin on the other side of the room.

Shikara picked it up and drop-kicked it into the waste-paper bin on the other side of the room.

At that moment she became aware of an intrusive feeling in her head, a swelling of power, a disturbance of the smooth concentric rings of force that protected her. Someone was trying to trace her again. This was the third time in the past few weeks, and she had *Counteracted* the first two with enough power to fry the average brain. Excellent! She was just in the right frame of mind to deal with anyone who dared to invade her privacy.

*

In an expensively furnished room in a southern city, six smartly dressed men were sat around a highly polished semicircular oaken table, watching as the black-robed old hag in the corner muttered and mumbled and added various powders and liquids to the cauldron that bubbled in the fireplace. It began to glow, and silvery smoke drifted out in a gentle stream, seeming to be sucked into the centre of the plain white wall that faced the six men. As it absorbed the smoke the wall too began to glow, and a coruscating whirl of colours expanded from a single dot in the centre until the whole surface of the wall was a seething psychedelic maelstrom.

Suddenly the colours imploded into a moving image of a young woman, beautiful but angry, who glared at them. Before any of the men could speak she stabbed out an imperious finger, and a bolt of light exploded out of the wall and hurtled across to smash into the old hag's startled eyes. For a brief moment the hag's head seemed to expand to twice its size, and then it exploded, showering the room and the six men with thousands of sticky little gobbets of brain. The image of the young woman smiled and ran one hand through her mane of auburn hair, then turned her disdainful gaze upon the men. Her eyes began to glow with an eldritch light and five of the men sat frozen in fear, but the sixth spoke quickly.

'Shikara, I beg of you, listen. We represent an extremely powerful organisation, and we have a proposition to put to you. If you agree to help us, it will bring you fame, wealth, and more power than you have ever thought possible. All men will look up to you and –'

'*All* men?' she cut in sharply. The sixth man nodded, then swallowed with some difficulty and eased a finger around the inside of a collar that suddenly felt far too tight. There was a pause that seemed to the six men to go on for ever, and then Shikara's image smiled and the light in her eyes died.

'Tell me more,' she said.

OUTWARD

The origin of the Vagen sea-raiders is, perhaps, one of the strangest tales of all. During the First Age, the centre of the civilised world was Perplec, on the southern coast. This city had grown rich from trade, and many were the businesses that flourished here. The wine-bars and cafés teemed with thrusting young executives all doing lunch, and for the most part life was easy at that time.

But then there came an era of recession to the city, and the lunches stopped. Now the talk was all of resources to be maximised and costs that must be cut. And in the drive for maximum efficiency a strange new ritual arose. The 'outward bound' course was developed, and the higher echelons of management all talked of building teams and bonding folk together. Many was the middle-aged executive who found himself marooned upon a cold and windy beach with others from his place of work, but minus any food or shelter for the night. Many was the sales-rep who spent a miserable weekend fighting mock battles in some rain-drenched woods, in order to achieve his full potential and bond him with his colleagues.

And though the vast majority of folk hated and despised these courses, yet there were a few who revelled in the challenge that they brought. For there were some young bankers who could march all night on just one slice of bread, or advertising men who found they loved to stalk a rival through the woods and 'kill' him with a rubber arrow tipped with paint. And they began to think, if we are all so talented at fighting, or surviving in the wild, then why are we all working for a bank?

And thus did they begin to put their talents to good use, banding together at the weekends to form sea-borne raiding parties, up and down the coast. At first this was a hobby, but as time passed it turned into their main employ. They left

their homes in Perplec, settling in the Maelvanta Islands,
and lived by raiding and by piracy, a tribe of warriors all
rooted in the middle-class.

Thus by the Second Age were they renowned, and people
went in fear. And yet their ancestry of middle-management
is plain to see. Their name, the Vagens, comes from the Old
Southron words vah geni, *meaning 'waste of space'.*

The Pink Book of Ulay

Marten sat on a tree-stump near the top of the hill and gazed out
over the emerald-green water of the bay. From here it was possible
to see maybe fifteen of the other islands on a clear day, although
in the scorching heat of this particular afternoon only a couple
could be discerned through the haze. But Marten didn't even
notice them. He was deep in thought.

To look at, Marten was probably everyone's idea of a typical
Vagen warrior. Well over six foot in height, he had neat blond
hair, smiling blue eyes, skin tanned to the colour of oak, and a
moustache that curved down past his mouth as though it had
melted at the edges. His body was fit and well muscled, and he
looked rather like Adonis might have done if he had gone in for
body-building and taken a bit more care of himself. He was
dressed in the smart-but-casual style that was typical of the
Vagens – neatly pressed cotton trousers, tasteful linen shirt, and
hand-stitched leather boots that were both supple and stylish. But
(and it was a but that really annoyed him), despite his looks
Marten wasn't a Vagen warrior at all.

Vagen, yes. He'd been born in the village twenty-one years
before, son of Lobbo the Relaxed. But warrior, no. Unfortunately
that hadn't been allowed. Despite the fact that it had been his
ambition since he was three, and despite the fact that he was
strong, fast and brave, the village elders had told him that what he
was best suited for was the challenging and responsible position
of goatherd. What they didn't tell him, but what was clearly
understood, was that he couldn't be a warrior because he was,
quite simply, working class.

Vagen society was riddled with class consciousness. Every
warrior was the son of a warrior, and could trace his ancestry right

back to the Leaving of Perplec, all those years ago. If you weren't related to one of the old families then you weren't good enough to be a fighting man, and as Marten couldn't trace his ancestry back more than two generations, that was that.

His main problem was that, unfortunately, no one knew who his paternal grandsire was. His father had apparently been conceived under a table in the Great Hall after a feast to celebrate a successful raid. All his Gran could tell them was that it had been one hell of a party, the lights had gone out, and that the guy had had a beard.

Lobbo the Relaxed had grown up to become the village rat-catcher, and although he was thoroughly liked and respected by just about everyone, his son still wasn't considered good enough to be a fighting man. And so despite his natural abilities, Marten had been put in charge of the goats.

He hadn't fretted or sulked, though. He had adopted his father's relaxed attitudes and gone to work with a will. But inside he was determined to show them all, to be the best *klatting* goat-herd the village had ever seen, to be so *klatting* good that some day they would realise that he deserved his chance as a warrior. And so he decided to revolutionise the field of goat-herding, to reorganise it from the bottom up.

Unfortunately, while Marten was lying on the hill-side one day, his brain busily engaged in working out all sorts of wonderful schemes for grazing rotation, breeding improvements, and increasing milk yield, the goats grabbed their chance and wandered off into the mountains. It took fifteen men a whole week to round them all up and bring them back to the village. Marten was immediately demoted to chicken-boy.

Grabbing at this second chance to show what he could do he quickly reorganised the entire flock (which had until then been allowed to range freely, laying their eggs wherever they liked), and installed them in predator-proof cages in a massive barn. Each chicken was imprisoned in its own small cage, with food and water handy, so that it didn't need to waste energy in running about looking for food, it was perfectly safe, and its eggs could easily be retrieved. Unfortunately, the chickens were thoroughly peeved at being deprived of fresh air, light, exercise and freedom, and retaliated in the only way they knew how. Within three days the village's egg production had gone from sixty a day to zero.

Marten was demoted to driftwood collector, on the grounds that even he couldn't upset driftwood, and it would be unable to run away from him. However, it only took a few months before his highly ambitious Driftwood Drying and Storage Warehouse caught fire and started a conflagration that burnt down half the village. Marten was again demoted, this time to the lowest possible level. Cesspit attendant.

At first he seemed to have found his métier, but then came the fateful day when a build-up of volatile gases caused by his Waste Reclamation Scheme suddenly exploded, covering the entire village in an inch-deep layer of excrement. After the village elders had fished him out of the sea (where an irate and extremely foul-smelling mob of villagers had thrown him) they told him that he was reinstated as goat-herd, on the grounds that when he did this job the first time at least he hadn't destroyed half the village. However, they went on, if the milk-yield fell by the merest fraction, or if a single goat got lost, then his next job would be as part of the foundations for the new harbour pier.

Wisely, Marten had decided to stop trying to impress. But it rankled. He might have let his enthusiasm run away with him, but he just knew that when it came down to planning raids, or fighting, or navigating the longships through unfamiliar coastal waters, he would be as good as any Vagen warrior. In fact, thought Marten as he watched a familiar flaxen-haired figure jogging into view on the coastal path below, I'd be way, way better than some. It isn't fair. It just isn't fair.

The flaxen hair belonged to Marten's best (indeed, only) friend in the village, Dene, son of Denhelm. It was fair to say that Dene looked the part of a warrior, but deciding which part he looked was much harder. He was a thin, weak, short-sighted maladroit who suffered badly from sea-sickness, and was about as suited to the Vagen raiding ethic as a tortoise would be to basketball.

As a child Dene had always wanted to work with animals, but as he was from one of the oldest families in the village and had a string of ancestors who had all been warriors before him he had no choice but to follow them. As a result, he was the only man in Vagen history to win the uncoveted 'Crap Warrior of the Year' award four times in succession. Whereas most of his comrades had a strong preference for swords (and in particular the newly launched Orcbane XN Terator), Dene was equally at home with any weapon – about as at home as the average penguin would be if it fell into an active volcano. As his sword instructor had said (before he had his breakdown and took early retirement), he'd seen lettuce that were more of a threat.

At first Dene had merely been a figure of fun for the rest of the tribe. When he went on his inaugural raid, they had almost split their sides laughing at his desperate attempts to defend himself from the vicious attack of a nine-year-old girl armed with a rolling-pin. His choice of booty had also caused great amusement. While the rest of them returned to the ship laden with gold and silver ornaments, silks, carpets, pottery and other artifacts, Dene had returned with a puppy. And when he'd told them all that he was going to call the puppy Mittens, on account of her little white paws, one or two of his comrades had been helpless with laughter.

But after a while the laughter had begun to fade. The other Vagens had started to realise that he was no longer a figure of fun but a downright liability. He couldn't fight, he wouldn't kill, and he didn't seem to have the first idea about looting or pillaging. He didn't even have any dress sense – he'd gone on one raid wearing a yellow cardigan that his mum had knitted him. Quite frankly, he was a total embarrassment, and the sooner something was done about him, the better.

Dene would probably have been demoted to some demeaning farming job (a move that would have absolutely delighted him) if it hadn't been for his father. Denhelm was a widely respected old warrior, and one of the village elders to boot. And so a compromise had been reached. Dene had become acolyte to Sadric the Priapic, the village priest. There was a tradition amongst the Vagens that the priest should accompany each raid, to propitiate the Gods and ensure success. Sadric had been getting on a bit and preferred to stay at home and indulge his dubious pleasures, so Dene had taken over as Acting Priest for the duration of every raid. This meant he still travelled with the raiders (and so saved face), but he was allowed to stay on the longboat instead of charging about cutting people's heads off and setting fire to their huts like the rest of the tribe, and that had suited him down to the ground.

The other thing that had suited him about being a priest was all the contact with little furry animals, although priests were usually expected to sacrifice them, not take them home and keep them as pets. All in all Dene had been pretty happy with his new position – until he'd begun to get a bit better at it, and things had started to go wrong.

Initially, he had been so inept that it made no difference at all. His sacrifices and rituals had been conducted so badly that they had produced no effect whatsoever, but as the Vagens were remarkably good at pillaging and looting anyway, they hadn't needed divine intervention. But then, as he had improved, his actions had begun to have some effect. Alas, it hadn't been the effect he was looking for.

The Vagens have an extensive and varied range of deities, from the kind and benevolent to the cruel and malevolent. The invocation of a particular God's assistance requires a series of prayers and rituals specific to that God. Vary things just one iota, and your prayer may get misdirected. Dene, without meaning to, varied things a lot.

The worst example came during a five-boat raid down the south coast, attacking the villages in the marshy area known as the Maremma, in western Brannan. As they had sailed south, Dene had managed to overcome his habitual sea-sickness, and had busied himself at his little altar at the front of the leading boat, conducting a ceremony to invoke the aid of Benefera, Goddess of Good Luck. But with his usual squeamishness Dene had only stunned his sacrificial chicken instead of killing it. As a result, the whole ritual was delivered up to Cloaca, the Goddess of Amoebic Dysentery, whose reply was immediate and thorough.

The raid had become without a doubt the most unpleasant in Vagen history. The few warriors who were still able to stand when they reached Brannan were so weak that they were soundly thrashed by a bunch of old men and women in the first village they came to. They had returned home covered in disgrace (and a lot of other stuff besides).

Overnight Dene became the most unpopular Vagen since Hari the Shipwright. Because of his father he was still taken on raids, but he was banned from conducting any but the simplest of religious rituals, and some raid leaders wouldn't allow him to do

46

anything at all. When the village Headman's son, Krage, had led a raid he'd had Dene put in a row-boat and towed twenty feet behind the longship. The little boat had pitched and yawed like a funfair ride, and Dene had been as sick as a *barrot* for the whole journey.

It had been Krage who had given Dene the scornful nickname of Plonker, which had joyfully been taken up by the whole village (with the sole exception of Marten). But, thought Marten, as he watched Dene trip over a small tuft of grass and fall headlong into a patch of nettles, you can't let friendship blind you to reality. Plonker was, alas, a sadly accurate nickname for a man who was totally incapable of crossing a vast empty field without knocking something over.

He watched as his friend fought his way clear of the nettles and began to climb the hill towards him. Marten thought that he recognised the signs. Dene, who had been happy and carefree for the past few days, now had a preoccupied air. As he climbed he was muttering to himself and moodily swiping the flower-heads off the top of the spiky *bullow* plants with a stick as he passed them. There could only be one reason. Krage was due back.

As Dene came closer the goats, which had been milling about eating grass in their usual supercilious fashion, perked up and trotted down to meet him. For some reason they all seemed to love him, and he in his turn liked them, and had a pat on the back or a scratch on the neck for each. Even more baffling was the fact that he could tell them all apart and had a name for each one. This amazed Marten, as the goats were so matted and hairy that the only way he could even tell the males from the females was by the smell. The females smelt appalling. The males smelt much, much worse.

Eventually Dene managed to push his way through the flock. Sitting down on a tussock beside Marten he gazed out to sea. He still looked preoccupied.

'So,' said Marten, casually, 'Krage's home from the raid, is he?'

'Yeah. Fjonë saw the ships heading along the south coast of the island from the cliffs. They should be putting into harbour about now.' Dene poked moodily at a few goat droppings with his stick and looked of puzzled. 'How did you know that?' he went on.

'Your face. I can read you like a book.'

'But you can't read.'

'Well, books, no. But I can read you. Since Krage took old Sadric with him on the raid last week, and insisted you stayed here, you've been as happy as a goat in, er . . .' Marten paused and cursed himself mentally. One of the problems with being a goatherd was that the goat motif tended to take over your life. Sometimes it could ruin a good conversation. 'Well, you've been very happy. But I can tell Krage's due back because you're looking as miserable as, er . . .' Marten dragged himself away from another goat reference. '. . . as miserable as a wet chicken.'

'Oh, Krage's not so bad.'

'Not so bad? He makes your life a misery. He's always picking on you!'

'I wouldn't say that . . .'

'I would.'

'Well, he does like his little joke . . .'

'Little joke? You mean like that time when he tied you upside-down to a tree with an apple balanced on your crotch and fired arrows at it?'

'I wasn't hurt.'

'Or the time he got you pissed and then set fire to your bed while you were sleeping it off?'

'He's just a little high-spirited, that's all.'

Marten shook his head in exasperation. Dene seemed to have the ability to find good in anyone. Despite the fact that Krage bullied him remorselessly, he still somehow managed to be in awe of the guy, almost to admire him. Mind you, most of the tribe admired Krage. Strong, self-confident, a born warrior and a natural leader, he was considered a certainty not only to follow his father Kaal as the next Headman, but also to become the next Chief Executive (the name given to the overall Vagen leader, chosen from the Headmen of all fourteen villages). Marten was amongst a small minority of people who thought that Krage was a cruel, self-centred psychopath. However, he had to admit that when you made your living through raiding, looting and pillaging, to be cruel, self-centred and psychopathic was a definite advantage.

'Fjonë said that they were flying the black flag,' Dene went on, after a while.

'Good,' said Marten, automatically. The black flag was flown at

48

the mast-head of a returning boat to indicate a particularly successful raid. 'That means there'll be a feast tonight.'

'I know,' replied Dene. He tried to smile happily, but missed by a long way. At feasts Krage always got drunk. When he got drunk he got mischievous. And when he got mischievous, it was Dene who suffered. It had been after the last feast that the setting fire to his bed incident had occurred.

Marten clapped him on the shoulder sympathetically. 'Look,' he said. 'Why don't you stay here and look after the goats for me? I'll nip down to the village and find out what's going on, what time the feast starts, and that. Then we'll slide into the Great Hall after it's begun. If you keep out of Krage's way you'll be all right.'

Dene nodded doubtfully, and Marten smiled and clapped him on the shoulder again. Then leaping up he strode off down the hill.

Dene watched him go, enviously wishing that he had just a fraction of the self-confidence and strength of his friend. He sighed and leant back with his hands clasped behind his neck to watch the sky, but immediately jerked forward with a pained cry and stared mournfully at the dozens of small spines imbedded in the backs of his hands. With unerring aim Dene had lain back on the biggest *bullow* in the field.

The full moon edged out from behind the clouds that littered the dark night sky, and its reflection laced across the waters of the harbour like a streak of butter smeared across a blue-black sheet. The longships moored at the quayside jostled and rubbed together uneasily as the waves lapped past them, and their carved dragon-headed prows bobbed and nodded at each other as though in some strange courtship ritual. Then the moon disappeared again behind the thickening clouds, and the first faint tendrils of sea-fog came creeping quietly across the sea and began to wind about the wooden hulls rather hesitantly, as though worried that they might be in trouble for being late.

As Marten walked down the deserted main street nearly every hut in the village was quiet and lifeless, but the Great Hall made up for that. Light and noise poured from every door and window of the vast building. There was singing, shouting, pounding on tables, beating of drums and clashing together of drinking mugs. Like everything else they did, when the Vagens feasted they did it thoroughly and efficiently.

Marten smiled to himself as he strolled down the narrow path that led to Dene's hut near the edge of the village. He loved a good feast. It had been going for an hour, and the booze would have been flowing like water. Everyone else would be well oiled by now, and he and Dene would be able to slip in unnoticed and join in the fun.

He pushed open the rickety door of Dene's hut and paused. His friend was sat cross-legged in front of the little altar he'd built against one wall of the main room, muttering to himself. A grubby white cloth was spread across the altar, and on it were a bowl of water, a pewter plate and a couple of flickering candles. To judge from the smell of the acrid smoke they were giving off, the candles seemed to have been made from male goats.

Dene looked up nervously, and then relaxed as he saw that it was just his friend.

'I'll only be a moment,' he said. 'I'm just making a quick offering to Galvos.' Then he turned back and began muttering again.

Marten watched fascinated as his friend lit an incense cone from one of the candles and placed it on the plate. Dene still took his duties as priest very seriously, despite the fact that after the rather unpleasant incident with the frogs a few weeks ago the entire village had warned him that they would sacrifice him on his own altar if they ever found him conducting another ritual. It was a shame that he kept screwing up because he really had thrown himself into it. He had spent hours listening to Sadric (at a safe distance), reading books on the subject, and generally learning everything he could about the vast pantheon of Midworld deities.

Marten had talked to him about it quite a bit, and had learned a fair amount himself. He found it fascinating that the particular Gods worshipped by a tribe or nation varied in direct correlation to the characteristics of the worshippers. For example, the Buranya (a level-headed and generous tribe from the island of Emba Razindi) have a set of rather touching deities such as Lamos, the God of Party Hats, and Feth, the God of Cuddles, whereas the tribe of Fallon (savage and barbaric nomads from northern Baq d'Or) worship a disturbing pantheon that includes

Vangel, the God of Tooth Extractions and Root Canal Work, and Vai'ha, the Goddess of those Little Pointy Slivers of Wood that you Stick under Prisoners' Finger-nails. Vagen Gods tended mainly to be concerned with financial transactions, status, and the better things in life, although they did have a number of distinctly unpleasant deities as well. It was these latter ones who, for some reason, Dene seemed unable to avoid tuning in to lately.

Marten watched as his friend finished the ritual, muttered the final words, and then ducked and looked warily around. He seemed relieved to find that nothing untoward had happened, and scrambled to his feet.

'OK. Are you ready now?'

Dene sighed. 'As ready as I'll ever be.'

'Ah, don't worry. Krage will be too busy celebrating the success of the raid to worry about you. And anyway, he's been away for days. He'll only have eyes for his wife Kamila tonight.'

And with this reassuring but inaccurate forecast, Marten led his friend out through the door into the thickening fog.

By the time they had reached the Great Hall the noise level had risen to a point where even an orc might have found it a bit on the raucous side. Wine, beer and conversation were flowing like water from a burst dam, and insults, jokes, and bits of food were being thrown about with reckless abandon. The atmosphere was heady with the smell of spilled ale and roasted meats, and the aromatic fragrance of pipe-herb and elf-weed mingled with the acrid smoke from fifty brightly burning wall-torches to create a dense but oddly enjoyable fug.

The village elders were sat at the head table, which was raised on a small stage at one end of the room. In front of this were the tables at which all the warriors sat with their friends, families, and hangers-on. To one side a group of the more macho members of the recent raid were busily recounting their exploits with casual bravado to a captivated audience of attractive young women. You could have scooped the pheromones out of the air about them with a bucket.

In the centre of the room was the massive open fireplace, in which huge logs burned and crackled. Six-foot high flames sent out solid waves of heat into the already torrid atmosphere. (It was traditional to have a fire at a feast, no matter how warm the weather was, although some of the village do-gooders were starting to make waves about the number of old people carried off each summer by hyperpyrexia.) Then on the other side of the fire came the tables and benches that accommodated the rest of the tribe – the tillers of fields, tenders of goats and catchers of rats.

There was always a fair amount of social mixing at feasts as some of the warrior class preferred, like Dene, to sit with friends at the lower tables, but snobbishness and class consciousness were still prevalent in Vagen society. Members of some of the older families in particular frowned upon this intermingling, and there had been many cases in the past of people being ostracised by their family for marrying 'below the fire'.

Marten and Dene pushed their way past the scurrying serving-boys and sat on one of the lower benches, near Marten's parents. They grabbed mugs of ale from a passing tray, and then waited for their chance to seize portions of bread, cheese and roast fowl as vast platters of food were borne hither and thither. Having managed to fill his wooden plate Marten drained his mug in a single draught and grabbed a replacement. He turned happily to the man beside him, only to smother a curse as he realised he'd sat down next to Twbi the chicken-boy.

If there was one person who dreaded feasts more than Dene did it was Twbi. He was a man who loved his job and whose life was dedicated to the chickens in his charge, and sitting here watching so many of them being carted around on vast trays with their legs in the air, roasted to a crisp, was almost more than he could stand. But he couldn't keep away. He liked a good time as much as the next man, and he just adored the taste of roast chicken. It was a dilemma that was almost too much for him to bear.

He was currently staring at the remnants of the carcass on his plate with a mournful expression, and looked like a depressed blood-hound that has just had its dinner stolen. Marten decided to try and cheer him up a bit.

'Hi, Twbi. Enjoying the party?'

Klat! Wrong question! Twbi looked at him with eyes brimming like saucers full of water and shook his head. Marten rushed on.

'So, Krage's done it again, eh? What a guy! Heard any good stories about the raid yet?'

Twbi shook his head, but the mournful expression left his face to be replaced by something a touch more animated. Now he looked like a depressed blood-hound that has just picked up a trail.

'Not really,' he drawled in his slow, sad voice, 'but there's a rumour flying around that Krage and Kamila have had a huge row.'

'You're joking!'

'No. Apparently half the village heard.'

Marten craned his neck and tried to peer past the leaping flames of the fireplace to the other end of the hall. He could just see Krage sitting in the place of honour at the second table, laughing and joking with his cronies, with Kamila sat beside him, talking to some of her friends. However, there did seem to be a marked stiffness in the way her back was turned towards her husband. Interesting!

'Any idea what it was about?'

'I think so. While Krage was away, Kamila has been hanging round with his sister, Klaer. And you know what *she*'s like.'

Marten did know, only too well. Klaer was a tall slim brunette with the face of a fallen angel and the speed and co-ordination of a *lenkat*. She was a better fighter than most of the men in the village, and had recently started a campaign for women warriors to go on raids. Marten thought she was the most wonderful person he'd ever clapped eyes on, but unfortunately, as village goat-herd, he couldn't do much about it. At the age of sixteen he had once managed to have a quick snog with her at a party, and Krage had taken him outside and warned him that if he ever so much as touched his sister again he, Krage, would personally drag him down to the harbour and drop him into the deepest part with a large boulder attached to his feet.

'Kamila wants to go on a raid, but Krage's put his foot down again. You know his line. The day that a woman can beat him in combat, then they can go on raids. Until then, a woman's place is in the home.'

Marten was just going to ask what Klaer's response to all this had been when Twbi's face fell again.

'Oh, no!' he moaned. 'I don't believe it!'

Following his gaze, Marten found he was staring at a large

platter of steaming chicken that had just been placed on the next table.

'That looks like Muriel!' cried Twbi, aghast. 'They can't have roasted Muriel! Oh, *klat*!'

Rising, he strode across to the next table and picked up the platter. Ignoring the indignant cries of the people sitting there he brought it back to Marten's table and plonked it down, then resettled himself on the bench.

'It is,' he muttered. 'It's Muriel. I don't believe it. She was one of the best. Always pleased to see me, she was.' He patted the crisp skin of the steaming fowl gently with one hand. 'I'm sorry,' he muttered to it. 'Oh, by the way, this is Marten.'

'Hello, Muriel,' Marten responded instinctively, then looked round furtively to see if anyone had noticed he was talking to a roast chicken. He felt a complete idiot, but then he'd never been on first name terms with the main course before. Embarrassed, he turned away to talk to Dene, and found his friend was slumped so low down on the bench that he was almost completely under the table.

'What's wrong?' he asked.

'Ssh!' hissed Dene, throwing him a look of pure panic. 'Don't look at me!'

'OK, OK!' Marten stared down at his plate and wondered why it was that he couldn't have normal friends like everyone else.

'If you look at me he might see I'm here, and I don't want him to know.'

There was no need to ask who 'he' was. Only Krage could induce this level of fear in Dene. Marten was just about to try to reassure his friend when he babbled on.

'He's had another row with Kamila, Ceb says,' he continued, nodding at the fat balding Vagen who was sitting opposite him, 'and he's in a really bad mood. He's going to take it out on me. He's told everyone that he's going to drop me into the cesspit! I don't want to be dropped into the cesspit, Marten!'

'Look, don't worry. He won't do anything yet, and the Raid Award Ceremony will be starting shortly. You can slip out while that's going on. Hide in my hut, he won't find you there. OK?'

Dene nodded doubtfully. At that moment Kaal, the village Headman, rose from his place at the centre of the top table, and as he cleared his throat an expectant hush settled over the Hall.

'Ladies and Gentlemen,' he began, 'and I apologise if I've left anyone out . . .'

The usual ripple of amusement ran through his audience. He always began the award ceremony like this, and they all loved it.

'What about old Sadric?' someone yelled. 'He's no gentleman!'

'Once again,' continued Kaal, 'we are gathered here to celebrate the completion of another stunningly successful raid. This magnificent feast – and hey, I think we should take time out here to thank Fjonë, Leusi and all the girls for the hard work they've put in to preparing the food . . .'

He began to applaud the group of women who were gathered about Kamila, and everyone joined in. Some of the women stood up and acknowledged the applause with half-embarrassed bows and grins, but Marten noticed that Kamila herself didn't even begin to smile. Nearby, Klaer was staring at Kaal with total disdain.

'Thank you, girls,' went on Kaal, with a sincerity that was almost believable. 'What would we do without you? We love you!'

At this point Klaer stood up and stalked haughtily towards the door, but with the exception of Marten no one even watched her go. They were all too intent on Kaal. Marten glanced around, and then carefully leaned down towards Dene, who by this time had slipped completely under the table.

'I think you'll be all right to sneak out now,' he whispered. 'They're all watching Kaal.'

Dene's head slowly emerged like a tortoise coming out of a long hibernation. He peered round doubtfully, then took a deep breath and crawled out.

'See you later,' he hissed to Marten, and then he stood up and slipped nonchalantly between the packed tables to the door. Marten waited resignedly for the crash of breaking pottery or the clatter of a knocked-over table to focus everyone's attention on his friend, but somehow Dene made it out of the Hall without a single mishap.

Wonders will never cease, thought Marten. Maybe that ritual to Galvos worked, after all. Dene must be getting the hang of being a priest at last.

So thinking, he drained his mug, pulled a moist, tender leg off Muriel (ignoring Twbi's aggrieved stare), and settled back to listen to Kaal announcing the winner of the Best Dressed Raider category.

Dene was so lost in his thoughts about the unfairness of life that he had been walking for a couple of minutes before he realised that the sea-fog had turned into a dense blanket so thick that he couldn't see more than a few feet in any direction. Suddenly he realised that he didn't have the faintest idea where he was. He was no longer walking on the compacted earth of the village streets, but through long grass and weeds.

Realising that he must have left the village he turned and tried to retrace his steps, but after a couple of minutes he was still as lost as ever. The fog was, if anything, thicker, and had a damp, cloying feel that irritated his nose. The temperature had dropped right down, and the chill of the fog seemed to be soaking into his bones like spilt wine into the earth.

He paused, and listened. The fog deadened everything and he could hardly make out a single sound above the continuous rhythm of the sea which, diffused by the fog, appeared to drifting faintly in from all directions. But then, suddenly, he thought he heard a distant cheer off to his right. With a relieved sigh, he turned towards it and set off again through the swirling greyness.

In the Great Hall the award ceremony was nearing its climax, and excitement was running high. The prestigious Most Innovative Slaying award had gone for the third time running to Mykel, this time for doing something highly unpleasant to a shepherd with his own shearing clippers. Now Kaal was about to announce the recipient of the Most Promising Newcomer.

'. . . and the winner is . . .' Kaal paused for maximum effect. You could have cut the tension with a fork. '. . . Nyjal, for the rescue of his brother, Jorg!'

There was another huge cheer, and to tumultuous applause the grinning Nyjal leapt up from his place and almost ran up the stairs to the stage. Kaal held up an authoritative hand, and the applause died down.

'As you may have heard, some of the boys ran into a little

trouble during a routine predatory incursion of a coastal village in Brannan. Unbeknown to them, the village was a base for a tribe of half-orc reivers, and their resistance was of an incrementally higher level than anticipated. As a result, five of our boys were injured, and Jorg was captured. This being at a critical time-phase of the overall pre-planned raiding structure, it was deemed necessary to negativise any organisational mass response and proceed to the next target. Nyjal, however, volunteered to undertake a solo incursive venture over a twenty-four hour period, and as this dovetailed neatly with the projected space-time schemata for the main body, permission was given. Nyjal, tell us about it.'

Nyjal stepped forward a trifle nervously, and brushed his hair back with one hand.

'Well,' he said, 'it was all pretty straightforward, really. After my ship put me ashore, I made my way back to the village. It was dark and there were only two guards, so when I'd dealt with them I had a good look round. There was rather a lot of blood splashed all over a table outside one large hut, so I went inside – and that's where I found Jorg. Or rather, what was left of him.'

'They'd killed him?'

'That's right. Killed and butchered him. I found his remains in the larder.'

A big 'AAH!' ran around the assembly. Despite their warlike nature, all Vagens loved a good sob story. Kaal let the tremor of sympathy die away, and prompted Nyjal.

'So then what happened?'

'Well, I killed the half-orcs who were asleep in the hut, and then I found a big bag, put all of Jorg's remains in it, and set off for the rendezvous spot. The ship turned up on time, and I guess that's all, really.'

'And where's your poor brother now?'

'Well, I knew he wouldn't have missed tonight for anything, so I brought him along. He's over there, by my seat.'

All eyes swivelled to stare at Nyjal's table. One of his friends held up a lumpy and blood-stained bag, from the top of which a white waxy foot protruded. There was an amused hum of voices, and a ripple of applause broke out.

'Nyjal,' continued Kaal in a deeply sympathetic tone, 'you

must have been very upset when you found your brother was dead.'

'Oh, I was terribly cut up about it. But nothing like as cut up as he was!'

The shout of laughter that greeted Nyjal's joke threatened to lift the roof off the hall. With a flourish Kaal presented him with his award and shook his hand, and Nyjal made his way back to his seat to thunderous applause, beaming all over his face.

Kaal waited while the noise died down, and looked round the hall proudly.

'And now,' he continued, 'we come to the final and most prestigious award, Warrior of the Raid. I won't waste any time. I'm sure you'll understand a father's pride when I tell you that the winner is, for the fourth consecutive time, Krage!'

Another tumultuous burst of applause greeted this not totally unexpected announcement, and Krage rose from his place and strode easily to the stage, accompanied by loud cheers. A smile played about his mouth, but somehow it didn't seem to reach his dark, rather cruel eyes. There was a faintly menacing air about him. He looked like Keanu Reeves might have looked if he had sold his soul to the devil in return for a lot more muscle.

At his lowly table near the door, Marten was joining in with the applause, but only half-heartedly. Like many of the tribe, he wasn't too fond of the gratuitous violence that had crept into the raids recently. That was Krage's influence, of course. There was a sadistic side to the guy's nature that seemed to relish killing, but Marten had to admit that Krage was a remarkably talented warrior. That was why the tribe would usually vote for his raids, that and the fact that he was Kaal's favourite son. Not forgetting, of course, his undoubted bravery. And the fact that he had an uncanny instinct for finding plunder. And, of course, his popularity. He had a knack of getting on with just about everyone. It was a shame that he seemed to have it in for Dene. Still, thought Marten, as he tucked in to Muriel's last few remnants and settled back to listen to Kaal's acceptance speech, at least he can't do anything tonight. Dene will be safe enough at my place.

Dene would have been perfectly safe at Marten's place, if he could only have found it. Unfortunately, he couldn't even find the village, let alone a single hut. The fog had really closed in around him, and its thick, clammy tendrils were clinging to him as though they were scared of the dark. He seemed to have been wandering around for ages, getting colder and colder and more and more lost. Still, the grass under his feet was shorter now. Maybe that meant he was close to the village.

You tosser, he thought to himself. You can't even walk down the main street without cocking it up. What would Krage make of this, eh? He'd never let you forget it. But look on the bright side. It could be worse. Krage could have dropped you into the cesspit by now.

At that moment the solid earth beneath his feet suddenly vanished, to be replaced by empty air. With a startled scream he toppled forwards. For one brief instant he was horrifyingly convinced that he was falling from one of the massive local cliffs, but then he plunged headlong into something that was appallingly smelly and slimy, but comfortingly shallow.

Dene had saved Krage the job and had dropped himself into the village cesspit.

Marten sat slumped forward, head resting on his hands, a smile on his face and his stomach full to bursting-point. He was thinking how lucky goats were. Apparently they had four stomachs. No wonder they were able to spend all day eating. Lucky beggars. And even when they were full they could bring a bit back up and eat it all over again. Chewing the cud, it was called. Marten thought he wouldn't mind eating Muriel again. She'd been one of the nicest bits of chicken he'd ever had.

The award ceremony was over now, and everyone was sitting round knocking back the ale and listening to the village story-tellers. (Everyone, that is, except Twbi, who had tearfully removed all the chicken bones from Marten's plate and gone off into the night to give them a decent burial.) It was traditional after a feast to have the storytellers recount a couple of the epic tales of Vagen heroes that had been handed down from father to son over the ages. They were currently relating the Epic of Grim Kamban, and had just got to the part where, after the slaughter of his wife and children by his enemies, Kamban arrives home to find that the Building Society have repossessed his hut.

As usual, Marten could feel a lump forming in his throat and tears pricking at his eyes. God, those old heroes had suffered! It made you realise how lucky you were, really. All in all, things could be a lot worse . . .

As far as Dene was concerned, things were about as bad as they could get. He was cold, he was soaking wet, he smelled awful, and a fair bit of the contents of the cesspit had lodged inside his clothes. And on top of all this, he was still lost. The fog still swirled about, although not quite so thickly, as though it was trying to edge away from him, but it was still effectively blanketing out both sight and sound. The only noise he could hear was a loud but diffuse buzzing, caused by several thousand flies which had caught his magnetic aroma and would dearly loved to have located him, but which were as lost in the fog as he was.

I must be close to the village, he thought. I've been walking gradually downhill for a while. Hang on, the grass has disappeared. I'm walking on stone. At last! I must be on the quayside . . .

For the second time that night Dene suddenly found that the solid ground beneath his feet had vanished, to be replaced by thin air. This time, however, he managed to fall into the bracingly cold water of the harbour.

Well, he thought, as the sea closed over his head, at least I know where I am. Pity I can't swim, though . . .

Then he heard a splash close by, and suddenly someone had grabbed him and was dragging him towards the surface. Then his head was clear and he was spluttering and coughing, and hauling oxygen into his lungs.

'Relax. Don't struggle,' said a calm, authoritative voice in his ear, and he found that he had been turned on his back and was being towed towards the harbour steps by a pair of strong, slim and undeniably attractive arms. Whoever had saved him certainly knew what they were doing, and so Dene relaxed as ordered and gazed thoughtfully at the hands that were pulling him so competently through the water. There was something familiar about them. Now, where had he seen them before . . .

Then it came to him. That distinctive black gemstone ring on the right hand – it was Klaer! With a sinking heart Dene realised that he was being rescued by the sister of the man who made his life a misery. This was probably part of some horrid plan of Krage's.

'Hang on,' he said. 'If it's all the same to you, I think I'd like to drown, please.'

And he started to struggle again.

In the Great Hall the Epic of Grim Kamban had come to its heroic end, and to lighten the mood the storytellers had followed it with the legend of Weird Eddie and his Herbal Tobacco. This was always massively popular, especially the part where Eddie discovers the strange mushrooms. As they came to the finale (where Eddie, convinced that he can fly, launches himself off the cliff-top and plummets five hundred feet down and straight through the hull of his enemy's ship, taking it with him to the bottom of the ocean) a concerted sigh of emotion swept through the hall, followed by a generous round of applause. The storytellers had done a good job.

Once again Kaal rose and lifted his hands for silence. He had one more task to perform before the feast broke up and everyone could stagger drunkenly off to their beds. The four candidates for leader of the next raid had to be chosen.

This was traditionally done by drawing lots. In one empty wine-sac went the names of all previous raid leaders who were still active. From these two names would be drawn. In a second wine-sac went the names of any warriors as yet inexperienced in leading a raid who had been proposed and seconded for the task. Two further names were drawn. The four candidates then had ten days to work out the scope, aims and logistics of their raid. On the eleventh day all four would appear before the assembled mass of Vagen warriors to make an in-depth presentation, after which the assembly would vote on which raid was to be undertaken. It was a good system. It was democratic, it ensured that there would be an experienced leader to vote for, and yet it allowed talented newcomers their chance. It was only unfair if you happened not to be warrior class.

Marten watched the proceedings blearily from his lowly table. He'd always drunk a little too much by this stage of the feast, to help drown his sorrows. He found it very difficult sitting there watching and applauding and all the time *knowing* that his name was never going to come out of the hat. He sighed and switched his gaze to his father, a few seats away. To his amazement Lobbo grinned happily at him and gave him a thumbs-up sign.

Good grief, Marten thought, even my own father doesn't understand. Feeling very sorry for himself he listened miserably as Kaal called upon his daughter-in-law, Kamila, to draw the names. And as if to rub Marten's nose in it, the very first name out of the wine-sac was Krage's.

It's a fix, he thought, as the hall exploded yet again with cheering. Look at them! Kamila's trying to hide a smile, and Krage is grinning all over his face. I bet they staged that argument, just to cover up her fixing the draw! Why doesn't my father say something? He can always tell when someone is up to no good, he's never been wrong.

But Lobbo was sat at his place watching the proceedings with a look of mischievous anticipation on his face, like a practical joker waiting for someone to come through the door with the bucket of water balanced on top of it. Marten gazed at his father, puzzled, and let his thoughts drift downwards in a depressing spiral of maudlin self-pity. He hardly noticed the roars of approval that greeted the selection of the next two candidates: Harald Silverbeard, a grizzled and wily old warrior, and Mykel, one of Krage's closest friends.

Then his attention was dragged back to the present. His father was staring fixedly at the stage with a tense expression on his face, and was gripping the table edge so hard that his knuckles were white. He seemed to be riveted by Kamila, who was groping around in the wine-sac for the fourth name with a look of rapt concentration on her face. Marten watched too as she selected a folded-up piece of paper and handed it to the smiling Kaal, who unfolded and read it. Instantly, the smile was wiped from his face to be replaced by an expression of distaste.

'And the fourth candidate is . . . Dene, son of Denhelm,' he read out icily, in a voice like an elven princess who has just discovered that the love-letter from her handsome prince is, in fact, an extremely filthy limerick. For a moment there was total silence, and then the hall erupted with laughter.

Plonker? Lead a raid? This was almost as funny as the bit in the legend where Weird Eddie, stoned out of his mind, muddles up a consignment of best Razindi Gold with a sackful of manure, and as a result his entire tribe end up smoking vast amounts of dried camel crap.

As the hall rocked with laughter Kamila looked blankly around, as though puzzled at this response, and Marten was probably the only other person in the place who saw her briefly meet Lobbo's gaze over the heads of the crowd, and who noticed the minuscule nod and wink of acknowledgement that his father gave her.

What the *klat* was happening? Marten shook his head and then rubbed his cheeks with his hands in a vain effort to clear his brain of the befuddlement caused by beer and by events. Then clambering to his feet he staggered across to Lobbo, who rose to greet him.

'Father, what's going on?' he demanded. 'How on earth did Dene get chosen?'

'Denhelm, his father, proposed him,' Lobbo answered, calmly. Now that Dene's name had been announced he looked more like his old, relaxed self, but there was still an air of suppressed excitement about him.

'But no other warrior would ever second him!'

'It's only the proposer who has to be a warrior. Anyone from the tribe can second a proposal.'

'It was you!' Marten stared at his father's calm face and felt puzzlement and, yes, anger that his father would set Dene up for such humiliation. 'But he won't be able to do it,' he raged. 'He's hopeless! He couldn't even lead a goat out of . . . out of . . .' Again his similes failed him.

'He doesn't need to!' Lobbo cut in. He glanced warily around and then took his son by the shoulders and continued in a lowered and oddly urgent voice.

'All he needs is a second-in-command who can plan, lead and fight as well as Krage.'

'Like who?'

'Like you, son.'

Marten felt as though his stomach had suddenly dropped down through his feet, leaving a yawning gap behind it. The shock was so severe that his central nervous system seemed to have packed in completely. His mouth worked desperately as he tried to form a coherent word, such as 'What?' or 'Me?', but his tongue appeared to have tied itself to his tonsils.

'Gnak?'

'Yes, you.'

'Zglop!'

'Dene would be a figurehead, because our laws say that only a warrior can lead a raid. But he can take with him *anyone he wants.* So you would be the leader in all but name.'

'Plish?'

'Because there are some in the tribe who are worried about the direction in which Krage would lead us. You are seen as our best chance to challenge him.'

'Fglump?'

'No, you have more support than you realise. But you must not waste time. You only have ten days to plan your raid and work out a presentation that will impress the tribe. So don't stand there gawping like a rat in a spotlight, go and tell Dene what's happened.'

Marten found himself staggering out of the Great Hall into the swirling fog with his brain racing. How the *klat* was he supposed to organise and plan a raid in ten days? They needed a longboat and crew to scout out potential areas, and there wasn't a single warrior in the village who would be prepared to crew for them. And it would be no use going to the other villages. Dene and his reputation had achieved cult status amongst all the Vagens now. It was hopeless. Hopeless.

No, he thought, as he strode down the dark, shrouded alley that led to his hut, it's worse than that. Because when we do our presentation, there isn't a man who won't laugh us off the stage. We're already scorned. We're going to be faced with total derision. Damn Dene and his father! And mine!

He stalked up to his hut, yanked open the door, and then skidded to a halt in the portal. For inside the brightly lit living room a soaking-wet Dene was sat on a chair with a look of complete and utter stupefaction on his face. And standing beside him looking relaxed, efficient and totally devastating was Klaer.

'We've been waiting for you,' she said, throwing him a smile that hit him like a thunderbolt. Marten searched desperately for something witty and charming to say, and found that his tongue was still locked into his tonsils.

'Glashk.'

'I see it worked, then,' responded Klaer, throwing him a cool smile. 'Dene's been picked as a candidate for raid leader, right?'

Marten just nodded. At least his neck still worked.

'Well, you'd better get busy,' Klaer continued. 'There's a lot of planning to do before the ship sails tomorrow.'

By sheer will-power Marten hauled his tongue free.

'Yeah,' he said. 'However, the problem is that they may have to provide us with a longship, but there won't be any men willing to crew it.'

'You won't need 'em. You've got women.'

'What?' Marten shook his head in blank incomprehension.

'You've got me, you've got Kamila, and you've got eighteen others who I've trained myself. We can sail the ship, we can scout, and we can fight. This is the chance we've been waiting for. We're coming with you to plan the raid, and if the village won't listen to our presentation, then we're going to take a ship and do the raid ourselves. OK? Or do you have a problem with this?'

There was only one way for Marten to answer her. Striding forwards, he held out his right arm and they shook hands, warrior with warrior.

'Here's to sea, sword and success,' said Klaer, in the traditional Vagen way, and Marten echoed her. Then they turned to Dene, expecting him to join in, but there was no response.

Dene, son of Denhelm, Vagen warrior and prospective raid leader, had fainted.

VELENTÁRI

*The constellations in the northern skies were named by the
Elves during the First Age, when both Frundor and Baq d'Or
were elven realms, and mortal man had yet to set foot north
of the Great River Leno. In those days the Elves were an
innocent race, and child-like to the point of soppiness. This
explains the rather embarrassing nature of many of these
constellations' names. For example, Cuniculus Laneus (The
Fluffy-wuffy Bunny), Agnellus (The Little Baa-lamb), and
Agnus Complexis (The Great Big Cuddly Baa-lamb).*

*In contrast, the more southerly groups of stars were
named by the human astronomer and depressive Tycho
Sourpuss, who, although remarkably talented in the field of
star-gazing, was a bit of a hypochondriac. The most familiar
of these constellations are probably Infectius (The Disease
Carrier), Acne Major (The Large Painful Boil), Acne Minor
(The Small Red Pimple), and Phthirus Pubis (The Crabs) . . .*

The Pink Book of Ulay

The prisoner was feeling very unsettled. Something was wrong.
At first, the four chill stone walls of the cell had been a welcome
change after the obscene luxury of that woman's rooms upstairs,
but now that he had been here a while they were beginning to
close in on him. He no longer felt safe here, and was getting an
urge to do something about it. But what?

He rose from the straw palliasse and examined the bricked-up
window. It was situated just above head height in the wall
opposite the door. Suddenly an all but forgotten anger rose within
him and he was beating and pounding furiously at the bricks with
his fists.

After a while he stopped, panting slightly, and stared closely at
the brickwork with a frown of concentration on his face. Then he
crossed to the tray that was on the floor by the door, picked up the

metal spoon, and began scraping away at the mortar between one of the bricks and the window-frame. As he worked at it the thin hairline crack that he had spotted deepened almost imperceptibly, until at last he was able to work the tip of the spoon into it. He paused for a moment and then gave the spoon a twist, and a small lump of mortar shot out and hit him on the nose.

Blinking, he stepped back and stared at the thumb-nail sized hole in amazement, then reached out a trembling hand. Warm air blew down and ruffled the tiny hairs on the backs of his fingers. Standing on tip-toe, he pressed his eye to the hole and peered through.

The broken-away piece of mortar had uncovered a small fissure alongside the brick, a fault-line that ran diagonally upwards to the other side of the brickwork. Through it the prisoner could see a tiny segment of dark sky, in which burned a single star, as red as flame. He gazed at this distant light for what seemed like an eternity, and a dull ache of longing began in his heart. He yearned to be free, to be outside under the night sky, and again the image of the slim female warrior came into his mind.

With a sigh he threw himself down on the straw palliasse. Who am I? he thought. Why am I imprisoned here? He felt that he had about as much grasp of what was going on as a *bewildebeest*.

'Why can't I work out what's happening to me?' he cried out to the little mouse that had crept out of a small hole in the cell floor and was sniffing around his empty plate. The mouse looked up at him with dark bulbous eyes and whiffled its nose.

'Because you're drugged up to the eyeballs,' it said, and then started to scratch its ear with a tiny paw.

'What?'

'You heard me.'

'How do you know?'

'Because I can smell it on your plate here.' The mouse paused, and regarded him with its head on one side. 'Anyway,' it continued, 'you must be on drugs. You're having a conversation with a mouse.'

It scurried back to its hole and dived in, and then popped its head back out.

'And if I was you,' it added, 'I wouldn't sit around waiting for that crazy bitch to get fed up with me. I'd get up off my palliasse and *do* something while I still can!'

With that it disappeared, and the prisoner was left wondering if he was hallucinating. He stood up and peered up through the window crack at the star again. Hallucination or not, that mouse was right, he thought. You'd better start doing something about this whole situation.

Tyson sat by the campfire and gazed up at the star, red as flame, that shone low over the Azure Mountains to the north. She knew it to be the pole star, Velentári (Old Elvish for Baby's Nose), though she preferred the Southron name of Gazhnektûl, the Eye of the Piss-head. It glittered malevolently, sharp and bright as a ruby, for they were high up in the mountains now and the skies were crystal clear. Tomorrow they would reach the high mountain valley where the city of Drolic lay, and she could cross another magic supplies shop off her list. But she was running badly behind schedule now.

She frowned across at the sleeping form of Arvie, who was lying wrapped in his blanket on the other side of the fire with his eyes closed and his mouth open, making a noise like a buzz-saw cutting up granite. Talk about a liability!

When they had left the chain-ferry, the Iduinian border patrol had warned them that, because of a vast increase in the depredations of Vagen sea-raiders, most of the country's militia had been sent to the west coast. As a result, brigands and robbers were flourishing in the eastern mountains. Hearing this, Arvie had insisted on travelling with Tyson to protect her. Normally she would have had a very short, sharp rejoinder for anyone who assumed that because she was female she needed protection, but Arvie was so obviously concerned for her welfare and so determined to help that it would have been like kicking a puppy. She'd tried telling him that she had changed her mind and would be going to Drolic instead of Tena, but he had still insisted on escorting her as far as the Drolic turn-off, and so she had made the best of a bad job and set off with the overweight sales-rep tagging along.

The problem was, not only did he bore her rigid with his inane chatter, but he also slowed her right down. On the first day they made barely twelve miles, and she had decided that next night when they had made camp she would just slide quietly off and leave him. But then they had been ambushed.

It was nothing too serious. Seven leering thugs with swords in their hands had suddenly appeared from behind some rocks and ordered them to stop. Tyson had been waiting for them to come a little closer so that she could deal with them, but Arvie had pushed past her with a very blunt and rusty dagger in his hand and a look of shit-scared determination on his face. It had been quite touching, in a way. It had also been a total waste of time, as the leader of the bandits had simply swiped the dagger out of Arvie's hand and held his sword up to the rep's throat. So then Tyson had got serious. Several seconds later, four of the thugs were lying on the ground, blood spouting from their slashed-open throats, and the other three were fleeing in terror.

As she wiped her sword clean on the leader's jerkin, she had noticed that Arvie's face had gone the colour of camp-fire ash and he was trembling like a jelly in an earthquake. When she'd held out her hand to help him up he had winced, and taken it as gingerly as if it had poison spines. And when at last he'd met her gaze it was with the expression of a young and innocent fly who has just discovered the depressing truth about his best friend, Willy the Spider.

The incident had knocked the stuffing out of him, and he'd decided to abandon his sales trip and head back home to his wife and family. Unfortunately, home was in Vabyus, a mountain town beyond Drolic. Tyson had found that she was stuck with him for the rest of the journey, and after such a graphic demonstration of the dangers of the area and his ability to withstand them she couldn't bring herself to slide off and leave him.

Tyson wasn't sure whether it was loss of face, whether he was scared of her, or what the reason was, but for the past few days Arvie had been withdrawn and taciturn, and about as much fun as a verruca. Still, tomorrow she could say goodbye and get on with her search. She sighed, and looked up again at the pole star. She still had a man to rescue. She hoped.

Tarl kept his eyes fixed on the flame-red star that seemed to be hovering above the crest of the hill, and concentrated on putting one aching foot in front of the other. Behind him he could hear the gentle clip-clop of Puss's hooves as the donkey picked its way up the shale slope. Tarl was tired, dirty, sweaty and unhappy. Even worse, he was sober. They had been out in the wilds for a few days now, trekking across sun-baked countryside and through dusty, sweltering hills, and he was missing city life. Also, he wanted a drink. Or several.

Tarl had come across numerous theories about drinking. Most of the people he had hung round with were devotees of the Big Bang theory. They liked to go out every now and then on a massive binge, get totally pissed, and have a really good time. But Tarl himself was a believer in the Steady State theory, which he practised whenever possible. He liked to have a steady flow of alcohol washing around his system, which was kept topped up by a regular (and frequent) intake of interesting drinks. It worked very well until moments like this, when there was no alcohol to be had, and reality thrust its ugly face into his life. Still, it could be worse. There was nothing much wrong with him at the moment that a good stiff drink wouldn't cure.

Tarl suddenly became aware that he had reached the top of the hill, and that the ground in front of him had levelled out. He paused, waiting for Puss to catch up, and looked back at the dark mass of the rest of the Gemae Hills, undulating away to the south behind them. *Klat*, he thought, that's one hell of a walk. No wonder my feet are hurting.

Puss came ambling out of the darkness and stood looking up at him.

'You're not going to start on again about wanting to ride on my back, are you?' it said.

'Well, it would have made life a little easier, that's all.'

'Easier for you, maybe,' snorted the donkey. 'I told you, I'll carry you half the way if you carry me the rest.'

'Look, normal donkeys carry people about all the time.'

'And normal people have a bath occasionally.' The donkey paused, its nostrils whiffling. 'Mind you, there's something round here that smells even worse than you do,' it added.

Tarl sniffed the air. An acrid, smoky stench was drifting across the hill out of the darkness towards them.

'Oh, yeah,' he said. 'Sort of a dirty, greasy, burning smell, like . . .'

'Like if your hair was on fire.'

'Oh, thanks.'

'Or what's left of it. Slap-head.'

'Now, you listen here, fuzz-face!'

But with a snort of amusement the donkey trotted off, and Tarl staggered tiredly after it. Just once, he thought to himself, I'd like to come out ahead in one of our conversations. It's not a lot to ask.

Then the ground before them fell away suddenly, and the two travellers came to a dead halt and stared down speechless at the view spread out before them. Neither of them had ever seen anything quite like it. Tarl had heard about Yai'El. Everyone had. But nothing had prepared him for the reality – especially as seen at night.

The city squatted in the edge of the sea as though someone had tried to throw it away in the ocean, but hadn't had the strength to hurl it far enough. Originally founded on dozens of tiny islands in coastal marshlands, over the years its citizens had dredged or drained the marshy bits and built on the islands until they had arrived at the modern Yai'El; a vast city rising from the waves, connected to land by a single narrow causeway and criss-crossed by a complicated and confusing network of canals, waterways, drains and bridges. But the feature that had made the city famous, and had become one of the seven wonders of the world, was the Night-fire.

As Yai'El had expanded, its builders and surveyors had discovered that hidden beneath the ancient marshes now covered by sea were vast deposits of Flame Ether, a gas that ignites and burns in air. By an ingenious system of underwater pipes these deposits had been connected to storage tanks in the city, which were in turn connected to a network of 'street-lamps', thirty-foot high posts with a thin jet and a stop-cock at the top. When darkness fell, the city lamp-lighters would go round opening these stop-cocks, and as the gas flowed out it ignited, burning with a red flame and illuminating the city pathways and canals below.

To Tarl and Puss, watching from the hills above, the hundreds of naked red flames that writhed and twisted above the street-lamps gave the city an unearthly, almost evil, look. Their reflections danced in the dark waters of the canals like sprites, and the smoke and fumes that they gave off settled about the houses and buildings like an ugly black gossamer veil. Tarl thought that it looked like some infernal vision of hell. He fell in love with the place instantly.

As they gazed, entranced, they could see the tiny figures of the night watch pacing backwards and forwards on the causeway.

'Well,' said Puss, 'the lights are on but, unlike you, there's someone at home. Shall we take a closer look?'

'No, let's wait for daybreak,' said Tarl. He was never too happy about marching straight up to places and announcing himself. For some reason, people often mistrusted him and threw him out. He preferred to sidle cautiously up in the midst of loads of others, and slip in unnoticed.

And so they settled down and waited for dawn to come up over the city that, had he but known it, was going to provide Tarl with one of the biggest surprises of his life.

The prisoner woke up to find a single ray of light lancing into the cell through the crack in the window. On the floor by the door his empty tray had been replaced by one containing bread, cheese, grapes, and wine. Sitting beside it were a couple of mice. One of them had a little white streak down one flank, and the prisoner recognised it as the one which he had imagined he was talking to the day before.

'Ah, you're back, are you?' he muttered.

'Yep,' came the unexpected reply. 'And I've brought my cousin Bernie with me.'

The second mouse nodded its head anxiously. It was brown all over, and considerably plumper than the first one.

'Oh. Any particular reason?'

'Well, as I said yesterday, your food's being drugged. If you want to do anything about that, then you're going to need a food taster to find out what has and what hasn't been affected. I mean, you can't stop eating everything, you'll get hungry. And if you need a taster, Bernie's your mouse. He just loves his food. Or anyone else's, come to that.'

'Won't eating drugged food affect him?'

'Yeah, but Bernie likes his food so much that he doesn't care. In

72

fact, he prefers it. He reckons that there's nothing better after a big meal than a bit of a sleep. Isn't that right, Bernie?'

The plump mouse nodded eagerly. It seemed to be quivering with anticipation.

'So, if it's all right with you, he can start,' finished the other.

'Fine,' smiled the prisoner. 'Be my guest.'

'Okay, Bernie, do your stuff,' said the first mouse, and with a little squeak of excitement Bernie scuttled onto the tray and started sniffing at the bread. After a moment he paused, head on one side, and then he nibbled a bit of it, squeaked excitedly again and started on the cheese.

'Apparently the bread's okay,' said the first mouse, and then added, 'and so is the cheese.' Bernie, after a couple more squeaks, had jumped up, caught the rim of the wine-mug with his front paws, and was now balanced precariously on the rim and lapping at the wine with great concentration. He shook his head, squeaked angrily, and then dropped down and began sniffing at the grapes.

'He says the wine is crap,' continued the mouse, 'but it isn't drugged. Ah, now then. What have we here?'

Bernie was studying the grapes with a look of rapt concentration. Gingerly, he took a small bite from one of them and began to chew. A happy little smile crossed his face and then his tiny black eyes closed, and he slumped on his side and began to snore.

'There you go,' said the first mouse. 'Drugged to the eyeballs. Told you so. Don't eat the grapes, and you'll be okay.'

It took Bernie's tail in its mouth and dragged the sleeping mouse across the floor to the crack in the flagstones.

'See you tomorrow,' it added, and pulled its friend out of sight.

The prisoner sat and pondered for a few moments. Well, either I'm hallucinating, he thought, in which case I must be drugged, or else that mouse *has* been talking to me, in which case I suppose I'd better assume it knows what it's on about. Either way, I'd better leave the grapes alone.

And with that he picked up the bowl of grapes, and began stuffing them one by one out of sight through a small hole in the wall above his mattress.

Tyson strode quickly along Third Circuit, threading her way

through the hustle and bustle of the busy town. The morning sun was already hot, but up here in the mountains it was a dry, comfortable heat, alleviated by the gentle breezes that seemed to waft down every now and then from the snow-covered peaks that surrounded Drolic. Everything seemed fresh and clear, and the air smelled of the pine-forests that covered the slopes of the mountains to the west.

To her surprise she realised she was humming. Still, it wasn't difficult to work out why she was feeling so good. She had at last managed to dump Arvie, who had been clinging to her like a maremma-leech ever since Dubbel. The moment that they had safely passed through the town gate she had slipped off down a back alley while he was pointing out to a merchant the disadvantages of the particular make of wheel on his cart. Now she had to move quickly. He knew she was looking for Shamen Corner, so she wanted to get there quickly and then drop out of sight until it was time to move on.

The shop shouldn't be too difficult to find, either. Drolic was laid out in a very logical way. The old town was built on the top of a sheer-sided hill, like an acropolis, and was known to the locals as High Drolic. The rest of the city was built round the base of the hill on a series of circular streets. Third Circuit was, quite simply, the third street out from the hill, and Shamen Corner's address of East 17 simply meant that it was the seventeenth house in the eastern section of that street.

Minutes later she was standing outside the gaudy shop front, glancing nervously around. She still had an uneasy feeling that Arvie was going to catch up with her. He had been very keen for her to meet his brother-in-law, who was editor of a daily newspaper in High Drolic. He'd told her that the guy would love to do an article on such a talented woman warrior, and would probably be able to help her in her quest.

'He hears everything that goes on,' Arvie had said, 'and it's a very influential paper around here. Don't underestimate the power of the *High Drolic Press*.' But Tyson reckoned that Arvie was just desperate for an escort on the last stage of his journey, from Drolic to Vabyus. Well, tough. He would just have to hire one.

With a final glance round she pushed open the door of Shamen

74

Corner and entered to the sound of a tinkling bell. Inside it was pleasantly cool and dark. Both sides of the store were lined with shelves stacked with row upon row of tins, boxes and packets. Down the centre ran a double line of tubs and bins, each of which had a scoop resting on top of it. Above them a sign saying *pick'n'mix* hung from the ceiling.

Tyson smiled to herself as she noticed that one of the tubs was labelled 'Grated bull's pizzle'. She pulled off the lid and nearly fell over as the smell hit her in the face with the force of a brick thrown from close range. The tub was almost full of an off-white gritty-looking powder that stunk worse than a posse of elderly male goats the morning after a night on the tiles. Retching, she slammed the lid back on and took a couple of deep breaths, then wandered along the shelves looking at the tins and boxes.

She was just peering at a packet of Gatt and Boulder's Woofle Dust and wondering what the hell it was when a bead curtain behind the counter clattered back and the shop assistant walked through. He was a young elf, tall and slim, with the liquid copper eyes and beautiful features characteristic of his race. As he spoke Tyson could just make out the soft burr of Nevin, the elven realm to the south-east of Behan.

'Good morning. Can I help you?'

'You could start by telling me what the *klat* woofle dust is.'

'Ah. Well, it's one of the basic ingredients of low-grade spell-casting. Its recipe is a closely guarded secret. I'm a little dubious about it myself. It's dangerous.'

'You mean powerful?'

'Oh, no, it's junior league stuff compared to some of the things we stock. No, but there have been quite a few recorded cases of regular users suffering strange side-effects. Loss of voice, juvenile behaviour, an urge to squirt water at people, that sort of thing. I reckon it will be added to the dangerous substances list soon.'

Tyson replaced the packet on the shelf hastily, and strolled up to the counter. There were several boxes resting on it. They were full of sweets; she recognised sherbet dips, love hearts, arrow bars and swizzles. She grinned happily. They took her right back to the tiny sweet-shop on the corner beside the council hall in Welbug when she was six years old. Her Dad had always let her buy something on the way home after her weapon practice.

'Swizzles! I used to be mad on them when I was little!'

'Here. Have a packet. On the house.' The elf handed her a little paper-wrapped tube of the sweets. 'We have them here for the kids,' he added.

'You get children coming in here?'

'Yeah, loads. They're fascinated by magic, and they all want to be able to do some. They're looking for spells to turn their big brother into a frog, or to make school disappear, or to get their homework done. We just give them some sweets and tell them to come back when they're eighteen, and they go away happy. Well, you can't be too careful, you never know when you might get a kid in who has the Power. There was a case up in Malvenis a few years ago. This little girl got her hands on some dried dragon-blood, and turned her child-minder into a rusk. He got sucked to death by her baby brother.'

'Nasty.'

'Mmm. But I reckon you're probably old enough to trust. So, how can I help you?'

Quickly Tyson outlined her quest and the reasons behind it, and the elf listened to her thoughtfully.

'In a nutshell,' she finished, 'I'm trying to track down someone pretty powerful who might have put in a bulk order for all the basic stuff. Just as though starting up from scratch. Have you had anything like that recently?'

'Well . . .' The elf paused and looked at her doubtfully. 'I'm afraid we have a policy of total discretion here.'

This was the point where Tyson would normally have explained just how dangerous a policy of total discretion could be for shop-holders from whom she wanted information, as it tended to start her off on a policy of total destruction. But there was something about this elf that she liked and trusted. She leaned forward and looked him straight in the eyes.

'I swear I'm not after revenge or anything like that. I just want to rescue my guy.' She paused. 'He's a good man,' she added tiredly.

The elf watched her closely for a moment, and then seemed to come to a decision. He nodded slowly.

'Yeah, as it happens, we have had an order like that. A few

weeks ago. We got this FACS⁵ from out of the blue requesting a lot of gear. Everything from run-of-the-mill basic ingredients to really powerful major-league enchantment stuff. I mean, dragon's teeth, for Braal's sake! We haven't shifted any of them since Badedas the Barmy blew himself up forty years ago. There just isn't anyone around who has the Power to cope with 'em. And she orders fifty! I mean –'

'She?' Suddenly, every nerve in Tyson's body was alert.

'Oh, it was a woman all right,' the elf told her. 'I can always tell. But I don't know who. We haven't got any regulars with that sort of Power.'

'Could it have been a beginner? Someone just starting up who's got a bit over-ambitious?'

'No way! She knew exactly what she was doing. You could tell from the way she collected the gear. We'd piled it all in the centre of the floor, as requested, and then ffft! A *Teleport* spell just whips it out of here in the blink of an eye, without even disturbing one speck of dust! No, a beginner would have taken half the floor with them.'

'And you don't know where the stuff went to?'

'Well, she didn't give an address, but . . . Look, don't quote me. This is one powerful sorceress, and I don't want her turning her attentions this way. But a few days ago we got an order by FACS for a batch of ground *lenkat* testicle. Just a few ounces, to be teleported to a location in Cydor. I'm sure it was the same person. The aura of the FACS was identical. I've got a touch of the Power, you see. I can pick up on these things.'

'Whereabouts in Cydor?'

'Somewhere in the southern foothills of Tor Yaimos, in the Chrome Mountains. North of the Yaimos Desert.'

Tyson nodded her thanks and strode to the door. Then she paused and turned back.

'By the way,' she said. 'What do people use ground *lenkat* testicle for?'

'It's a powerful aphrodisiac. You can make very strong love potions with it. They say that after a single sip even a eunuch could get an er –'

The door slammed shut, cutting off the rest of the elf's words,

⁵ FACS – Far-away Communication Spell

and Tyson was hurrying down the street towards Westgate. This has got to be it! she thought, and her heart leapt. She's got nowhere with him! He's not fallen for her long hair and her pneumatic tits, so she's gonna use a potion on the poor guy. I'm really going to have to move it now. Ronan's stubborn enough, and his resolution is rock hard. Unfortunately, if he drinks that potion it won't be the only thing that is . . .

Tarl leant on the old stone bridge and watched the procession of gaily decorated barges floating by below on the murky brown waters of the Central Canal. In the first one sat a young bride and groom, both grinning from ear to ear and acknowledging the cheers and waves of all the onlookers. Each was dressed in the traditional white, and the barge itself could hardly be seen, it was so covered in flowers and ribbons. The heady smell of *taboghee* blossom drifted up as they passed and enveloped the bridge.

'Ah!' said Tarl, sentimentally. 'Just look at that. You know, there's something about weddings . . . they always make me cry.'

'It's probably fear,' said Puss, coldly. Tarl frowned down at the donkey, which was lying with its head between its hooves, the very personification of boredom.

'All right, all right,' he muttered. 'We'll go and get some food in a minute. Just let me soak up the atmosphere a bit, will you.'

The donkey sighed ostentatiously and raised its eyes heavenwards, but said nothing more, and Tarl turned happily back to his contemplation of passing Yai'El life.

The previous night, watching the city aflame in the dark from his vantage point in the Gemae Hills, Tarl had thought it looked beautiful. Close up, it was even better. The old, weathered redstone buildings glowed in the sunshine as though lit from within. The streets pulsated with life as locals, travellers and tourists mixed and mingled in a maelstrom of humanity, and the canals and waterways teemed with boats and barges of every size and description, all busily ferrying people and goods from place to place. Wherever you looked there were bars, cafés and open-air restaurants.

Tarl sniffed the air. Like most city centres at lunchtime, it was filled with the mouth-watering aromas of freshly cooked food and recently brewed coffee, yet behind this was an underlying smell that he would come to recognise as being peculiar to Yai'El. It was a mixture of smoke, stagnant backwaters and the sea.

For a moment he drank it all in, and then his eyes lit on a quiet, shady alleyway that ran off at an angle from the quayside nearby. According to the street-sign on the wall it was called Balin's Shank, and there was something alluring about it, something that seemed to beckon silently but irresistibly. Tarl, who had an internal compass that switched on automatically in unfamiliar towns and guided him unerringly to the best pub, just *knew* that this was the way to go.

'Come on, fuzz-face,' he said. 'Walk this way.'

'If I could walk tha—'

'Shut it.'

Together they ambled into the shade of the alley. After a few paces it bent to the left, and instantly the hubbub of the city faded to a distant murmur that was all but drowned out by their footsteps.

'So,' said Puss, conversationally, 'now that we're actually in the city, any signs of that thick blanket of magic that you were on about, back in Atro?'

'Shh! Quiet!' Tarl gestured frantically for the donkey to shut up and looked nervously around, as if frightened that they would be overheard, but the few doors and windows that pierced the crumbling walls of the houses lining the alley were closed and shuttered. They might have been the only folk in the city.

'It's *klatting* well everywhere!' he hissed. 'The air's saturated. Look!'

He held his hands out and Puss saw that tiny little pinpoints of light were coruscating around his friend's finger-tips.

'Someone somewhere is just leaking Power,' Tarl continued, 'so let's not do anything to attract their attention. Don't say the M-word, don't even think it, OK? Just forget it. We're going to have to play this very, very carefully indeed.'

He turned and stalked off down the alley, and the donkey followed, its little hooves clip-clopping on the stone paving. After a short while the alley twisted to the right, and they found themselves walking along the edge of another canal. This one, however, was much smaller, and had an air of decay about it. Discarded rubbish poked through the green scum and the rotting weed that lined the surface, and the putrefying body of a pi-dog[6] floated near the foot of a flight of crumbling steps that led down to the water. Two others were scampering up and down the steps, whimpering with hunger and vainly trying to reach the body of their fellow, but as Tarl and Puss approached they slunk away into the shadows, growling.

'Yeuch!' said the donkey, looking down at the floating corpse and crinkling its nose up fastidiously. 'What a stench! Those dogs must be desperate.'

'I've seen you eating things that smelt worse,' said Tarl.

'Well, I've seen you chatting up things that smelt worse.'

'No, you haven't.'

'Oh yes I have.'

'When?'

'That time in Atro.'

'What time?'

'The night that you had a drink in every bar on the Vendai Strip, and ended up pissed as a *vart* in the Mortal Sindrome.'

'Ah. *That* night. You would remember that.'

'Well, I'd never seen anyone trying to take their trousers off over their head before . . . let alone succeeding.'

'That was quite clever, wasn't it?'

'The other people at the table didn't think so. You kept treading in their food.'

'They didn't have to complain to the management, though. Party-poopers!'

'Well, they were trying to have a romantic candle-lit dinner together.'

'Yeah, and that *klatting* candle set fire to my trousers.'

'You could have chosen a more tactful way of putting it out. Something a bit less . . . biological.'

'Well, I'd had a lot to drink.'

'I think they could tell that.'

Tarl smiled to himself and stared down at the scummy green canal. It was exactly the same bilious colour as a Gutwrencher, one of his favourite cocktails. He was just wondering if he ought to have one in the first tavern that they came to when there was a

---

6 So called because their appallingly hard life means that they frequently lose limbs in fights or accidents, and it has been discovered that, on average, they have 3·14159 legs.

swirl in the water and something large and dark briefly broke the surface before disappearing again. The water eddied gently for a moment and Tarl wondered if he'd imagined it. Then he realised that the body of the pi-dog had disappeared.

'*Klat!*' he exclaimed. 'What was that?'

The donkey was peering at a faded notice on a post at the edge of the canal. 'Danger,' it read out aloud. 'Beware of the *skarrads*. Beware of the drain-worms. Beware of the *falanas*.' It peered over the edge of the quayside at the deceptively still water. 'Well,' it continued, 'if it's got big sharp teeth and an attitude, it appears to be in here. Looks like a nice relaxing swim is out, then. Shame.'

'Wow!' Tarl shook his head, impressed. 'Some waste-disposal system, eh? Come on, I can sense a really good bar not far from here.'

He led the way farther along the shadowed alley, which twisted and turned as it followed the quayside. Then the canal branched off, disappearing into a low, dark tunnel beneath a dilapidated abandoned warehouse, and the alley jinked to the left between high walls of crumbling stone. As they turned the corner the hum of human activity fell on their ears, and then after some fifty paces the alley opened onto a large, sunny square lined on all four sides with bars and restaurants. In the centre was a massive fountain. A jet of water sprayed high into the air from the open mouth of a life-sized marble statue of a mountain-troll, at whose feet four entwined dragons disgorged crystal-clear streams into the ornate marble basin below. There were people everywhere, sitting in groups or strolling in the sun in twos or threes, laughing and joking. Tarl noticed that most of the men wore their hair unfashionably long and were bearded, and that many of them were wearing trousers of a rough blue cotton and jerkins made from soft black leather.

Tarl gazed around for a moment or two, then sucked in his breath and nudged Puss.

'Hey, look over there,' he said, pointing to the far side of the square, where five horses were tied to a hitching-post outside a tavern called Huge Eddy's Maelstrom Bar. All five were gleaming chestnut thoroughbreds, large, powerful and muscular, and were the centre of an admiring crowd.

The donkey sniffed, unimpressed. '*Klatting* prima donnas,' it said. 'Look at them, lapping up the attention. I'd like to see them face down a *lenkat* in the Cumanceum.'

Tarl grinned. 'Listen,' he said. 'That bar over there is packing out the vibes. I'm going to have a quick drink and see what's going down. You have a sniff round the square and use that nose of yours to find out which joint serves the best food, OK? I'll see you by the fountain in ten minutes.'

The donkey trotted off with its tongue literally hanging out, radiating waves of hunger, and Tarl strolled across the square, threaded his way through the seats outside the bar, and plunged into the dark interior of Huge Eddy's.

He had to pause for a moment until his eyes had got used to the low level of light and his ears had got used to the high level of noise. The place was well named. It was a whirlpool of people, a tightly packed swirl of folk of every description crammed into one long room, a torrent of sound and smoke and smells. A lot of the customers were dressed in the blue trousers and black jerkin style, and nearly all of them were talking about race-horses. There were conversations going on about which breed was the fastest, which was the most reliable, or which could accelerate the quickest.

Tarl eased his way to the bar, behind which the staff (three humans, an elf and two hobbits) were dashing about at breakneck speed, serving people and perspiring heavily. Tarl, with the ease perfected during a lifetime of drinking, caught the eye of the dwarf who was standing beside the till overseeing the bar-staff, and nonchalantly waggled his thick wad of banknotes.

'Hi,' he said. 'My name's Tarl.'

'I'm Huge Eddy,' growled the dwarf. He had a dark forked beard, and a battered face that looked as hard as the hobs of hell. An evil-looking battle-axe was thrust through his stout leather belt. 'Wanna drink?'

'Yeah. Got any Low In Brow?'

Huge Eddy's face moved as close to a smile as it was capable. 'A man of taste, huh?' he growled, and began to pull a foaming mug of ale from one of the beer pumps.

Tarl hid his satisfaction. His first priority on entering a new tavern was always to get matey with the landlord, just in case any trouble arose later. He was well aware that Low In Brow was a

Dwarfish lager brewed beneath the Chrome Mountains, and that all dwarves were very fond of it.

'You in town for the races?' continued Huge Eddy.

'The races?'

'The Thoroughbred Trophy.'

'Oh . . . yes. Yes, that's right.' Light dawned for Tarl. He pulled the mug towards him and took a deep, thoughtful draught of beer. So it was Thoroughbred Trophy week, was it? That explained a lot. He had heard of these races, where huge, powerful horses raced around the streets of Yai'El. By tradition, anyone could enter, and what with so many amateurs trying to control such big fast steeds around a twisting, turning course of narrow alleys, quaysides and streets, dozens died every year. It was reckoned to be the most dangerous sporting event outside of the Terrordrome in Velos.

Huge Eddy eyed the wad of notes as Tarl peeled one off and stuffed the rest back inside his jerkin.

'If you're betting on the races,' he said, 'then maybe you should talk to some of the riders. There's five of them over there in the corner. They're riding in the Beltane Sprint this afternoon.'

Tarl tried to peer across but couldn't see past the throng of people, so taking his mug he wormed his way through and, to his delight, found himself watching a card game. A couple of dwarves, a fat, heavily perspiring merchant and three grim-faced women warriors were playing Cydorian Sweat. Tarl's fingers began to itch and he flexed them idly, yearning to feel the smooth shiny surfaces of the cards flicking out from under his finger-tips. He had just decided that he would ask to sit in as soon as the first person dropped out when he realised that they were playing with mage-cards. Immediately the itch in his fingers stopped. *Klat!* he thought. I'm not going to get burned with them again!

The problem with playing cards with strangers, as lots of people have found to their cost, is that you may run up against someone who cheats, either by sleight of hand or by use of magic. And so, some years ago, the Confederation of Master Wizards got together and came up with the idea of magical tamper-proof packs, known as mage-cards. They cost a lot more than a normal pack, but when you use them you can be sure that the game is straight. Tarl had never forgotten the time he'd first encountered them, during a serious game of draw poker in an orc speakeasy in High Meneal. He was just dealing himself a full-house when two of the cards started squeaking, 'He's dealt me off the bottom! He's dealt me off the bottom!' He'd been lucky to get away with his life. Since then he'd kept clear of mage-cards. It wasn't that he invariably cheated every time he played, but he did like to feel that he had an edge if necessary.

Sighing, he switched his attention to the onlookers. Two more women warriors were standing near the three playing cards, drinking and talking desultorily together, and Tarl reckoned that the five women must be the riders of the horses outside. One of the two standing had brown hair shaved very short, with a dagger pattern shaved even shorter on each side of her skull. Six or seven silver bands hung from her right ear, and small silver pins were inserted in pierced holes in her nose, eyebrow and cheek. She wore rough black leggings and a black sleeveless tunic of orc design, and her tanned right arm was tattooed with a multi-coloured snake. Her companion was very tall, with long fair hair and pale skin, and was dressed in dark-brown warrior leathers. Both had bows slung across their backs, and broad-bladed swords hung in sheaths from their waists.

Tarl sidled up to them and pasted his cheesiest, most ingratiating grin in place.

'Hi,' he said. 'You girls own those horses outside?'

The woman with the short brown hair fixed him with a stare from ice-blue eyes. 'What if we do?' she answered in a voice as safe and welcoming as a scorpion with chronic back-ache.

'Oh, nothing. I was impressed, that's all. They're beautiful horses, really beautiful. Er . . .' The ice-blue eyes seemed to be boring a hole straight out of the back of Tarl's skull. He shifted uneasily. 'Um . . . my name's Tarl, by the way.'

'I'm Ravannon. This is Blue Sonjë.' She indicated the tall fair warrior. Tarl stared up at her.

'Blue Sonjë? Why do they call you that?'

The tall warrior turned a pair of flint-like green eyes on him. 'None of your *klatting* business, you *wegging* little *spav*. So *klat* off.'

Tarl blinked. He was impressed. He hadn't heard language like this since he worked amongst orcs.

'Coo, you don't half remind me of a friend of mine,' he burbled. 'She's a warrior too. Tyson, her name is. We've been –'

'Tyson?' Ravannon cut in. '*The* Tyson? Tyson of Welbug?'

'That's right. We've been travelling together.'

'You move in exalted circles.' Ravannon grinned and held out a hand. 'Any friend of Tyson's is OK with us,' she added as she and Tarl shook hands. 'Right, Sonjë?'

'Too *klatting* right. No shit.'

Ravannon put an arm around his shoulders and lowered her voice. 'So, you want to know about the horses, eh? Thinking of having a bet on the race this afternoon, are you?'

'Maybe just a little flutter. You know.'

'OK. Well, I'm riding Night Hawk. He's a nice horse, but too young. He needs the experience. He'll be better next year. Sonjë's on Silver Wing. He's too slow for a sprint. He'll be more suited to the All-night Endurance, on Sunday. Bathsuke over there rides Fire Blade.'

She indicated one of the card-playing women, a small slim warrior who seemed to have an awful lot of money piled in front of her. As they watched she laid down her cards with a flourish and began to scoop in the kitty.

'He's too big for her, really,' Ravannon went on, 'but she's not here for the races. She comes to play cards.' Tarl felt a quickening of interest. A card player, eh? And she was pretty good-looking, too.

'Now Judge there has a fair chance,' continued Ravannon, indicating the black woman sat next to Bathsuke. She had long snake-like dreadlocks that reminded Tarl of Ronan, and he felt a twinge of guilt as he watched her shuffle and deal the cards like an Orcville professional.

'She's a good rider,' Ravannon continued, 'and Law Master is a fast horse. He's one of the favourites, but personally I don't think he'll win. He's got big, wide hooves, and I don't think he'll take the corners well. No, if you want to make any money, bet on Kaz the Knife there. She's got hands like steel, she knows the course inside out, and she's riding Slingshot. He's fast. Real fast. Right?'

'Yeah. Thanks. Look, can I buy you all a drink?'

'Go ahead. We're gonna be starting a second table of cards, if you want to join in. Then after the race we're gonna be having a bit of a party back here. You'd be welcome. You could tell us what Tyson's been up to lately. We heard a rumour that she was behind the destruction of Nekros . . .'

Tarl stood there in a daze, his mind whirling. *Klat!* He'd fallen on his feet all right this time! Thoroughbred Trophy week was one long festival, and it sounded like these women knew how to party. And thanks to Tyson's reputation, he was accepted. Booze and cards and who knows what else. That Bathsuke was a real babe . . . He was staring at her when she looked up, saw him next to Ravannon, and gave him a real slow burner of a smile. *Klat!!* he thought. I'm in!

He eased his way towards the bar, nodding absently to the small slight figure that bumped into him and muttered an apology, and it was only a few seconds later that the warning light flashed in his befuddled brain. Cursing, he thrust his hand inside his jerkin, but it was too late. His entire wad of banknotes had gone. He swore again and gazed frantically around, but the small slight figure had vanished, taking all Tarl's money with it.

Dipped! You pranny, how could you be so careless, he thought. Well, easy come, easy go. Let's not panic. Better find Puss, then we can separate some gullible stranger from a small amount of cash, bet it all on Kaz the Knife there, and be back in time for the party. OK, let's go.

He pushed his way to the door and emerged blinking into the sunshine. Puss was standing patiently by the fountain. Its tongue was still hanging out, and a small puddle of drool had collected on the ground underneath.

'Hi,' said Tarl. The donkey looked at him with its head on one side and screwed its eyes up.

'Ah,' it said, 'now I know the face. Hang on, it will come to me in a minute. It's been such a long time.'

'I was having a drink and I got talking.'

'Trying to do two things at once, eh? Your brain probably overheated.'

'Quit it, will you. I'm not in the mood.'

'Well, now you've actually got here at last, you can put your hand in your pocket and buy our dinner. I recommend Bofur's Bistro over there.'

'Too late. Someone else has had their hand in my pocket first.'

In a few pithy words Tarl told Puss what had happened. The little donkey looked up at him sourly.

'You're not fit to be let out alone,' it said. 'Honestly, I've had fungal infections that were smarter.' It sighed. 'Well, I don't know about you, but I've got to eat something. I'm famished. We'll have to use Plan B. Come on.'

They walked across to the west side of the square, and went up a couple of steps and through a swing-door into the narrow-fronted bistro. It was crowded inside. At every table the red-checked table-cloths were covered with dishes and plates of food, and candles wedged into wax-streaked wine-bottles guttered smokily. The smell of garlic, fresh bread and coffee made their mouths water.

Tarl stopped next to an elderly man who was tucking in to a thick juicy steak with relish[7] and turned to Puss.

'The food looks good,' he said in a loud voice.

'Yeah,' replied Puss, 'but when you're as hungry as I am any food looks good.'

'I suppose so. I mean, I've eaten some pretty bad things when I've been really hungry. Rats and stuff.'

'Me too.'

'What's the worst thing you've ever eaten?'

'Ooh.' The donkey pretended to think for a moment. 'I think it would have to be when I was young, and I had an owner who lived in the Nevacom Plains. They had no food at all, so they had to live on the millions of flies that were attracted by the cesspit.'

'They ate flies?'

'Oh, not raw. No, they invented scores of recipes. I think the worst one was probably the Crème Brulée.'

The donkey paused. There wasn't a sound in the whole bistro. Every eye in the place was on them.

'You take a few hundred nice fresh wriggling maggots, put them through a blender, then sieve them to get rid of the skins. Put the lovely creamy maggot-insides into a ramekin, and sprinkle a layer of mixed fly legs and wings on top. Sear under a very hot grill, and there you are. It was truly revolting. I don't think anyone actually managed to keep one down. There was

---

[7] Gusto Relish, an unpleasant sauce made from old tomatoes that is often used by cheap restaurants to ruin food.

something about the consistency of the stuff as it slid off your tongue and clung to the back of your throat . . .'

The donkey paused again as the stampede of footsteps faded, and then the silence was broken only by the *whuff-whuff* of the oscillating swing-door and the sound of dozens of people retching outside.

Tarl looked around the deserted bistro. 'Well, if they don't want all this nice food . . .' he murmured, helping himself to a plate of *mulampos*.

'. . . it would be a shame to let it go to waste,' the donkey finished for him. It was already halfway through the elderly man's steak.

Six minutes and three meals each later they slipped out through a side door into a narrow alley, and quietly worked their way back into the square. It was still full of people, many of whom were standing staring across towards the front of Bofur's Bistro and pointing.

'I don't think we'll eat there,' a doubtful voice said, 'not if that's what the food does to you.'

Tarl grinned and led Puss over towards the fountain. He was about to outline his plans for the rest of the day when a strange feeling began to creep over him. It was as if dozens of tiny ants with ice-cold feet were crawling over his skin. He could feel every hair on his body slowly rising to stand on end, and the air seemed to thicken until he could hardly drag it into his labouring lungs.

The donkey looked at him with concern.

'What's wrong?' it asked.

'It's close . . . very close . . . the magic . . . *klat* . . . can't breathe . . .'

A tight steel band seemed to be slowly enclosing his throat, squeezing, squeezing, but then all of a sudden there was a massive explosion on the east side of the square, and at the same time the pressure around his throat eased instantly, as though the band had snapped.

Everyone was staring across the square and Tarl, wild-eyed and panting, stared with them. At first there was nothing to be seen save for a small cloud of red smoke, but then the smoke seemed to twist and writhe, coalescing into the shape of a crimson serpent, long and slim and fierce, which undulated through the air above the heads of the crowd.

Then all at once the square was filled with illusions. Tarl stared in disbelief as nine or ten hooded and cloaked figures slipped out of a side alley and threaded their way through the hypnotised bystanders, for he appeared to be the only person in the square who was aware of their presence. Each of the figures seemed to be the centre for a different illusion. Around one, silver and gold dragons danced and played, their massive wings reflecting brilliant shafts of sunlight, their plate-sized eyes whirling like many-faceted jewels. Around a second, a dazzling kaleidoscope of colours shifted and flowed in a coruscating, mind-blowing psychedelic stream. Above a third floated a profusion of impossibly beautiful naked bodies, toying and stroking and playing with each other in a display of hypnotic eroticism.

The intensity of the magic took Tarl's breath away, as did the sheer effrontery of the figures producing it. For as they moved through the square, effortlessly casting their sorcerous illusions, they were robbing the captivated crowd blind. Tarl watched with reluctant admiration as they moved from spectator to spectator, rapidly frisking them, lifting a jewel here, cutting some purse-strings there, and their spellbound victims noticed nothing.

The nearest of the black-robed figures was projecting fire-spells, weaving fantastic patterns of incandescent flames in the air. A small group of merchants next to Tarl gazed open-mouthed in wonder as rivulets of molten gold rippled up and down their arms, whilst the slight creator of the enchantment deftly removed purses, rings and gold chains, slipping them inside the dark, flapping cloak.

From the moment the illusions had begun, Tarl had been aware of the Power within him sloshing around like water in a bucket. He had a near-overwhelming urge to join in, to let loose that Power. He fingered the ring in his pocket, the one he hadn't dared to use since Anthrax had warned him of its potential. Don't be a pranny, he thought. You'll get fried. But then the slight figure was moving towards him, head down, examining the contents of the wallet that it had just removed from its last victim, whilst absently controlling images of birds of flame that weaved in and out above the heads of the crowd.

Tarl could never work out later whether it was stupidity, pride, or something outside controlling him, but suddenly the ring had slipped onto his finger and he was silently rapping out Words of Command. At once the flame-birds fused into a pulsating ring which rocketed skywards in a pillar of fire, glowing red and orange, then shimmering yellow-green, its top churning in a furious cloud of energy that moved through blue to violet and then exploded in a vast and thunderous ball of white light. There was a collective gasp throughout the square, and the black-clad figure gazed up in sudden awe at the illusion which had been wrested so powerfully from its grasp, then turned to look at Tarl.

He found he was staring into a pair of huge brown eyes set in a thin, waif-like face belonging to a girl of no more than twenty. There was something about the eyes that seemed to grab his heart and shove it up through his throat until it was beating furiously somewhere between his ears. His head pounded, and he felt as if his stomach had been scooped out with a shovel and the resulting void was being slowly and persistently stroked with a fur glove.

The girl suddenly grinned mischievously and thrust the wallet into his hands, then pulling her black hood about her face she threaded her way through the still-enchanted crowd. Tarl watched as she rejoined the other dark-robed figures and they slipped into a side-alley and vanished from view.

Gradually, the illusions faded, and the crowd let out a sigh of regret and began to stare about them in confusion, like people emerging sleepily from a dream. The donkey was shaking its head from side to side as though trying to clear it, and Tarl suddenly realised that he was the only person in the whole square who had the faintest idea what had happened.

'My purse has gone!' yelled someone.

'My rings – and my chain!' came a second cry. All over the square people were angrily discovering that they had been robbed.

'Oi! What are you doing with my wallet!' yelled a third voice, and Tarl turned to see a merchant pointing at him with an accusing finger. He looked down and realised with horror that he was still clutching the incriminating evidence that the girl had thrust into his hands.

'Thief! Here's the thief!' The cry rang out from those close by and was taken up by the rest of the square. The nearby merchants drew their swords as one man and began to surge forward, and

Tarl realised that he was as popular as a *lenkat* in a crèche full of babies. He decided to bluff it out.

'Hey, wait a minute,' he yelled, 'you all saw those fantastic illusions, right?'

The crowd paused doubtfully. One or two nodded.

'So you must be aware that you're not just taking on any old bozo here. That was pretty powerful stuff.'

There was a contemplative silence for a few seconds.

'He must be a witch,' said one of the merchants.

'A warlock,' corrected one of his companions, pedantically.

'I hate witches,' continued the first merchant.

'Warlocks.'

'No, I really do. I reckon we should burn him!'

'Yeah,' said the guy whose wallet Tarl still clutched in a shaking hand. 'Burn him, but get my wallet back first.'

'Burn him,' the rest of the crowd began to chant. 'Burn him! Burn him!' And they surged forward once more.

So Tarl did what any powerful witch or wizard in his situation would have done.

He ran for it.

The prisoner sat bolt upright, instantly passing from deep sleep to total wakefulness. A finger of sunlight was shining down through the fissure in the bricked-up window, but he didn't need that to tell him that it was late afternoon. He *knew* it was, just as he knew that he was a warrior, and that his name was Ronan, Vanquisher of Evil . . .

His memory had come back! He could recall everything about Shikara, and Tarl, and Tyson. Especially Tyson. Not only that, but every sense seemed to have regained its old sharpness. He was totally aware of his surroundings and, most important of all, he could utilise every piece of information gleaned during his drug-dulled sojourn in the impossibly feminine apartments upstairs. All at once he knew exactly how to escape from this hell-hole.

At last! he exulted, swinging his feet off the palliasse and standing up. No more foul drugged dreams! No more hallucinations!

The little mouse sitting beside his food tray looked up at him.

'So you're better then,' it squeaked.

Ronan sat down again with a sigh, and watched as the second (and by now rather plump) mouse struggled out of the hole in the floor and waddled over to the tray.

'I thought I was,' he said.

'No, you are. I can see that,' squeaked the first mouse, as the other started sniffing and nibbling at the various foods. 'But you've got to keep your strength up, so Bernie here needs to keep tasting. Don't want to get drugged again, do you?'

Ronan watched as Bernie tested everything on the tray. The plump mouse gave the food the all-clear, but having sipped the wine began to get very excited.

'He says that the wine is very, very high class,' said the first mouse, 'but there's something in it. Some sort of magic potion.'

Bernie, squeaking with emotion, had fallen off the rim of the wine-mug and was busily trying to climb on top of his friend.

'Bernie! Leave it out, will you!' said the first mouse, uncomfortably. Bernie started emitting little crooning noises and tried to nibble his friend's ear.

'If I'm not mistaken,' said the first mouse, 'I think we're talking about . . . Bernie, quit it, or I'll break your goddam neck for you . . . We're talking about a love potion here.'

He skipped to one side, causing Bernie to slide off, and started squeaking furiously at his amorous companion, who lay there with glazed eyes, panting. But then he suddenly paused, his head on one side, and seemed to be listening intently.

'Someone's coming,' he squeaked. 'I'm off!'

Like a flash he disappeared down the crack in the floor. Ronan lay back against the wall.

OK, he thought, act drugged, and then as soon as whoever it is has cleared off again, I can get on with escaping. Then he felt something tickling his foot. He looked down. Bernie had wrapped his tiny front paws around Ronan's big toe and, with his eyes closed in ecstasy, was busily humping it and uttering little breathless squeaks which were coming a bit too close together for comfort.

Klat! thought Ronan, I'd better not even wet my lips with that wine! It's lethal. Gingerly he reached down with an expression of distaste on his face, lifted the mouse by its tail, and pulled it free. Then he held it over the crack in the floor and dropped it through.

'What is it about this place?' he muttered. 'Everyone is sex mad.'

'Good, isn't it?' came a low, sultry voice from behind him, and turning, he saw Shikara standing in the doorway. She was wearing something sheer and diaphanous that almost totally failed to hide any of her curvaceous body. In one hand she was holding a bottle of champagne and in the other a suggestively shaped cylindrical object that Ronan (who was still something of an innocent and who had met quite a lot of Hobbits) thought was called a bilbo.

'*Klat!*' said Ronan.

'That's the general idea, babe,' said Shikara, and closed the door behind her.

Tyson would probably have had no problems travelling to Vabyus if it hadn't been for Arvie. Hauling him as far as Drolic had delayed her so much and left her feeling so impatient that she was striding along the road with none of the precautions or care that she normally took. Even though he wasn't there in person, he still seemed to drag her down like an overweight millstone. The guy was the perfect cure for loneliness. After several days with him, she would never complain about being on her own again. He'd had a lasting effect on her, and somehow she just knew that for the rest of her life she was going to feel a desperate need to strangle someone whenever she heard the words 'have you heard the one about the . . .'

By the Gods, it was good to be travelling fast again! Up here in the high mountain passes the air was as fresh and invigorating as a glass of ice-cold water. Ahead of her the path snaked westwards around the lower spurs of the mountains, occasionally dipping down into tiny ravines to cross the gushing crystal-clear springs that hurled themselves down to the tree-filled valley below. Snow-covered peaks thrust skywards on every side. To the right was Tor Kemada, and to the left was the icy grandeur of Tor Villandene. Ahead of her lay the craggy, darkly glowering Tor Antino. This was Tyson's goal for the night, as at its foot, where the road reached the river Vabyus, was a staging-post for weary travellers, the Kwent Inn. An extremely violent place, she had heard, but entertaining, and she was looking forward to lodging there for the night.

She was just day-dreaming of a hot meal, a mug of beer and some interesting conversation with a fellow-traveller or two who might be psychopathic axe-murderers but at least wouldn't try to tell her crap jokes or sell her cartwheels, when the path curved away to the right round a massive outcrop of rock. She followed it blithely round without any of her usual care and found herself face to face with four tattered, grimy bandits. Three were brandishing swords while the fourth held a bow with an arrow fitted to the string.

Klat! she thought. This area really needs cleaning up.

Then she realised that she knew one of the swordsmen. He had been one of the treacherous councillors who had worked for Nekros back in Welbug. The man stared at her and grinned wolfishly.

'Tyson!' he drawled. 'This must be my lucky day.'

'Gawulf,' she said, leaning nonchalantly against the rock. 'Well, well.'

'Barga,' the man said to the archer, 'don't relax for one second. You have no idea just how dangerous she is. That little crossbow at her belt is lethal, and she'll have knives hidden in each boot and in her back-pack.'

Barga eyed her suspiciously, and raised his bow so that the arrow was pointing at her heart.

'She doesn't seem worried,' he muttered.

'Worried?' laughed Tyson. 'Why should I be worried? I sorted out your boss, Gawulf, and your boss's boss too. Four pathetic minions with brains even smaller than their dicks shouldn't be too much of a problem.'

She was trying to needle them, and was readying herself to move as soon as a chance showed itself, but Gawulf raised a calming hand.

'Easy, lads,' he said, then turned back to Tyson. 'You and I have a score to settle. I could be living in luxury back in Welbug. Thanks to you, I've got nothing! Well, I'm not going to mess about. I know how dangerous you are.'

He gave her a look of grudging respect.

'Kill her,' he snapped to Barga, and the archer grinned with pleasure and drew back his bowstring.

Tarl dodged the clutching fingers of a couple of laughing young warriors, ducked under a wild sword-sweep from an irate red-faced merchant, and leapt onto the rim of the fountain basin. People yelled threats and orders as he dashed along it, vaulted over the head of a dwarf who was shouting furiously, swerved between a couple of fat tourists (who grabbed at him, missed, and collided) and, yammering with fear, ran for the shelter of an alley near Huge Eddy's.

With a sinking heart he saw that a grinning soldier was standing in his way, sword drawn. Tarl tried desperately to think of a spell but his befuddled brain remained resolutely empty. The soldier swung his sword back and Tarl just had time enough to realise that he was about to have his head cut off when someone came hurtling out from behind a horse, yelling 'I've caught him, I've caught him,' and threw themselves on the soldier. The two of them crashed to the ground, and Tarl hurdled them without hesitating and kept on running. Snatching a quick glance back he was startled to see Ravannon rolling in the dust on top of the soldier. She was still yelling at the top of her voice, but paused to wink at Tarl and silently mouth the word 'Run!' at him, before yelling 'I've caught him!' again and rubbing the soldier's face in the dirt.

With half the square pounding after him Tarl needed no second bidding. He hurtled down the alley at a speed that would probably have won the Beltane Sprint, dived headlong into a deeply shadowed side alley, hurtled round a bend, and slid to a screeching halt. In front of him the paving came to an abrupt end at the edge of a wide, deserted canal. A set of steep steps led down to the scum-covered surface, but although there were a couple of ancient rusting mooring-rings here, there was no sign of a boat. Faced with a choice of swimming or retracing his steps, Tarl turned, but before he could move the chasing mob surged round the corner. Seeing their quarry trapped they stopped, panting, and began to edge slowly forwards.

'Look, I can explain!' whimpered Tarl. 'You've made a big mistake!'

'Someone's made a mistake,' said the man at the front of the crowd. He was a small, inoffensive-looking guy, but there was nothing small or inoffensive-looking about the wickedly sharp sword that he was waggling. 'And it isn't us who's made it,' he continued. Then he strode slowly but purposefully forwards, and the rest of the crowd came with him.

Back in the square, the few people who had got left behind or who had been trampled in the chase were muttering to each other and dusting themselves down. Beside the fountain, Puss was having a drink of water and thinking dark thoughts about the sanity of donkeys that got themselves mixed up with prannies like Tarl. And on the far side of the square, two men were watching the donkey thoughtfully.

'Here, see that tatty brown donkey?' said the first.

'Oh yeah. Yeah, quite sweet, isn't it?'

'I've been watching it. It got left behind by that little thief when he scarpered. And I reckon it would be just about perfect for tomorrow's ceremony.'

'Looks a bit fierce, though.'

'We'll just act friendly, like. By the time it realises what's going on, it will be too late.'

The second man grinned evilly, and then the two of them walked slowly across to the unsuspecting Puss.

As Shikara advanced into the cell, Ronan backed away. Somehow, his attitude wasn't quite what she had been expecting. The seductive smile on her face flaked off like old paint and she glanced down suspiciously at his tray.

'You haven't touched your wine,' she said accusingly.

'I don't feel like it,' he muttered.

'Drink it!' she ordered. Ronan could feel the Power in her voice. Rather than attempting to disobey her and finding himself literally forced into obedience, Ronan stooped down, picked up the mug of wine – and then before she could stop him, he had emptied it down the crack in the floor.

Shikara glared at him, ignoring the excited squeaking that began to emanate from the crack, and Ronan felt a faint, almost unnoticeable tingling inside his head. She was probing his mind!

Desperately, he tried to keep it blank, but to no avail. A look of astonishment crossed her face.

'You bastard!' she hissed furiously. 'Not to want me, that's one thing, but how dare you pity me! You pathetic innocent, with your brave notions of fidelity and love, trying to save yourself for that skinny bitch of a warrior. You don't know what you're rejecting! You could be the most powerful man in the world, at my side!'

Gleefully, she boasted of her plans for the immediate future, outlining the scheme dreamt up by the six well-dressed men and gloating over the power that she would wield.

'Even now,' she scoffed, 'they have no idea what they've started. They think to use me in their schemes, like they used that . . . that pathetic *animal*, Nekros. They'll soon find out just who is using who!'

She paused abruptly, gazing angrily into space, and the only sound that could be heard were dozens of little gasps, squeaks and pants coming from the crack in the floor, where some sort of murine orgy appeared to be under way. Ronan stared at her unfocused eyes and at the vein that throbbed rapidly in her temple. Five hundred years spent under an enchantment inside a magical sword might have stoked up her libido, but it certainly hadn't done her sanity any favours.

Suddenly she switched her gaze back to Ronan, and the lazy, feline light was back in her eyes. She reached out one hand and traced a pattern on his chest with one long red-painted finger-nail.

'I have to leave here tomorrow,' she purred. 'Tonight, I'd hoped for an evening to remember . . .' She looked Ronan up and down like a starving woman eyeing up a jumbo hot-dog, and suddenly her eyes were full of bitter scorn. 'But look at you! That wine was supposed to put some lead in your pencil. By the five great demons! I've seen more lead in a soap bubble! You're worse than a senile old man. In fact,' she continued, warming to her theme as her voice changed to an ugly snarl, 'you *are* an old man! *Aetate provectior fieristi!*'

At these words, Ronan felt his skin begin to wrinkle and dry out, and his back began to stoop. Aches and pains sprang up in every joint of his body. Little clumps of coarse white hairs eased themselves out of his nose and ears, and lumpy tumours and warts erupted on his face. His hands started to shake uncontrollably, his eyes began watering, and his lower jaw began to tremble. By the Gods, he thought, what's happening to me? My mind is going again. I can't remember . . . can't remember . . .

Shikara studied her handiwork with grim satisfaction, tinged with just the smallest amount of doubt. In seventy seconds he had aged as many years. That would teach him to reject her advances all right, but it wasn't really very likely to increase her chances of getting a night of unforgettable debauchery out of him. Well, maybe she would turn him young again when she got back from the east. Maybe she would just swallow her pride and use a straightforward spell on him. An *Uncontrollable Lust*, possibly, or a *Transform into Rampant Shag-monster*. Or maybe she would just turn him into a field-mouse instead, for being such a pain.

As the cell door slammed angrily and the footsteps faded away, Old Ronan lowered himself shakily onto his palliasse. She had been a pretty young girl, whoever she was. Had she told him her name? He couldn't remember. What a shame she had gone. There was something he had wanted to tell her. Something that was important. Very important. So important that he wanted to tell everybody he met. Now what was it? Oh yes. That was it.

'I'm ninety-two!' he said out loud to the four stone walls, and his quavery old voice was thick with pride.

In the tenth of a second that she had to evaluate her position, Tyson was forced to come to the unhappy conclusion that she would be able to deal with the four bandits, but was going to have to take an arrow through the body to do so. Mentally cursing the carelessness that had got her into this position, she was about to draw the Crow when Barga lowered his bow, his head on one side.

'Someone's coming,' he said, and indeed, beyond the outcrop of rock the sound of galloping hooves could be heard.

'Sod that! Kill her!' yelled Gawulf. But before anyone could move, the approaching rider swept round the outcrop. He was astride a large black stallion, urging it on with hand and heels, his dark cloak billowing out behind him, and in his left hand he held the reins of a second horse, the twin of the first, which galloped alongside. As he saw the scene in front of him he let out a roar of rage, twitching his reins to drag his mount sideways, straight towards Barga. The archer yelled with fright and loosed his bow, but the arrow whirred over the rider's head as he ducked, and then the two horses were trampling Barga to a crumpled wreck beneath their hooves.

Gawulf and his two remaining companions stood rooted to the spot in shock for perhaps half a second, and then Tyson was amongst them. A thrown dagger took one of the men in the throat, slicing his jugular and piercing his larynx, so that his scream of pain was a mere hiss of air. Her sword plunged through the stomach of the second to sever his backbone, and he dropped soundlessly to the floor as though his strings had been cut. Gawulf managed to haul his sword into position barely in time to parry her first lightning slash at his neck, but then it somehow twisted out of his grip and there was a flash of metal, a horrible burning sensation across his neck, and for some reason blood was fountaining out of his throat and his chest was soaked and everything was misty, so misty that he couldn't seem to see or hear anything, and he felt so very, very tired . . .

'Welcome to hell, baby!' breathed Tyson, and bending she wiped clean her blade on the back of Gawulf's ragged jerkin. Then she turned to thank her rescuer, who had reined in his horse and was trotting back. To her amazement, she saw it was Arvie. *Klat!* she thought, leaning tiredly on her sword. The only guy in the world who would make taking an arrow through the body seem preferable to being rescued. Well, I've got to be polite, but I am *not* travelling with him, no matter what he says. Screw him.

'I reckon you came along just in time,' she called. 'Thanks.'

'Well, I was a bit worried when we got separated,' he answered, 'So I hurried up to High Drolic and talked to my brother-in-law. I've borrowed these two horses off him, and I'd really appreciate it if you'd ride with me. They're good mounts. We can ride on from Vabyus down to Asposa, and you can get a boat from there while I bring the horses back. We could be there in a day, it will be much faster for you.' He looked at Tyson's stern, set face, and a nervous note crept into his tone.

'Listen, I want to apologise,' he continued. 'I know you're desperately trying to get somewhere in time to rescue your friend, and I realise that I've slowed you down because I'm overweight and unfit, and I must have driven you half mad with my incessant chatter and my lousy jokes. I want to make up for it. Believe me, I ride better than I walk.'

He fumbled to a stop, gazing down at her like a vast puppy trying desperately to work out just what its master wants it to do. Tyson sighed. Be firm, she thought. Tell him. Go on.

'I'd love to ride with you,' she said, and only someone more observant than Arvie would have realised that she had the fingers of both hands firmly crossed behind her back.

Tarl backed slowly towards the canal, desperately wishing that the fizzing sparks would stop flying out from his finger-tips, and wondering where the hell Puss had got to. The crowd followed him even more slowly, as though worried that he might yet have some wizardly trick up his sleeve. Unfortunately, he was well aware that his unpractised magical ability was nothing like strong or reliable enough to take on several hundred people. His choices seemed limited to two. Get in the canal or get killed.

Deciding that the first one might be slightly the best bet, he began to edge his way down the crumbling stone steps. Foul-smelling water trickled from the rusted, crud-encrusted metal grating that covered a sewer outlet in the wall at the foot of the steps, just above the canal surface. Tarl was about to hurl himself into the putrid waters in a panic-induced dive when another massive scaly body briefly swirled the surface before disappearing into the murky depths.

Klat! he thought. No way! He turned to run back up the steps, but then the suffocating sense of imminent magic grabbed him again. Panting, he stared in incomprehension at the myriad dots of light which were shooting out from his fingers like sparks from a knife on a whetstone, then looked up in fear at the advancing crowd. Suddenly, all the power in his body seemed to syphon out through his hands, shooting up into the sky in a vast fireball which burst in a flash of blue-white flame and an explosion like thunder. The whole crowd ducked, gasping, and Tarl sagged to the damp green stone, totally spent.

Then the rusting metal grating of the sewer outlet at the foot of the steps swung open, and a hand beckoned urgently. Panting, and with his heart beating at the tempo of some mad orcish drummer, he dragged himself down the last few steps. As he clambered through the dank, noisome entrance, the hand swung the grating firmly shut behind them. Just enough light crawled through for him to see a shadowy figure leading the way further into the sewer, and Tarl staggered blindly after it.

On the quayside above, the crowd picked themselves up after the fireball and peered down at the canal. On the bottom step was the wallet that had been stolen. In the scummy water, a couple of large *skarrads* lazily broke the surface and then disappeared. But of the thieving little wizard there was no sign, and the crowd turned away, muttering with disappointment, and went about their business.

ERUPTION

. . . but although most orcs are as psychopathic and degenerate a species as you will ever meet, by far the worst are the Uttuk tribe of the Irridic Mountains. Their lives are devoted entirely to fighting and partying. Uttuk babies are weaned at fifteen months from breast-milk (which is 4% proof) to a strong barley-wine (about 12%) called **Rashgak Krazatukul** *(which, roughly translated, means 'this should shut the little bugger up for a bit'). After that they never look back. At sixteen they undergo a rites-of-passage trial in which they are required to pass through the Labyrinth of Bloodeagle (a huge subterranean disco-bar), where they are made to sample every one of the hundreds of drinks available. Those who survive this test are fêted as adults by the rest of the tribe.*

Interestingly, the Uttuk words for 'adulthood' and 'cirrhosis' are the same, and it has been found that the average adult orc liver is so hardened by years of alcohol abuse that a filed-down segment will cut diamond. This has necessitated the addition of an extra level to the Moh scale of hardness[8]; 11 – cirrhotic orc-liver.

With this in mind, you should be wary indeed of accepting an invitation to an Uttuk party. At best it will leave a six-month gap in your life about which you will remember very little (and those moments that you do recall will be a source of acute embarrassment for the rest of your days). At worst, it will be an effective (though oddly enjoyable) method of suicide.

Orcwatching – Morris the Bald

[8] A scale used to measure minerals, and not to be confused with the Moe scale of hardness, which is used to measure aggressive combat ability. (Moe Crudnik was a Behavioural Scientist at the University of Unch Haven who was barred from every tavern on the campus for getting drunk and picking fights with anyone whose face he didn't like.) On the Moe scale, 1 indicates a stoned old hippy, while 12 represents a cave-troll with a grievance.

The orc party had been going on for fifteen weeks now. It had begun far to the north when Chigger had got together with his mates Shanker, Pustule and Spavin for a minor celebration near their lairs in the mountains to the south of Weldis. One thing had led to another, and they were still drinking in their favourite bar (the Troll's Haemorrhoids) when a band led by an *Uttuk* called Clyster had come in. Clyster had a bit of a reputation as a party-giver, and so when he had suggested moving on they had decided it might be fun to join in.

It turned out that Clyster was just one of many recruiting officers for a human called Nekros, who had some major plan in progress. They had actually begun to march on a city called Minas Tryk with a view to laying siege to it, just as orc raiding-parties used to do in the old days under celebrated leaders like Gaz the Tall, but someone had screwed up somewhere and the siege had never materialised. Instead, the party (now some several hundred strong) had crossed the River Leno at Westbridge and headed southeast to the Irridic Mountains. There they had staggered from drinking-den to drinking-den, and although as with all orc parties the mortality rate was high, other parties kept merging with theirs and their numbers grew and grew.

Last week they had reached that well-known orc night-club, The Severed Gonad, which was situated in a vast cavern under Tor Menting, at the south end of the Irridics. Or more accurately, it *was* a vast cavern. (Most orc drinking-dens were just a huge empty cave with a massive bar along one end.) The place was dark, smoky, and stiflingly hot, thanks to the many fissures in the rock floor through which yellow flames licked up, providing heat, light, and an almost overpowering stench of burning sulphur. There was no furniture in the Severed Gonad, but this was normal, as any place optimistic or foolish enough to provide chairs or tables would invariably find that they had all been smashed to tiny fragments over people's heads in the first couple of hours. If you wanted to sit, one area had small stone stools carved out of the rock floor, but most orcs preferred to stand – or rather, to mill about in laughing, shouting, vomiting groups.

Chigger was standing at the edge of the cavern, looking round. Nearby a group of snarling *Kulashaks* were quarrelling, fighting and thrusting coins into the massive Auto Mage-deck that was pounding out the deafening, stomach-churning rhythmic beat of 'Totally Pissed as a *Vart*', a recent hit for Bonny the Tiler. Beyond them another group were playing Blind Orc's Leap, a favourite drinking game in which each competitor is blindfolded, drinks a pint of beer, and then has to jump over one of the flaming fissures. A great roar of laughter went up as a sudden belch of fire incinerated a competitor, and Chigger grinned tiredly and turned his attention back to his friends, who were talking excitedly.

The word on the floor was that another raiding-party was imminent, and that they would be crossing the River Derchey and attacking Brend, in Behan. What's more, the rumour went on, this raiding-party would be huge, with parties from several other orc drinking-dens merging with them, and it would be led by a human general! And so Chigger joined in with the speculation of his friends, laughing and joking, and trying to hide the rising tide of panic that threatened to overwhelm him. For Chigger had a secret, deep, dark and terrible, that he couldn't admit even to his greatest friend. Chigger loathed the orc life-style.

To be honest, he quite enjoyed nipping out for a quick three-day drink with his mates, and when he did, his wife, Pellagra, hardly had time to notice he was gone. But these massive four-month jobs were purgatory, and he simply loathed the fighting. He would much rather have been at home, playing with his two little orclets, Kibes and Pessary, or putting up a few shelves, or decorating the rutting-room. But to admit it to anyone, or even to try and slide off before the party was officially declared pooped, was asking to be dropped down the nearest fissure and instantly incinerated. And so Chigger grinned and yelled and drank like a good orc should, and quietly prayed for a miracle to put an end to the party so that he could go home to his family.

In the expensively furnished room in a southern city, the six smartly dressed men were again sat around the table. They were awaiting the arrival of Shikara, and awaiting it with some trepidation, for she had been giving them one or two little problems. In fact, the leader of the six was beginning to think that they had made a bit of a mistake in having anything at all to do with her.

He drummed his fingers on the neat memo-pad in front of him

and looked thoughtfully across at the hag who was uncertainly stirring the cauldron in the corner of the room. The six men were dependent on hag-magic to work the intricate communications network that was at the heart of their empire. Unfortunately, every time they had talked to Shikara recently she had been in a foul mood and had taken it out on whatever hag they had been using at the time. They were now running very short of hags. In fact, the current one was really far too young and pretty to warrant the description of hag at all. It was a well-known fact that hag-ability was in inverse proportion to ugliness. The uglier the crone, the more powerful her spells, and a good-looking hag, whilst easy on the eye, was not at all good for the reputation of their company, professionally speaking.

All at once there was an explosion of air and a blinding flash of light, and Shikara stood in front of them, her long dress billowing about her, her auburn hair floating in the breeze of her material-isation. They sat blinking, rooted to their chairs with surprise, as papers gusted to the floor around them, and Shikara smiled to herself with satisfaction at the effect her entrance had made. Then her eyes fell on the young hag.

'Oh, dear,' she said. 'Oh dear, oh dear. You really are much too pretty for this job.' There was another flash of light, and the girl turned in an instant to a withered old crone with wrinkled skin, thin lank hair, warty nose and rotting teeth. The six men gave a collective sigh of satisfaction, but the hag took one look at her aged, shaking hands and fled weeping from the room.

'Right, then, gentlemen,' Shikara purred. 'To business.'

As the leader of the six men expounded on their plans and gave the details of timings and logistics, Shikara prowled about, her face furrowed with concentration. Eventually, as he finished talking, she gazed into the eyes of each man in turn.

'It is a good plan,' she said, 'and I can read plainly in your minds your belief in it. I can also see the fear there, for now you begin to realise my power. And in one mind I can see something else. Something more unpleasant . . .'

Suddenly she was staring fixedly at the vice-chairman, who sat on the leader's right.

'Lecherous and perverted thoughts and fantasies about me are something that I don't object to, in the mind of the right person. In fact, I quite often approve. But in the mind of such a fat and ugly old toad as you, they are nothing more than a gross insult. You must learn respect.'

Her eyes flashed, and the vice-chairman's face sagged. He sat rigid in his seat, the skin of his face grey and sweating, his fat little hands clutching the table-top so tightly that his fingers were yellow. He began to make an unnerving whimpering sound, and his piggy eyes glazed over with a pain so intense that the other five were unable to wrench their horrified gaze away. The acrid stench of hot urine filled the room, and then Shikara clicked her fingers and he slumped down in his seat, panting as though he had run a mile, and sobbing.

'Yes,' said Shikara thoughtfully. 'Respect. You must all learn respect.' And then she was gone, with no explosions, no flashes of light, just a faint swirl of wind that gently rustled the papers which had blown onto the floor.

The leader of the six men leaned back in his chair and wiped his suddenly moist brow. He had a horrible feeling that, this time, they might possibly have bitten off a good deal more than they could chew.

The party in the Severed Gonad had reached fever pitch. Word had spread round that they were definitely leaving to join with a massive raid into Behan the very next day, and as a result the alcohol was flowing like water from a burst dam. The Auto Mage-deck was operating at a sound level that was causing nose-bleeds in anyone within thirty feet of it, while several hundred voices were raised in a raucous sing-along to an old orc favourite. 'It started with a cyst,' they bawled. 'I never thought it would grow to this!' The games too were getting wilder and more lethal by the moment, and Chigger had counted seventeen orcs who had disappeared down fissures in the last quarter of an hour alone.

Then all at once there was a small clap of thunder, and a human female appeared out of nowhere. She materialised on the bar-top, clad all in shining black leather armour, with a small, almost dainty, sword in one hand. The laughing and yelling died away, to be replaced by puzzled muttering as the assembled orcs noticed her. Who the *klat* was she? What was she doing here? Did she have the slightest idea what she was letting herself in for? The hum of muttering grew in volume as some of the orcs warmed to the theme of what to do with her, then died away as she opened her mouth and spoke.

'I am Shikara. I am to lead you on the raid.'

There was a stunned silence, into which a large *Uttuk* near the bar shouted a suggestion so obscene yet imaginative that all the other orcs burst into laughter. Shikara stared at the *Uttuk* for a moment, and then her eyes flashed with a brilliant red light and two tiny points of flame rocketed out of them and smashed into the orc. For an instant he seemed to swell, and then he exploded in horrible slow-motion, showering every other orc in the cave with steaming little red gobbets of hot orc-flesh.

There was a brief awed silence, and then the orcs burst into spontaneous cheering. That was more like it! A leader who could explode you so entertainingly with one quick flash of her eyes was someone to follow into battle, all right! And so every orc settled down to listen to her with something akin to hero-worship. Every orc save one, that is. For Chigger looked at her long, soft, glowing hair and thought how horrible it looked compared to his beloved Pellagra's greasy, lank black locks. He looked at her soft full lips and remembered the rough caress of Pellagra's scabrous, slimy mouth. He looked at her two horribly large, round breasts that looked as though they had been artificially inflated, and thought of Pellagra's beautiful hairy, flaccid, scaly paps. All five of them. And it was all he could do to hold back the tears.

UNLIKELY

Many unlikely raid leaders have there been in Vagen history. Eric the Green, who got seasick just stepping over a puddle, Lars Blood-face, the legendary drinker, whose shaking hand and blunt razor made shaving such a perilous deed, and Flokki Mummy's-precious, whose mother followed him everywhere and insisted he wore clean underwear whene'er he led a raid . . . But most unlikely by far was Dene the son of Denhelm, whose first foray began with the laughter of the whole tribe ringing in his ears . . .

The Pink Book of Ulay

At first, Marten and Klaer had a bit of a problem in getting Dene moving. He had been in a state of shock since the night before, when they had broken the news to him that he had been nominated as one of the candidates for raid leader. Marten had been woken at dawn by Klaer hammering on the front door. The two of them had found Dene hiding under the spare bed, and it had taken a lot of persuasion and a few firm thrusts with a broom-handle to persuade him to come out. He had eventually emerged covered in dust and cobwebs, like a small and very frightened Miss Haversham, and had made a run for the door. But outside he had found a small crowd of villagers who had gathered to jeer and poke fun at him, and the massed chants of 'Plonker! Plonker!' had driven him straight back inside.

Recognising a severe attack of stage-fright, Klaer had gone straight to work on building up his confidence, and Marten had helped by pouring him a quintuple whisky. However, he hadn't made allowances for the fact that in the past few months Dene hadn't spent more than ten minutes at a function before fear of Krage had caused him to run for cover. He had hardly touched a drop of booze in this time, and had lost whatever head for alcohol he had once possessed. As a result the whisky had gone straight to his head, effecting a complete change of mood. Two minutes after draining the glass in one gulp, he had marched confidently but erratically out of the door and down to the harbour, with Klaer following him like a sheepdog following a high-spirited and recalcitrant sheep.

However, she needn't have worried. When they came to the quayside they found that Klaer's friends were bustling about their longship (the *Shorn Teal*) getting ready to sail, and Dene had thrown himself whole-heartedly into helping them. As he knew bugger-all about the intricacies of getting ready for a sea voyage this wasn't a lot of help. Still, he strode about issuing orders and trying to help (while Klaer followed him, countermanding the orders and rectifying the attempts at help), and the crowd that had followed him down to scoff found that there was little to scoff about. Suddenly Dene seemed to have donned the mantle of leader.

Meanwhile Marten, influenced by the impending voyage in the company of twenty of the village's most attractive women, had been home and shaved in the way that rumour had it Krage shaved – dry, using his dagger's edge. Unfortunately, Martin's rather soft skin wasn't quite used to this sort of treatment, and instead of an attractive designer stubble, Marten had come out with a face like an abattoir table. Ah well, he thought to himself as he surveyed the wreckage of his handiwork in the mirror, I look just like Lars Blood-face. Maybe I can become a legend like him. (Lars had led a series of highly successful raids that had looted breweries the entire length of the western coastline.) Sighing, he took one last look at his reflection and then slung his kit-bag over his shoulder and set off for the harbour.

When he arrived at the quayside, the air was full of the fresh salt tang that accompanied most high tides. The remaining members of the crowd took one look at him and quickly faded away, for his face reminded them more of Cyd the Vicious, a warrior who had ritually mutilated himself before every raid, and whose violent nature had been deemed a bit much even for the Vagens. Marten stood at the top of the stone steps that led down to the longship and watched Kamila, Fjonë, Leusi and the others bustling about. Dene was striding around the ship issuing orders like a true leader and only occasionally tripping over things, and Klaer was following him and making sure he didn't screw anything up.

'Someone make fast that horsey,' Marten heard Dene shout.

'Hawser,' Klaer corrected him.

'Stow all the whores by the bollocks!'

'Oars, Dene. And those metal things are called rollocks. With an R.'

'Sail the main-hoist!'

'Oh, God! Kait, brew some strong black coffee, would you?'

As Marten watched the preparations, he began to wonder if he was really needed. The others seemed to be managing fine without him, and despite his father's words he didn't have any great plans or ideas of where to go. Who the hell am I kidding, he thought. I'm just a simple . . .

'Goat-boy!'

The words were hissed fiercely into his ear from a range of about two inches, and Marten leapt like a mountain goat with nerve trouble. Krage was standing right behind him with a look of ice-cold fury on his face. He took hold of Marten's collar and jerked him forward. Marten found he was staring into Krage's eyes so closely that they seemed out of focus.

'I don't know what you think you're up to,' Krage hissed, 'but you'd better be careful. I don't like this business of the women going off on raids. That's man's work. Once you and Plonker have finished playing around on this trip of yours, you'd better not try for a repeat. Understand? Or I might have to do something about it.'

'But . . .' began Marten, but Krage tightened his grip and dragged him even closer so that their noses were touching. Marten winced. Krage appeared to have been eating *pasaroni* a bit too recently for comfort.

'And one other thing,' Krage continued. 'You'd better be very, very careful on this trip. Because if Kamila is in the slightest bit hurt or damaged, I will kill you. And if my sister is in the slightest bit hurt or damaged, I will kill you. In fact, if they are in any way worried, frightened or upset, I will kill you. That is, if Klaer doesn't kill you herself. I will also kill you if you lay so much as a finger on either of them. Understand?'

Marten nodded, and Krage released him abruptly, threw Dene a look that, had he seen it, would have had him cowering under the bed again, and stalked off.

Marten watched him go feeling a little bemused. Why did Krage think he was up to something? It hadn't been *his* idea for the women to come on the raid . . . although Klaer had known that Kamila was going to pick Dene's name, as had his father. Had they been planning it together?

At that moment Lobbo himself appeared, ambling along the quay towards his son in his usual laid-back manner. He smiled as he approached and lifted one hand slightly in a lazy gesture that might just by stretching the imagination have been described as a wave.

'Hey, son, how's it going? All ready for the big trip?'

'Well, as it happens, no.' Suddenly Marten could feel all his doubts and worries flooding to the surface. 'I'm sailing off into the blue with a crew of women and the worst raid leader since Horalf the Foot-fetishist, we've got ten days to plan a raid so attractive that the tribe will vote for us ahead of Krage, the most successful raid leader in years, I haven't the faintest idea whether to sail north, south, east, west, or upwards, and you ask me if I'm ready?'

'Hey, hey, calm down!' Lobbo said, placing a supportive hand on Marten's shoulder. 'Listen, we're not sending you out there blindly. Things are happening in Midworld. I've heard a lot of . . . messages. Trust me. I can't give you an exact set of guide-lines. You're going to have to play it by ear. But sail northwards up the coast, towards Yai'El. Stop and talk to people. And watch out for a very unusual donkey.'

'A donkey? You're joking! I don't want to sound ungrateful, but that isn't going to make much of a presentation, is it? Come on, lads, vote for our raid, we've found a small-holding and we can probably get away with a few dozen eggs and some straw!'

'Hey. Trust me.'

Marten stared into his father's level gaze and slowly subsided. He had to admit that, over the years, when it came to knowing what was happening, Lobbo never seemed to have put a foot wrong. In a quiet, unassuming way, the man was always right. He sighed. 'North, you reckon. OK.'

Lobbo smiled up at his son and gently squeezed his shoulder. At that moment, the sound of cheering broke out further along the quay. Turning, they saw that a crowd had gathered to watch

Harald Silverbeard's longship, which had left its mooring and was pulling strongly for the harbour entrance, its twenty oars flashing in and out of the water in perfect unison. A shouted command drifted back over the water, and at once the massive blood-red sail unfurled from the single yard-arm. For a while it hung flapping limply, but then as the longship pulled clear of the protected harbour waters it suddenly billowed out, and the ship leapt forward. Another command drifted back, and as one the oars lifted from the water and were pulled inboard.

Then a second and much louder cheer went up, and Marten saw that Krage's ship was under way.

'You'd better get moving,' suggested Lobbo, and Marten realised that everyone in the *Shorn Teal* had completed their preparations and was standing watching him and his father.

'Yeah. Right. Um . . . OK.'

'Take it easy, son. When you plan the raid, remember that a lot of our people are fed up with easy pickings. They want to be warriors, not murderers. And listen to Klaer. She's knows what she's doing. You'll make a good team.'

Marten embraced his father roughly and then climbed down the steps and swung himself aboard. The others were scrambling to take up their positions; Fjonë in the lookout position, high on the prow behind the carved dragon-head, Dene in the traditional leader's position at the steering-oar near the rear, and the other women seated at the oars. Marten clambered across to the last unoccupied position at the rear on the right, in front of the steering-oar.

'Throw it out!' yelled Dene.

'He means cast off,' muttered Klaer, and Lobbo bent and lifted the mooring-rope free of its post. The women along the port side thrust their oars against the dark stone walls of the quay, and the longship moved slowly out into the harbour.

'Pull!' called Klaer, who was acting as stroke, and Marten thrust his oar down with all-consuming enthusiasm. Unfortunately, no one had ever taught him how to row. The blade bounced off the surface of the water, swung upwards in a scything curve and smashed straight into Dene's face. With a grunt he fell backwards, dragging the steering-oar with him, and the longship lurched wildly across to the right. Before anyone else could react

Klaer had pulled her oar inboard, leaped out of her bench, dragged Dene off the steering-oar and hauled it towards her, bringing their ship veering back to the left.

'Just look at the *Shorn Teal*!' yelled someone on the quayside. 'She moves more like a ruptured duck!'

Laughter rang out across the harbour and Marten, whose face had gone a colour that would have matched Harald Silverbeard's sail, was painfully aware of twenty pairs of furious female eyes boring into him. He put his head down, concentrated on getting his rowing right, and wished (not for the last time) that he was safely back on dry land with just his goats for company.

On the quayside Lobbo watched and shook his head wryly. Not a good start. Still, not to worry. He had a feeling that things would turn out well. And when it came to having feelings about things, Lobbo had a rather unusual record. He had, quite simply, never been wrong.

Lobbo the Relaxed had been born with a quite remarkable talent. He could read other people's minds. From an early age he'd found that he could pick up their thoughts and emotions as easily as he could hear them speak. And not just humans, either, but elves, dwarves, orcs, and even animals. In fact, as a child he had been a little frightened by the furtive images of greed, lust, anger and hatred that churned about in the average human brain, and had spent a lot of time listening to the more pleasant driftings that went on in animal minds.

Then he had discovered that he could broadcast his own thoughts and emotions, although the fact that other people weren't blessed with his talent meant that they had no idea where these thoughts were coming from. This could have been a powerful weapon in the wrong hands, but luckily Lobbo had a calm and unambitious nature and a conscience that restrained him from abusing his talent. However, he did enjoy broadcasting the odd rude images into the minds of his grandmother's maiden friends and watching their faces, and whenever any of the men who were paying court to his mother called at their home he would stir up the dog's emotions with canine lust and push it into conducting a brief but enthusiastic affair with the visitor's leg.

On reaching adulthood he had moved gradually into the field of rat-catching, advertising himself as an environmentally sound pest controller. He had no need of poisons, powders or chemicals. If someone had a houseful of mice, Lobbo would stroll along in his usual relaxed way and broadcast a mental message to the mice that they were upsetting the householders, and that it would be awfully nice of them to move on. If that didn't work, he would broadcast a warning that pretty soon they would be living in a house which was brimful of traps and poisoned baits, and that it might be a little dangerous, so why not move on to somewhere a little safer? This frequently did the job, but if he was faced with stubborn, devil-may-care mice, it was occasionally necessary to move on to stage three. This involved broadcasting a sudden very loud thought to the mice while they were half asleep. In cat language. The effect on a dozing mouse of a loud miaou right inside its brain can only be described as devastating, and invariably next day a little posse of grey-haired, shaking mice would move out in search of a good nerve specialist. Lobbo was quick, effective and safe, and very popular.

As he grew older, he began to realise that there was no limit to the range of his talent. He could pick up thoughts from a long way away, and once he had been inside someone's mind he could always pick them out again. It was like knowing their address. Gradually he started letting his brain swoop out further and further, skimming through the thoughts and images in the minds of people in villages, towns and cities all over Midworld. It was addictive. All human life was there. And as his mental range expanded, so did his knowledge of the events and goings-on in the world, and the folk of the village began to discover that if you wanted to know what was happening, Lobbo was your man. His reputation increased even further.

Then one night, after a particularly powerful elf-weed cigarette, Lobbo was drifting lightly through the thoughts of a nearby village when he came across something very puzzling. Someone was bemoaning the loss of their chief, Klyv, in a recent raid, and yet Lobbo had been called to Klyv's house that very day to persuade a stubborn rat to vacate the premises and the chief had been perfectly well. It was only after Klyv's death a month later that Lobbo had realised that he had picked up thoughts from the future.

With practice he began to be able to distinguish past, present and future, and to visit each at will. The future was by far the most difficult, as it involved using a lot of elf-weed and he was generally wrecked for a couple of days afterwards. Also it was vague and tenuous, and later events could often change it, but even so he began to get a reputation as a bit of a soothsayer.

And so when some of the village elders had begun to get a little worried about the direction in which Kaal and Krage were taking the tribe, it was quite natural for them to consult Lobbo. In his search for a remedy he had cast his mental net even further afield and found that there were other minds out there drifting and probing like him. They were as aware of him as he was of them, and some of them he avoided, for there was an evil feel to them. Others he had made contact with, and these had included a wizard named Anthrax, in the far-off city of Welbug.

Lobbo had spent a long time communicating mentally with Anthrax, and had discovered that there were massive forces at work in the world, forces which in the near future could have an ill effect even on the Vagens. Anthrax was trying to find some way of counteracting these forces, and so the two of them had cobbled together a plan. It was dangerous and could easily go wrong, but desperate times require desperate remedies. They had to do something, and this was the best that they could do.

And so Lobbo had had a few quick words with Klaer and her friends, and in return for a place on the raid they had ensured that Dene had been picked as prospective raid leader. It was the best way of getting Marten in a position of influence on a raid, and Lobbo's visions of the future had shown him that his son could have a pivotal role to play. Unfortunately, some of the visions of possible futures had also shown Marten as one of many Vagen bodies lying dead upon a battlefield.

Klat! thought Lobbo as he strolled back to his house with a heavy heart, if the tribe realised what I'm letting them in for, I'll be at the bottom of the harbour with a lead weight round my neck faster than you could say 'glug'. But if Marten does die, then I won't *klatting* well care . . .

CONTACT

Be very careful about how drunk you get in the pubs in Yai'El, because they have a very sly and underhand way of dealing with anyone who is getting a bit too raucous. They give you a free drink. What they don't tell you is that they spike the drink with one of the nastier drugs such as Qwertyuiopamine, a very powerful hallucinogen, so named (legend has it) because after first sampling it, its inventor passed out with his head on the typewriter.

I discovered all this in the Tern and Turtle, a big old inn on the Far Canal. One moment I was doing this very complicated dance-step along the top of the bar, the next moment I was being locked in the cleaning-stores cupboard by the barman, and a whole rainbow of coruscating colours was flashing in front of my eyes. I remember sinking into a deep sleep, and dreaming that I was trapped in the desert with no food or water save for a packet of large and very chewy marshmallows. All these huge, fantastically coloured monsters were trying to get them off me, but although they were difficult to eat as my mouth was as dry as a bone, I scoffed the lot.

When I woke up in the morning, I was still locked in the cleaning-stores cupboard, and all the toilet-rolls had vanished . . .

Tarl's World-wide Guide to Free Booze

Tarl was dreaming, and he wasn't enjoying it one little bit. It was one of those dreams where he kept making things worse for himself by opening his big mouth all the time. He was in one of his favourite pubs, The Ruptured Colon in Setel, but it had been turned into a courtroom and he was on trial for his life. The lawyers were orcs, as were the jury and all the spectators. On the wall behind the bar was a board on which was chalked 'Today's

Special: Char-grilled Tarl', and nearby his own Defence Council, dressed in a chef's uniform, was setting up a large barbecue and sharpening a huge man-sized spit. In front of Tarl the Prosecuting Council, a massive *Kulashak* in a white wig, was pacing up and down and reading aloud various quotes from the Tarl Apprecia-tion Society Magazine, *Tales from the Drunken Bum*.

'Tarl, it is alleged that on every day of your miserable little life you did wilfully and with malice aforethought fail to buy your round. How do you plead?'

'Like this,' answered Tarl, clasping his hands together in supplication and trying to look appealing, but to no avail. The jury were handing round plates and unfolding napkins.

'To ensure a fair trial,' continued the Prosecuting Council, 'we have arranged for the presiding judges to be representatives of our greatest enemies, the Dwarves. This way, you can be sure that they are not biased. Do you have anything to say?'

Tarl looked across to the bench and saw three stern-looking Dwarves sitting there. Great, he thought, they must be on my side.

'Well, I guess these little things are sent to try us,' he heard himself saying. The judges looked daggers at him. 'I suppose I should be thankful for small mercies,' he babbled on, 'but I'd like to request that you don't give me a fine, as I'm a little short at the moment.'

'Guilty!' snapped the first judge.

'Here, that's a bit low.'

'Definitely guilty!' snarled the second judge.

'You must be out of your tiny mind.'

'Totally and completely guilty!' roared the third judge.

'Shouldn't you be in the small claims court?'

The Prosecuting Council advanced on Tarl brandishing a huge bowl of sage and onion stuffing and a large wooden spoon.

'If you'd just like to bend over, please,' he said, and the dark-robed orc guard behind Tarl got hold of his shoulder and shook him . . . and shook him . . .

And then Tarl woke up. He was lying on a pile of straw by a broken packing-case in a damp, mildewed cellar, and a dark-robed figure was indeed shaking his shoulder. For a brief instant he nearly made a right mess of the straw, but then the events of the previous day came flooding back into his memory.

Of course! He'd been chased by that mob and trapped, but then at the last moment this very same figure had popped out of nowhere and led him to safety along a bewildering maze of foetid sewers and subterranean passageways. By the time that they had finally emerged into a deserted alleyway through a rust-covered manhole it had been night-time. There was no moon, but the lurid red haze in the sky from Yai'El's Night-fire had provided some illumination. However, Tarl's rescuer had kept well clear of all the street-lamps, leading him through dark deserted streets and darker alleyways until at last they had stopped by a wooden door so old and swollen that it seemed to have fused with the lintels on either side. Tarl would have sworn that nothing less than an axe would have shifted it, but his guide had muttered a few words and the door had swung silently open of its own accord. They had stepped through and gone down a set of dust-covered stairs, and it was only as they had entered the damp cellar at the bottom that Tarl had noticed that although they had no torch, he could see clearly. His guide was using a *Light* spell! The realisation that he was blindly following a magic-user of un-known power had been enough to cause total panic to well up inside him, but before he could so much as beg for mercy the dark-robed figure had lowered its hood, and Tarl's jaw had hit his chest with an audible thud.

His rescuer was the thin, waif-like girl who had been controll-ing the fire illusions in the square, and whose theft of the wallet had landed him in such trouble. Close to, Tarl could see that she was a few years older that he had thought, but her small stature, thin features and huge, brown child-like eyes made her look young. As he had studied her doubtfully she had smiled at him, pushing the dark-brown curls of hair back from her face, and all of a sudden his heart had started tap-dancing about inside his rib-cage.

She had told him that her name was Guebral, and had apologised for the mess that she had left him in. She had added that she'd seen that he was a magic-user, and had expected that he would have been able to get himself out of any predicament. Tarl had told her that he wasn't so much a user as an abuser, and that he was to magical ability what an orc party was to interior design.

She had giggled deliciously, and Tarl's heart had decided to join forces with his stomach and started leading the rest of his internal organs in a raucous conga around his body.

He'd taken an instant decision to trust her, and had told her a few stories about his journey with Puss. He'd made her laugh several times, and this had made him feel as though someone had replaced all the blood in his veins with vintage champagne. But then she had got serious, and had warned him that he wouldn't be safe out on the streets of Yai'El.

'They'll have wanted-posters up shortly,' she'd said. 'We've run a wad of fizzes like yesterday's. The affoes are getting wazzed off. You'd better stay here. No one can get through the door, I've put a *Hold Portal* spell on it. You'll be safe enough, and I'll come back tomorrow.'

'Who's *we*?' Tarl had asked her, and she had smiled again.

'The Dead Boys,' she'd answered enigmatically. Then she'd left, and Tarl had sat on the pile of straw and thought about all she'd said. He'd had a bit of a problem understanding the odd streetspeak she was using, but he'd thought he got the gist of it. He had lain back, wondering who the 'affoes' were, and the next thing he had known he was on trial in the Ruptured Colon . . .

He sat up and started to brush the bits of straw out of his hair and off his clothes. He felt hot and dirty, his clothes were soaked with sweat, and his mouth felt as though a gang of orcs had been holding a party inside it. He swallowed with difficulty and grimaced. Guebral smiled sympathetically at him.

'Sounds like you were having a bad dream,' she said. 'Don't you like sage and onion then?'

'Depends on how I get it,' Tarl answered guardedly. 'Look,' he added, 'I think I probably owe you my life or something. I was about to dive into that canal when you turned up yesterday.'

'That's pretty lethal.'

'I know. I've seen some of the creatures that swim about in it.'

'Oh, they aren't so dangerous. It's the pollution you have to watch out for. The canals are full of crap. Literally. Things are so bad that the city kids grow up believing that fish are small round brown objects that float on the surface.'

'Remind me to give a wide berth to the seafood restaurants, then,' Tarl muttered, and Guebral flashed him another of her smiles. Instantly, his heart started a new and even more energetic dance routine.

'So, what's the news then?' he added, a little gruffly.

'They've got wanted-posters of you all over town. They're offering ten silver *tablons* for your arrest.'

'*Ten*?! By the Gods! That's more than they were offering for Mad Bastard Mazhgan or Cedric the Scimitar when I was in Orcville! Your Dead Boys must have really pissed them off.'

'We've done our bit. Come on, we'd better get moving. We've got to go and find someone in the Temple soon.'

Guebral turned to go, but Tarl stayed exactly where he was.

'Hang on,' he complained, 'there are wanted-posters of me all over town, and you're suggesting that we go out into the streets in broad daylight?'

'Don't worry. I . . . changed their perception of you. The posters look nothing like you, believe me.'

Tarl looked doubtful, but followed her up the steps and out through the metal door. Bright sunlight was pouring down and he was shocked to realise that he must have slept for more than twelve hours. They walked along the quiet alley and round a couple of corners, and then all at once they emerged onto a quayside above a wide canal that was teeming with boats. They pushed through the throngs of people that were bustling about, past shops and carts piled high with that morning's produce, and then Guebral stopped beside a barrow laden with fruit. Tarl winced and looked about nervously as a tiny bright-red fire-bird the size of his thumb suddenly materialised above the entranced barrow-boy's head and swooped about his shoulders, hissing and chirping, but no one else seemed to notice Guebral calmly removing two apples from the barrow. Throwing one to Tarl she bit into the other before leading the way farther along the quay, and Tarl followed her looking about as carefree and innocent as a mass-murderer.

After a few hundred yards the quay opened out onto a massive piazza. On the corner a number of passers-by were staring at a notice-board fixed to the wall of a severe stone building. Tarl followed Guebral as she pushed her way through them. Reaching the front he looked at the board, and only just managed to retain control of his bladder as he realised he was looking at a wanted-poster of himself, and that the building was the headquarters of the Yai'El City Police. For an instant he thought he must have walked straight into a trap and tensed himself for the pointing fingers and grabbing hands, but then he realised that although Guebral was watching him with a sardonic little smile, no one else was paying him any attention whatsoever. As he stared at the poster he could see that the artist's impression wasn't quite right, and the description below the picture was even more misleading. It was as if they had been trying to depict his imaginary brother, a younger, taller, more handsome brother, who might have been a male model, or a warrior, or hero.

'It looks nothing like me!' he exclaimed with relief.

'Yeah. So stop creeping around looking as guilty as an orc in a kindergarten, okay? Now, come on.'

They worked their way out of the crowd and Guebral led the way across the piazza. Tarl saw that their destination was a large building on the far side which, from its suggestively shaped cuneate portal and distinctive bell-tower, he recognised as a temple belonging to the Order of the Seventh Day Hedonists. Several monks of the Order were milling about in front of the doorway in their distinctive orange robes, propositioning the passers-by, and the huge phallic-shaped brass bell was tolling away at the top of the campanile. *Dong*, *dong*, *dong*, it went, and Tarl had to admit that the sound really was rather fitting.

As they neared the door Tarl began to feel a little uneasy. He knew the conditions that had to be met if you wanted to enter a Hedonist Temple, and he found the idea of Guebral being involved in such goings-on highly disturbing. He was about to stop her and find out why they were doing this when a little clutch of illusions suddenly appeared in front of her. Tarl smiled as he saw she had created a small flock of beautiful bird-sized naked women that swooped and fluttered on dainty white-feathered wings, like angels. The flock flew across to the monks and began weaving an intricate pattern above their heads, chirping and moaning as they did so. The monks watched them, totally entranced, reaching up their hands to try and clutch the vision, but the tiny bird-women stayed always just out of their reach, and Tarl and Guebral slipped past them unnoticed and entered the Temple.

Immediately, the sweet, cloying scent of burning musk-wax candles assaulted their noses with all the subtlety of a clout round the head with a slab of concrete. Guebral pulled Tarl into a small side-chapel.

'Right,' she said, 'we've got a few minutes before the Brothers start gathering for Pierce. Stay here while I have a quick look round. And if anyone challenges you, call. Leave the sparking to me. I mean, the spell-casting. OK?'

Tarl nodded and she slipped away into the main body of the temple and disappeared beyond the rows of couches, her feet making no sound on the fur-covered floor.

Tarl kicked moodily at the silken drapes that covered the small altar-bed in front of him, and looked up at the statue that stood in a niche in the wall behind it. According to the inscription below, it was a statue of Saint Kylie. Tarl grinned. He'd never heard of her, but any saint who wore clothes like that was okay with him.

Joking apart, however, he hoped that Guebral found whoever she was looking for quickly. He didn't want to be here when the Brothers gathered to celebrate one of their rituals. He had heard far too many unpleasant things about what happened during the seven Orders of the Day: Matings, Preen, Pierce, Sex, Moans, Whispers and Comply. Once, when he was a younger, more curious lad, he had allowed himself to be talked into attending a Seventh Day Hedonist service. Oddsong, it had been, followed by communion, the ritual where everyone present takes the host. He could still remember the expression on the face of the unfortunate man whose turn it was to be host. Not that all of their rituals were so unsavoury, though. Tarl was definitely quite taken with Preconfession. The idea of thinking up something sinful to do, confessing it to one of the Brothers, receiving absolution, and then going out and committing the sin with a clear conscience was quite attractive.

Tarl wrinkled up his nose and glared sourly at the unsubtly shaped wax candles burning in their sconces in front of the altar-bed. They didn't half stink! Glancing round, he crossed to an insects-burner that was hanging from a bracket on the left-hand wall. Taking a small coin from his pocket he thrust it into the slot in the vending-machine that stood beside the burner and pulled out a paper bag full of sweet-locusts and spice-flies. The bag hummed and buzzed agitatedly as he threw it into the glowing embers of the insects-burner, and then the paper caught fire and the buzzing rose to a frantic level, to be followed by little tiny popping noises as the insects ignited. A couple of flaming flies flew out of the burner and spiralled down to the floor, leaving tiny plumes of smoke trailing behind them, and then the fragrant cinnamon-smell of the spice-flies and the rose-petal odour of the sweet-locusts eddied forth, drowning out the musk-candles with their fragrant scent.

'Tarl! Here!'

Guebral's urgent voice echoed through the temple, and Tarl dashed out, past the rows of couches and chaises-longues, past the main altar-bed and the huge statues of Saint Timothy the Onanist and Saint Hilary of the Bounteous Favours, and came to a screeching halt in front of the entrance to what an inscription on the archway proclaimed was the Chapel of Depraved Tastes.

Inside, Guebral was kneeling on a raised platform, and beside her, held in position by golden chains, was Puss. Guebral was gently stroking its head and whispering reassurances. Tarl gasped with relief, and then swore violently as he noticed some splashes of fresh blood on the platform.

'*Klat!* Puss! Are you okay?'

The donkey lifted its head.

'Oh, don't worry,' it said. 'It's not *my* blood. There was an awful lot more of it, but I got a bit thirsty, and it's nearly all gone now.'

Tarl cursed himself. He'd been so busy worrying about his own predicament that he hadn't even considered the possibility that his friend might also be in trouble.

'But what happened?' he asked. 'Why are you here?'

'Well, after you'd run off without so much as a "see you later", these two guys in orange robes found me and led me off. I thought I'd fallen in with the right crowd. I mean, these Seventh Day Hedonist people are supposed to like a really good time, right? I thought they must be taking me along to a party, with lots of nice food and stuff. It was only when they started putting these *klatting* chains on me that I realised they had something else in mind. Well, you know my philosophy. Never bite the hand that feeds you. But if it doesn't feed you, bite it as hard as you can, it might be all you're going to get for a while. So I did. Got a couple of fingers. Nice plump juicy ones, too. And if another one of those sick bastards had come anywhere near me with no clothes on, I'd have bitten off more than his fingers next time!'

Tarl could feel a cold fury welling up inside him. He shook his head angrily and dragged his sword free to slash at the chains, but Guebral lifted her hand to restrain him, then whispered something and the chains just fell away from Puss as though all of a sudden they had got rather tired.

'Come on,' she said. 'Let's get out of this hell-hole.'

Turning, she led the way out of the chapel, and with a surge of hate-fuelled strength Tarl slashed violently at the gold chains with his sword, and yanked them free of their mountings. Then stuffing them in his pocket he followed Guebral, with Puss trotting at his side. The temple was still deserted, and they sped silently across the floor to the exit. Guebral held up a warning hand, then peered carefully around the edge of the doorway, but the monks outside were still totally entranced by the flock of tiny bird-women flying and swooping above their heads, still just out of reach.

'Let's go,' said Guebral. 'Nice and quiet, OK?'

Puss nodded, but there was no answer from Tarl, who was standing with his head on one side, as though concentrating on listening to something.

'What's up?' asked Guebral.

'What?' he muttered absently. 'Oh . . . sorry . . . I thought I heard baaing. Er, yeah, let's get out of here.'

Quickly they slipped out into the bright sunlight, and Guebral led them along the piazza past a gaily playing fountain and into the calm shaded shelter of another alleyway. As they walked along they passed few people, but snatches of quiet conversations drifted out from the shuttered windows that overlooked the alley, and birds sang in the small trees and leafy greenery that stretched out over the walls of hidden gardens.

As they walked, Tarl was trying to puzzle things out.

'What I can't understand,' he said at last, 'is how you knew where to be to save me, and then found out where Puss was. I mean, you do seem to have some pretty cool powers, but . . .'

He trailed off. Guebral was looking almost embarrassed, and seemed to be weighing up her reply.

'I waited after we had fizzed the square and . . . watched you. I'd seen that you were a sparker, but you were a blanko to me . . . that is, a stranger. When the affoes chased you I felt guilty. I pre-thought, and knew where you would go, but as I went there I watched the square. I can watch places in my head, it is one of my sparks. I saw the Brothers lead Puss away, but I knew that he would be safe until this morning. I pre-thought it.'

Tarl shook his head in admiration. He was new to this magic lark and didn't know much about it, but he reckoned he could tell a natural talent when he met one. There was just one other thing bothering him.

'But why did you save me? I mean, you don't know me . . .'

'You're a sparker. And the affoes thought you were one of us. A Dead Boy. So they would have killed you. And it was my fault. I gave you that wallet.'

'Why do you call yourselves the Dead Boys?'

'Because the affoes hate us and fear us. We're different. If they ever catch us they will snuff us like they would snuff a cockroach. They want us all dead.' She stopped, and stared straight at him. Tarl was mesmerised by her huge, brown, guileless eyes.

'You can leave Yai'El, and you will be safe,' she continued. 'Or you can stay in the city and take your chance. But someone will recognise you soon. You will spark, you will not be able to help it, and they will snuff you if they can. Or, if you wish, you can come with me.'

'Where to?'

'I go to a tavern I know, for a mug and some stape.'

'Stape?'

'Food. Then maybe I play a hand. And then later, I go back to the Graveyard. That is what we call the place where we live.'

With an effort Tarl dragged his eyes free from hers and looked down at Puss.

'I think we'd better discuss this,' he said. Guebral nodded, and Tarl wandered a few paces away, with Puss following. He crouched down and started gently scratching the donkey's ears.

'Well, I reckon we should go with her,' he whispered.

'What? Walk into danger and the threat of death, when we could just leave town?' The donkey put its head on one side and looked at Tarl consideringly. 'You sad man,' it went on, 'you just want to get inside her pants.'

A huge wave of anger flooded over Tarl. 'You . . . you . . . manky little dung-ball!' he stuttered, almost incoherent with rage. 'She is . . . she is . . . don't you *dare* talk about her like that!'

'Ow! Let go! You're hurting my ears!'

'Hurting them! I ought to tie them in a knot and stuff them down your throat!'

'Well, if you want to tie knots, try tying one in your dick, 'cos if you're not careful it's going to get us into trouble!'

'*Klat!* That girl saved your life, you ungrateful little mongrel! Or at any rate, she saved your . . .'

'All right! I know! But look me in the eyes and tell me you don't fancy the pants off her.'

'Listen, carrot-breath, get it though that minuscule brain of yours that this isn't like that. Guebral is . . . is . . .'

Tarl shook his head, unable to find the words to express his feelings. Indeed, he didn't really understand these feelings in the first place. Normally he knew exactly how he felt with women. If someone fancied a quick bit of fun, fine. If they fancied a slow bit of fun, even better. But Tarl didn't believe in getting involved. That way you got hurt. He liked to say that he didn't go in for casual sex – he did it on the back doorstep and then left quickly. The first (and indeed, the last) thing most women said to him after love-making was, 'That was . . . hang on, where've you gone?'

But all of a sudden here he was with a brain full of the most unaccustomed thoughts and feelings. Strange day-dreams were floating through his mind, in which he was saving Guebral from hordes of savage monsters, or rescuing her from a pack of rampaging orcs, or – God help him! – buying flowers for her. Well, stealing flowers for her, anyway. God, what was wrong with him?

Sighing, he stood up.

'Just don't talk about her like that. OK?'

'Oh, shit! You're in love!'

'No, I'm not!'

'You're staring at her with the look you normally reserve for bottles of five-star brandy.'

'Look, I don't know about love. All I know is that, as the man said, those are the sweetest eyes I've ever seen.'

'Yeuch! Good job I haven't eaten for a while.'

'She is the loveliest . . .'

'OK, OK! We'll go with her. But don't go all broody on me. And I'm warning you, if you start writing poetry I'm going to bite your pathetic little hand off.'

Tarl made a tired and dismissive gesture and walked over to Guebral. She smiled uncertainly at him, and his heart began doing the lambada with his tonsils.

'We're with you,' he said. 'Let's go.'

The North Star was in a pretty rough area of town, and reminded Tarl of a few taverns he'd visited in Goblin City. It was the sort of place where if you want to attract the barman's attention, you throw a bottle at his head, and where going to the gents to urinate is regarded as a sign of weakness.

The place was quite full, and as they entered every conversation in the place stopped and every eye swivelled to check them out. However, the clientele seemed reassured to see Guebral, and the hum of conversation quickly rose to its previous level. She peered round, then motioned to Tarl to buy the drinks and wandered across to talk to a group of shady-looking men seated in one corner.

Tarl ambled up to the bar and looked at the menu, which was chalked on a blackboard next to a sign that promised live entertainment. The choice of food appeared to rest between horse stew, dog stew, cat stew, oysters, or pork chops. Tarl watched as the barman emerged from the kitchen doorway brandishing a plateful of oysters, which he handed to a large dock-worker who was standing at the end of the bar. Crossing to the blackboard he scrubbed out the word 'oysters'.

Behind him, greasy black smoke began to pour out through the kitchen door. The barman sniffed the air and leapt back through the door, cursing. A few seconds later he re-emerged muttering to himself and rubbed out the words 'pork chops'.

Deciding that he had better make a move before every single dish had been scratched, Tarl ordered three bowls of horse and two pints of the only beer available, Whitebeard's Nether Scrapings. He was leaning on the bar peering sadly at his pint (which was cloudier than a bank holiday) when a large black cockroach eased itself out from a crack in the wood and waddled across towards his beer. Tarl lifted his mug and brought it sharply down on top of the insect, which made a loud crunching sound. Then lifting his mug again he scraped its base against the edge of the bar, and the remains of the cockroach slid off and fell behind a barrel of beer with a soggy squelching sound. The barman scowled at him, so Tarl tried on one of his range of cheesy grins for size.

'Er . . . nice beer!' he lied jovially. The barman scowled some more and said nothing.

'So . . . what's the Live Entertainment, then?' Tarl continued.

'You just killed it,' the barman snarled, before pulling the notice off the wall and dropping it in a bin.

Tarl turned away nervously and found Guebral standing behind him.

'There's a card-game starting up later,' she told him. 'I'm joining it. You'd be welcome, too. But be warned, they use mage-cards here.'

Tarl was about to point out that he had no cash when the weight of his tunic pocket thumped gently against his hip and he remembered the gold chain that he'd taken from the temple.

'Fine,' he said doubtfully. 'Deal me in. But we'd better eat first. I've ordered horse. I hope you don't mind.'

'Nay,' she smiled, then repeated it in a more horse-like manner.

The stew, when it came, was much better than Tarl had expected, and the portions were generous. On the floor beside their table the donkey was tucking in to its plateful with evident enjoyment, and kept muttering to itself. Tarl strained his ears to listen.

'Well, this will teach you,' he heard Puss mumble to the stew. 'You think you're so smart, because you're big and muscle-bound and fast. Well, ha-*klatting*-ha. You weren't smart enough to keep out of the butcher's shop, were you, eh, bugger-lugs?'

As they finished their meal, Tarl found he was telling Guebral about the events of the past couple of months, and of his search for his friend, Ronan while she listened, fascinated.

'When I found that huge cloud of magic hanging over Yai'El I thought perhaps I'd found Shikara,' he finished, 'but I guess it must have been you and the Dead Boys. So I'll have to keep looking.'

'That was a neat spark that Anthrax pulled on Puss,' Guebral replied, 'giving him speech. I'd like to try that.'

'Is it a spell . . . a spark . . . you can do?'

'It is now. You see, I only have to see someone or something who has been sparked, and I can read on them the imprint of how it was done. Then I can do it myself.'

'You're joking! You mean that just by looking at Puss you now know how to do a *Spell of Animal Talking*?'

'Yes. Watch.'

She looked across to the table where the docker was half-way through his plate of oysters, and whispered something. The docker levered the shell of another oyster open and raised it to his lips.

'Don't eat me!' squeaked a terrified little voice, and the docker paused and looked round.

'Please! I'm too young to die. I don't want to go like this, I've got my whole life in front of me!' the voice continued. The puzzled docker peered underneath the table, then picked up his plate and looked at it suspiciously.

'Yes, leave him alone!' joined in another voice. 'Pick on someone your own size!'

'Like a giant clam,' added a third, 'or a shark or something!'

The docker scratched his head and shrugged, and then tossing back his head he tipped the oyster into his mouth. It disappeared with a shrill 'Aaargh!' that tailed away to nothing, and all the other oysters on his plate started a tremendous yammering and wailing. Embarrassed, the docker pushed his plate away.

Tarl could hardly contain his laughter. 'Seafood, yes,' he gasped. 'But hear-food . . . that's a new one!'

Guebral grinned. 'Shall I get them to clam up?' she asked.

Tarl pulled a face and then asked, 'Hey, did you hear about the oyster that went to a disco?'

Guebral shook her head.

'He pulled a mussel,' finished Tarl. Guebral giggled, and the sound made Tarl glow with pleasure. Careful, mate, he thought. She does wonderful spells, she's saved your life, she plays cards, and she's got a great sense of humour. She even laughs at your jokes. Puss could be right. If you're not careful, you could get really hooked. Better play it cool.

*

Six hours later, as they left the card table and staggered out of the tavern into the chill of the evening, Tarl was feeling about as cool as an erupting volcano. Quite simply, he had never met such a talented card-player as Guebral. It had been a pretty fierce game with some good players, and he had come out slightly ahead, but she simply hadn't put a foot wrong. She shuffled and dealt like a croupier, worked out odds faster than a bookie, and played with a verve and flair that Tarl hadn't seen since he worked as a gambling-chip for Mavrik the Half-orc in the Life and Death Stud Poker game at Gashnik's Palace, back in Orcville. And she could hold her drink as well! She'd had as much as he had, yet she was still in total control. Wonderful!

Puss too was feeling rather taken with her. She had suggested that the donkey might like to go and visit the horses in the stable at the rear of the tavern. Puss had spent a very happy hour explaining to a captive equine audience exactly what sort of dishes were being served in the kitchen just a few paces away, and asking them if any close friends had gone missing lately.

And so the two of them contentedly followed Guebral as she led them deeper into the back-alleys of the city. At first they passed a number of people, revellers happily heading out to enjoy an evening in one of the numerous restaurants or taverns. But after a while the passers-by became less frequent, and the ones they did meet were more surly, scowling threateningly at them and laying their hands on their sword-hilts. Occasionally one would snarl a warning at them. There were half-orcs, Southrons and others equally dangerous, but no one approached them, and Guebral ignored them all.

The area they were now walking through was ancient, and totally run down. The pale stone of the deserted houses was crumbling and weather-beaten, and mosses and weeds grew from the gaps in the mortar. Rotting timbers poked through the slateless roofs like the rib-cages of corpses on a battlefield after the vultures have finished, and dark empty windows stared like eyeless sockets. The canals here were still and stagnant, and the green scummy water was full of discarded rubbish. Broken slats of wood, empty bottles and rusting bits of metal poked through the surface, and the bloated corpses of dead pi-dogs floated like croûtons in thick pea soup. The noisome stench of rotting flesh and excrement filled the air, mixing with the thick oily fumes from the street-lamps to produce an all but unbearable miasma.

Tarl buried his nose in the sleeve of his jerkin, but as they gingerly crossed the sagging remnants of a wooden foot-bridge that still clung doggedly to the mouldering quayside the smell that rose from the canal beneath was so overpowering that he almost retched. Beside him Puss was trotting along with his muzzle so tightly wrinkled up that it looked like a prune.

'*Klat!*' the donkey muttered, 'I didn't think it was possible for anything to smell worse than your feet.'

Tarl glared at it through streaming eyes. 'Listen,' he replied, 'if we're talking about foul smells, it's no picnic being in the same room as you the day after you've scoffed three plates of *mulampos*!'

Guebral turned left and led them along a weed-grown, uneven quayside, beside the ruins of what must once have been a massive warehouse. A cluster of ancient, verdigris-covered gas-pipes, each the thickness of a man's thigh, ran above the quay on rusting metal gantries, and the gas inside each one gurgled and chuckled to itself eerily. Every so often another pipe would snake across the canal and join the ever-thickening cluster.

At the far end of the warehouse ruins the thin vertical tube of a street-lamp poked upwards from the pipes. It was nearly dark now, and the smoky red glare of the night-fire cast a pool of hellish light into the evening gloom. The canal bent sharply right, and was closed off by a rotting lock gate from another canal that was wide enough for sea-going vessels, running directly from the distant ocean to plunge into the heart of the warehouse ruins. The quayside path terminated in a flight of wooden steps that led up to a foot-bridge across this canal. The gas-pipes curved sharply upwards, following the framework of the steps, and then straightened out again, crossing alongside the foot-bridge at a height that would allow clearance for the mast of a ship.

Guebral led them up the steps. Tarl was about to ask her where they were going, but as they reached the top the sight that met his eyes quite literally took his breath away, and he stood rooted to the spot with horror. From this height he could see that beyond the ruins of the warehouse was the vast gas storage plant which collected and processed the Flame Ether from the sea-bed. Huge spherical metal tanks were connected to each other apparently at random by hundreds of pipes, and in several places gouts of flame belched skywards at irregular intervals from the nozzles of towering metal chimneys. Tarl could feel the heat even at this distance, and the rhythmic pulses of dozens of hidden pumps made the bridge vibrate. A black pall of smoke hung heavily over everything, and an infernal red glow lit the plant and its surrounds. It looked like a badly constructed model made out of huge straws and ball-bearings by giant children, who had then sprayed it dark red and set it alight.

However, it wasn't the gas-works that had horrified Tarl, but the sight that could be seen in the rubescent glow that it cast. At the base of the steps on the other side of the canal a path led across a stone-flagged yard to an arched doorway in the side of the warehouse. The yard was littered with bones; human skeletons, dozens of them, stripped bare of flesh by the hordes of rats that scurried about them, yet still clad in ragged fragments of clothing. Around the edges of the yard they were few and far between, but closer to the warehouse they increased, until in front of the doorway they were piled on top of each other in a ghastly rat-infested osseous mountain. Many still held rusting swords or staves in their bony fingers.

Tarl took a deep, quavering breath, then looked down as Puss nudged him. With a toss of its head the donkey indicated the sea-canal, and Tarl gazed down to where it entered the shadows of the warehouse ruins and ended in what had once been a massive loading-bay. There were rats here, too, hundreds of them, swarming around the stone quay and swimming in the foul water. But there was a circular area at the end of the canal which they seemed unable or unwilling to enter. There was a hazy appearance to this circle, as though the air around it had solidified slightly, and inside it were twenty or so small boats, all pointing inwards as though they had just reached the warehouse. In the boats were more human corpses, not skeletons this time, but foul-fleshed, bloated and putrefying. These too held swords and staves, as well as the remains of wooden torches. From where they stood Tarl and Puss could hear the vexed and hungry squeaking of the rats.

Guebral turned and looked at them dispassionately.

'Welcome to the Graveyard,' she said.

'Twice the people of Yai'El have come against us,' she told them, 'once by foot and once by boat. We were younger then and there were fewer of us. They had already cast us out and driven us from their sight, for we were different and they hated and feared us. But that was not enough for them, they wanted to kill us, too. So we defended ourselves. Now they leave us alone.'

They were walking along a passageway inside the warehouse ruins. Ahead and behind them it was pitch black, but again there was a faint luminescence around Guebral that enabled them to see. Coming to the shattered remnants of a wooden door they passed through and climbed several flights of stairs. At the top was an open archway that led into a massive room. Here the ceiling had collapsed, taking half the floor with it and leaving the room open to the sky. It had begun to rain, and the remnants of floor that clung tenaciously to the walls were wet and slippery. Skirting the huge hole in the centre of the room, Guebral led them to a door at the far end, and passing through they turned right, went along a short passage, then through another door on the left.

Tarl stopped and peered around uncertainly. They were in another vast room, but this one still had its ceiling. Instead, nearly the whole of the left-hand wall had fallen out, leaving a stunningly hypnotic view over the son-et-lumière display of the gas-works. Lurid red light poured in and illuminated a jumbled collection of the most bizarre furnishings that Tarl had ever seen.

The room was lined with items constructed from rusting metal, splintered wood and other refuse. Tables, chairs and couches littered the floor, and home-made steps rose at weird angles to meet with shaky-looking platforms that were fixed to the three remaining walls or hung from the ceiling high above. Some of these platforms held pieces of furniture, others had been screened off from view by partitions or had been turned into aerial shacks of plywood and corrugated iron. It was as if someone had tried to build a shanty-town up the walls, but had reserved the floor as a kind of common-room. The whole place looked like something that might have resulted if Escher had taken up home improvement but had been really crap at it.

Tarl sniffed and grinned happily to himself. In here the smell of smoke from the gas-works was all but wiped out by the thick, aromatic smell of elf-weed. Nine or ten black-clad figures were lounging around on the couches in the centre of the floor, but as Guebral led Tarl and Puss across they rose to their feet. One, a tall, slim youth with spiky black hair and a sarcastic grin, stepped forward and bowed low in a mocking salute.

'So,' he said, 'you're the blanko sparker who saw us fizzing the square. Gueb told us about you. I'm Raze. Welcome to the Graveyard, our humble abode. I'm afraid it isn't much –'

'You're telling me!' muttered Puss.

'– but it's home to us,' Raze finished.

Tarl listened carefully as he was introduced to the other members of the Dead Boys and tried hard to fix their names in his memory. Remembering people's names was not a trick that he had ever got the hang of. In fact, for most of his life he had been so drunk that it had normally taken him about twenty minutes to remember his own. However, he managed to get a handle on a few of the others.

There was Stipe, a skinny shaven-headed skull-faced man wearing a strange and battered hat. There was Gutter-rat, a thin girl who was only about ten years old, and whose language was even worse than that of Blue Sonjë. There was Pinball, a powerful and handsome black guy, whose only unusual feature was that his eye-sockets held a pair of gleaming metal ball-bearings instead of eyes. There was Image, a small but wirily muscular man with long hair and large gold earrings, who was sat on a rickety chair by a small table. Every inch of his skin seemed to have been decorated with tattoos, some of which were so rude that they opened Tarl's eyes wide with surprise. And there was Shiftfister, a pallid youth with bleached blond hair shaved to a stubble, a thin mouth set in a permanent snarl, and a pair of prosthetic hands constructed out of metal and wire.

Tarl grinned and nodded to everyone, but he found it difficult to keep from staring at Pinball's blank metal eyes or Shiftfister's chrome hands. He kept dragging his gaze back to Raze or Guebral, but his eyes kept sliding back of their own volition. Shiftfister held one of his hands up right in front of Tarl's embarrassed gaze.

'Pretty, huh?' he said. 'It's all right, you can look. No cack.'

Tarl stared at the hand. The metal base slipped over the flesh of the wrist like a glove. The fingers and thumb were made from segments of polished chromium linked together like the bones of a real hand, and moved by tendons of bronze wire. Shiftfister flexed it, and the fingers moved smoothly back and forth with a faint whirring sound.

Guebral moved to stand beside Tarl, and linked her arm through his.

'The affoes cut off his hands when he was young,' she said. 'They thought without hands he would be unable to spark.'

'Affoes?'

'Aphotics,' replied Raze. 'Non-sparkers. The normal, quiet, every-day man in the street. Our magic scares them – even though none of us had ever harmed them. Until they tried to harm us.'

'It was the same for Pinball,' Guebral continued. 'When he was fourteen someone caught him sparking. They saw the glow in his eyes – and so they put them out.'

'Can you really see with those?' Tarl asked Pinball, gazing at his gleaming optics.

'Better than you can, guy.'

'Really?'

'Damn right.' The shimmering metallic spheres seemed to whirl in their sockets as they examined Tarl. 'You've got black hair – what's left of it. And about four days of stubble on your chin. A mole on your neck. Another one on your shoulder under your jerkin.'

Tarl's eyebrows shot up as he realised that Pinball could actually see through his clothes.

'Don't look so surprised,' Pinball continued. 'You've got a very interesting ring in your pocket. Oh, and ever since Guebral got hold of your arm you've had a large and persistent erec—'

'All right! All right! I believe you! Ye Gods, you don't have to rub it in!' Tarl had gone bright red. He didn't dare meet Guebral's gaze. 'So how does it work? Is it magic?'

But as soon as he had asked he knew the answer. Of course it was magic. He was suddenly aware of the Power in the place. It was like the noise of a big city, there in the background all the time, but unnoticed. Now he had noticed it, he was aware of just how much there was. These guys were powerful magicians, the

135

lot of them! This was the source of that magical field he had sensed, all right.

'It's Goetetics,' answered Raze. 'The technology of magic. We have a . . . contact. The Glimmer King. He's a renegade half-elf who imports illegal high-tech magical items from the Forbidden Lands across the western ocean. A spark-runner. He liaises with a couple of dwarf techno-mages who have a goetetic workshop somewhere under the Chrome Mountains. They produce some pretty amazing stuff.'

'But it's powered by magic, right?' Tarl asked. 'You're all wizards.'

A wave of laughter greeted this remark, and Tarl looked from one to the other, puzzled. Guebral squeezed his arm in support.

'Get real, guy!' laughed Stipe. 'Do we look like a gang of sad old wrinklies, sitting round wearing pointy hats and long beards, muttering incantations?'

'All those self-important old farts are only interested in one thing, and that's power,' said Image, and Tarl saw that he was rolling a very fat elf-weed cigarette on the table in front of him. 'But we're different. We're narcomancers.'

They looked at Tarl expectantly, but he stood there blinking, not at all sure what the hell they were talking about. Goetetics? Narcomancer? That sounded like a wizard with a very short temper.

'Why should we waste our time doing cacky enchantments?' said Raze. 'We've got the Power, why not use it to have fun? There's a whole world out there for the living, and you can experience any little bit you want through narcomancy. You can watch other people, *be* other people, do anything you wanna do.'

He paused, and Tarl gazed at him with interest. This sounded right up his street. Then the silence was broken by a gentle asinine cough.

'Er, I don't want to lower the tone of the conversation or anything,' murmured Puss, 'but what time are we eating?'

'Hey, you hungry, kid?' asked Image, ruffling the donkey's tatty mane.

'Nothing much gets past you, does it?'

Image grinned wryly and stood up, and Tarl watched his body, fascinated. As he moved, his muscles rippled, and the numerous

136

tattooed figures seemed to be doing even ruder things to each other. He crossed to a large table and picked up one of the many dishes that littered it. Puss trotted across with its tongue hanging out in anticipation as Image placed the dish on the floor, then snorted with disgust as it saw that it contained cold, thin, watery gruel.

'Not quite what you want, eh?' drawled Image. 'I thought so. I reckon you'd like something a bit more . . . meaty?'

He squatted down, held out the elf-weed cigarette, and looked inquisitively at Guebral, who clicked her fingers. At once a small flame appeared right in front of him, and he lit the cigarette from it and inhaled deeply. Then he blew out the flame and took a second deep inhalation. For a moment he sat there, seemingly waiting, and then his eyes glazed over and his body stiffened.

'What's happening?' Tarl whispered to Guebral.

'He's mind-surfing. Grazing the thaumatosphere.'

'Do what?'

'Watch.'

Image remained absolutely motionless for several seconds, and then his eyes refocused and he smiled a satisfied smile. The bowl of gruel suddenly vanished, and in its place was a large platter on which was a steaming haunch of roast venison.

'There you go, kid. Fill your boots,' invited Image. Puss fell on the massive joint of meat ravenously, and the Dead Boys stood and watched it, smiling and passing the elf-weed cigarette back and forth.

'Ah, it does like a joint,' said Tarl fondly.

'Don't we all,' said Guebral. Tarl took her by the arm and drew her to one side.

'Look,' he muttered in a low voice, 'I'm all in favour of having fun, but I don't quite get what's going on. Why did Image graze on the, er, tomato-sphere before producing that food for Puss?'

'Thaumatosphere. Look, when you spark you can't create things out of nothing. If you produce a big dish of venison, it must come from somewhere. We like to check and make sure no one gets hurt by our sparks. Image mind-surfed until he found what he wanted out there. And he replaced it with the gruel. Image,' she called raising her voice, 'where did the stape come from?'

Image grinned, causing two tattooed men on his cheeks to

137

become hugely erect. 'A fat old money-dealer, sitting at his table counting a big stack of coins before his dinner. We'll see how he likes the taste of cold gruel, eh?'

'You see?' Guebral said to Tarl. 'You saw us fizz the square. We don't want to hurt the affoes, but we take what we need to live from them, and we like to annoy them, and remind them that we're here. That money-dealer will know it was us.'

'And the, er, thaumatosphere?'

'You've used it yourself. Remember when you told me you'd used a *Mindsweep* spark and found a vast cloud of magic over Yai'El? Well, when you did that your mind was travelling through the thaumatosphere. It's difficult to describe, but you could say that it's the plane that the magic moves through. Elf-weed frees your mind so that it feels as though your whole body is there. You can go anywhere.' She paused, her head on one side, and watched Tarl consideringly. 'Do you want to experience it?'

Tarl nodded, and taking him by the hand Guebral stepped forward and plucked the elf-weed cigarette from Raze's fingers. Then she led Tarl across to a ladder that ran up to a platform near the ceiling.

'Follow me,' she ordered, and began to climb.

The platform was set out like a small room, with a carpet, a bed against the wall, and a couple of oaken storage-chests. Guebral sat down on the floor with her legs folded under her, and Tarl followed suit. Her eyes, huge and serious, bored into his.

'Right,' she said, 'when you start, let your mind go where it wants. It will probably head for old haunts. Hop about. Enjoy yourself. But watch out. There are other people and things out there. If you feel another presence, don't go near it. Get out fast. OK?'

Tarl nodded, and she handed him the cigarette. He took a couple of inhalations and waited until he felt the effects, then muttered the words of the *Mindsweep* spell. He gazed at Guebral as his mind seemed to be slowly drifting upwards, and then all at once it felt as if his mind had reached back down and hauled his body sharply up after it. Guebral vanished, and in her place was a whirling kaleidoscope of colour. He was shooting along faster than a dragon flies, past other thoughts and entities that he could sense but not see, heading faster and faster towards . . .

All of a sudden Tarl is sitting at a card-table in the centre of a plush gambling salon, surrounded by well-dressed and wealthy merchants and beautiful women. He watches as the cards flash from the hands of the dealer across the green baize, and feels the soft supple leather of the table edging under his hand. In front of him is a large pile of gambling-runes. He sees that the cards are the distinctive mantologistic pack used for the game of Guts. Glancing down he sneaks a look at his two hole cards – the headless orc and the one-legged orc. A waitress who would make Shikara look totally emaciated appears at his side with a trayful of drinks. The dealer turns up the shared cards – and they include the one-armed orc, the blind orc and the death of orcs! The other two shared cards are the death of trolls and the death of elves. Someone else at the table could have four deaths, but Tarl has an unbeatable top flush of orcs! The perfect hand! Beside him the waitress pours him a large Elf's Pecker, and the crowd round the table gasps as he pushes forward a pile of runes equal to the maximum bet. Beside him the waitress stoops to whisper an outrageously erotic suggestion in his ear . . .

Then he is standing on a balcony in a tall red-stone tower at one corner of a massive castle built on the edge of a cliff. Below him the castle walls fall sheer to the cliff-edge, which in turn falls away to the pounding surf below. He looks out across the sea to the sun which is slowly setting on the horizon, sending a shaft of gold lancing along the waves towards him. Beneath him to one side, in the castle courtyard, servants are scurrying hither and thither, laying cloths and plates on serried ranks of trestle tables, and beyond them others are tending roaring bonfires and laboriously turning two giant spits on which an entire ox and a wild boar are roasting. The smell of cooking meat drifts up to him, making his mouth water. And then a pair of soft arms reach around him from behind and start to stroke his chest . . .

Suddenly he is in a bright and airy room, looking out from a window over a city of glittering crystal towers and white marble walls. Turning he sees the massed ranks of champagne and brandy bottles waiting on an exquisitely carved *mastic* sideboard. In front of the bottles are small golden plates containing an interesting and brightly coloured array of tablets and pills. In the centre of the room is a vast bed covered in soft furs, and beside it is a small table, on which is a large tray of fruit. He walks across, picks up a strawberry and pops it into his mouth. The flavour is intense, so intense that he squirms with pleasure, savouring the juice on his tongue. The door opens, and a tall, slender woman with long auburn hair enters. She is wearing a black velvet choker about her neck, and nothing else. Tarl realises that he too is naked. She crosses to him, her wide mouth parting in a knowing smile, her soft brown eyes aflame with anticipation. He puts a strawberry between her lips and she sucks it into her mouth, slowly but oh, so meaningfully. A small dribble of juice escapes and runs down her chin . . .

But something is calling him from outside the window, pulling him against his will, something he dare not turn to look at, something horrible and foul. It is creeping nearer and nearer behind him, and he knows he must not look on it, yet he cannot stop himself from turning . . . But then a voice is calling him. 'Come back, Tarl. Come back. Come back . . .'

All at once Tarl found himself sat on the platform, bathed in the red glare from the gas-works. Guebral was holding him by the shoulders, gently rocking him back and forth and repeating, 'Come back, Tarl, come back,' in a soft, insistent tone. He blinked and shook his head, still dazed. It had all seemed so real!

Guebral studied him for a moment, then relaxed and let go of his shoulders.

'So,' she said, 'how do you feel?'

'I feel good!'

'I knew that you would.'

'That was incredible! Was I dreaming?'

'No, it's all real. You're seeing things that are happening, but you're seeing it through someone else's eyes. You're sharing their experiences.'

'Do they realise?'

'As far as we can tell, no.'

Tarl sat back and thought about it. He had never been averse to a small spot of voyeurism, but this was major league stuff, in spades, redoubled. It was highly enjoyable, but there was something about it that for some reason unsettled him.

'With all the Power that you have, you could go out into the real world and experience it all for yourself.'

'But that would mean mixing with the affoes, and sooner or later they would kill us. This is safer.'

'It's not like that in other cities. Folk don't give a toss if you've got magical powers . . .'

His voice trailed away, as he realised that Guebral was staring fixedly at him. The pupils of her eyes had grown large, and her lips had parted slightly. When she spoke, Tarl could hardly hear her over the racket his heart had started kicking up.

'Have you got a woman in your life?'

'No. Definitely not.' Tarl shook his head so hard he went momentarily dizzy.

'You're not married? Or engaged?'

'No.'

'You're sure?'

'There isn't a woman anywhere who will have given me so much as a thought recently.'

'Good. That's important.'

Guebral leaned forward and gazed deep into his eyes. He stared back at her, mesmerised, as the tip of her tongue gently moistened her lips, then she leaned forward – and there was a sudden fuzziness in the air beside them on the platform, as though a tiny whirlwind had suddenly materialised. It was accompanied by a loud buzzing noise. Tarl and Guebral watched as the air fizzed and whirled about, and then all at once it solidified into the half-size image of a woman dressed in warrior gear, slim and tanned, with her dark-brown hair cut short in elven fashion. She was sitting cross-legged, and from the light that played on her face they could tell that wherever she was, it was still daylight there.

'Tarl, I have no way of knowing if this charm of yours is working or not,' said the image, staring blindly at them. 'I hope you can see me. I don't know if you can, or even if you're alive. Or sober. I don't know where you are. I could be making this appeal to a pub full of people. Or to a flock of sheep. But I need you. I need you badly.'

The image paused, and Guebral gave Tarl the sort of look that people normally reserve for the dog when it has just ruined the new carpet.

'It's only Tyson!' he babbled. 'She's just a friend! Honestly!'

'I think I've found Ronan,' the image continued. 'There's a house at the foot of Tor Yaimos, on the northern side of the Yaimos Desert. I think it's Shikara's base. Meet me there in two days' time.'

Then her image wavered and suddenly imploded into a puff of grey smoke which drifted up towards the ceiling and vanished. Tarl turned to Guebral.

'She *is* just a friend,' he said, 'but she needs my help. Shikara has more Power than you could shake a stick at. I have to go. And it's going to take me at least three days to get there.'

He stood up reluctantly, and Guebral rose with him.

'I know you're telling the truth,' she said. 'I can see it inside you. And I can see fear. And cowardice. And lust.'

A donkeyish bray of laughter echoed up from the floor far below.

'But I can see a lot of other things as well. Pain. Loneliness. And love. So go and help your friends. There are a lot of big, fast horses in town at the moment. With one of those you could make it in a day and a half. So we will steal one for you . . . Tomorrow.'

She leaned forward and kissed him, ever so gently, on the lips. Tarl could feel passion rising so overwhelmingly that it was making him tremble. He drew back and studied her face. She was so beautiful and so vulnerable that she made his heart ache.

'Why?' he said. 'Why me?'

Guebral gazed into his eyes.

'Because deep down inside you're a good man,' she said. 'And God knows, there aren't many of them about.'

And taking him by the hand she led him slowly across to the bed.

Tyson watched as the flame of the small fire burned down, and the ashes of the spell-charm that Tarl had given her days before blew away on the wind. Sighing, she stood up and stretched. The non-stop ride had left her a bit stiff, but Arvie had been as good as his word, and they had reached the River Errone well before night-fall, despite his insistence on taking a slight detour to show her the famous waterfalls, the Torrents of Vabyus. She had bought a ticket on the downstream boat and then lit a fire and used Tarl's magical charm, reckoning that it would save time to do it now, rather than later when she had actually found Ronan. She had a good feeling about this lead.

Kicking the glowing embers out, she wandered across to the jetty. The boat wasn't due to leave for another hour, but already a good number of people were standing around waiting to board. Tyson sat on a bollard and stared out across the wide, fast-flowing River Errone. It was getting dark now, and on the other side of the river the industrial area of the city of Asposa was ablaze with light. The sound of dozens of buzz-saws drifted across from the massive timber-yards that lined the north bank. The town was famous for the quality of its wood; oak, ash, birch and beech from the forests to the east, cedar and pine from the dense Azure Wood that lined the mountain slopes south of the river. Upstream from the timber-yards was the water-purifying and bottling plant owned by the Saran Company, which was named after Sara, the famous actress who announced to a surprised world that her youthful good looks were due to her habit of regularly drinking Errone water. Now the purified and bottled river water was sold throughout Midworld.

Tyson stared down at the swirling muddy river, wondering how the hell anyone could have possibly wanted to drink the stuff. And then she realised that the hum of conversation around her had died away, and that everyone was looking up at the sky and pointing. Following their gaze she saw a sight that filled her with foreboding.

The sky to the east was dark, but above their heads it was still lit by the recently set sun. And out of the eastern darkness were flying flocks of birds of every type and species, not in their hundreds or even thousands, but in their hundreds of thousands, a great swarm of birds fleeing to the west away from some unknown danger in the east. As they flew overhead the sky darkened with their numbers, and the rustling and murmuring of a million wings drowned out the sounds of industry from across the river.

And then, far away in the east, a light sprang up, a fire flickering and burning far away upon a distant hill-top in the dark. Seconds later it was joined by another one to the north-east, and then a third, far to the north. The hum of conversation rose again, but this time there was an apprehensive note to it.

A worried-looking oarsman from the boat hurried past, and Tyson caught his arm.

'What is it?' she asked. 'What is that flame?'

'The beacons! The warning beacons on the Damon Hills and beyond! They haven't been lit for a hundred years. It means that orcs are on the march! May the Gods protect us! Orcs are in Behan!'

ORC ARMY

In our next issue, we'll be looking at the latest summer fashions, and guess what, girls, the colour this season is . . . black! Surprise, surprise. We'll also be taking a look at the worrying problem of battered babies, and our resident chef will be telling you how to keep them crisp and firm on the outside, but light and fluffy inside.

Hurl (the Magazine for Today's Orc)

When the orcs had come surging out of the Severed Gonad, they were close to three thousand strong, and armed to the teeth. After her speech Shikara had vanished in a sudden blaze of flame that had badly burned the five orcs standing nearest to her (to the huge amusement of the rest), and then a group of sales-orcs from the Weldis Blade Company had turned up. They had brought a huge consignment of their goods with them, and the excited orcs had spent vast sums on re-arming themselves with the very latest weapons.

Pustule and Spavin had bought Ferder Lances, spears with long spiked shafts and wicked saw-edged blades. Shanker, a keen archer, had bought an all-metal Plaquet Bow and a hundred arrows. And Chigger, after much deliberation, had spent nearly all of his cash on just about the best sword an orc could buy; the Man-Hoover, one of the wonderful Astral range designed by Amtus the Berserker, a famous orc warrior, one of the few orcs to be mentioned by name in the pages of *The Pink Book of Ulay* . . .

Mad Amtus, as he was known to his fellow orcs, had a workshop inside the factory of the Weldis Blade Company. The fame of this orc warrior had spread throughout the land, and his workshop became a place of pilgrimage for others of his race. And many was the orc who boasted that he had visited Mad Amtus Swords.

Most fearsome of the weapons he devised is probably the

Astral range, swords with jagged tungsten blades that have been irradiated to give out a faint light, like starlight, that is enough for an orc to be able to see in the dark, although insufficient for human eyes. The top of this range is the Man-Hoover, a blade that emits a keening wail pitched at a frequency that causes fear and discomfort to humans. This hellish and frightening wailing has been the last noise heard by many a human sentry on a dark and moonless night, and it has been said that the worst sound a man can hear is the sound of orc Astral Man-Hoovers in the dark . . .

The orc raiding-party had hit the road before day-break, and when an orc raiding-party hits the road, it stays hit. They had merged with another party that was marching down from east of the Irridic Mountains, and a while later had met a third coming out of the Eastern Wastes from the Great Desert (a huge underground orc brasserie, so named because firstly, it does wonderful puddings, and secondly, its owner couldn't spell 'dessert' properly). As they flooded out of the mountains' foot-hills onto the Derchey Plain they were joined by a mass of Southrons marching up-river from their far-off land beyond Nevin.

As the sun rose in the sky their spirits rose with it, and as they marched they roared out some of their favourite battle-songs. Many chronicles and sagas have suggested that orcs are daylight-hating creatures who fear the sun. This is patently untrue. It's just that they spend most of their time indoors mainly because there are so very few alfresco night-clubs that open during the day, and when you have a hangover that feels as though a five-ton woodpecker is trying to bore into your skull, bright sunlight is not the most welcome thing in the world.

As they neared the city of Derchey, they found more allies waiting for them. There was a group of *Uttuks*, tall powerful orcs who had brought with them a wagon-train of siege equipment, ten massive wagons each pulled by a brace of half-tamed *megoceri*. There was a troop of Southron cavalry mounted on the vicious mutant horses known as Freaks, which snarled and reared and snapped with their razor-sharp fangs at anyone who went near. And waiting with the Southrons was Shikara, mounted on a white stallion and dressed in jet-black armour that fitted her remarkably well.

Leaping from her horse onto one of the wagons, she used a *Fireball* spell to blow up a small orc at the front of the crowd in a loud and soggy explosion, just to get the attention of the rest, and then when all the cheering and laughing had died down, she addressed them.

'A few miles down-river lies the city of Derchey,' she told them. 'Asleep in the sun, ripe and luscious, just waiting to fall into our hands. A city full of food, and booze, and yet more booze. But there is one thing even more important in the city. The bridge. The only bridge over the River Derchey for a hundred miles. Beyond it the whole of Behan and Cydor awaits. Fat, wealthy towns like Brend, Far Tibreth and Ilex. Once we cross that bridge nothing can stop us. So when we take Derchey, you can have your fun, but only for a few hours. *We keep moving!* And we are going to make the most successful raiding-party in history, one that will make the legendary Gaz the Tall look like a party-pooper! Are you with me?'

The roar that greeted this could have been heard miles away, and Shikara glanced nervously to the north-west, hoping that the sentries on duty at Derchey's town gates weren't too alert. Quickly she issued orders to her lieutenants. The Southron cavalry wheeled round and galloped away, and behind them the foot-soldiers, nearly ten thousand strong by now, set off at a run. A fully tanked-up orc is capable of running flat out all day long, needing only a couple of brief stops to be sick. This means that an orc army can cover the ground very quickly. (It also means that they are ridiculously easy – and very unpleasant – to follow.)

The first warning that the four town-gate sentries got was the sight of a distant cloud of dust approaching. As it was more than forty years since they had needed to close the gates in the face of an invading army, the first thing that went through their minds was that it looked as though the wind was getting up a bit, and perhaps they would be better off in the guard-house with a nice cup of tea. The second thing that went through their minds was that the dust-cloud was moving awfully quickly, and weren't there rather a lot of horsemen in front of it? The third thing was the thought that the horsemen looked pretty damn unfriendly, and *klat!* we'd better shut the gates. This was followed almost immediately by the last thing to go through their minds – four well-aimed and extremely sharp arrows.

Then the horsemen burst through the town gates, their horses snapping and slashing at the running townsfolk with lethal teeth, ripping and tearing flesh, and arrows from their small but deadly bows cutting down the few who tried to withstand them. A small group of riders reined in their mounts and waited in the open gateway, their bows at the ready, but the rest galloped on through the packed streets, cutting down the fleeing citizens with their razor-sharp scimitars. They drove a wedge into the town, reaching the Derchey bridge in but a minute. Here a small group of thirty armed townsfolk tried to make a stand behind a hastily formed barricade consisting of a couple of carts, but the horsemen charged them in two waves, the first one leaping over the pitiful barricade before turning to charge again, and the defenders found themselves trapped between the two. Arrows pierced their limbs, scimitars laid open their flesh like the quivering meat upon a butcher's table, and the slashing fangs of the blood-crazed Freaks ripped great chunks from their faces and bodies. Minutes later, the bridge was secured, and all that was left of the defenders were a few slumped and mangled corpses on which the mutant horses grazed contentedly.

The Southrons guarding the open gate didn't have long to wait before the first of the orc foot-soldiers arrived. They were jogging at the double and singing one of their favourite war-chants, '*Kalgazh buhr nazh gashbul nakkerz*' (or, 'Last one in the city gets his testicles ripped off'). They burst into the town like a malodorous flood, sweeping through the streets in search of opposition, but there was virtually none. For years, Derchey had been a peaceful and sleepy border city, and the town guard were poorly trained, ill equipped, and burdened under the full weight of Behanian bureaucracy, which insisted that before any off-duty guard members could receive their weapons from the town armoury they had to fill in weapon application forms in triplicate, a task very difficult to do when your arm has been bitten off at the elbow by a mutant horse. And so the city capitulated, and the orcs spread out through the streets in search of loot, plunder, and most importantly a little bit of fun.

*

When orcs have fun it can be extremely perilous for anyone in the vicinity. Their idea of a good time invariably involves the use of alcohol, shouting, danger, and sharp implements. A good insight can be gained by consulting orc literature on the subject . . .

Another excellent game is Stab-in-the-dark. For this, one person (the Player) is blindfolded, and a second (the Target) sits with his hand outstretched on a table, palm down and fingers spread wide. The Player is then given a sharp dagger and must attempt to stab the point of the dagger into the table-top between each of the outstretched fingers in turn as quickly as possible. If he hits a finger with the dagger he must start again. If he hits two fingers or the main part of the hand he is disqualified, and becomes the next Target . . .

The above extract is taken from
Old Ratshagger's Book of Party Games for Six-year-olds . . .

Chigger and his friends were in the party that stormed the Castle Gates (an up-market tavern on River Street). After the long march from the mountains they were very, very thirsty, but having been warned that they only had four hours to relax, they quickly got down to the business of having some proper fun.

Firstly they divided up the plunder between themselves. There were twenty orcs, but only nineteen barrels of beer in the cellar, and so they drew lots to see who was the unlucky one[9]. This turned out to be a small orc called Syph, who was forced to console himself with the dozen or so bottles of wine that they'd found. Then they got down to the serious business of party games. The pub landlord was killed when his head smashed into the brick wall during a game of Spin the Human, so they cut him down and moved on to playing Chicken. The barman chosen as the target lasted a full forty minutes before a badly aimed knife went straight into an eye-socket. Then they moved on to Blind-orc's Buff, and this lasted until the current blind-orc (Spavin) managed to smash another orc's brains out. (The *buff* in this game is a large fearsomely spiked metal mace weighing about ten

---

[9] Drew lots of obscene graffiti all over the walls, that is. The orc whose pictures or scribblings are judged to be the least filthy and obscene is, by common consent, the loser.

kilograms.) Finally, when the beer had just about run out and it was time to go, the eighteen remaining orcs set fire to the pub and staggered out. It was probably just plain absent-mindedness which caused them to forget that they'd locked Syph in the cellar, and either he was too drunk to scream or else the crackling of the flames drowned him out.

It was the same throughout the city. Whilst most of the townsfolk cowered in their homes in comparative safety, Derchey's population of taverners, wine merchants and bar-staff was virtually wiped out in a few hours. And as evening fell and the orcs poured out into the streets at the appointed hour, yelling and singing, flames licked from the windows of every licensed premises in the city.

But then there came a sound from the east, the rhythmic sound of distant feet marching closer, accompanied by the beating of drums and the harsh braying of war-trumpets. The orcs in the street fell silent, wondering what this might portend, but Shikara ceased her pacing on the battlements above the east-gate and peered into the gathering gloom, smiling with satisfaction.

For marching up-river towards the city there came a horde of Easterlings some five thousand strong, grim-faced and fierce, with their blood-red banners trailing in the evening breeze as they came to join Shikara's army. And after them there came a host of orcs from the north, four thousand strong, who said that an orc called Kev had invited them to the war-party, and although they hadn't brought a bottle, they'd all got their own swords and could they come along anyway?

And so it was that, an hour later, there issued forth from the west-gate an army some twenty thousand strong, orcs and Southrons and Easterlings, well armed and savage. At their head rode Shikara on her white stallion, and behind them they left a town in flames. And as they marched on Brend, no creature was safe. Man, animal or bird, everything that they came across became a target for their arrows or their spears. If it was alive, they killed it, and if it was inanimate, they burned it. To their rear, the smoke and stench of their passage floated up into the skies like the tail of some foul comet. And ahead of them all living things fled, bearing warning of the death and destruction that bored its way deep, deep into the heart of Behan.

LOST

The island of Emba Razindi in the Western Ocean was notorious amongst sea-faring folk for the dangerous waters surrounding it. Full of fierce currents and hidden reefs, they were the haunt of smugglers, wild and savage men who ran the notorious Razindi Gold elf-weed to the mainland in their swift, sleek ships. Many a good sailor died there, swallowed up by the treacherous seas or murdered by pirates or smugglers, until eventually it came to be regarded amongst sea-faring folk as an act of the utmost recklessness to venture into these waters. And many was the poor widow too proud to speak of the Emba Razindi seas that had caused her husband's untimely death . . .

The Pink Book of Ulay

As the *Shorn Teal* sped swiftly eastward through the night, Dene leant against the neck of the carved dragon-head prow, peered uncertainly forwards into the swirling sea-fog, and fretted to himself. After a couple of days of sailing through some of the most dangerous seas in the world, he was getting just a teeny bit worried. They had eight days left, eight days in which they had to find some target or group of targets worthy of a Vagen raid, plan and cost this raid, prepare a detailed breakdown of the logistics involved, and then get home and deliver a presentation that was sufficiently interesting and entertaining to persuade the rest of the tribe not to condemn them to death on the spot.

So far, they hadn't found a target worthy of the name. The big cities were far too well defended, and the rest of the coast-line seemed to be raided out. Every village they came across was virtually destitute, with half the buildings burnt down, and at the first sight of the *Shorn Teal*'s dragon-headed prow the villagers grabbed whatever few pitiful belongings they retained and high-tailed it into the nearest hills or forests.

Mind you, he thought, it hadn't been a total waste of time. Two days cooped up in a ship with eighteen women had taught Dene a lot. He had little experience or understanding of the opposite sex, and had come to think of them as being somehow slightly different. The past couple of days had shown him just how different they really were.

For example, they were tidy in a way that seemed totally beyond the ability or understanding of men. The ship was neat and clean, with everything stowed away where it belonged. Dene couldn't understand this at all. He'd always been on male-only raids before, and thought that after a couple of days it was compulsory for the decks to be knee-deep in old food, empty beer-bottles, broken fishing tackle and solidifying lumps of spit.

Not that they hadn't had any fun. He'd discovered that most of the crew could drink him under the table. They favoured a strange cocktail of rum mixed with the juice of blackcurrants, which Dene had always heard the men of the village speak of dismissively as 'no drink for a man'. Now he understood why. After a few of those a man completely lost the use of his legs, and could be quite violently and spectacularly sick. However, he had been delighted to find that the women weren't interested in any of the macho stuff that usually went on whenever Vagens had a few drinks. No one had done any oar-walking, or diving into the sea from the top of the mast, or even challenged him to arm-wrestle and half broken his wrist for him. There had been a lot of scurrilous and very rude gossip, though, and he had been surprised (and not a little embarrassed) at how near the knuckle it got.

He had also been surprised at what had happened when his habitual sea-sickness had struck on the second day. Instead of laughing at him or throwing him overboard, Kait had disappeared into the covered galley area for a few minutes and had emerged with a herbal remedy of hers that had actually made him feel better.

Mind you, he had still managed to get himself thrown overboard, and had come to the conclusion that you had to be very careful what you said. It was obvious that Fjonë for some reason hated any mention of waterfowl – or at least this was the only interpretation he could place on the events of last night. The off-duty crew members had all been having a few drinks, and he and Fjonë had been talking about the fact that every peasant in the coastal villages had learnt to run for their lives as soon as they saw the give-away dragon-head prow approaching. Dene had suggested that they should have a different emblem as a figurehead, something that was not so aggressive and macho, but more loveable and cuddly. A teddy-bear, perhaps, or a bunny-rabbit. Fjonë had told him that he had to be joking. Dene, warming to his theme, had suggested they could try something that looked humorous, such as a puffin. Fjonë had told him that, raid leader or not, there was no way in which they would allow him to place a puffin-head on the prow of their ship, even if it was named after a bird. There had been a short silence, and then Dene had muttered, half to himself, 'I suppose a duck's out of the question,' and that was when Fjonë had thrown him overboard. Later, after the others had fished him out, she had been most apologetic, but Dene had decided that women were a funny lot, and he was going to keep his ideas to himself in future.

At the steering oar, Marten too was fretting, but for a very different reason. He had stopped worrying about what was going to happen in eight days' time, as he'd come to the conclusion that he'd be dead by then. For in the past forty-eight hours, the mild passion that he had felt for Klaer when they boarded the ship had turned into complete and utter infatuation. Whenever she was within eyeshot, he couldn't take his eyes off her. When she wasn't, he kept seeing her face in front of him. And sometimes other bits as well. His private parts seemed to have taken on a life of their own, and he'd had to spend a lot of the day walking round the ship with a shield strategically held in front of him. He just knew that sometime in the next week, when she was stood looking at him with those huge eyes of hers, he was going to find it impossible to stop himself from grabbing and kissing her. And he knew how any of the women would react to an approach like that. He'd seen what happened when Fjonë thought Dene had merely made a dubious suggestion. If Marten actually *did* something he was damn sure that he would get cut off in his prime. He'd seen how sharp that knife of Klaer's was.

And so the *Shorn Teal* ploughed on into the night with a lookout who couldn't see for fog and fretting and a steersman whose attention was firmly fixed on one of the sleeping blanket-covered bodies on the deck in front of him. This would have been a recipe for disaster if they hadn't known exactly where they were, and where they were heading. But one of the surprises of the journey so far had been the discovery that Dene had a natural aptitude for navigation. Give him a sextant and a chart, show him the pole star, and he could tell in seconds exactly where they were and how far away land was. Half an hour before, Marten had given him the chart and the sextant, and Dene had predicted that on the current course and speed they would reach land near Yai'El in approximately four hours' time.

Unfortunately, what Marten hadn't allowed for was the fact that Dene was totally crap at astronomy. It hadn't entered his mind that anyone might not know which the pole star was. Dene had, alas, taken his sextant reading on the star Yellopus in the constellation of The Septic Goitre, an error of some twenty degrees. As a result, his reckoning was a good thirty miles out. The first inkling Marten had of this was a strangled and panic-filled shout from Dene.

'LAND –'

Then the *Shorn Teal* stopped dead, as though it had run full-tilt into something immoveable (which it had), and tilted sharply to one side. Marten was thrown forwards and went crashing down amongst the shipped oars. The sleeping bodies were sent sprawling along the deck in a chaotic mass of arms, legs and blankets, and Dene shot over the front of the ship almost as precipitately as if he'd just propositioned Fjonë again. There was a moment's pause, while everybody dragged themselves to their feet and stared around in confusion, and then Dene's head popped up over the front of the ship and peered at them through the tendrils of fog.

'– AHEAD!' he finished, somewhat belatedly, and then fell backwards as Klaer's well-aimed beer-mug bounced off his head.

Ten minutes later, the two friends were wandering shame-facedly up the sandy beach on which they had run aground, Klaer's fierce diatribe still ringing in their ears. Both had been reinforced in their views by the tirade of anger which she had vented on them. Dene didn't particularly like being called a half-witted, cretinous nematode with the brain-power of a retarded amoeba and the leadership qualities of rotting wood, but it was certainly preferable to being buried head-down up to his waist in the sand, which is what the guys would probably have done. And Marten, although Klaer's scorn had cut him to the quick, had been so turned on by her fierce brown eyes flashing fire at him that it had been all he could do to prevent himself from committing suicide by grabbing her then and there. Luckily his hands had been fully occupied in holding a large rock in front of his groin (as in all the excitement he'd left his shield on the ship) or else he might have made a total prat of himself.

As they reached the top of the beach the drifting fog deadened the sound of the pounding surf, although they could still hear the occasional female voice lifted in imprecation against the sort of totally blind *pillock* who could steer a ship straight into an entire continent without even noticing it. There were palm trees growing thickly here. Their fronds rustled in the almost imperceptible on-shore breeze that wafted the tendrils of fog up the beach, and a faint smell of decaying vegetation assailed their nostrils.

Dene threw himself down on the sand and scowled back down the beach.

'*Klatting* fog!' he muttered. 'I'm sick of the stuff! Every time I go out, it's foggy. I can never see where the hell I'm going. Fog, fog, fog. And if it isn't foggy, there's a mist. And on the few occasions that I manage to get to a decent-sized town, it's full of smog. It's not *klatting* fair!'

Actually, it *was* fair. Although Dene didn't know it, he had cocked up yet another ceremony some months previously. An invocation to Noax, the God of Dogs, had ended up with Nebula, the Goddess of Fogs, and she had generously granted her supplicant the gift of plenteous damp and misty weather whenever he was out and about.

But as Dene sat moodily sifting sand through his fingers and complaining, Marten wasn't listening to him. His attention was elsewhere, as he thought he had heard a faint, furtive noise in the trees in front of him. The hairs on his neck rose, and he laid his hand on the hilt of his sword and half drew it from its scabbard. Apart from Dene wittering on beside him he could hear nothing

155

more, and yet the silence felt oppressive and threatening.

'Dene,' he whispered, 'we'd better get back to the –'

And then the trees seemed to erupt with half-orcs and in an instant Marten was fighting for his life.

Half-orcs, the result of unions between humans and orcs, tend to inherit characteristics from both races. This is generally to their advantage, as they have the height and strength of humans, and the cunning and stamina of orcs. Unfortunately, though, they tend to inherit the uncontrollable desire to party that is typical of orcs, along with the sadly limited alcohol tolerance of humans, and this usually results in the most god-awful semi-permanent hangovers. Thus as a species they tend to be remarkably short-tempered and aggressive. A few of the most obnoxious end up in cities, where they invariably find employment as night-club bouncers, but most end up in semi-nomadic tribes of brigands or outlaws. They are frequently skilled and lethal fighters.

When the pack of perhaps fifteen of them burst out of the fog, Marten had little time to think. He had no experience of battle, and all his training in the past had been either alone, or as a child with others. To his amazement, his body reacted as though born to fight, and he found that he was standing over Dene wielding his sword in a two-handed grip, its blade a whirling barrier of death. He could hear himself roaring threats and defiance, and at his feet Dene was yammering what sounded like another of his invocations. Yet Marten was aware that, although four of the half-orcs already lay headless before him, there were too many of them. In a matter of seconds, one would find a way past his blade, and then he would be cut to bloody ribbons. But suddenly all his foes were backing off, hands clutching their guts, near-comical expressions of pain on their faces. Three or four threw up copiously, and as the others moaned and whimpered in agony, the sour smell of vomit was joined by an almost overpowering stench of excrement. Bent double in pain, puke dribbling from their mouths and with ordure-stained trousers, the band of half-orcs reeled back into the night, and Marten, gagging from the mephitic odour, staggered down the beach and sank to his knees as reaction set in.

Beside him Dene appeared to be having hysterics, and Marten was just about to comfort his friend when he realised that he was actually laughing.

'I don't believe it!' spluttered Dene, 'It worked! I don't *klatting* well believe it!'

'What worked?'

'My prayer. Krage once told me during a raid that my prayers were more like curses, and that I should save them for our enemies. So I did. When those guys just attacked us, I yelled out the prayer to Benefera, the one I used during the raid on the Maremma, when our whole raiding-party went down with dysentery. But I made it really powerful. It worked. They had the same reaction our tribe did, but much stronger.'

Marten looked at him and shook his head.

'There is something seriously wrong with your technique,' he said, 'if that is what happens to the people you pray for. Don't ever pray for me. OK?'

Rising, the two of them wandered back down the beach to where their crew-mates were standing looking worriedly at the front hull of the ship. The receding tide had left it clear of the sea, and there was a head-sized hole beneath the waterline. Klaer looked at them coldly.

'Ah,' she said. 'The guys who put the w in dead wreckoning. Not content with ramming a beach, you had to hit the only large, jagged rock on the whole of that beach . . .' She paused, taking in Marten's blood-stained sword, and in a few quick words he told her about their encounter with the half-orcs. She looked at him with a new respect in her eyes, and feeling that old familiar stirring again he crouched down and started to clean his sword with a handful of sand.

'So that's what all the shouting was,' she continued. 'I thought you two were having a manly it-was-your-fault-no-it-was-yours type of argument. Well, that gives us problems. We're running out of time, it's going to take at least five days to repair the ship, and now we've got a tribe of half-orc brigands for neighbours. Great. I don't suppose you have any idea where we are?'

With the help of the sextant (and Marten to point out exactly which star was the pole star), Dene was able to work out that they were on the coast of Cydor near the Gemae Hills, about twenty miles southwest of Yai'El. With time running out, they decided to follow Lobbo's advice and head for the city. However, the ship had to be repaired, and with the half-orcs around it was necessary to keep a strong force to guard it. In the end, as Marten and Dene had already proved themselves capable of dealing with the brigands, it was decided that the two of them would set off for Yai'El alone, and that everyone else would stay behind to mend the hull.

And so half an hour later, the two men hefted their packs onto their shoulders and said goodbye to their companions. One by one they shook hands with the others, until only Klaer was left. Marten didn't dare meet her gaze as she took his hand. Just that brief amount of contact was enough to set his pulse racing. But then she suddenly leant forwards and kissed his cheek.

'Good luck,' she said briskly, before turning and leaping back aboard the beached ship.

And so Marten set off into the fog. He had just a week to find some irresistible target for a raid and then convince the tribe of this irresistibility. He was on foot in a dense fog in a strange land apparently awash with savage half-orcs, there was a large hole in the bottom of his ship, and his only companion was an incompetent maladroit whose only talent was for being crap at everything. Strange, then, that as he set off on the twenty-mile hike to Yai'El, he should be singing like a skylark that has just won the lottery . . .

LOYALTY

The Yaimos Desert . . . a dry and barren region south of the Chrome Mountains, in Cydor. Few creatures can live in these burning wastes, and those that do survive have been forced to adapt in order to conserve water. For example, the Banded Ruby-neck, a venomous snake that bites and kills anyone it finds who has left the taps running, or the Cydorian Sidewinder, a snake that needs no water at all, having adapted to survive on neat alcohol (hence its curious sideways gait). The Sidewinder is quite lethal, having breath that can kill a small rodent from five feet away.

But most unusual of all these adaptions must be the Desert Daisy, an intelligent plant with mental powers so strong that it is able to move around in search of water by levitating itself. It is thought to be Midworld's only example of a self-raising flower . . .

The Pink Book of Ulay

Tarl leant nonchalantly against the white stone wall, ostensibly reading the tatty hand-written menu pinned to the doorpost of Scoffuluvv, a run-down and malodorous café on the east side of the small square. In fact, he was intently watching the three horses that were tied up outside Sigarni's, a nearby winebar. The early morning sun slanted obliquely down, leaving his side of the square in shadow, and Tarl was confident that their owners hadn't even seen him standing there.

The first horse was all skin and bone, and looked like a skeleton shrink-wrapped in brown plastic. It had a filthy old blanket across its back, on which someone had embroidered the words 'My other horse is a thoroughbred'. Tarl thought it looked like the equine equivalent of the small brown donkey that was salivating all over the pavement beside him. However, the other two horses were a different matter. Both were large, sleek, muscle-bound beauties that were obviously in town for the Thoroughbred Trophy races. Tarl had watched their two owners entering the winebar, and knew that the bay on the left was called Zephyr, and the chestnut was named Virago.

The donkey whiffled its nostrils hungrily as it stared through the café door, and then sighed and looked up at Tarl.

'Made your mind up?' it enquired.

'Yeah. The chestnut, I think. It looks more manageable. How about you?'

'The thirty-ounce steak on table four. It's so rare it's a collector's item, and he hasn't even touched it yet.'

'OK. Let's go for it.'

Tarl glanced across to the south side of the square, where the main street exited. Guebral was nonchalantly leaning against the corner, and seeing him look across she gave him a small, almost imperceptible wave. Tarl nodded calmly back, but his heart beat a little faster inside. *Klat!* he thought, what a night! What a girl! He couldn't get over those huge eyes of hers, and as for—

'Hoy, Romeo! Concentrate.'

Tarl muttered an apology to the impatient Puss, and dragged his attention back to the present. Casually he wandered across to Virago, while Puss disappeared inside the café. Looking round to make sure he wasn't being observed he untied the reins from the hitching post, and then sauntered round to stand beside the great horse. For a few seconds nothing happened, and then there was a yell of anger from the café, and Puss came tearing out of the door with a huge pinky-brown steak hanging from his mouth like a giant tongue.

Tarl leapt into Virago's saddle, dragging the horse's head round with a vicious tug of the reins, and dug his heels into its side. The great horse reared up and then took off after the donkey, which had gone clattering into the street to the south. As they shot past her Tarl blew a kiss to Guebral, and then he was haring after the donkey, which was going so fast its hooves were raising sparks off the cobbles.

Quickly Tarl risked a look back. Their getaway hadn't gone unnoticed, and people had come storming out of both café and winebar, but pursuit was impossible. All the other horses in the square were bucking and leaping in fear as a winged stallion of fire soared and dived about their heads.

'Nice one, Gueb,' he muttered. 'Wait for me, sweetheart. I'll be back.'

And he put his head down and steered Virago after the fleeing donkey as it sped through the streets towards the causeway that led to the mainland.

Tyson watched the boat while it churned southwards down the Yarrone towards Atro, then she hefted her pack onto her shoulders and set off towards the distant Chrome mountains. The ground beneath her feet was rough and uneven, and damp with early morning dew. Behind her the eastern sky was clear, and the newly risen sun was warm on her back, but ahead a bank of thick cloud was edging nearer from the west, and the sky above the mountains was grey and leaden.

Tyson was tired. She had slept little during the down-river cruise, preferring to join the mass of passengers lining the railings on the top deck to stare at the warning beacons burning in the night on the mountain-tops of Behan and Cydor to the north, and Iduin to the south. The talk was all of the orc incursion, and rumours were flying thick and fast.

'They say there are thousands of them, armed to the teeth . . .'

'Orcs won't swim or use boats, you know. They must have captured the bridge at Derchey . . .'

'We'd be safe in Iduin, then. There are no bridges across the Errone this side of the Inland Sea . . .'

'No, I heard that Southrons are with them, and that a huge Southron army is on the march from the deep south, heading towards Brannan . . .'

'I met a magic user in Asposa who said that they're led by a vastly powerful sorceress. He reckoned no one could withstand them . . .'

'One of the sailors told me that the orcs will march west and join forces with the Vagens. Nowhere will be safe . . .'

Eventually she had wrapped herself in her blanket and curled up in the lee of the cabin, but sleep had been impossible. Her brain had been whirling around trying to make sense of this invasion. And now, as she strode away from the river towards the distant mountains, she was still trying to puzzle it out.

There had been rumours of massed orc movements a few months ago, when she had been desperately trying to defend Welbug from the machinations of Nekros and his allies, but since his death everything had gone quiet. Now it rather looked as though whoever had been backing Nekros had gone quietly on with their plans, and had found a new figurehead.

Tyson shook her head in perplexity. Well, whatever was happening in Behan was no concern of hers. Welbug, her home city, was on the other side of the Great River Leno and was presumably safe for the moment. Time to worry about the orcs after she'd rescued Ronan. Let's face it, she thought. I'm about to try and rescue the object of lust of a very powerful, sex-starved and rather unbalanced sorceress, and if I'm lucky I may have the help of a small brown donkey and the worst spell-caster since Salemon the Shite. Why should I worry about orcs? I'll probably be dead in two days' time . . .

The town of Brend stood where the roads from Derchey, Far Tibreth and Rednec met in the centre of the Behan Plain, north of the Damon Hills. It was an old and historic town, but its stout stone walls were high, and were guarded by formidable towers. Never had the walls or the massive oaken gates been breached in combat, and never had the city fallen to siege, as Brend was the distribution centre for produce from all the surrounding farmlands. Its massive store-houses were always full of food, and water was no problem, as within the walls were numerous artesian wells of crystal-clear water which had never yet run dry.

When news of the fall of Derchey had reached the town, riders had been sent out to warn the other cities of Behan, and to muster the Behanian militia. But Brend itself stood calm before the approaching storm. All day a stream of people from the surrounding farms poured through the great gates in search of safety, and as the afternoon wore on this slowed to a trickle, then ceased altogether.

Then, in late afternoon, a distant murmur could be heard. The citizens and soldiers lined the battlemented walls to gaze eastward. At first it was difficult for them to see, for the sun had been swallowed up by thick, glowering clouds that inched across the sky from the west. But then slowly their foe came into view, not as they had expected, an army marching in column with banners flying and drums pounding, but as a broad and straggling destructive swathe that swarmed in a wide band across the fertile countryside, burning and trampling the fields and orchards as it went, for no more reason than pure malice and the sheer enjoyment of destruction.

On the battlements, a young farmer watched the columns of smoke pouring up from his fields of wheat and turned to the old man next to him in frustrated anger.

'Why do they destroy so much? Surely they realise that they will need food soon, or their army will die. Why do they not gather it in as they come?'

The old man smiled a humourless smile.

'They are orcs and Easterlings,' he answered. 'They know that there is food in the city. They believe it will fall soon, and then they will eat their fill. They look forward to eating fresh meat. Meat that runs on two legs.'

He looked at the farmer with pity in his eyes.

'You should have fled while you had the chance,' he added, and then turned his stony gaze back to the black tide that flowed unstoppably towards the town.

Tarl was speeding along the main Yai'El to Dol Dupp road with the wind in his hair and a smile on his face. Virago was incredible, the smoothest ride he'd ever had. Well, on horseback, anyway. He peered back over his shoulder and giggled uncontrollably. There was no sign of Puss. At first the little donkey had set a fair pace, but after a mile Tarl had just let Virago steam past. As he'd done so, he had seen the furious look on the donkey's face. He'd yelled some comment about dawdling along, and had thought he'd heard Puss bray something about hares and tortoises, but he was well ahead now. He'd stop in a bit and let his friend catch up. Better not rub its tatty muzzle in it too much, though. He didn't want Puss to bite Virago's leg off.

Then suddenly from behind him he heard a familiar loud wailing sound, and his heart sank.

'Oh, no!' he thought. 'The *klatting* highway police!'

With a sinking heart he slowed Virago down, and sure enough, when he looked round he saw a vast black horse pounding after him, with the unmistakable figure of a Cydorian Highway Patrolman urging it along, one arm whirling as he swung the air-siren with which the Patrol always delighted in announcing their presence.

Tarl pulled Virago up and slipped out of the saddle, and the patrolman reined his horse in ahead of them at the side of the road, dismounted, and swaggered back. Tarl took in the gleaming black boots, the smooth white helmet and the impenetrable black glasses and cursed mentally. This meant trouble.

'In a hurry, sir?' The flat, uninterested tones held a vein of sarcasm that the patrolman made no attempt to disguise.

'Er, well, I'm supposed to be meeting a friend, but I'm a bit late . . .'

'Have you any idea just how fast you were going, sir?'

Tarl shook his head. He hated patrolmen who called him 'sir', like that, because it was obvious that although they were saying 'sir', what they actually meant was 'you little piece of shit'.

The patrolman walked slowly around Virago studying the horse, and then casually kicked one of the massive hooves before addressing Tarl again.

'This your horse, is it, sir?'

'Yes. Well, I'm minding it for a friend. You know.'

The patrolman nodded, as though this had confirmed all his worst fears. Pulling a thick sheaf of parchment out of the pocket of his smartly pressed jacket, he started to leaf through it. Tarl squinted at the upside-down pages and could just decipher enough to make out that it was a list of 'wanted' descriptions.

In the distance, a little figure came into view trotting along the road at a deceptively fast pace. The patrolman looked up briefly and then went back to his descriptions, and Tarl watched hopefully as Puss trotted towards them. But, to his horror, the little donkey went straight past him, and Tarl thought he heard a muttered aside about *klatting* hares screwing up again. But then Puss skidded to a halt and ambled over to the police-horse.

'Ah!' said the patrolman, and Tarl switched his attention back. The man had found a description on the very last page that interested him. He studied it for a moment, and then looked Tarl up and down.

'Height,' he muttered to himself, 'negligible. Colour of eyes . . .' He paused, and stared at Tarl. 'Bloodshot. Hair . . . not much.'

Tarl squinted at the page, and saw to his horror that the description was of a man wanted for robbery, deception, and illicit spell-casting the previous day in Yai'El. It was him to a T. He glanced across to Puss and nodded almost imperceptibly.

'Right, chummy, you're nicked,' said the patrolman, and with one snap of his jaws Puss bit right through the hamstring of the big black horse's hind left leg. It screeched in agony, and as the startled patrolman swung round Tarl leapt into Virago's saddle, kicked the horse into a gallop, and pounded off down the road with Puss alongside. A crossbow quarrel hissed past him, missing by a good two feet, and then they were round a bend and out of sight.

Tarl slowed Virago down, making sure that the pace wasn't too hot for Puss, and the little donkey grinned up at him.

'I'm not going too fast for you, am I?' it asked.

Tarl shook his head and laughed. 'Thanks for your help back there,' he called.

The donkey snorted. 'No problem,' it said scornfully. 'Police-horses – the only animals in the world with a prick halfway up their back!'

After another mile or so Tarl reined in again. Ahead of them the road to Dol Dupp stretched on into the distance, with the shimmering ocean on its left and the Chrome Mountains towering above it on the right. A rough track branched off to run eastward along the foot of the mountains, skirting the edge of the Yaimos Desert.

'I reckon this is our turning,' said Tarl. 'We're making good time. Tomorrow with a bit of luck we'll come up against Shikara.'

The donkey looked at him darkly. 'Ever had the feeling you're stepping out of your league?' it asked.

'All the time, mate. All the *klatting* time. But somehow I've always survived.'

And with that he turned the horse's head to the east, and they set off along the track.

'Tarl is riding to his death,' said Guebral, and stared at Pinball, waiting for a reaction. He was sat on the floor, with his back to the wall and his face in shadow, but the dull red light from the gas-works glinted on his metallic eyes as he stared levelly back at her.

'You cannot be sure of that,' he said.

'I have been mind-surfing, farther than I have ever been before. I've seen things that may be. I must help him.'

'He has the ring.'

'It won't be enough.'

'Then go.'

'But even with my help, in a few days' time he and thousands of others face death unless you help too. You, Raze, Shiftfister and all the Dead Boys.'

'We do not help affoes.'

'We don't go out of our way to harm them, either. Refusing our help when it could save them would harm them. And anyway, Tarl isn't an affo.'

Pinball was silent. In the centre of the vast room, the other Dead Boys were laughing and yarning. Guebral fidgeted on the rough wooden seat and dragged a stray curl of hair back behind one ear. Pinball sighed, and his metal eyes whirled like molten rubies.

'The others won't want to help.'

'Talk to them while I'm gone. If things go right I will be back in a few days.'

'And if things go wrong?'

'Then it's been nice knowing you,' she smiled, and suddenly she just wasn't there any more.

The eight members of the Ruling Council of Brend stood on the battlements of the city walls beside one of the massive towers that flanked the city gate, peering out confidently at the distant mass of orcs. Since their arrival the previous day the besieging army had ringed the city, ensuring that nothing and no one could get in or out, but had kept their distance. Now, however, they seemed to be forming up into an attack formation, but the councillors weren't worried. They had every kind of defence available on the town walls, they had a mass of defenders armed to the teeth, and they had five resident wizards of varying ages and powers who had been hurriedly conscripted from their homes and now stood conferring beside the councillors.

Meanwhile there had been a mass of feverish activity over by the cluster of wagons a quarter of a mile away. The besiegers had been putting together some form of siege weapon, a mobile tower of wooden scaffolding mounted on vast wheels. Now it was being laboriously pushed towards the gates by a seething mass of sweating, straining orcs. It rumbled forwards, inch by inch, escorted on either side by several large *Mazhkunuzg*, the powerful orc mages, who held in their taloned hands jet-black stone wands. A massive hammer hung vertically within the framework of the tower, its solid metal head cast in the shape of a demonic skull. The orcs had named it *Guragazul*, or MC Warhammer, and underneath it was a huge siege mage-deck, its directional speakers pointing forwards towards the town walls.

In front rode a single small black-armoured figure on a white stallion. To the rear, the mass of orcs, Easterlings and Southrons waited, silent now, watching as the tower edged inexorably forwards, and there was no movement amongst them save for their red and black banners fluttering in the breeze.

On the town walls, the leader of the council turned to a waiting messenger.

'Pass the word to make sure the burning oil and the fire-arrows are ready,' he ordered. The messenger sped off, and the eldest of the wizards cleared his throat and spoke.

'There is powerful magic protecting that tower,' he said. 'Your fire-arrows won't get through without a counter-spell.'

'Which, I take it, you can provide?'

'I believe so,' replied the eldest wizard.

'We have seen nothing so far that worries us,' added a second.

'Piece of piss,' stated the youngest.

'Hm,' said the eldest, a little tight-lipped. 'I think, gentlemen, that if we work together we might accomplish our desired aim. I can see no more than ten orc mages down there. In unison we should be able to break through with a *shatter* spell strong enough to destroy that infernal machine.'

He held up his staff and the councillors watched, intrigued, as the other four wizards grasped hold of it together, closed their eyes and muttered an incantation in unison.

It was difficult to describe what happened next, it happened so quickly. The leader of the council was left with the impression that an almost invisible flash of lightning had shot out from their staff towards the siege tower, but that it had rebounded from the figure on the white horse and come hurtling straight back at them. But whatever the cause, the five wizards suddenly screamed in unison as matter burst from their ears, eyes and mouths, and then they fell to the floor as though pole-axed. From the foul and bloody mess around their heads it looked as though something had exploded inside their skulls, blasting their brains out through every available orifice in sticky, quivering fragments.

The leader of the council stared aghast at their remains. There was an eyeball beside his foot that seemed to be staring up at him accusingly. Shuddering, he dragged his gaze around to the approaching siege-tower. It was well within range now.

'Fire!' he yelled, and a barrage of flaming arrows erupted from the walls and battlements, but to his horror every arrow seemed to bounce off the air around the wooden structure as if they had hit some invisible barrier. Slowly and unstoppably the tower ground onwards, crunching across a litter of spent arrows, inching nearer and nearer to the city gates, and behind it the ranks of orcs jeered and yelled, and then began one of their favourite war-chants, 'Grakutul khumb zul klattuk razuluk' ('You're going to get your klatting heads kicked in').

The defenders on the walls roared defiant threats at them, but wave after wave of their arrows merely bounced off the invisible barrier around the attackers, and the tower rumbled into the shadow of the town walls, stopping right in front of the gates. Torrents of boiling oil poured down towards it but fared no better than the arrows, and the toiling orcs that had pushed the tower into position looked up and jeered at the defenders, knowing they were safe behind their impenetrable barrier of magic.

Gradually the defenders fell silent. A feeling of unease was spreading amongst them, a gnawing doubt that threatened to turn into panic. Every eye was drawn to the figure on the white horse waiting beside the tower, for it seemed to be the source of an almost tangible cloud of dread which wafted up to engulf them. Meanwhile, the orc mages scrambled about the huge head of the hammer and the mage-deck, readying them, and the vast mass of the orc army waited just outside of bow-shot and roared their daunting chants.

Then the mage-deck burst into life with a vast throbbing beat so deep that it was sensed more than heard, and the walls beneath the defenders' feet seemed to vibrate in rhythm. The figure on the white horse removed its helm and shook out a mane of long auburn hair, and they saw with disbelief that it was a woman. And then she raised one arm and the mighty metal head of the warhammer was drawn slowly backwards. The orc mages stood together chanting, their black stone wands raised with tips touching, pale red fire flickering along the shafts. Then white flame lanced from the woman's hand and merged with the pale fire from the orc mages' wands to dance about the head of the hammer, which swung forwards and hit the massive city gates with a mighty crash. There was a brilliant flash of white light and a huge explosion, and the gates were instantly vaporised.

The watching orcs roared and swarmed forwards. A few fell, brought down by arrows from the city walls, but only a very few, for the defenders were suddenly seized by an overwhelming and all-consuming fear, and throwing down their weapons they fled from their posts, seeking refuge in the city. Orcs, Easterlings and Southrons poured through the open gateway, swords in hand, driven by blood-lust and hunger, and spread out through the streets in an orgy of death and destruction. And so began the rape of the city of Brend.

Tarl was getting decidedly saddle-sore. As saddles went, this one was a beauty, all soft supple leather and luxurious padding, but it had obviously been designed with someone a lot bigger than Tarl in mind, and he was starting to resemble a wishbone. The insides of his thighs felt as though they had been sand-blasted.

They were quite high up in the foothills of the Chrome Mountains now. Puss was leading the way, following a track that wound between large boulders and outcrops of rock along the side of the hill. Below them to the right, a thin strip of silver marked the course of the stream that collected water from the mountains and ran eastward to become a tributary of the Errone. Beyond this, the burning hot expanses of the Yaimos Desert stretched away southwards as far as the eye could see.

Then the donkey stopped, and Tarl rode wearily up alongside it. The track continued ahead of them, but a rougher path branched off to the left here, disappearing over the brow of the hill and heading for the imposing, snow-covered peak that dominated the other mountains to the north.

'I guess this must be it,' the donkey said.

'Yeah. That's Tor Yaimos, all right,' replied Tarl. 'Beautiful, eh? Just beautiful!'

He was going to elaborate further when all of a sudden there was a pop of displaced air and Guebral was standing right beside them. Tarl was so surprised that he fell off Virago. He lay there on the ground, staring up at her with an expression of total stupefaction.

'Gueb! What are you doing here?'

'What do you think she's doing, you wazzock?' snorted the donkey. 'Having a brisk walking tour of the mountains? Going on a skiing holiday? Or could it possibly be that she's come to help us? No, no, surely nothing so *klatting* obvious!'

'I was worried for you,' Guebral told Tarl.

'We would have been OK,' he answered, but secretly he was pretty relieved. He had no illusions about the strength of his powers compared to Shikara's, and he was beginning to have enormous respect for Guebral's abilities. *Teleporting* from Yai'El to within four foot of him showed an accuracy and control that was far beyond his own. Also, he found it surprisingly moving to find that someone actually cared what happened to him. He stood up and took hold of her hand, and the donkey made a noise like an orc retching.

'If you two start snogging, I'm off,' it warned them, and turning its back pointedly to them it stalked off up the track. Grinning, Tarl and Guebral followed it, arm in arm, and Virago ambled docilely after them.

As they breasted the crest of the hill the path levelled out in front of them, running straight for a couple of hundred yards before disappearing into the edge of the thick woodland that covered the lower slopes of Tor Yaimos. There wasn't a house to be seen and Tarl paused uncertainly, but the donkey snuffled eagerly at the ground for a moment before looking up.

'Tyson's been along here,' it said happily, and Tarl felt a wave of relief wash over him. Eagerly he strode out along the track, and the others followed. As the path plunged into the densely growing trees it was like entering a tunnel, and it took a few seconds for their eyes to get accustomed to the gloom. But when they did, Tarl saw a sight that cheered him up immensely, for there ahead of them, sitting on a shapeless hummock at the edge of the track and cleaning a blood-stained dagger, was Tyson.

The donkey trotted ahead and pushed its head at her, and she grinned and scratched its tatty ears. Then she looked up.

'Hey, Tarl!' she greeted him. 'How's it hanging?'

'All the better for seeing you, Tyse!' he yelled back, and then wished he hadn't as Guebral's nails almost went through his palm. Hurriedly he introduced the two women.

'So,' he continued, after they had shaken hands warily, 'you think you may have a lead on Ronan, eh?'

'I know I have.'

'What makes you so sure?'

'My chair,' said Tyson, getting up, and the others saw that the hummock was the body of a soldier, dressed in an embarrassingly brief leather uniform that showed off his bulging muscles and hairy chest, and rather crudely emphasised his sexual organs.

'By the Gods!' exclaimed Tarl. 'What's he wearing?'

'Something dreamt up by the bitch-queen herself. Apparently she's got a bit of a male harem in her castle.'

'A castle, eh? And Ronan's in there too?'

'So this guy said. Ragnar, his name was. One of Shikara's guards, now retired. He'd tell you himself only he got a little cocky and tried to jump me.'

'Did he say if Ronan has . . . er . . .' Tarl dribbled to a halt, unable to think of a tactful way to phrase the question.

'Has he succumbed? No, the great lummox wouldn't play ball,' Tyson said proudly. 'So she's got him locked up in the dungeons. This guy spilled his guts in more ways than one,' she added, prodding the soldier with her toe. 'He told me how to get into the castle and how to find Ronan. Problem is, there are a lot of magical defences to crack, so we're gonna need all the Power you can muster.'

'Me? Oh, she's way too powerful for me,' said Tarl, and Tyson's face fell like a lead weight. He rushed on, 'No, Gueb's the one you want. She's a natural!'

Tyson looked from Tarl to Guebral, and then shrugged.

'Okay,' she said. 'Follow me.'

Leaving Puss to guard the horse, she led them along the track for a couple of hundred paces to where a second track branched off. They followed this for a while before she angled off to the left, leading the way through dense undergrowth for maybe fifty yards, and eventually stopping behind a vast and ancient oak tree.

'Well, there it is,' she said, and Tarl craned his head around the trunk. There, in the centre of a clearing, was their target.

It was a small castle that looked like something dreamt up by Mervyn Peake in one of his gloomier moods. Built from dark, damp, depressing stone, it had crumbling turrets that seemed to sag under the overpowering weight of some terminal depression, and gates of twisted and blackened oak that had obviously come from trees which had found life a great trial. Above the main gate large stone replicas of a death's head moth and a couple of scorpions had been fixed to the outer wall, in a macabre attempt at decoration. Black pennants with rampant white horses on them hung limply from the towers as though they didn't quite have the energy to move in the breeze – anything so optimistic and jolly as fluttering was obviously way beyond them. Around the castle the earth was scorched and bare. No plants grew within fifty paces, and at the edge of this area the trees and undergrowth had begun to shrivel and blacken, as though they had lost the will to live. The overall effect was about as uplifting as bubonic plague.

Tarl pulled his head back.

'Charming,' he said. 'What a wonderful place for a holiday.'

There were a couple of guards moving around on the towers, and so they decided that their best time for a rescue attempt was after dark. Making their way back to Puss, they sat under the dense forest canopy chatting and waited for nightfall. Tarl started to tell Tyson about his adventures. He had got as far as the illusions that the Dead Boys had used in the square and was telling her about the fireball he had created when Guebral cut in.

'That ring,' she said, 'can I see it?'

'Sure,' said Tarl. Fumbling in his pocket he pulled out the heavy golden band and handed it across. Even in the murky light of the wood the silver and platinum tracery glittered and shone like starlight, and the green stone that was set within the twists of gold gleamed like a *lenkat*'s eye. Guebral examined it for a few moments.

'Where did you get this?' she asked. Quickly Tarl told her of Ronan's battle with Nekros, and of Shikara's appearance.

'. . . yet when she turned Nekros into a rat, Ronan couldn't bring himself to kill the thing,' he concluded. 'But then this perambulating gut of a donkey ambles across, picks it up and eats it!'

'Very nice it was, too,' said Puss, taking over. 'But as I was chewing there was this hard crunchy bit. I nearly broke a tooth on it. So I spat it out, and it was this ring.'

'It was the torque that Nekros had been wearing around his neck,' explained Tarl. 'It had shrunk with him.'

'And you say Shikara had known Nekros before?'

'Yeah, and was well pissed off with him. Why, is this important?'

'Damn right it is!' Guebral held up the ring with a triumphant grin. 'This used to belong to her. It has the same feel about it as the Power that seeps from that castle. Shikara has greater Power than anyone I've ever met, but she is not there at the moment, and with this ring I think I can undo any sparks or traps that she has left behind. I think we can rescue your friend.'

'Keep it,' said Tarl. 'It scares the crap out of me anyway.'

He watched Guebral as she slipped it over her right forefinger, and then turned to Tyson, who had started removing the clothes from the dead castle guard. 'I don't want to spoil your fun,' he said, 'but it's getting dark. We should be starting soon.'

'I know,' said Tyson, 'but this guy may come in useful. We need them to open the door, and they'll be expecting him back.'

'But he's dead!'

'Yeah. But you're not,' said Tyson, with a sly grin. Tarl began to back away from her, shaking his head.

'Oh, no! No, no! I'm not wearing that kinky stuff! No way!'

'We need someone to pass for that guard,' said Tyson.

'Please, it will really help,' said Guebral.

'Go on, I could do with a good laugh,' said Puss.

'Forget it!' yelled Tarl.

Ten minutes later, he stepped out from behind the tree where he had insisted on changing. The brief leather costume had been designed with someone a lot more muscle-bound in mind. It certainly wasn't meant for someone whose legs, as Puss had once put it, would make a flamingo's look chunky. It sagged loosely about Tarl, exposing large areas of pallid skin-and-bone and small areas of wrinkled hairy bits. He looked like a male stripper with a slow puncture.

Both Tyson and Guebral managed to keep a straight face, although neither dared look at the other. Puss, however, was a different matter, and the forest echoed to the braying of a donkey that is laughing so much it is in serious danger of doing itself an injury.

'Oh, my God,' it gasped, 'it's the Incredible Stick Man,' and it rolled on its back, waving its legs in the air and literally snorting with amusement. 'How on earth can you fancy *that*?' it gasped to Guebral.

'I've always liked the consumptive poet look,' she replied. 'Anyway, it goes beyond mere external appearances. I can see what's inside.'

'So can I, unfortunately,' said the donkey, looking askance at Tarl's clinging leather briefs. 'It's put me right off my supper.'

Tarl gave it a look and then stalked off towards Shikara's castle with as much dignity as he could muster, which wasn't much at all, really. Tyson and Guebral followed him, grinning openly, and Puss was again left to look after Virago.

They stopped at the edge of the trees and peered out. It was dark now, but they could clearly see two oddly dressed guards on duty at the main gate, where a couple of flaming torches had been thrust into sconces on either side of the massive doors. However, Tyson didn't seem interested in this entrance, but led the others through the edge of the trees until they were opposite the rear of the castle.

'There it is,' she said, pointing to a small postern-door in the base of one of the towers. 'That's our way in.'

Quickly they sped across the open space into the shadow of the castle and pressed themselves against the wall beside the door. It was of solid oak, with huge black metal hinges and a small spy-hole set in the centre. On Tyson's instructions Tarl stood in front of the door clutching his stomach and doubled up as if in agony, so that all that could be seen in the dark was a shadowy figure with pale skin gleaming through a scanty but distinctive uniform. Then Tyson rapped out a strange rhythm on the door, and pressed herself against the wall again.

'Who goes there?' called a voice from the other side of the door.

'Ragnar,' gasped Tarl. He could tell he was being inspected through the spy-hole. Then there was the sound of bolts being drawn, the door opened, and another guard popped his head out.

'*Klat*, Ragnar, you look like sh—'

The guard's voice stopped dead as the edge of Tyson's hand smashed down on the back of his neck. He fell to the ground, and the three of them hastened through the door and shut it behind them. They were in a long stone passage lit by a single guttering torch jutting out from the wall.

'Right,' whispered Tyson. 'Ragnar told me the way to go. Leave any guards to me. Guebral, can you take care of any magical traps?'

'I'll *Scan* ahead of us as we go,' Guebral answered.

'Fine,' said Tyson, and with her dagger in one hand and the Crow in the other she set off down the corridor. At the far end was a door, and she gradually eased it open and peered through. It led into an empty store-room. They hastened through and up a flight of spiral stairs set in the wall before emerging into another long corridor. This one was wider and more brightly lit, and was lined along one side by a series of statues, all of naked and seriously excited males. Turning to the left they crept along, but when they were half-way to the door at the end it opened, and another guard walked through.

He was dressed even more briefly than the others, in only a tight leather pouch and a black studded collar. A sword hung in a scabbard that hung from the waist-band of the pouch, and his muscled body gleamed with oil. As he saw the intruders his hand flew to the handle of the sword and his mouth opened, but before any sound could emerge a bolt from the Crow had smashed into his throat, and he sagged to the floor, dead.

Quickly, Tarl grabbed him by the arms and dragged him behind one of the statues. The smell of the man's after-shave was almost overpowering. Then they hastened to the door at the end, but as Tyson reached out to open it Guebral stopped her.

'There are sparks here,' she said. 'Two of them. Very strong ones, a *Hag-spell* and a *Warning*. Any woman but Shikara who enters this room would age in seconds, turning into an old crone, and Shikara would know of this instantly. Wherever she is.'

'Can you fix it?'

'I can . . . dismantle them. Wait.'

Guebral's eyes closed, and her face slowly tautened with effort. For a while nothing seemed to happen, and then her eyes flickered open again, and she let out a gasp and sagged tiredly against the wall.

'It is done,' she said, 'but it was not easy. She is powerful, very powerful.'

Tyson eased open the door, and they found themselves in a deserted room that was full to bursting with soft furniture, plump pillows and muslin drapes, all of them pink. It was like being inside candy-floss. Tyson led them across to yet another door, which opened on cold stone steps leading down into darkness. A dank, mouldy smell drifted up.

Tarl went back to the corridor and took one of the torches from its wall-bracket, and holding this before them they went down the steps. At the bottom a cold dark passage lined with doors stretched out before them, but Tyson led them straight along it to a thick wooden door at the end. Hanging from a hook in the stone wall beside it was a vast key, but as Tyson reached for it Guebral stopped her again.

'If the man in this cell is Ronan,' she said, 'then I'd better warn you, there is a spell on him. He is not how you remember him. I can change him back, but we had best get him out of here first.'

Tyson nodded calmly, but inside her chest her heart had started pounding, and she felt sick. Taking the key she unlocked the door, and then they pushed it open and, holding the torch aloft, stepped into the cell.

Sat on a bench against the wall was Ronan – but a Ronan who looked about ninety years old. His dead-white dreadlocks hung limply about his shoulders, his face was lined and wrinkled, and his rheumy eyes blinked and watered in the sudden light as he stared at them in disbelief.

'Tyson? Is it you?' he said, in a thin quavery voice that shook even more than his hands, and his breath rasped and wheezed in his throat as he hauled himself painfully to his feet. Tyson took his hand, and then brushed the white hair back from his face and kissed his forehead. Last time she saw him she would have needed to stand on a box to do so, but now he was so stooped that she could easily reach. To her surprise she found that the tears were pouring down her face.

'It's me,' she said. 'Hush, love, we're going to get you out of here.'

'And my friends,' he mumbled. 'Don't forget my friends.'

Tyson followed his gaze and saw two little mice sitting on the floor by the bench and looking up at her. Bending, she scooped them up and thrust them inside her leather jerkin next to her skin. Then, with her on one side of Ronan and Tarl on the other, they helped him up the steps and back the way they had come.

The journey back through the castle was uneventful, although at the feeble pace that was all Ronan could manage, it seemed to take a lifetime. They came across one other guard, but before he could react Tyson's thrown dagger sank up to the hilt in his eye-socket, and he died without a sound. The guard at the postern-door was still out cold, and they slipped unnoticed past him and out into the night.

At last they reached the safety of the trees, and stumbled through them to where Puss was waiting. Tarl disappeared again to change into his normal clothes, and Ronan, who was gasping like a fish out of water, sagged tiredly to the ground. His eyes were closed, and his skin had taken on an unhealthy greyish pallor. Tyson was desperately worried that he might be about to have a heart-attack. She grabbed Guebral by the wrist and swung her round.

'You said you can reverse this,' she hissed. 'How?'

'As with the other sparks in the castle, I can see how Shikara did it as plainly as if it was written on his face in ink. I simply have to . . . wash it away. Then he will change back. As will his friends.'

'Friends? What fr— Oh, the mice!' Tyson could feel them warm against the skin of her breast. She reached inside her jerkin and pulled the two small rodents out. They each had their eyes closed, and she could have sworn that they were blushing. She placed them carefully on the ground and they sat there, trembling, unable to meet her gaze.

Guebral crouched beside Ronan and stared at him with a look of concentration on her face. For a while nothing seemed to be happening and Tyson shifted impatiently, but then suddenly, almost imperceptibly, she saw that the lines in his face were smoothing out and the snow-white dreadlocks were gradually darkening. Slowly the years seemed to slip away from him, and Tyson found that for the second time, the tears were pouring down her cheeks. Kneeling down behind him she put her arms round him and supported his weight. His eyes opened, and he stared up at her with dawning recognition.

'Hiya, Muscles,' she said, with a catch in her voice.

'Hey, babe,' came the almost inaudible reply, and all at once Tyson felt as though the ton weight that she had been carrying around for the past few months had suddenly disappeared from her shoulders. The sun seemed to be shining, the birds were singing, and she felt like going out and getting blind, stinking drunk. Well, plenty of time for that later, she thought. First, I'm going to find that fat cow Shikara and cut her *klatting* bum off.

Tarl, meanwhile, had returned from behind his tree, and was watching Guebral as she turned her concentration on to the two mice. Their outlines seemed to shimmer and blur and they began to swell, then all of a sudden there was a whoosh of expanding air and in their place stood two adult dwarves, as naked as the day they were born, with only their long black beards to maintain their modesty. Tarl stared in amazement as they bobbed and bowed to Guebral, stammering out broken words of thanks and almost weeping with gratitude.

'Hey, who are you two?' he asked, and they immediately started bowing to him instead.

'I am Bernie,' said the plumper of the two, 'and this is Bumfur. We run a magical research laboratory in our city of Zanadakan, beneath Tor Enshal.'

'Hey, I know,' said Tarl, clicking his fingers and smiling at Guebral. 'Goetetics and stuff, yeah?'

'That's right. Well, some weeks ago a human messenger arrived at the gates of our city, bringing the news that Shikara had returned after all these years, and requesting us to come to her. Our fathers used to trade with her, long ago, and so we came . . .'

His voice trailed off, and Bumfur took over.

'We came with our cousin, Bovrel. Shikara wanted to know of all our latest discoveries, but this was not the charming woman of whom our fathers spoke. She was cold and implacable, demanding that we make a gift of our knowledge. But she did not deign to hide the cruel and malevolent thoughts in her mind, and seeing them we refused. She cast us into her dungeons, threatening us with torture and death, but try as she might, she could not persuade us. So then she cursed us, changing us into mice . . .'

His voice in turn faded away, and he stared miserably at the ground. There was a brief silence.

'So what happened to Bovrel?' asked Tarl.

'The cat got him,' whispered Bernie.

There was another silence. Tarl was staring rigidly at the ground in front of him, trying to control himself. He didn't dare meet Puss's eyes for fear of bursting into fits of laughter, but he could sense that the donkey, Guebral and Tyson were all on the verge of corpsing.

But then Ronan pulled himself unsteadily to his feet, and advanced on the dwarves with his hand outstretched.

'Bumfur, my friend, I owe you and Bernie my freedom. Without you, that fell witch would have lured me into her control. I am for ever in your debt.'

He shook hands with the two dwarves and then turned to the others.

'These are two brave and loyal friends,' he said, and then clapped Bernie on the back, adding with a sly smile, 'but don't let this guy anywhere near your feet.'

Bernie went bright red and stood there with his cousin grinning shyly, covered in embarrassment, beard and little else, as Ronan outlined how the two of them had roused him from his drugged state. The others crowded round to congratulate them, and there was much joking and laughter, but then Tyson brought them all sharply down to earth.

'We'd best be well away from here before the bitch-queen from hell catches on,' she said, 'otherwise we'll all end up as cat food.'

The dwarves were eager to return to their people and invited the others to come with them, but Guebral was insistent that they head back to Yai'El, and Tarl backed her up. Ronan looked with interest at the waif-like woman who his friend had so obviously fallen for. There was much here he wanted to learn about, but that could wait. His transformation had drained him, and he needed all his breath for the journey ahead.

And so Bernie and Bumfur strode off north-west through the

trees, while the others set off downhill towards the Yai'El road. Just before they finally disappeared from sight the two dwarves turned to wave, and shouted something down to them. Tarl, who had sharper hearing than the others, thought it sounded like something about taking care of Shikara, but his mind was dwelling on Guebral, and he paid it no attention. Which was a pity, because if he had taken in what they said, they could have done something about it, and that might have saved an awful lot of lives . . .

In the expensively furnished room in the southern city, the six men were again seated about the table. They were animatedly discussing the progress of their plans when there was an urgent knock at the door. A messenger scurried in and handed a sealed piece of parchment to the man at the head of the table, who opened it and scanned the contents.

'Gentlemen,' he announced in serious tones, 'I regret to inform you that our strategy seems to have gone somewhat awry. Brend has fallen with scarcely an arrow fired or a sword drawn. There would appear to have been something of a massacre in the city. And, most unfortunately, I am informed that our warehouse there has been looted and burned to the ground.'

The others were totally silent. He paused and tapped the table thoughtfully with one fingernail before continuing.

'In retrospect it would appear to have been a mistake to employ Shikara. She seems to have adapted our plans for her own ends, and I am of the opinion that there is little we can do about it. She is out of control, and I rather fear that there is nothing that can stop her . . .'

Although it was night, the sky was red from the countless fires that burned within the city walls. Half of Brend appeared to be aflame, and the acrid smell of wood-smoke mixed with the stench of seared and burning flesh.

Shikara sat waiting on her horse outside the western walls of the city as her lieutenants harried and chivvied her army into one cohesive whole again. There were orcs milling around everywhere, yelling and shouting and waving bottles and flagons of drink. Many of them were carrying severed human limbs that had been roasted or barbecued, from which they were occasionally tearing great mouthfuls of meat. Others had human heads impaled on their spears, which they thrust up and down as they leapt about, and the heads waved and nodded to each other in a macabre dance, their eyeless sockets gazing blindly into the night.[10]

Shikara moodily watched these gruesome results of her labours, and for the first time felt a vague unease at the sheer scale of death and destruction she had helped unleash. She glanced round at the city cemetery spread out behind her. After tonight, they were going to have to extend it to about four times the size. Well, serve them right! And serve those six sad old men right as well, thinking that they could use her in their plans. Suddenly Shikara could feel the familiar red mist of anger rising again and threatening to engulf her. That's all men ever did, use you and then cast you aside. But she would show them, she would show them all!

Then she thought back to Ronan, the warrior who had released her from her enchantment, only to spurn her advances. Odd how she should feel more guilty about the *Spell of Ageing* that she had cast over him than about the destruction of an entire city. What a waste of a wonderful body . . . By the Gods, she fancied him! Ah, well, perhaps he might be feeling differently when she changed him back. If he hadn't died of old age in the meantime. That would be a shame. Maybe she'd better check. It was about time she checked on things back home, anyway.

She reached down into her saddlebag and pulled out a small sphere of rose-coloured crystal that fitted snugly into her palm. Holding it in front of her face she breathed on it, and a spark of light flared up deep inside it. For a few moments the spark sat there, glowing, and then it suddenly expanded into the moving image of a man sat at a table. It was Carlin, the impossibly handsome leader of her castle guard, who at this moment looked more like the impossibly worried leader of the guard. Shikara stared at him for a couple of seconds and knew straight away that here was a man who had bad tidings to report, and who realised that he was in deep, deep do-do.

'OK, what's the problem?' she asked him.

'Well, er, I don't quite know how it happened, but, er . . .'

[10] Human eyes are a great orc delicacy. When buying a dead human from their butchers, it is a favourite joke of orc housewives to ask him to leave the eyes in, 'So it will see us through the week.' Orcs and humour don't really get on.

'Spit it out, man, while you still have a tongue to spit with!'

'It looks as though someone has, er . . .'

'Has what?'

'Well, someone has rescued the prisoner!'

'WHAT??'

'The, er, the black warrior in the dungeon. He's been rescued. By someone.'

'*Tute homo tristis, mus fieristi!*'

'Squeak! Squeak, squeak, eek!'

Shikara watched the impossibly handsome little mouse as it ran in horrified circles round the seat. It was just as well that she had cast a *Hidden Eye* spell on Ronan. It meant that she could watch him wherever he was – so now it would act as a handy trace. She muttered the necessary words and waited patiently as the crystal whirled and fizzed to itself, then sat forward with a muffled curse.

In the depths of the crystal she could see Ronan slumped like a sack in the saddle of a horse that was ambling along a track through the southern foothills of the Chrome Mountains. He looked dead beat, and the only things that were preventing him from falling off were the arms of that *klatting* warrior woman who had been permanently and annoyingly in his thoughts ever since Shikara had carried him off. Following them was the puny gimp who had been in the hut when she had re-emerged and taken her revenge on Nekros, and with him was a donkey and some other skinny waif of a girl.

So! She, Shikara, wasn't good enough for him, hey? And yet he was off like a shot with that skinny, flat-chested warrior woman! Well, someone was going to pay for this!

She looked around, and her gaze fell on the cemetery again. Perfect!

'*Vivat mortui! Huc venitis, nothi iniucundi!*'

A wind as cold as an Orcville winter morning began to eddy around her, gaining speed and causing her hair to leap and float about her head. Suddenly this wind whooshed off towards the cemetery so fast that you could see the movement of the air. It swirled about the graves nearest the gate, collecting dry leaves and dead grass and whirling them upwards like a small tornado. And then all at once it split into four fingers, each of which plunged into a grave with a noise like a gigantic arrow thudding into flesh.

For a moment all was still. Even the revelling orcs nearby had paused and were staring open-mouthed. And then the earth in the four graves began to churn and seethe, spilling outwards and upwards like a small volcano. A hand erupted from one, a black and rotting hand with foul and noisome flesh. Rivulets of soil ran off the putrefying torso that emerged from a second grave as the occupant sat upright. For a moment it remained there, and then it raised one hand and scratched at the remnants of its head as though puzzled. When it took its hand away, all the finger-nails remained lodged in the rotting skin of the scalp. It looked at its hand for a moment and then shook its head, and the tattered knots of hair still clinging to the skull came free and fell to the ground, their roots still buried in clumps of rotting flesh. The corpse sighed, a sound like poisonous gas escaping from a pipe, and then it hauled itself free of the constraining earth and stood up, and the other three followed suit.

The stench of decay filled the air as all four corpses staggered uncertainly towards Shikara. It was totally silent now, save for the sounds and cries emanating from the city. Fear had rendered the watching orcs speechless, and many fell to their knees and hid their faces from the loathsome sight. Even Shikara looked a touch uncertain, but deep down inside she was feeling a fierce exhilaration. Yes! she thought. Bugger of a spell!

The leading zombie lurched towards her and then stopped expectantly, with the others behind it. She saw with revulsion that its stomach was grossly distended with the gases of putrefaction. She was about to speak when suddenly the rotten, fragile skin of its stomach split, and the foul gases escaped from inside it with an audible *pfthhht*. Shikara nearly gagged, and the corpse waved a disintegrating hand in front of itself in an ineffectual attempt to dispel the noxious vapours.

'Oops! Pardon me!' it said, in a slow croaking voice. And then its hand fell off and hit the floor with a soggy squelch.

Shikara turned and shouted a brief command to the commander of the Southron cavalry, and he in turn snapped out an order. Four of his men dismounted from their mounts and led them forward to stand beside Shikara. Bending, she took the reins from the hand of the first Southron cossack and held them out to the zombie.

'Here,' she said. 'Take hold of these.'

'What with?' asked the zombie peevishly, holding up the stump of its arm.

'Don't get smart with me!' snapped Shikara, before mentally transferring a clear picture of Ronan and his four companions into the fetid semi-liquid mush that was the remnants of the corpses' brains. 'Take the horses and track these people down. Kill all but the tall black warrior, then bring him to me. Now go! Ride like the wind!'

It took all the strength and experience that the Freaks' cossack owners possessed to calm their near-frantic, unwilling mounts enough to allow the zombies to clamber into the saddles. Then they released them, and with a terrified whinny the first horse plunged away, galloping furiously to the west with its fell rider urging it on, and its fellows following close behind.

Shikara smiled grimly to herself. On the back of the terrified Freaks, the zombies would reach the Chrome Mountains in a day. They would soon run their quarry to earth. Zombies never stopped, their pursuit was remorseless, and they carried the *Touch of Putrefaction*, so that any mortal flesh they touched would begin to decay. Apart from herself, they were probably the most lethal things loose in Behan at that moment. She almost felt sorry for Ronan and his friends.

Wheeling her horse about, Shikara began to yell orders to her lieutenants, and the business of rounding up her army resumed at an increased pace. She wasn't going to let the defiance of one stubborn, bone-headed (though undeniably attractive) guy deflect her from her aim. Within two days she meant to be at the gates of Far Tibreth with her army. Then, when the town fell, they would have cut a swathe of destruction right across Behan, and Cydor would be lying defenceless before them. News of her exploits would have spread, and the city councils would be only too glad to negotiate. It was about time that they were all brought under one ruler.

However, perhaps she might need to destroy one or two more towns first, just to rub it in. And just to show them all that here was a woman who wouldn't be pushed around. And, if she was totally, brutally honest with herself, just for the sheer wonderful hell of it.

Shikara was starting to enjoy herself.

ENDANGERED

. . . but still more needs to be done to combat the rise in organised crime. Recent figures show that, in the past year, rape has increased by 19%, looting by 17%, robbery with violence by 23%, and drug dealing by a staggering 47%. And that's just in the police force.

Yai'El Police Gazette

Marten was completely and utterly furious. He couldn't believe that things had gone so wrong – or that Dene could have been so thoroughly stupid. He could happily have belted the prat, and he probably would have done so if his arm hadn't been twisted right up into the small of his back by a large and unpleasant police officer who appeared to have rather a lot of cave-troll blood in him.

Everything had seemed so promising at first. It had taken them a couple of days to find their way along the coast, but they hadn't run into any more half-orcs, and after sundown on the second day they had breasted yet another hill and found the city of Yai'El stretched out below them, looking like a gigantic burning rag washed up against the shore. They had both been fascinated by the sight of the Night-fire and had stood staring at it for what seemed like ages.

Marten had noticed that the gate at the end of the causeway was guarded, and had wanted to wait for daylight before entering the city, but Dene had been eager to press on and had talked his friend into agreeing. And so they had gone marching straight up to the gate police and announced themselves. Dealing with highly suspicious armed police was a situation that so obviously needed to be handled with tact and diplomacy that Marten didn't even bother warning Dene to be careful. It was self-evident that, as members of a tribe that had been ransacking the coast for years, they needed to use some discretion.

And so the police sergeant had produced the night-duty log-book, and his conversation with Dene had gone like this:

'Name?'

'Dene, son of Denhelm.'

'Occupation?'

'Apprentice priest.'

'Age?'

'Twenty-one.'

'Tribe, or city of origin?'

'Vagen.'

'GRAB THE PILLAGING BASTARDS!'

And now they were being marched through the city streets beneath the red glow of the street-lamps to the headquarters of the Yai'El City Police. Even though it was night there was no chance of escape, for they were being escorted by five burly policemen, three of whom were armed with lethal crossbows, and the streets were too brightly lit to have much chance of making a run for it.

Marten cursed. Even if they ever got out of this, they had no chance of getting back to the village to make any sort of presentation, and he was going to end up being dropped into the harbour with a large boulder tied to his feet. The only bright spot was that exactly the same thing would be happening to Dene. Or, as he was going to be known to Marten from now on, Plonker.

The rain was coming down onto the foothills so fast that it gave the impression it was suffering from vertigo and couldn't wait to get its feet on the ground. Ronan was slumped over Virago's neck and seemed to have passed out, and Tyson's arms were aching with the effort of holding him on. He had been shivering for a while, but now he had stopped. She pressed her fingers against his neck. Her hand was cold enough, but it was like touching a block of ice.

Worried, she stopped the horse and waited for the others to catch up. Guebral and Tarl were supporting each other and were soaked to the skin. It was pitch dark, but even so she could just make out what a state they were in. Neither of them had an ounce of fat on them, and the wind that had sprung up was obviously cutting them to the core. Puss, too, was in a sorry state. The little

186

donkey had been keeping dry by ambling along beneath the great horse and using it as an umbrella until, without warning, Virago had urinated copiously. Now Puss was a sticky, smelly mess, and was cursing monotonously.

'We can't go on much further,' Tyson yelled. She virtually had to scream to make herself heard above the wind. 'Ronan isn't going to make it. We've got to find shelter.'

'OK!' yelled Tarl. Next to him Guebral closed her eyes, and her face went blank for a few seconds before they snapped open again.

'There's a cottage of some sort about four hundred yards over there,' she shouted, pointing to the north. 'It seems to be deserted.'

'That'll do. Can you lead the way?'

Guebral nodded and set off up the hill with Tarl beside her. The horse followed them automatically, and Tyson concentrated on keeping Ronan in the saddle. The wind was ripping at them now, trying to strip the very clothes off them, and driving the rain into their sides like stones from a sling-shot. Their feet slipped and stumbled on the uneven, soaking ground, and then all at once they were sliding down into a hollow, and the intensity of the wind dropped.

In front of them they could see the dark outline of the cottage. It was built of stone, with a single timber door in the centre and a wooden lean-to against the lee wall. Guebral wrestled with the latch while Tarl helped Tyson to slide Ronan down from Virago's broad back. Half leading him, half carrying him, they guided him through the doorway, while Guebral led the exhausted animal round to the lean-to. It was obviously used as a stable, and inside it was dry and, if not exactly warm, at least it was out of the wind. There was a trough of water and even some hay in a wall-manger. The great horse hardly had room to turn round, but she made it as comfortable as possible before dragging the rickety door shut and following the others into the cottage.

Inside she found them crouched shivering in the dark. Tyson had been trying to undo her pack to get at her tinder-box with fingers that were so cold they refused to work, and Tarl was so tired and bemused that he hadn't even thought of using his Power. So Guebral made a *Light* spell, and in the resulting radiant glow they examined their refuge.

The cottage had two rooms. The main living area had a stone fireplace to one side, with a long wooden bench in front of it. Two more benches ran along either side of the table that was the room's only other piece of furniture. In the hearth sat a blackened and ancient cooking-pot, in which rested tongs, spoons and a couple of long skewers. The second room was much smaller, and contained only a tiny fireplace and a roughly constructed wooden bunk.

To judge by the smell and the droppings, the cottage was probably used by the nomadic goat-herds whose flocks roamed the slopes of the surrounding mountains. It had obviously been left ready for the next occupant as there were logs piled in both hearths, and it was but the work of a moment for Guebral to build a couple of roaring fires. If there was one thing she was good at, it was producing fire out of nowhere.

Then they dragged the wet clothes off Ronan and wrapped him in whatever dry garments they could muster from their packs. He was still asleep, and as cold as ice, but his breathing was regular. Between them they managed to carry him to the cot in the small room, and Tyson covered him with the only dry blanket and then sat down beside him.

Seeing the worried look on her face, Guebral laid a hand on her shoulder.

'Don't worry. It's only the after-effects of the transformation. And he has lost fitness while he was so aged. A day or so of rest will cure him. The day after tomorrow he will be fit again.'

Tyson nodded, smiling, but her eyelids were beginning to droop. It was days since she had slept properly. Guebral and Tarl watched for a moment as she too fell instantly asleep, and then they trudged tiredly into the other room, where Puss was lying stretched out in front of the fire. Steam was coming off the little donkey in great clouds, and the room smelt like a burning urinal.

With the last of her energy Guebral did a *rose-scent* spell, and then sank onto a bench, with Tarl beside her. She had meant to do a few other things, to use her Power to dry their clothes and cook food, but she was exhausted. The *rose-scent* had used up the last of her reserves. She closed her eyes, and the last sensation she was aware of was Tarl's arms around her, hugging her to him.

Tarl smiled fondly and gently eased her slim form down to lie stretched out along the bench. Then he sat himself down on the floor between her and Puss. There were dozens of questions he wanted to ask her. She had the most amazing powers, but seemed hardly aware of them. Still, plenty of time tomorrow, he thought as he nodded off. We've rescued Ronan, and got away with it. We're safe at last.

But then Tarl didn't know about the zombies . . .

The two dwarves might have introduced themselves to the others as Bernie and Bumfur, but that was just the old dwarvish distrust of strangers at work. Not that they hadn't trusted Ronan, but dwarves don't like to hand over too much information about themselves to new acquaintances. They might have given the impression that they were just a couple of average dwarves who had been chosen as emissaries to Shikara because they were experts in the field of goetetics, but there was a little more to their visit than that.

They had been selected because the Shikara of old had been an admired and respected neighbour of the dwarves, if not exactly a trusted friend, and thus merited ambassadors of a certain rank. Bernie and Bumfur (their 'outsider' names) were in fact nephews of the Tarse (or King) of Zanadakan, the dwarvish city beneath the Chrome Mountains. Bovrel had been one of his sons.

When they returned to the gates of the vast underground city, the news spread like wildfire. At first there was great celebration, but when word got round about Bovrel's death, the mood changed. War-drums began to sound, battle-axes were honed and chain-mail was cleaned. A mood of seething anger changed quickly into a burning desire for revenge. Within hours, a couple of hundred grim-faced heavily armed dwarves were streaming through the gate of the city and marching off downhill through the woods. Few things have been discovered which are deadlier or more implacable than a dwarf with a grievance. One of them, however, is two hundred dwarves with a grievance.

Shikara was about to discover an age-old truth. As has been said before, you don't *klat* about with dwarves.

There were quite a few people in the world who wouldn't have shed too many tears if Shikara had fallen off a cliff. However, one of those who would have been least upset was the orc, Chigger. Whilst most of his friends were having the time of their lives, he had come to look upon the massive war-party as one long nightmare from which he couldn't seem to wake up. He was, though he wouldn't dare to admit it, sick of the sight of beer, his feet were killing him from all the running, his friends kept trying to force bits of roast human on him (and back home he was secretly a member of ORGASM, the Orc Revolutionary Group Against Sentient Meat), and, worst of all, he was going to have to try to explain to an unbelieving Pellagra just why he had gone out for a couple of days and disappeared on a bender that lasted for four months. The one thing she had always said she loved about him was that he wasn't like the other male orcs. He didn't go out drinking for years at a time, or crap on the furniture, or eat the children if he came home and found that his dinner wasn't ready. *Klat!* She'd be heartbroken. Or furious. Or both. And she would probably have moved out by now.

Anyway, it probably didn't make any difference in the long run. Chigger had a feeling that he, like many of his comrades, wouldn't be going home. They were settling down to besiege another city – what was it called? Far Tibreth? – and although they had pissed on the first two towns, this one looked like being a completely different prospect. The seamless stone walls were huge, crowned at regular intervals with massive towers, and were lined about five deep by defenders bristling with weapons. The gates were solid metal, and were protected by a moat and drawbridge. As at Brend there was a group of magic-users on the wall above the gates, but this time there were more of them, and rumour had it that they included old Ruddyguts the Wrinkled, probably the most experienced wizard south of the Great River Leno. And if that wasn't enough, Southron outriders had come in a few minutes ago, and rumour was spreading that a group of a thousand Behanian cavalrymen were riding to the relief of the city, and were just a few miles away.

No, Chigger wasn't amongst Shikara's most adoring fans. But then it didn't really matter, because every last one of the thousands of chanting, singing orcs, Easterlings and Southrons around him thought that she was the greatest thing since malt whisky. And they were going to do what she asked even if it meant marching into the gates of hell itself.

Marten was sat on the floor of the cell, staring blankly into space. His brain was still refusing to accept what had happened. They would come before a magistrate, the duty sergeant had told them, in eight days. *Eight days!* By the Gods! Well, that was it. Their trip was over!

Dene was squatting on the bench beneath the barred window, and was rocking backwards and forwards, muttering to himself. Then he got up and squatted down next to Marten.

'Listen,' he hissed. 'We've got to escape!'

'Brilliant! Why didn't I think of that?'

Dene either ignored or didn't notice the strong tone of sarcasm.

'We could overpower the guards . . .'

'How? You going to take your socks off?'

'Well, I thought –'

'No, you didn't,' interrupted Marten, furiously. 'You never *klatting* well think! You just go through life like some kind of human muck-spreader, and everyone you go near ends up with shit all over them! I have seen shellfish that would make better leaders than you! I've had haemorrhoids that were more fun to be with! Now, for the last time, will you *klatting* well LEAVE ME ALONE!'

And with that Marten pointedly turned his back on his friend, and Dene, ashen-faced, tottered back to the bench on legs that had suddenly turned to rubber, and slumped down in a miserable, dejected heap.

Tarl had been put in charge of the cooking, which was rather like making a cave-troll head of ballet, but there wasn't much alternative. The donkey, which had provided them with three wild chickens by its usual method of ambling up to the unsuspecting birds like any normal donkey but then biting their heads off, had gone in search of a pool to bathe in, as it still smelt like a small brown urinal. Ronan had woken up at last, but was still very weak, and both Guebral and Tyson had been keen to stay in the small room and look after him. That had left Tarl, and so he had set to work with a will, but with very little ability.

Outside, the wind had dropped now and the rain had eased off, but the sky was crammed full of ominous black clouds, and although it was mid-afternoon it was nearly dark. Tarl was crouched in front of the fire in the main room, humming to himself as he watched the chickens sizzling on the spit. There was a thump on the door, and sighing he rose and opened it apprehensively. Puss pushed past him, and as he shut the door again Tarl sniffed delicately and smiled.

'Ah, you don't half smell better. What a relief! You were pretty high, you know.'

'That's rich, coming from you.'

'Do you want something to eat?'

'No thanks, I've just had something.'

'Are you sure?'

'Yes. I distinctly remember eating it.'

The donkey ambled across to the fire and stood watching the chickens on the spit.

'You know,' said Tarl, 'there's a secret to good chicken.'

'Oh, what's that?'

Tarl looked sadly at the birds, which were still cold and raw on one side, and were beginning to blacken on the other.

'Buggered if I know,' he replied.

'It might help if you turned the spits round.'

'That's a thought.'

The donkey shook its head.

'I've heard of cordon bleu,' it said, 'but your cooking should be cordoned off.'

'Oh, very funny.' Tarl picked up the big wooden spoon, scooped up some of the melted fat that had collected in the tray in front of the fire, and poured it over the birds. This was a tactic he'd only recently been told about. Before that, when he had heard people talking about basted chickens he had just assumed that they didn't like chickens very much.

'I could do with a beer,' he added.

'You drink too much.'

'It relaxes me.'

'Yeah. You frequently get as relaxed as a newt.'

Tarl grinned and reached out a hand to scratch the donkey's neck.

'Always got to have the last word, haven't you?' he said.

'Yes,' said the donkey.

Meanwhile, in the other room the two women were listening to Ronan's slow recounting of his time in Shikara's care.

'. . . and then she lost her temper,' he finished, 'and I have no memory of anything after that. I guess that's when she cursed me.'

'I've undone the curse,' said Guebral, 'but there is a memory erasure there, too. I can remove that, if you want.'

Ronan looked uncertainly at Tyson, and then nodded, and Guebral closed her eyes. For a few moments her face was a mask of concentration, and then Ronan suddenly exclaimed out loud.

'*Klat*! It's all coming back! She started boasting about her plans, and about how powerful she would be. She wanted me to be her male concubine.' Ronan paused, a little confused. He had thought that a concubine was a small spiky animal. 'She had backers behind her. Six very powerful men, the same ones who were backing Nekros! By the Gods! They've got a huge army on the march! Thousands of orcs have been massing under the Irridic Mountains. By now Derchey will have fallen. The whole of Behan and Cydor could go up in flames!'

'Who are these men?' asked Tyson. 'What do they want? Power?'

'No, not power. Not just power. Profit. They're the members of the board of the Orcbane Sword Corporation.'

'And they're starting a whole war, just to sell a few swords?' asked Guebral.

'Not just a few,' mused Tyson. 'Their salesmen were in Welbug when trouble was brewing. Nearly everyone in the city bought themselves a new weapon. I guess they must be missing out a little using an orc army, though. Orcs wouldn't be seen dead holding an Orcbane sword.'

Ronan shook his head tiredly.

'That's all been thought out,' he continued. 'Shikara said that Orcbane own the Weldis Blade Company. They don't publicise the fact, but every sword that Weldis sells is money for Orcbane.'

'They must be six satisfied men at the moment, then,' Tyson muttered, but Ronan shook his head a second time.

'I doubt it,' he said. 'Shikara's taken their plan and altered it to suit her own ends. They just wanted to create a demand. Shikara just wants to destroy.'

At that moment there was a loud crash from the other room, and they heard a shout of dismay from Tarl.

'Talking of destruction,' said Tyson, 'it sounds like Tarl having problems with the dinner.

In the main room Tarl was having problems all right, but not food-related ones. The chickens had been going really nicely now he'd got the hang of rotating the spit, and he had been about to take them away from the heat when there was another knock on the door. Putting down his spoon he had gone to answer it, expecting to have to pacify an indignant goat-herd, but the minute he had lifted the latch the door had been thrust violently back to crash against the wall, and that had been when Tarl had given his shout of dismay.

For standing in the doorway were the remnants of what had once been a human being. The putrefying flesh of the face was pitted with holes, and a worm was burrowing into one cheek. Soil-stained rags of clothes hung loosely, and the noisome stench of decay hit Tarl in the face with the power of a slab of concrete. One eye had fallen backwards from the socket, and Tarl could actually see it where it had lodged behind the two rotting holes that were nostrils. The other eye glittered with a malevolent humour.

'Surprise!' the zombie said, and then it shuffled forwards into the room, and three similar nightmares followed it in.

The dwarves from Zanadakan may have been fired up and hell-bent on revenge, but they didn't let that blind them to reality. They knew full well that even though they were several hundred strong, Shikara was a powerful sorceress who would have left enough potent magical defences behind to make storming the castle in her absence a highly risky job. And so they contented themselves with burning the place to the ground instead. A few of Shikara's guards tried to fight their way out, but the whirling dwarf battle-axes made mincemeat of them. And then the dwarves stood patiently outside as the roaring flames leapt from the castle windows to the sky, and the screams of the guards trapped inside gradually faded to nothing. And when all that was left was a smoking stone shell, the dwarves shouldered their axes and marched steadily back to their city under the Chrome Mountains.

*

The rumour that a thousand Behanian cavalry were riding to the relief of Far Tibreth was only partially correct. Firstly, there were only six hundred of them, although they were some of the best-trained warriors in Behan. And secondly, they were riding to Far Tibreth, but not to relieve it. They were riding to join Shikara's troops, part of the vast plan worked out by the six members of the board of the Orcbane Sword Corporation.

The spies and agents of the board had been busy in Behan. There was a lot of unrest and dissatisfaction with the government, especially amongst the warrior class, and the agents had stirred and fermented it until they had produced a cadre that was ready and waiting to take over. This cadre of warriors had been told about the orc army that would march through northern Behan en route to Cydor, and knew that if they were left in control of the cities of Brend and Far Tibreth after the orcs had moved on, many others would flock to join them, and the centralised government in Rednec would be too tied down by red tape and bureaucracy to do anything about it.

And so, as arranged, they had come to join Shikara's army. As they approached, a small welcoming troop of Southron cavalry rode out to meet them. The leader of this troop, a Southron Captain named Kabila, stood in the stirrups of his Freak and addressed the Behanian riders.

'Hail, fellow warriors! Our leader, the sorceress Shikara, bids you welcome! She wishes to address you herself, and asks that you leave your horses in the care of those who have been detailed to tend to them. The place of honour has been left for you, and she would be honoured to tell you of her strategy for the taking of the city of Far Tibreth! If it pleases you, follow me!'

With that he wheeled his Freak about and cantered eastward around the orc army, which was lined up to the south of the city gates. The leader of the Behanians, a podgy, aggressive warrior named Julian, gave the command to follow, and as one man the Behanians swung their horses to the right and cantered after him.

To the rear of the great army, a thousand orcs had been detailed to tend to the horses, and were waiting with leather buckets of water and bales of hay. A large space had been cleared through the centre of the horde, and beyond this Shikara was stood on one of the transport wagons, waiting to speak to her forces. The

Behanians dismounted, handing their reins to the waiting attendants, and then swaggered forwards into the space between the two walls of orcs with a confident arrogance. Julian stared up at Shikara, and let his eyes wander over her body. He had no intention of taking orders from a mere woman, but it might be interesting to hear what she had to say. Maybe they could work together. In a number of different ways.

Shikara looked down at Julian and his troops with an eager anticipation. So they had turned up! Those sad old men had planned this campaign well! These Behanians were going to play a very important role in the taking of the city. She smiled secretly to herself. It just wasn't going to be the role that they or the sad old men had planned for, that was all.

Chigger stood in the ranks of the orcs, clutching a bow looted from a Brend warehouse, and waiting for the command. Every orc in the army knew that on the word *attack* that was exactly what they had to do. Apparently surprise was going to be very important.

'Greetings to our noble allies,' began Shikara. She could feel the eyes of the Behanians roaming over her body, and could read their dismissive scorn as easily as if they had voiced it. That was going to make this even more enjoyable.

'There is no need for me to waste time. I would just like to assure you that you are vital to our plans, and that you will need to use your heads in this attack . . .'

At this last word the Behanian warriors were stunned to see that the bows held by the orc troops to both sides were suddenly pointing straight at them. For a brief instant it was as if they were caught in between two gigantic hedgehogs, and then with one massive *twang* a thousand arrows were loosed.

Many of the Behanian rebels were killed by the first volley, most by the second or third. A few drew their swords and charged, but the best orc marksmen had been detailed to wait for such an attack, and not a single Behanian got close enough to draw blood.

From her position on the transport wagon, Shikara watched the massacre with undisguised pleasure, her mouth slightly apart, her breathing coming a little faster. Then, when the only movement amongst the slaughtered warriors was the spasmodic twitching and jerking of limbs, she gave the awaited signal.

Immediately, a few hundred sack-carrying orcs drew their long, serrated knives and began to move amongst the bodies, conducting their grisly business. As they did so Shikara barked out another order, and more orcs ran to remove the tarpaulins covering the siege engines which they had laboured through the night to piece together.

One of her most loyal lieutenants ran to a wagon that was parked a good way from the others and climbed into the driving seat. Shaking the reins, and trying unsuccessfully not to retch, he urged the oxen forwards, and the seething mass of flies that had been swarming across the contents of the wagon took off as one. As it lurched slowly towards the siege equipment they followed it like some foul trail of buzzing, germ-infested smoke, a fitting prelude to the obscene horror that was to follow.

Marten was still sat staring blankly at the floor of the cell and feeling totally wretched when he realised that everything had gone rather quiet. Looking up he saw that Dene was sitting on the bench with his eyes closed, his lips moving soundlessly, and his face screwed up in concentration. Even stranger, the two police guards who had been playing dice at the end of the room had slumped to the floor, and were lying there, motionless.

Scrambling to his feet he grabbed Dene's shoulder and shook it. Dene's eyes popped open and he gazed blankly at Marten, and then he caught sight of the two policemen and immediately began to babble excitedly.

'It's worked, *klat*, it's worked. Look at them, Marten, they're out cold, I really did it, I knew I could! I realised that we had to escape, and so I tried praying for the guards, like I did with the half-orcs, only I prayed for them to be well, and the opposite has happened again, and they've got ill –'

'They're dead, Dene,' interrupted Marten, looking at his friend with something approaching awe. This was some talent he was developing. Death by Prayer.

Dene stared uncertainly along at the bodies, the wind completely taken out of his sails.

'But . . . I never . . . *klat!* Still, at least we can escape, right?'

'How?' answered Marten. 'The guards have the keys to the cell, and they're twenty feet away.' He paused as an idea struck him.

Crossing to the bench he stood on it and peered out of the barred window. Great! They were only on the first floor!

'Listen, Dene,' he said, 'I want you to pray for this window. Pray for its structure and strength. Pray for it to be long-lasting and firm. Pray hard!'

Dene stared up at him, bemused, but then closed his eyes and did as requested, sending an intense and passionate plea to Fenester, God of Windows. But as usual, he got the words wrong, and the prayer was misdirected.

Somewhere in one of the slightly more run-down backwaters of Valhalla, Stannemalus, the God of Rust, Verdigris and Metallic Corrosion, was just cutting his toe-nails when he became aware that someone wanted some help really badly. Touched by the passion of the request, he fired off an instant reply.

Back in the cell, Marten watched with disbelief as the bars of the window began to rot before his eyes. In the space of ten seconds they turned from strong, stout metal rods to fragile brown sticks that crumbled to dust in front of his eyes.

Marten drew a deep breath and blew the remnants of the bars away, and then grinning he hauled the startled Dene up to the gaping window.

'Brilliant!' he laughed. 'Now, let's get out of here! Jump for it. It's only fifteen feet.'

And thirty seconds later they were dodging their way through the crowded street below. Or rather, Marten was dodging, and Dene was limping after him. Typically, he had managed to fall awkwardly and had broken a leg and several ribs. But for once, his luck was in. The leg and the ribs all belonged to the frail old lady who he had landed on, and he had merely twisted an ankle.

Tarl backed slowly away from the zombies, with Puss beside him. The stench of death and corruption was overpowering, and he almost vomited. He couldn't take his eyes off the worm in the first zombie's cheek, which he could actually see feeding on the decaying flesh.

The donkey was snarling, its lips pulled right back to expose its razor-sharp teeth. Suddenly it sprang at the nearest of the foul creatures. Tarl gave a cry of horror and grabbed at the donkey's tail, yanking it backwards and bringing Puss crashing to the floor just as the zombie lashed out at it. He hauled the donkey back and it scrambled to its feet and turned to him, eyes blazing.

'What are you playing at? People have had their faces bitten off for less than that!'

'Don't go near them! Don't even let them touch you!'

'They're only zombies, for *klat*'s sake! Dead-heads. Mush-for-brains. Stomach-farters. Remember how Tyson killed one back in Welbug? They fall to pieces if you so much as breathe on them. Look, an arm's dropped off that one!'

Tarl got hold of Puss's tatty mane and hauled him backwards out of reach of the leading zombie.

'Listen, carrot-breath,' he snarled, 'these ones are lethal! Trust me, I can feel the Power of the mage-spell that's driving them. They'll snap your spine for you – and their merest touch rots your flesh!'

'So how do we kill them?'

'I don't know!'

Tarl backed away another couple of paces and found that the wall prevented him from retreating any further. Wondering how the builder of the cottage could have been so stupid as to forget to provide a window so that people could escape from marauding zombies, Tarl slid along the wall, his eyes on the walking corpses that stalked him, and found that he was trapped in the corner.

The zombies had spread out a little, and there was no way past them. With a shaking hand Tarl drew his sword, and the donkey bared its teeth and prepared to spring. But there was something in the gaze of the zombies that held them, something that seemed to prevent them from moving. The first one grinned with anticipation, and its lower jaw slipped quietly out of its socket and slid down the creature's neck, leaving a broad, slug-like trail. The zombie reached out a hand to grab Tarl by the neck, and as he closed his eyes the foul stink of rotting flesh enveloped him. And then the door to the small room opened.

Tyson was stood there, momentarily rooted to the spot, and then she disappeared sideways, unceremoniously shoved out of the way by Guebral, who raised one pointing finger.

'Down!' she yelled, and a ball of fire erupted from her hand. Tarl threw himself to the floor, taking Puss with him, and the fireball burst into the zombies. There was a soggy-sounding *whuff*, and all four ignited like paraffin-soaked torches. As they staggered about screaming, almost totally enveloped by the roaring flames, Tarl wriggled clear, desperately trying to avoid touching any of the distinctly unsavoury rotting feet. Tyson was steering Ronan out of the small room and towards the door, and Guebral hauled Tarl to his feet. Picking up the back-packs they followed the other two outside, with Puss trotting behind. Tarl pulled the door to after them and held it closed, and they stood there shivering with reaction and listening to the crackling of the flames and the agonised screams from within.

Suddenly the screams rose in intensity, merging to reach a high keening wail that set their teeth on edge. And then something smashed through the slate roof of the cottage and hurtled up into the sky like an invisible sky-rocket, to fade wailing into the east.

'Are you OK?' asked Guebral. 'They didn't touch you?'

'No, I'm fine,' Tarl answered, and then he sniffed and looked round nervously. 'Here, what's that smell? Are there any more of them out here?'

'No,' said Puss from the rim of the hollow, 'it's these poor things.'

The others crossed to where the little donkey was standing, and looked down. Lying on the ground by some rocks were four of the Freaks used by Southron cossacks. They looked as though they had been dead for weeks. The flesh of their sides and necks was rotten, and had been eaten away so badly that the bones of their ribs could be seen protruding like red-stained ivory cages. And yet, although they were so far gone that they could no longer move, they were still alive. Their glazed eyes were open and staring, and their labouring lungs were dragging in the air in harsh, gasping breaths.

Tarl turned away and was sick.

'These must have been the zombies' mounts,' muttered Ronan, and Guebral nodded.

'Their touch has done this,' she said, and turned to Tarl, who had straightened and was wiping his mouth with the back of his hand. 'That would have happened to you if they had touched you,' she added, and Tarl was instantly sick again.

'This is Shikara's work,' swore Tyson. 'I'm going to find that woman. And when I get hold of her, I am going to cut her *klatting* head off and stick it up her wobbly fat butt!'

'You won't need to find her,' answered Guebral. 'She's coming to find us. We need to get back to Yai'El. That is where this will all be ended.'

Tyson opened her mouth in another question, but Tarl forestalled her.

'Trust her,' he said. 'She knows what she's doing.'

Tyson stared at him thoughtfully for a moment, and then nodded and went back to rescue Virago from the lean-to. Tarl gave the dying Freaks one last glance and then turned away.

'*Klat*,' he muttered. 'Just a few months ago I thought the height of fear was short-changing an orc in the Blue Balrog club, back in Orcville. I didn't know the half of it!'

You don't know what fear is, mate, the donkey thought, but it said nothing, and just patiently followed the others as they climbed out of the hollow and set off for the comparative safety of Yai'El.

Shikara knew the moment the zombies were torched. A small segment of her Power had been driving them, and she felt the connection sever in the way a fisherman feels it when his line breaks and a fish escapes. And then, seconds later, the last sad remains of the zombies' tortured souls came wailing out of the west, passing way, way above her in the darkening sky and hurtling eastward to plummet down to their graves in the cemetery outside Brend.

However, this was only a minor setback, and she dismissed it from her mind. There would be plenty of time later to deal with Ronan and his pathetic cohorts, but for the moment she had more important matters to deal with. To her satisfaction, the city of Far Tibreth had just agreed to her demands, and its great gates were opening.

The Ruling Council of the city had not been too worried when, a few hours earlier, the tarpaulins had been dragged off the siege engines, revealing them to be large trebuchets. The city walls and towers were thick and strong, and it would take months of continual bombardment for the missiles to have any effect. And the Council knew that the besieging army didn't have months. Orcs don't hang around that long. Either the booze runs out or they get bored and head off to somewhere that's a bit more fun.

But within moments of the barrage beginning, their will was being tested. For when the first missiles had come hurtling over the walls to land in the streets of the city, they had found to their horror that, instead of rocks, the orcs were using the severed heads of the Behanian rebels. Six hundred of them had come hurtling in to bounce off roofs and skitter along the cobbled streets, and the townsfolk hid their eyes in fear.

And then Shikara had sent a messenger to announce her terms for raising the siege. She did not want to linger long there, she had told the Ruling Council, for she had other targets in the west. If she was made to stay and take by force the supplies her army needed, then every single person in the city would lose their head. But if they would send her out the supplies, she would march her army away.

The list of supplies had been long, but not impossible. Put simply, she wanted a wagon laden with gold and silver (for the Southrons and Easterlings), and fifteen wagons laden with just about every bottle or barrel of alcoholic refreshment that the city possessed. She had requested little in the way of food, for her army still had ample supplies, and now they also had six hundred live horses ready to slaughter. There are few things an orc likes better than a nice fresh quivering piece of raw horse-meat.

The Ruling Council had been split. Some had wanted to put their faith in the city defences, but others had heard rumours about the events at Brend and wanted to buy Shikara off. And so they had decided to consult old Ruddyguts the Wizard and his colleagues.

Ruddyguts had tutted and fussed at the very idea of capitulation and, dismissing all offers of help from his less-talented coll-eagues, had decided then and there that he would show this so-called sorceress a thing or two. Leaning casually on the battlements above the gate he had fired off a *Mind-scan* so powerful that to any recipient it would have felt like mental rape. Any recipient except Shikara, that is. Her responding *Counterblast* was so strong that Ruddyguts was thrown a good ten feet backwards. It felt as though someone had driven a row of ten-inch nails straight through his forehead and out of the back of his skull. Climbing painfully and shakily to his feet, he informed the dismayed Council that they were faced with an enemy who had more Power than any he had ever before experienced, and who could probably just walk in with her army any moment she liked.

The Council had sent a messenger straight out to Shikara saying that as long as she gave her word that no attack would ensue, she could have her sixteen wagons right away, and good luck to her. Shikara had immediately pledged that not one of her army would set foot inside Far Tibreth, and that not one more missile would be fired. And now, a mere couple of hours later, the gates had opened and the sixteen wagons were trundling out.

The orc army was kicking up the most tremendous racket, aware that there would shortly be a load of fresh drinks to enliven the raiding-party. Shikara smiled. They could be on the move again soon. The original plan had been to head west into Cydor and to make for Ilex, but she had a sneaking fancy to go southwest and destroy Asposa. That wouldn't be too far from home, either. Maybe she could order a couple of her favourite castle guards to meet her there. It had been a few days since she had last made love. Yes, that might be pleasant . . .

Shikara reached into the saddlebag and pulled out the rose-coloured crystal, but when it sparked into life her face froze in an expression of disbelieving fury. The view she was seeing was not of the castle rooms that she had expected, but of burnt and blackened passages, and of gutted rooms open to the sky, with here and there a charred and twisted shape that had once been one of her guards. Her home had been destroyed!

In a cold rage she spat out a word of command, and the crystal fizzed for a moment before presenting her with a view of Ronan and his friends heading west through the mountains, all apparently perfectly well. *Klat!* The zombies hadn't hurt a single one of them! Well, she would have to sort them out in person. She'd teach them to destroy her home. Meddling fools! They would be begging for death by the time she had finished with them! Heading for Yai'El, were they? Well, so was she now, and she was going to take her entire army with her. She would follow Ronan and his friends to the ends of the earth if she had to, to get her revenge.

Furiously she spurred her horse up to her commanders and hurled out her orders. As the last wagon trundled out across the drawbridge and the great gates swung hastily shut behind it, her army began to form up for the long march to the sea. Shikara looked back at the ranks of defenders lining the city walls, and felt the rage inside her begin to abate slightly. Look at them all, stupid fools. They thought they had bought her off. If they only knew the truth of it!

But the defenders hadn't the faintest inkling of the fate in store for them. They had no way of knowing that, before they had been fired, every single severed head had been taken across to the wagon that Shikara had brought with her for this very purpose, the wagon containing twenty corpses recently dead from the Grey Plague. Here the heads had been infected with this disease by the simple method of placing decaying human tissue inside the mouths of each one, after which Shikara had done a simple *Proliferation* spell. As a result, every head was a deadly bacteriological bomb, alive with the vigorous bacilli that cause this lethal and highly contagious disease. Even now, those unfortunates inside the city who had been detailed to remove the infected heads were beginning to suffer the initial symptoms that invariably led to death; the typical skin pallor, the swelling buboes, the muscle spasms, the vomiting and bleeding. Within twenty-four hours the necromantically strengthened bacilli would have affected half of the population, and few of them would recover. The city would be dying from within.

Shikara smiled grimly to herself. It wasn't much to hold on to, but it did make her feel just a teensy bit better. Now all she needed to cheer her up completely was to have the mangled and bleeding bodies of Ronan and his friends laid at her feet. Unfortunately, she would have to wait a few days for that, and in the meantime they would be enjoying themselves in Yai'El, blithely unaware of what was in store for them. Maybe she should send them a little foretaste, just to stir them up a bit. Yes, that might be fun!

Dismounting, she rummaged in her bag and drew out a small copper dish. Then she opened the locket that hung at her neck and took out the small hank of hair that lay coiled within, the hank of hair that she had cut from the head of her lover, Nekros, all those years before as he lay sleeping. She had saved Ronan and his friends from Nekros just a few short weeks ago. Now it was time to rectify that mistake . . .

TOGETHER

One of the most famous sights in Yai'El is the Bird Market in Maelvanta Square. Here can be bought almost any species of caged bird, from kalayas to kakokeets. But be warned. Although they are very beautiful, kakokeets make very bad pets. They are perfect mimics and are sold as 'talking' birds. However, being cooped up in cages tends to make them rather stroppy, and they generally try to wind their owners up. A kakokeet given as a present to a maiden aunt will tend to come out with the foulest orc drinking-songs, whereas one bought for an orc party will stick to religious madrigals. Their lives tend to be very short, and most end up barbecued on a stick by irate orcs, or flushed down the latrine by shocked old ladies.

The Rough Chronicle to . . . Cydor

To someone who had spent most of their life in a small island village, Yai'El was a seething, claustrophobic cauldron of people, and Marten was finding it totally overpowering. Since escaping from the police station, he and Dene had been wandering blindly around, desperately seeking something, anything, that would make a fitting target for a Vagen raid, but so far they had drawn a complete blank, and they were already a day late for their rendezvous with Klaer and the others.

Something was in the air, that was for sure. The city was full of warriors, although they had been told that this was because of the Thoroughbred Trophy races. And today, detachments of the Cydorian Guard had started arriving, ordered here to meet some threat, apparently. Rumour had it that a massive orc army was heading for Yai'El, but Marten was worried that someone had sighted the *Shorn Teal*, and that the soldiers might be mustering to deal with the Vagen threat.

They were currently sat at an open-air café table by the Bird

Market, drinking a couple of beers. Marten was watching the soldiers walking past, and was wondering if they were searching for him and Dene. Dene was watching the birds, and had been fulminating for ten minutes about the iniquities of keeping wild creatures in tiny cages. Marten had just decided that if his friend said one more word on the subject he would force his head inside one of the said cages when Dene suddenly changed tack.

'Ah, look at that sweet little donkey,' he said, and something clicked at the back of Marten's mind. Donkey? Hadn't Lobbo said something about a donkey? He watched as his friend bent down from the table to click his fingers at one of the tattiest creatures that Marten had ever seen. It was standing in the street beside them, nostrils whiffling, staring at the steak and chips that the man at the next table was eating.

'Izzum an ickle sweetie, den?' burbled Dene. 'Duzzum wantums neck scratched?'

The donkey turned a distinctly unfriendly eye towards him.

'Duzzum wantums *klatting* head bitten off?' it snarled, and then scowling it trotted off through the crowds.

Marten stared in amazement, his mouth agape. Look for an unusual donkey, Lobbo had said, and donkeys don't come any more unusual than one that swears at you. Hauling the bewildered Dene to his feet, Marten dragged him through the crowds in pursuit, desperate not to lose sight of the little creature. For the first time since they had set off from the village, it was starting to look as though there might be a touch of method behind all the madness.

Ronan and Tyson sat in Mithrills Galore, a wine-bar on the south side of Tor Antino Square, waiting for the others to show up. They had been watching the passers-by and chatting together, discussing what to do for the best about Shikara. Ronan was relaxed, contentedly revelling in being free, young, and in the company of his woman again, and wasn't really taking in much that was going on around them. But Tyson was, and she was worried.

She'd noticed that although the city was full of warriors here to race their mounts, instead of the usual carefree holiday mood they were all gathered together in muttering, frowning groups. Also, the Cydorian Guard seemed to be using the city as a mustering point, and a fully fledged general was sat on the other side of the wine-bar, talking to a couple of underlings and looking about as happy as an old and very sick horse that is on its way to visit a vet who it knows has shares in the local glue factory. It wasn't too difficult to work out what must be happening, especially as Guebral had said that things were destined to unfold at Yai'El – although she had since clammed up, saying she needed to talk with the rest of the Dead Boys, whoever they were. But it rather looked as though Shikara and her orc army were heading straight for the city.

At that moment Tarl ambled in, with Puss trotting behind him. He came straight over to their table, fell into a seat, and sank his waiting beer in one go.

'So. What's the word on the street?' asked Tyson.

'Shikara's on her way here, all right,' answered Tarl, 'and she's bringing one or two orcs with her.'

'How many?' interjected Ronan. 'Any estimates?'

'The Guards reckon about twenty thousand.'

'WHAT?'

'Even allowing for exaggeration, she must have an army some ten thousand strong.'

'By the Gods!' muttered Tyson. 'No wonder the cities have been falling like two-pins[11]!'

They paused as a tall, blond warrior with a drooping moustache sat himself down at the next table, glanced at them, blushed, and then buried himself in the menu.

'So,' continued Tyson, after a pause, 'what are we going to do?'

'Keep moving?' suggested Tarl, hopefully.

'Get something to eat,' suggested Puss, taking the short-term view of things.

'Fight,' stated Ronan, with conviction.

'Yeah, I reckon we need to face the bitch down,' agreed Tyson, 'but the Cydorian Guard will only have a couple of thousand troops available. They'll get slaughtered. We need more. How long have we got?'

'Three days, they reckon,' muttered Tarl, who was starting to feel dreadfully depressed.

---

[11] A rather boring form of skittles invented on the island of Kerti where, owing to the complete lack of trees, wood is in very short supply.

'There must be four hundred freelance warriors in town,' said Tyson.

'We need ten times that number,' answered Ronan.

'Ah, come on, guys,' begged Tarl, the Voice of Reason. 'We're gonna get slaughtered unless we can find several thousand fighting-men! What's the point in hanging around? No one's about to stroll up to us and say, "Guys, I've got an army I can let you borrow," now, are they?'

'Guys, I've got an army I can let you borrow,' said a quiet voice from the next table, and Tarl snapped his head round so quickly that he nearly dislocated his neck. It was the blond warrior. Ronan and Tyson glanced across, expecting to see him smiling at his little joke, but he seemed to be in earnest.

'Well, an army of sorts, if I can persuade them,' he continued. 'My name is Marten, by the way, and this is Dene.' He indicated a thin, flaxen-haired man who was just returning from the bar with two beers. The man nodded a greeting and managed to spill most of the beer down his sleeve.

'I think I must have been looking for you,' Marten continued, cryptically, and Ronan was just about to invite him to join them and explain what he meant when an ice-cold wind blasted in through the door of the wine-bar so strongly that people in its path were sent staggering. Then the air in the room seemed to split down the middle like a sheet being ripped in half as a lightning bolt blasted out of the floor to strike the ceiling, showering the customers with fragments of charred plaster. And there, hovering threateningly before Ronan, was the wafting spectral shape of Nekros the Black.

For a few stunned seconds no one moved, and the apparition stared balefully. But then the owner of the wine-bar came striding out of the back room.

'Oy! What the hell's going on in here?' he roared. Almost without looking Nekros stabbed one spectral finger in his direction, and black flames burst through the floor and enveloped him. The owner screamed and writhed as the dark fire licked about him, and then the flames began to sink back through the floor, taking him slowly with them, as though he was vanishing into some foul quicksand. For a few moments his tortured and burning face hovered above the floorboards, but then it sank from sight, and the screaming stopped abruptly. There was a stunned silence.

'Welcome to hell, baby,' drawled the apparition, 'as someone not a million miles away is fond of saying.' Its malevolent embers of eyes came to rest on Ronan, Tyson and Tarl. 'Ah, how delightful,' it continued. 'Unfinished business!' Hatred oozed from every pore of the shifting features as the spectre seemed to grow and swell, edging closer to the three of them until it towered over them.

'Before you ask,' it snarled to Ronan, 'Shikara sent me. She will be here herself in three days, at the head of an army that will tear this puny city apart. Such is her hatred that she would follow you wherever you run. She wants to be personally revenged for the burning of her home, so I am denied true vengeance. But I can . . . amuse myself with your friends.'

It leered foully down at them, and Tyson found that unspeakable terrors were forcing their way into her imagination. She tried to stand, but found that she seemed to be frozen into position. Anyway, she knew that she had no defence against such a magical demon.

'Can't you do something?' she hissed out of the side of her mouth to Tarl.

'I already have,' came the mournful, damp reply.

Then the door of the wine-bar opened again. The spectre flicked a disdainful finger at it, and a black lightning-bolt rocketed towards the figure standing there – and rebounded straight back, slamming into the spectre, which let out a surprised and painful yelp.

Tyson managed to haul her head round, although the air dragged at it like glue, and saw to her surprise that a single slight figure stood in the doorway. It was Guebral, and although her face looked drawn and frightened, her right hand was held up imperiously, and there was a golden ring on her finger that glinted in the light.

The spectre of Nekros stared at it with horrified recognition.

'Oh, shit!' it said.

And then an emerald mist began to seep out from the green crystal that was set in the ring, a mist that eddied and swirled across to the transfixed apparition, whirling about it in slow-motion and cloaking it in a verdant fog. Small dots of brilliant light began to sparkle in the fog, which then began gradually to contract, and as it contracted it squeezed the ensnared spectre, which threshed furiously but ineffectively about inside its misty cage. Slowly the mist condensed until it was a pulsating ball of brilliant green, and then suddenly it exploded into tiny emerald fragments of light, which instantly vanished into nothingness. At the same time, there was an inhuman scream of pure agony that cut out as suddenly as it had began, and everyone in the room found that they could move freely again.

A hubbub of relieved and speculative chatter broke out, and Tarl noticed that nearly every eye in the place was on them. He gave Guebral a weak but incredibly grateful smile as she sat down next to them.

'Thank you! From the bottom of my heart, thank you!' he babbled.

'If you hadn't noticed, that was Nekros,' Ronan told her.

'Ah. I thought he seemed a bit miffed with you.'

'What did you do to him?'

'I don't really know. I just . . . reacted.'

'Well, thank the Gods you did,' said Tyson. 'That wasn't a lot of fun.'

'Yeah, it was a little taxing,' added Tarl, wryly.

'And Tarl just hates it when a taxing spectre catches up with him,' interjected Puss, to a chorus of groans.

Ronan turned back to Marten and Dene, who had been watching events with complete bewilderment, and called them over, but they had only just dragged their chairs across when eight members of the Cydorian Guard marched up to the table.

'If you don't mind,' said the sergeant at their head, 'our general would like a little word with you. I think he'd rather like to know what's going on.'

Ronan and the others looked over to the general's table. He was studying them thoughtfully, and as they looked he raised one crooked finger and beckoned them. Ronan took in the seven Guards lined up behind their sergeant with hands hovering close to their sword hilts, and the fifteen or so other Guards in the wine-bar who were watching carefully, and decided that a little discretion was called for.

'We'd be delighted,' he said, and stood wearily up.

Royan Issimo had from an early age been a career soldier. Even in his rookie days as a Lieutenant in the Cydorian Guard, there had been a strange inevitability that, one day, he would make it to the position of General. And in the three years that he had been the supreme commander, he had found the job remarkably easy. It wasn't that he was a natural leader, or a superb strategist. There just wasn't much going on in Cydor for an army to do. They might have to chase after the occasional gang of marauding brigands and half-orcs, or drive off some Vagen raiders once in a while, but on the whole, the job was simply one of administration.

Or rather, it had been. But all of a sudden, with twenty thousand orcs on the rampage and heading straight for Yai'El, things were very different. General Issimo wasn't a bad leader, but he knew his limitations, and with a bare two and a half thousand men to face eight times that number of orcs, even the famous war-leaders of the olden days would have stood about as much chance as a slug would against the owner of the foot that is about to crush it.

What he needed was a miracle. Watching the strangers wiping the floor with that spectre in the wine-bar, he'd wondered if perhaps he might have found it, as they certainly seemed to know about the sorceress who was leading the orc army. Indeed, if the spectre was to be believed, they'd burnt her house down or something. But now, sitting in his office in the Guard Head-quarters and looking at the strangers, he wasn't so sure.

Four men, two women and a small brown donkey. True, two of the men looked the part of warriors, but the other two men looked like a part of a warrior that he wasn't going to mention in mixed company. Still, one of the women seemed to be a pretty competent warrior, too, and from the way that she had dealt with the spectre, the other obviously had a fair bit of talent. And he had to admit that the donkey had an unpleasantly sharp wit, and teeth to match.

Moodily he tapped the point of his dagger on his desk, leaving a series of tiny gashes in the polished blackwood surface.

'OK,' he said to Ronan, 'what do you know about this sorceress and her army?'

Quickly Ronan told him what he could remember about Shikara's appearance, his abduction, and the subsequent events. As he talked, the general listened intently.

'Oh, great!' he muttered, after Ronan had finished. 'She's that powerful, and you lot go and burn her *klatting* house down! Nice going! No wonder she's pissed off with you!'

'But we didn't! It was fine when we left it!'

'Well, someone did!'

'Er . . . I think I know who,' mumbled Tarl, and all eyes swung to stare at him. 'When we left them, Bernie and Bumfur yelled something about taking care of Shikara. You know what buggers dwarves are for revenge. They've probably come streaming out from under the mountains and burned down her castle and everyone in it.'

'Look, it doesn't really matter who is responsible,' said the general, 'the result is the same. We've got twenty thousand orcs coming straight at us and no way of stopping them.'

'Maybe it does matter,' mused Tarl, thoughtfully. 'For starters, we've got the Cydorian Guard. And there must be a couple of hundred freelance warriors knocking about the city. They'll fight, once they know that Ronan and Tyson here are taking part.'

The general sat up, suddenly alert.

'Tyson?' he said. 'Tyson of Welbug?'

Tyson nodded, and a slow grin spread over Issimo's face.

'Things are looking up already,' he said.

'And this guy,' continued Tarl, ignoring the interruption and indicating Marten, 'this guy was just about to lend us an army when your soldiers decided to gatecrash the party.'

'Oh, you just happen to have a whole army that you don't need, do you?' asked the general, raising a disbelieving eyebrow.

Blushing, Marten stammered out an explanation.

'Many of the tribe are unhappy with the raiding,' he finished hurriedly. The atmosphere had cooled noticeably when he had confessed to being a Vagen. 'This is our chance to make amends and show the world what we can do.'

'So how big an army are we talking here?'

'From my village, fewer than two hundred. But if I can organise a mass raid with warriors from every village then I could bring back two thousand fighting men.' Marten paused. 'And women,' he added, mentally apologising to Klaer.

'We still wouldn't have enough,' said the general.

'But that brings me back to the destruction of Shikara's castle,' said Tarl. 'Now, dwarves may be many things. Greedy. Vengeful. Single-minded –'

'Short,' interposed the donkey.

'Ah, but the best things come in small packages,' said Tarl, 'as I found out a long time ago. I used to know these two Hobbit girls. The Fallowfile sisters. Boy, were they fun . . .' He paused, with a fond expression on his face, and then glanced guiltily at Guebral. 'Hang on, I'm getting side-tracked. No, the thing about dwarves is that they always pay their debts. If someone they trust, such as Ronan here, was to go and point out to them that because they burned her castle down, Shikara is about to take it out on us, then there must be a good chance that they will come and bail us out.'

'We'd still be outnumbered by more than three to one. And what about this sorceress? The rumour from Far Tibreth is that even old Ruddyguts couldn't stop her.'

'You saw how Guebral here dealt with that spectre in the wine-bar. She's just *one* of the Dead Boys. If she can persuade the others to join us, they'll be more than a match for Shikara.'

'The Dead Boys? You mean those thieving renegade magic-users holed up in the old factory?'

'Er . . . well . . .'

'So, in a nutshell,' the general said, 'what you're suggesting is that I march my men out to confront this orc army trusting that the Vagens, who have been a thorn in our side for years, will suddenly come to our rescue, and that an army of dwarves will also turn up out of the blue to help us. You're asking me to do this knowing that if either of them fail to turn up, we will get cut to bloody ribbons. And you're suggesting that to defend ourselves against a sorceress who appears to have more power than just about anyone in the whole of Midworld, we employ a gang of outlaws who have been robbing the citizens of Yai'El blind for the past ten years. That is what you're suggesting, right?'

Tarl seated himself nonchalantly on the edge of the general's desk, and grinned down at him.

'Put it this way,' he said. 'What alternative have you got?'

*

Marten stood at the rendezvous point, a beach a couple of miles north of Yai'El, and prayed that Klaer hadn't given up on them and gone home when they hadn't turned up the previous day, but would keep coming back as arranged. He needn't have worried. At the appointed hour the newly repaired *Shorn Teal* nosed its way round the headland and into the bay, and minutes later the women crew were leaping down onto the sand and being introduced to Ronan, Tyson, Tarl and Puss. Klaer and the others listened open-mouthed as Marten nervously outlined the task ahead of them, and as he finished, to his surprise, they surrounded him, shaking his hand and thumping him on the back.

'This is exactly what our tribe needs,' Klaer kept repeating, and seeing the glowing admiration in her eyes Marten had a strange urge to climb to the top of the mast and hang upside-down from it, baying at the moon.

Ronan had decided that he had better visit the Dwarves' city alone, as their mistrust of strangers was well known. Guebral had stayed in Yai'El, but Tyson, Tarl and Puss had voted to go with the Vagens to offer whatever support and persuasion they could. They vaulted on board the longship, and then with Ronan's help Marten and Dene pushed the beached ship clear of the shingle. As it glided away the oars were unshipped and the two Vagens leapt for the stern rail. There was a loud *thud* and a splash, and after Klaer and Kamila had reached over the side and hauled the bedraggled and half-stunned Dene out of the sea the ship pulled away.

Ronan watched until it was out of sight, and then he led his borrowed horse up the beach, mounted, and set off for the distant mountains at a gallop.

They were beginning to run short of time now, and the off-shore breeze wasn't strong enough to take the Vagen ship along at the required rate to get home in time for the presentation, so Tarl dug a small, leather-bound book out from the bottom of his backpack, consulted it, and cast a *Summon Wind* spell. To his delight it worked perfectly, and as the ship leapt along through the waves he sat at the stern chatting with Dene. They had discovered that they shared rather a lot in common. Both were small and thin, with an eldritch power that for unaccountable reasons kept going wrong and dropping them in the mire, and they had both found that an awful lot of people seemed to have had it in for them for a very long time. Puss, uncharacteristically, lay quietly on the deck beside them, eyes closed, panting slightly.

Tyson, meanwhile, stood near the prow with Klaer and Marten beside her, watching the sea whirling towards them and enjoying the feel of the salt spray on her face. Her heart was heavy at having to part from Ronan so soon, but she was excited by the imminent prospect of taking on and defeating Shikara. The other two, however, seemed nervous.

'Do you think we can beat the orcs?' Marten asked her.

'Yes. With your help.'

'But if we lose, what will happen?'

'We won't lose. Anyway, your tribe will be safe on your islands. Shikara would never set foot on a boat. Every time one of the sailors called out "Avast behind", she'd think they were talking about her. But as long as your folk will help us . . .' Tyson saw the doubt on their faces. 'Is there a problem with this?'

Marten and Klaer looked at each other, and then Klaer began to tell Tyson about Marten's standing within the tribe, and about the opposition they were likely to face from Krage and his supporters. And as she talked, Tyson's brow furrowed and her expression grew thoughtful. This didn't sound good, it didn't sound good at all.

General Issimo marched along the quayside at the head of a detachment of the Cydorian Guard. As he marched he threw out commands to the scribe at his side, who hurriedly noted them down.

'. . . and lastly,' he finished, 'I want notices printed and pasted up all over town, so that no one can miss them. Notices to advertise for freelance warriors needed for imminent battle. Army rates of pay, but all successful applicants may select and keep their choice of weapons from our ultra-modern armoury consisting of the very latest in combat hardware.'

'But, my Lord,' interjected the scribe, 'we haven't got an armoury of the very latest in combat hardware.'

The general stopped and laid a hand on the scribe's shoulder. They were stood outside the gleaming metal doors of a vast new warehouse.

'No,' he agreed, 'but the Orcbane Sword Corporation have, and a lot of it is in this warehouse here. Crates and crates of high-tech weaponry, and they're going to lend it all to us. Permanently.'

He turned to the sergeant in charge of the detachment.

'Break the door down,' he ordered, 'and make it quick. We haven't got all day.'

And he stood back and waited patiently as the Guards set to work with a will.

Even with Tarl's wind-assistance, it was an hour after the appointed starting-time of the presentations when the *Shorn Teal* sailed into the village harbour. Although the place was crammed with longships, there wasn't a soul to be seen save for the agitated figure of Lobbo, who was pacing up and down on the quayside and looking about as un-relaxed as Marten had ever seen him.

'You've cut it *klatting* fine!' he yelled across the water to them as they neared the stone jetty. 'They're half-way through the second presentation. I've managed to get you scheduled last, but even so, an hour later and you would have been eliminated. In more ways than one, to judge from what Krage has been threatening!'

As the longship touched the quayside Marten leapt out, with Dene beside him. Tyson and Tarl followed, leaving Puss asleep in the stern. Lobbo clapped his son on the back, and then grabbed Dene by the shoulders and stared unblinkingly into his eyes.

'Well, your time has come. You were chosen raid leader, and you must make the presentation. By our rules, no one else can speak for us. And you have *got* to do it well, for the sake of our people. Krage has already made his. He wants all our villages to combine on one vast raid on the pirate bases around Emba Razindi, not to make the seas safe, but to take over their operations! He wants to take our tribe into drug-running and piracy! And such was the power of his presentation, the majority will vote for him unless you can provide something better, as will the representatives of the other villages! Harald and Mykel won't beat him. It's all down to you, Dene. Good luck!'

Dene had turned the colour of very old milk. He swallowed, and then shuffled off nervously towards the main hall with Marten and Lobbo on either side of him, whispering encouraging words. Tarl and Tyson followed.

'Did you find what you were looking for?' Tyson muttered.

Tarl grinned, and held up his small, leather-bound book.

'I certainly did,' he said. 'A *Charm of Silver-tongued Oratory*. As long as he summons up the guts to open his mouth, he should be fine. Are you ready for your bit?'

'Yeah. I've had a word with Klaer. She knows what to do.'

'Good. Well, this should be interesting, to say the least!' said Tarl, and they followed the others through the door of the Great Hall.

Inside, the place was crammed with Vagens. The whole village was there, along with representatives from every other island. Harald Silverbeard was just finishing the presentation of his Monastic Islands Summer-break, which appeared from his flip-charts to involve an awful lot of burning of monasteries and abbeys, and looting of religious treasures. He got quite a good round of applause, and was followed on to the dais by Mykel, who launched enthusiastically into the details of his Suntrekker Summer Spoils Special. The basis of his plan was to pillage the holiday villas and hotels along the beaches south of Perplec whilst picking up a pretty cool tan, and this got an enthusiastic response, especially from the younger Vagens. After promising that they would all get gold, silver and bronzed, Mykel left the dais to cheers.

Then it was Dene's turn. He mounted the rostrum to boos and cat-calls, and Marten half expected him to turn around and make a run for it. But there was something different about the guy. He looked nervous and a little unsure, but instead of launching straight into speech and being shouted down, he waited, surveying his audience calmly, and slowly the noise subsided.

'You all know me,' he began, 'and you all know that on every raid I have been on, I was totally . . . crap.' He said this with a disarming grin, and there was a shout of laughter from the audience, but a slightly surprised shout, because as they laughed they all suddenly realised that they were laughing *with* Dene, instead of at him.

'As a swordsman, I couldn't beat a bunch of watercress,' he

continued. 'For a while, I was a message-carrier. I was probably the worst carrier since Typhoid Betty. And then you made me a priest, and you all know what happened then. Crap really was the word . . .' He paused, and let the laughter die down.

'But I've been on a lot of raids. North, south, mainland and islands. And I'll tell you one thing. I'm proud to be a Vagen, proud at what we've done!'

This was good stuff, and the audience lapped it up, basking in a comfortable warm glow of satisfaction.

'Yes, I'm proud,' Dene continued, and suddenly his voice was harsh and full of contempt. 'Proud of how stealthily we have crept up to villages in the dark and massacred the peaceful folk who live there! Proud of how we burn their homes and steal their meagre possessions! Proud of how two hundred heavily armed Vagens have faced down an equal number of peasants, old men and children armed with pitchforks and kitchen knives! We brag to ourselves of what wonderful fighters we are, but when did we ever take part in a fair fight? When did we last march to a real battle? When did we last face a heavily armed and fearsome foe? Not in my lifetime!'

There was an angry hum within the audience, but no one dared to call out aloud, for what Dene was saying was uncomfortably close to the truth.

'But why is this? I know you for what you are!' All at once his voice was full of a patently honest admiration. 'I know that you are brave and noble folk! I know of your fighting ability. I know that the blood of our ancestors still flows within your veins! So why is it that when I visit the mainland, I hear the townsfolk talk of the Vagen barbarians? The Vagen pirates? Murderers? Cowards? Why do they talk of us so? Well, let us examine what my colleagues here have offered you this afternoon! A voyage to confront murderous and savage holiday-makers on the beaches of northern Iduin – how brave! A trip to massacre and rob some peaceful religious communities – how dangerous! Or the chance to supplant the pirates of Emba Razindi, and begin a life of piracy and drug-running – how noble!

'Well, I'm sorry, but I cannot offer you such things. No gold, no jewels, no fine wall-hangings or carpets to plunder and bring home, no peasants or old folk to slaughter. Not even a sun-tan. All

218

I can offer is death. Death in battle, but death with honour! Out there, to the north of Yai'El, a handful of men from the Cydorian Guard are marching to face an orc army led by a powerful and terrible sorceress, an army that is some *twenty thousand strong!*'

The audience gasped as one man, and Dene waited again until the hum of conversation had died away.

'With them, they hope, will fight the dwarves of the Chrome Mountains, and yet they will still be outnumbered some five to one. They have little hope, even though they have some of the most famous warriors in Midworld fighting for them, warriors such as Tyson of Welbug here!'

Tyson walked to the dais, stepped up, and surveyed the audience silently.

'They have little chance, even though they have powerful magic-users such as Tarl . . .'

Tarl stepped onto the dais next to Tyson. Well aware that he wasn't such a prepossessing figure as she was, he'd prepared for this moment. He thrust a pointing finger dramatically upwards, and a yellow fireball exploded out of his finger and rocketed upwards to blow a big hole in the thatched roof. Again, the audience gasped.

'They have little chance because they are so heavily out-numbered. But if we sail to ally with them, if we march into battle against the orcs, then they will have a chance! So that is what I offer! No gold, no silver, but the chance to test ourselves in battle, whether we live or die, and the certainty of more glory and honour than even our ancestors achieved!'

Dene grabbed one of Tyson's hands and one of Tarl's, and raised them aloft in his own.

'We sail tomorrow morning! Will you sail with us?'

For a moment the room was totally still, and then it erupted with cheering and shouting. Kaal, the village chief, climbed onto the dais and looked daggers at Dene, then raised his hands and signalled for quiet.

'We must choose, as always, with a show of hands. Remember, only people from this village who are eligible to partake in the raid may vote. Who votes for Krage?'

A number of hands went up as Krage's coterie of friends and hangers-on voted for him. Kaal counted carefully.

'One hundred and eight. Who votes for Harald Silverbeard?'

A single hand was raised.

'One. Who votes for Mykel?'

Again, a single hand was raised.

'One. Who votes for Dene?'

Again a number of hands went up, and as Kaal counted his face fell.

'A hundred and twenty-six.'

Once more the hall erupted with cheering and shouting, but through it all a single voice rang out, cutting through the clamour like an axe through soft-wood. It was Krage.

'You counted the women who voted for Dene. They may have crewed for him, but as women do not go on raids they are not eligible to vote. That means I win by two!'

A silence fell on the hall, into which Klaer spoke.

'You said the day that a woman beats you in combat is the day that we take part in raids.'

Krage turned to face her, smiling smugly.

'Sister,' he said, 'you could not beat me, and you know it!'

'I can, though,' said Tyson, stepping happily down from the dais. Krage looked at her as though she was something he had just stepped in.

'This is not your business,' he snarled.

'Tough titty, baby. You can either stick that fancy sword in me or you can stick it up your muscle-bound arse. The choice is yours.'

Krage looked round, but it was obvious from the faces of the watching Vagens that a refusal of this challenge would be attributed to fear. He was going to have to fight the *klatting* woman. Angrily, contemptuously, he dragged his sword from its scabbard, and waded in to the attack. Seconds later he found to his horror that he was fighting for his very life.

Tyson had been putting up with an awful lot of crap in the past few weeks, and she was just in the mood for taking it out on someone. To her surprise, she found that she was fighting more fluently than she could ever remember. Krage was no slouch, in fact he was very, very good indeed, but no one could have lived with her that day. However, she didn't want him thinking that she had won by a fluke, and so she deliberately held her hand. On four occasions the point of her sword stopped just short of Krage's neck or chest. Slowly she drove him backwards across the space that had formed in the crowd, until his back was against the wall by the dais. He was white-faced and sweating now, and fear lent weight to his attack. For a few seconds Tyson had to defend, but then Krage's sword whistled inches past her neck, and he looked down to see the tip of her blade resting right against his groin.

'Whoops,' she said, lightly, 'you almost joined us women then!'

And then she stepped back and with a lightning-fast two-handed blow she smashed his sword clean out of his hands. There was a silence that seemed to drag on for several seconds and then Krage smiled, and she was surprised to see a grudging respect in his eyes.

'We appear to be sailing to Yai'El,' he said, and the roar of approval from the assembled Vagens nearly took the roof off.

Guebral looked at the stubborn, set faces of the Dead Boys, took a deep breath, and tried again.

'Look around you,' she said, and with one sweep of her hand she indicated her scorn for the decrepit factory and their makeshift homes within it. 'Is this all you want for the rest of your lives? A cack existence in a cack-hole like this? There's a real world out there. In other cities, sparkers are welcomed and respected. And now we have a chance to show the affoes that they need us!'

She paused as an extra-large gout of flame shot up from the gas-works chimney, bathing the watching faces in crimson light. All of a sudden she was fed up with seeing people bathed in crimson light, and after the clear air of the Chrome Mountains, the sulphurous stench that permeated the air here was more than she could bear.

'Nothing we do will bring back Pinball's eyes, or Shiftfister's hands,' she continued, 'but we can prevent the same stuff happening to any other kids. There's an army of twenty thousand wazzed shittoes heading this way, led by a major-league sparker. No daiming. Without us, the affoes get ironed, and so does the city.'

'No loss,' muttered Image.

'Yeah, *klat* 'em,' said Gutter-rat.

Guebral looked at their blank faces and sighed. Reaching across she pulled a bottle from the crate that Stipe had brought in that afternoon, uncorked it, and took a swig. The harsh red wine bit at the sides of her tongue, and she screwed her face up. Then she settled herself back amongst the cushions on the ragged old sofa and readied herself to try again.

This was going to be a long night.

Ronan sat back on the horse and stared down into the valley below. The sun was low in the sky now, peering round the spur of a mountain to the west, and the valley was full of shadows. However, it was easy to see the wide, straight, stone-paved road that ran along the valley floor from the north-west, curving around the foot of the towering Tor Enshal above to run straight as a die to the sheer rock face of the mountainside. And here, carved from the living stone, were the great gates that guarded the Dwarves' underground city of Zanadakan.

Ronan could see a couple of Dwarf sentries on duty outside the gates, their halberds glinting in the last faint rays of sunlight. It looked as though he would just make it before night-time. It would be good to see Bernie and Bumfur, and to talk about their time in the cell together. Ronan grinned. He was dying to ask them about what had happened under the stone flags after he had poured the wine with the love-potion in it down the crack. But he had a feeling they might not want to talk about that.

As she waited for the Vagens to complete their preparations for the voyage, Tyson wandered about looking at the village. Everywhere she went, people stared at her in wonder, but most of them seemed too in awe of her to talk. The one exception, however, was Twbi the chicken-boy. She had stopped in the street beside his chicken-run, made a brief but complimentary remark about the birds, and had suddenly found herself embroiled in one of those interminable one-way conversations that are so difficult to get out of. After ten minutes she had learned everything that she could ever need to know about chickens, and yet Twbi was still talking. A fascinated crowd of Vagens had gathered around at a respectful distance and were chatting together excitedly, occasionally pausing to stare at her.

'Of course, Chanticleer, my prize cockerel, isn't with them at the moment,' Twbi gabbled on. 'I keep him in my hut. He's too valuable. But you should see him! He's so beautiful, all bottle-green and bronze plumage! Yes, you may think these chickens look good –'

At this point, one of those sudden lulls in the surrounding conversations occurred, and Twbi's next words seemed to ring out around the village as if the town crier had enunciated them.

'– but you should see my cock!'

Every eye for fifty yards turned to stare at them, and for the first time since she was about ten years old Tyson found that she was going red. Muttering something unintelligible, she turned and hastened back towards the harbour. As she reached the corner she risked a quick look back. Some of the villagers had picked Twbi up by the ankles and were dunking him head-first in something that looked suspiciously like a cesspit. Grimacing, she fixed her eyes in front of her and hurried off.

At the quayside she bumped into Tarl, who came running out of the Great Hall with Fjonë at his side.

'Hey, what's the rush?' she smiled, but then saw the worry in his eyes.

'Fjonë says there's something wrong with Puss,' he cried, and scurried off towards the ship. Tyson followed him along the jetty, and together they jumped down onto the deck of the *Shorn Teal* and made their way to the stern.

The little donkey was lying there on one side, its eyes open but glazed, its chest rising and falling with painfully laboured breathing. Tarl knelt beside it, but then recoiled, his nose wrinkled in disgust.

'*Klat!*' he muttered. 'What's that foul smell?'

The donkey lifted its head with an obvious effort.

'Bit ironic,' it gasped, 'that *you* . . . should be complaining . . . about *me* smelling . . .'

And then it rolled onto its other side, and both Tarl and Tyson gasped with horror. Half of the donkey's left flank appeared to have gone rotten. The hair had fallen out, and the flesh was foul and putrid, giving off a corpse-like stench.

'Oh, *klat!*' moaned Tarl, rocking back and forth on his heels. 'Oh, *KLAT!*'

'Sorry,' Puss continued. 'I'm afraid . . . that one of the . . .

zombies . . . managed to touch me . . .'

Tyson stared at the donkey, thinking back to the horrible fate that had awaited the four Freak horses which had been zombie-touched and feeling sick with apprehension. She grabbed Tarl by the shoulder and shook him roughly.

'You've got to do something!' she yelled.

He turned and looked up at her, and the fear on his face filled her with dread.

'I can't!' he wailed. 'It's way beyond my Power! There's nothing I can do! Nothing at all!'

Ronan couldn't believe his ears.

'What?' he demanded. 'What did you say?'

'I'm sorry,' repeated Bernie, 'but I don't think I can ask our king to grant you an audience. It wouldn't be worthwhile disturbing him. He isn't interested in battles and stuff like that.'

Ronan sat back in the cold stone chair in the cold stone room and stared at the plump dwarf. Despite the torches guttering in the wall-holders, the city carved out of the heart of the mountain was dark and depressing, and he couldn't wait to get outside to the daylight again.

'I thought dwarves were big on revenge and debts of honour,' he muttered angrily.

Bernie shrugged indifferently.

'To be honest, our king would rather enjoy himself. He likes a good time. He says that into each reign some life must fall.'

'I'm sure he'd listen if you and Bumfur had a word with him.'

'I don't really like to. We've already stuck our necks out, getting the guys to help us torch the castle.'

'Please, Bernie. I'm begging you.'

'I really don't think I can.'

'You owe me one.'

'No, we're quits. You may have brought us out of the castle, but don't forget that we brought you out of that drugged stupor. I risked my life testing your food back there.'

'Is that your final word?'

'I'm afraid so.'

'Really?'

'Yep.'

Ronan leaned forward and lowered his voice to a conspiratorial whisper.

'If you don't take my request for an audience to your king, then I am going to tell everyone in this god-forsaken city exactly what went on between you and my big toe in that dungeon.'

There was a sudden silence. Ronan thought he heard a pin drop in the next room.

'I'll just go and have a word with him. I won't be long.'

The embarrassed dwarf scurried out, and Ronan shifted restlessly in his seat. Time was running out. If he couldn't get a dwarf army on the march in a few hours, then it was going to be too late for everyone concerned . . .

The *Shorn Teal* sped northwards through the night like an arrow before the spell-summoned wind. In the stern, Tarl knelt with Puss's head cradled in his lap. The smell from the festering, rotting flesh along the donkey's flank was appalling, but somehow Tarl didn't seem to notice it. Puss's eyes were closed, and its breath was coming in rasping, painful gasps.

Tyson walked back and knelt beside them.

'Are you sure there's nothing you can do?' she asked.

Tarl bit back an angry reply, and took a deep breath.

'Positive,' he said. 'The dark magic is far too powerful. Maybe Gueb can cure it, I don't know. I've *Summoned* the strongest wind I can. She'll be waiting for us at the beach, and we'll find out then.'

Tyson rested a sympathetic hand on his shoulder, then stood up and left him kneeling there. Tears ran down Tarl's cheeks and dripped onto the ragged hair of the donkey's neck, and he smoothed them away with his hand.

'Don't worry, mate,' he whispered. 'Gueb will cure you, and then I promise you I'm going to get you the best steak you have ever eaten. In fact, I'm going to carve it out myself. Pure fillet of sorceress. And if you're not here to eat it, then I *klatting* well will!'

But the little donkey made no reply, and its breathing seemed to be getting more and more painful and laboured by the minute.

THE LAST BATTLE

On the coast of Cydor between the Grey Sea and the Chrome Mountains lies a narrow strip of land. Once covered by the sea, it was reclaimed many years ago and transformed into fertile fields by the local farmers. Here on these fields, which bear the name of the sea that once covered them, was fought the savage battle between the Alliance of the West and the forces of the dark sorceress, Shikara. Bloody and terrible was this battle, so that the name of the strip of land became synonymous with death and destruction, and men hid their faces in fear and loathing at the mere mention of Grey Sea Fields.

The Pink Book of Ulay

The orc army had hardly stopped for three days, and the long march was beginning to have an effect. A few of the weaker orcs had fallen out from exhaustion, collapsing as they marched to be ruthlessly trampled underfoot by their comrades. The rest were tramping on relentlessly, but were in a state of slowly simmering discontent that was threatening to boil over into something much uglier. It wasn't the fact that they were tired, weary, hungry and thirsty that was causing this. It was something much, much worse. They were starting to sober up.

Still, Shikara was none too worried. They were getting very close to Yai'El now, and her outriders were already reporting the progress of the pitifully small detachment of the Cydorian Guard that had set out to block her progress. In a few hours' time the vanguard of the orc army would swing southwards around the end of the Chrome Mountains and fall upon the Guards with all the ferocity of a pack of orcs that have been getting a little bored lately and want to have a bit of raucous fun. And then, after a brief and bloody massacre, the city of Yai'El would be lying defenceless in front of them, and the orcs could run riot for a couple of days and drink all they wanted, for she would have achieved her two aims. Firstly, she would be in a position to dictate whatever terms pleased her to the terrified rulers of Behan and Cydor, who would be only too happy to agree to them. And secondly, she would have the lifeless bodies of Ronan and his friends nailed to the city wall above the gate, as a warning to all of what would happen to those who dared to oppose her. Nailed upside-down to the wall, in fact. Naked. Minus heads. And minus every single internal organ. And one or two external ones as well, come to that.

With a smile of cruel anticipation hovering about her lips, Shikara led her impatient and thirsty army towards their destiny.

General Issimo stood in his stirrups and surveyed the terrain ahead of him. On his right rose the foothills of the westernmost Chrome Mountains. In front of him lay the Grey Sea Fields, a flat, cultivated strip of land barely a quarter of a mile wide. To his left, a sloping shingle beach could just be seen beyond the long, low dyke that ran along the edge of the fields to prevent the high winter tides from reclaiming them for the sea.

It would have to do, he supposed. There were worse places to make a stand. If just one of the two additional armies he had been promised actually turned up, they would have enough men to block the passage of the orc army and could make some sort of a show of resistance. And then, who knows? Maybe a miracle might happen. The orcs might not have the stomach for a fight – or maybe they would be tired out after the long march and unable to fight – or maybe they might all spontaneously explode . . . The General sighed. It had to be said that he wasn't feeling too optimistic about his chances.

Turning his horse he looked back over his army. He was already experiencing problems, and the day had only just begun. The Cydorian Guard were no problem. More than two thousand footmen and a couple of hundred cavalry, their faces were pinched and drawn and they looked, quite frankly, terrified, but then they knew that this was virtually a suicide mission. Each of them had friends and family in or near Yai'El, and to a man they were determined to do their best. He knew he could rely on them. No, the problem lay with the three hundred or so professional warriors who had signed on.

Issimo had been surprised and delighted at the response to his posters. Damn near every warrior in town for the races had joined up, and boy, did he need them! The mercenaries were superb fighters, each worth about four of his soldiers, and they all had horses. He was desperately short of cavalry, and his outriders had reported that the orc army included a large troop of Southrons riding the fearsome Freaks. He had heard of the devastating effect those savage animals had on infantry, and he desperately needed the mercenaries and their huge mounts to counteract this.

Unfortunately, he had since discovered that the excellent response was because he had been seen with Tyson of Welbug, who had a bit of a reputation for never backing a losing cause. But since she sailed off with the Vagens two days ago, a rumour had been going round that she wasn't coming back, and the mercenaries had issued the General with an ultimatum. If Tyson fought, they fought. If she didn't, then neither did they. Issimo looked across to where they were sprawled on the ground in a large relaxed group, laughing, talking or playing dice. Without those horses of theirs it would be a complete massacre . . .

And then there was a small explosion of air in front of him and his horse reared in fright, throwing him to the ground. For a moment he lay there winded, scowling at the slight, dark-clad figure that had materialised in front of him, and then he waved away her helping hand and stammered apologies and hauled himself to his feet.

'I wish you wouldn't keep doing that,' he muttered. 'It gets me every time.'

'I'm sorry,' said Guebral. 'Really, I am.'

'Look, if you want to make me feel better, then give me some news of your friends. Any sign of these Vagens turning up?'

'A ship will be coming into the bay in just a few minutes.'

'A ship,' the General repeated, stony-faced. 'A ship. One. Wonderful. How many fighting-men will that hold? Thirty? Forty? The orcs will be terrified!'

'The others are coming,' she answered, 'but later. This ship has come ahead because they need my help. I have a sick friend on board.'

Issimo could tell from her grave face that this was serious, and so he just nodded, and said nothing more. She turned and walked towards the sea and, dismounting, he followed her along the edge of a large patch of maize. They climbed the dyke together and stood staring out over the rolling waves. It was a dull grey morning with a sky full of lowering dark clouds, and the visibility was poor. Behind them they heard a deep roll of thunder echoing around the distant mountain-peaks.

'Here they are,' said Guebral. The General strained his eyes, but could make out nothing in the gloom. Then a gust of wind hit him, and at the same time the sleek shape of a longship appeared out in the bay, racing towards the beach faster than he had ever seen a ship move. For a moment he thought that it must break in half when it hit land, so fast was it moving, but then the wind died away and the ship slowed, gliding in to beach itself with a slight crunch.

Guebral was racing down to the sea's edge, her feet sinking into the wet shingle. Willing hands reached down and helped her up onto the deck, and she strode along the length of the ship to the stern. Tarl and Tyson were knelt there, and in between them was the still figure of Puss. Guebral could smell the foul stench of decay from ten paces away. Close to, the miasma rising from the putrefying flesh along one flank was almost too much to bear.

Tarl turned a tear-stained, haggard face to her.

'Can you save him?'

Guebral knelt and placed a hand on the donkey's chest. She could just feel the faint ragged beat of the labouring heart deep inside. Puss was still alive – but only just.

'I think so,' she said, and then concentrated all her thoughts on the horrible wounds before her. Her eyes closed as she let her mind wander across the rotting flesh, searching for the remnants of the dark mage-spell that drove the infection. Finding it, she followed all the faint tendrils of Power backwards, back towards their very beginnings, gently rubbing them out with her mind as she went, reversing their effects, and following them as they merged like strands of fungus until they were one vast plaited cord. Then all at once she could feel the explosion of evil Power that had infected the living flesh as the zombie had caught Puss with a single rotting finger *there* on the flank, and the spell had taken root. With one last mental flourish she wiped out the spell, and then opened her eyes.

Tyson and Tarl were staring in amazement at the donkey's side, and Guebral heaved a sigh of relief. It had worked! The foul smell still lingered on the air, but the rotting flesh had vanished, to be replaced by solid, hair-covered donkey-skin.

'I don't believe it,' Tyson muttered. 'It just – *un*-rotted – in front of our eyes!'

Tarl threw Guebral a look of such naked gratefulness that she was almost embarrassed.

'We were lucky,' she said, looking away. 'An hour later and Puss would have been dead. I could have done nothing then.'

The donkey still had its eyes closed, but its breathing was stronger, and its chest was rising and falling regularly. Then, with a visible effort, it forced one eye open.

'Can you tell slap-head here,' it wheezed, 'that all these tears of his are making a right soggy mess of my coat.'

Tarl didn't know whether to laugh or cry.

'You prat!' he gasped. 'You hairy-arsed, four-legged wol! Why didn't you tell us that you'd been zombie-touched?'

'I didn't know it was curable,' the donkey answered, heatedly. 'You were prancing round saying how lethal it is to be touched by one of those things. You want to get your facts right, mate!'

Unsteadily it hauled itself to its feet, staggered forwards a couple of feet, and then lay down with its head resting in Tarl's lap.

'You pranny!' muttered Tarl, stroking its neck.

'Bollock-brain!' murmured the donkey, and shut its eyes again.

'Come on,' said the grinning Tyson to Guebral, 'let's leave them to it.'

Together they walked along the ship and jumped down to the shore. General Issimo was waiting for them, and his face creased into an expression of relief when he saw Tyson.

'Thank the Gods you're back,' he said. 'Any news of the rest of the Vagens?'

'They're on their way,' she told him. 'Eighty-four ships. Two and a half thousand warriors. They'll be here in three hours.'

For the first time that day the general grinned.

'Wonderful! Now, do me a favour, come and have a word with the professionals back there and tell them you're staying!'

He walked back up the beach with the two women at his side.

As they came to the top of the dyke Tyson stopped and surveyed the terrain, visualising how the twenty thousand orcs might attack.

'Do you think we can win?' she asked baldly.

'If your friend Ronan turns up with the dwarf army that he promised, we have a chance,' answered the General. Then he lowered his voice. 'Without them, we've as much chance as a piece of steak has against a mincing-machine.'

'Then we should be OK,' Tyson answered, trying to keep the doubt out of her voice. The three of them stood there, staring hopefully up at the mountains, but there wasn't a hint or a trace of movement, save for a single eagle swooping above the towering peak of Tor Tiyachip. If there was a dwarf army on the move, it was keeping very quiet about it.

The rest of the Vagen fleet sailed into the bay two and a half hours later. Sunlight broke through the clouds as ship after ship came gliding around the headland and cut through the rolling waves, each one coming gracefully to rest alongside its predecessor against the wet, grey shingle at the sea's edge. Issimo watched with relief, and gave up counting after sixty. It seemed as though he was getting the first of the several miracles he required. There must have been well over two thousand Vagens disembarking and forming up efficiently on the beach. If they fought as well as their reputation suggested, then maybe they could give the orc army something to think about.

If they fought. At the moment that seemed to be in doubt, for there was some sort of altercation going on over by the leading ship. The tall blond warrior, Marten, seemed to be having a serious argument with another Vagen, a dark, muscular man with more stubble than a recently harvested field of corn, who was armed with a vicious-looking battle-axe. A number of those near by had stopped what they were doing and were standing listening with interest.

Issimo was about to ride across and see what the problem was when the deep, sonorous sound of a battle-horn being blown echoed across the fields. Turning, he saw in the distance a couple of his scouts riding frantically towards him along the base of the dyke. They were crouched low in their saddles, urging their tiring horses onwards, and on their heels came seven Southrons mounted on the horrifying Freaks, laughing and brandishing their barbed scimitars. As Issimo watched, the scimitars flashed downwards, and the rearmost scout disappeared in a welter of spouting blood and churning hooves. A couple of the Southrons hauled their mounts to a halt, and the two Freaks circled the writhing figure on the ground, their hooves trampling and their vicious teeth tearing and rending his flesh. The other five continued their headlong pursuit of the remaining scout, gaining ground with every stride. At Issimo's order a troop of Guard cavalry galloped off through the maize on an interception course. For a moment it seemed as though they would be too late, but then the Southrons wheeled their Freaks around and galloped off to the north, yelling insults over their shoulders, and leaving the Cydorians to escort the exhausted rider to the General.

He tumbled from his mount and fell gasping at Issimo's feet, trying to stammer out his message. The general crouched down and gently placed one hand on the man's shoulder.

'Easy, easy,' he said. 'You've got plenty of time.'

'But we haven't, sire!' the scout panted. 'The orcs are barely two miles away! They'll be here within the hour!'

General Issimo jerked upright and stared northwards. The rapidly improving visibility meant he could see farther now, and he could just make out a black cloud of smoke far away above the mountainside, as though the country beyond was on fire. *Klat*, they were close!

Vaulting onto his horse he shouted out a string of orders to his underlings, and then galloped across to where Marten was still arguing with the other warrior. Things looked bad here. Behind them, all the Vagens had stopped forming up, and some were even re-embarking onto their longships. Marten and the other warrior were stood face to face and were snarling threats and insults at one another.

'OK, lads,' called the general, dismounting beside them. 'Is there a problem?'

'No problem, general,' drawled the other warrior with a lazy smile, and Issimo found himself taking an instant dislike to the man. 'By the way, I am Krage, Warleader of this expedition. No, no problem at all. We were promised that we would be fighting alongside an army of two and a half thousand Cydorians, and at least an equal number of Dwarves. There are no dwarves here. If, as I am told, the opposing army is over twenty thousand strong, then fighting without the Dwarves is the equivalent of suicide. That wasn't part of the bargain, and so we're leaving. Good day.'

He turned away and Marten, almost incoherent with rage, grabbed his arm.

'No . . . you . . . we must fight!' he stammered, but Krage just shook his hand off contemptuously. Marten grabbed him again.

'Coward!' he yelled. The word rang out as clear as a bell, and every Vagen for fifty yards stopped what they were doing and stared. Slowly and very deliberately the furious Krage raised his battle-axe until it was half an inch from Marten's nose.

'Let me spell it out,' he hissed. 'We are not here to throw our lives away uselessly. With the Dwarf army, we would fight. Without it, we stand no chance. *I* was chosen as Warleader by Kaal, our Chief, and I say we leave. And as soon as we are back on the ship, you and I are going to settle our differences. For ever.'

Marten squinted at the razor-sharp blade and swallowed painfully. The sound could be heard twenty paces away. But then another war-horn sounded, a distant one, and mere seconds later its plangent tone was echoed by a host of others, and the Grey Sea Fields rang to their call. All eyes turned to stare up at the mountains above them, whence the noise came, but at first nothing could be seen. Then all at once a host of warlike figures began to issue forth from a high pass behind a spur of Tor Tiyachip. Sunlight glinted and flashed off countless axe-heads and chain-mail coats, and banners waved and fluttered as the figures streamed down towards the waiting army like water flowing down a dry river-bed after the first winter rains.

To Krage's complete and utter chagrin, the dwarves' army had arrived in the nick of time.

Ronan had waited impatiently for more than four hours before he had been granted his audience with the Dwarves' king, Rokan-wrolin. However, the instant he had met him, Ronan had realised that the guy was a kindred spirit, if not with him, then most definitely with Tarl. In fact, the king had remembered meeting Tarl in a Welbug casino some years before and losing quite a bit of money to him at Cydorian Sweat. So when Ronan had outlined the situation, the king had only paused for a few seconds before deciding that, debts of honour and responsibilities aside, decapitating vast numbers of orcs might be rather fun.

Once the decision had been made, things had moved at a rapid pace. Even so, Ronan had been worried that they might be too late, but Rokanwrolin had assured him that they knew exactly how far the orc army had progressed, and that they would get to the battlefield in time. And so it had proved.

As they emerged from the mountain pass Ronan was deeply relieved to see the Vagen ships drawn up on the shore below them. Now they stood a chance! He climbed onto a protruding rock as the dwarves streamed past and scanned the view below. He could make out Issimo's entourage at the centre of things, and there, seated on horseback at the general's right hand, was the familiar figure of Tyson. With a song in his heart and a smile on his face, Ronan leapt down from the rock and began to jog down the hill. (He had been forced to abandon his horse before entering Zanadakan. Dwarves don't bother with horses as, firstly, they live underground, secondly, they prefer to walk everywhere, and thirdly, they have a bit of a problem with clambering up onto the things.)

It took him a while to make his way down to the Fields and across to where Issimo was directing the deployment of the allied forces, and by that time most of the decisions had been made. In truth, the General had little choice in most of them. The Dwarves, natural mountain fighters, were positioned along the foothills on the right wing of the allied army. The Cydorian Guard took the central position on the Fields. The Vagens formed the left wing along the shore beside their ships, and Krage had split them into three groups. The first, some eight hundred strong, was led by Marten, and was strung out along the top of the dyke. Krage himself led the second and largest group, which curved out from the foot of the dyke towards the Cydorians. The third group was a reserve of two hundred, led by Klaer, and positioned on the dyke behind the front lines, ready for any emergency.

Although General Issimo had ordered his cavalry to merge with the mounted professional warriors as a mobile reserve behind his army, he himself had dismounted to fight in the front rank with his men, and Tyson had decided to fight alongside him. She figured that he was the most indispensable part of the Cydorian Guard, a figurehead and inspiration to his men, and she had appointed herself his bodyguard. Ronan, when he at last caught up with her, agreed, and so the two of them stood side by side in front of the general, surrounded by nervous and frightened guardsmen, calmly swapping details of the past couple of days.

Tarl, meanwhile, had left the recuperating Puss safely wrapped up in blankets in the stern of the Vagen ship. The donkey wasn't yet strong enough to defend itself, and orcs had been known before to break off in the middle of a battle for a quick barbecue. He had briefly joined Tyson, but she had found him a horse and told him to stay with the reserve, as his magical ability was too precious to risk in the front line. Relieved, he had cantered back to the mass of mercenaries. As he joined them a loud wolf-whistle had attracted his attention, and he'd seen Blue Sonjë and Ravannon waving at him. Pleased, he had joined them, but as he sat there listening as they talked about the Thoroughbred Trophy races, he was getting a little apprehensive. There were a number of familiar faces around him, but try as he might, he couldn't find the one face he was searching for. Guebral seemed to have completely disappeared.

The orc army seeped into view around the base of the distant mountain like some foul black tide, and like the tide, it just kept on coming. The northern sky was black with smoke now, and the pounding of the orc drums and the rhythmic tramp of forty thousand feet set the ground shaking. On it came, rank after rank, file upon file, and as it came nearer an unease settled upon the allies, a creeping, gnawing doubt that seemed to worm its way into the heart and mind of every soldier.

Then, a few hundred yards away, the army stopped dead. The drums, the chanting and yelling of the orcs, the waving of banners all ceased, and it stood motionless like some vast, malignant predator waiting to pounce on its prey. Hardly a sound could be heard, and the feeling of unease grew in the hearts of the human soldiers, moving from doubt through fear towards mortal dread. Tarl could see some of the Cydorian Guard beginning to edge backwards, and although he recognised this feeling as the result of some powerful mage-spell emanating from Shikara, he too was prey to it. The urge to run, to fling down your weapons and flee for your very life was becoming by the second more and more difficult to resist.

But then, just as Tarl thought that the whole of the Guard were about to turn tail and flee the battlefield without a blow being struck, there was a now-familiar *pop* of expanding air, and Guebral materialised in the open ground to the left of the cavalry reserve, along with seven other Dead Boys. She looked across and flashed Tarl a quick wink, but then her face became a mask of concentration that was mirrored in the faces of the other seven. Tarl could feel the waves of confidence and self-belief that welled up from them and spread outwards like water, flooding over the allies and washing away the doubt and fear. He grinned, and then standing in his stirrups he cupped his hands about his mouth, and his voice rang out over the plain.

'You're going to get your *klatting* heads kicked in!' he roared, and as heads everywhere turned to stare at him he repeated the chant. Ravannon and Blue Sonjë joined in, and seconds later virtually the whole of the allied army were waving their weapons in the air and hurling the orcs' own favourite battle-chant into their faces, and the mountains echoed with the noise.

On her horse within the ranks of the orcs, Shikara sat back thoughtfully. So her *Sap Willpower* spell was being countered, eh? There were obviously some useful magic-users on the other side. Still, she could tell that they were young and inexperienced. She would wear them down in the course of the day, but for the moment it was time for her army to do the work.

Raising one hand she gestured lazily. Orc commanders snarled out orders, and as the drums began to pound out once again the vast army ground forward to attack. Two large sections peeled away from the flanks, one heading for the high ground guarded by the Dwarves, the other for the Vagens along the dyke. But the centre section, almost half of the orc army, was headed straight for the pitifully small Cydorian Guard.

The allies waited, the Dwarves calm and confident, almost

exhilarated at the prospect of fighting with their age-old enemy again, the Vagens nervous but excited, the Cydorians grim and scared, yet determined to sell their lives dearly. Arrows showered out from the approaching orcs, hitting a man here and there, but most thudded harmlessly into shields or bounded off helm or chain-mail. And then with a deafening roar the orcs charged.

To the rear, Tarl stared nervously forwards and tried to make out what was happening. Beyond the frail lines of Cydorians he could see the black banners of the enemy waving in what seemed to be their thousands, and the shock-wave as the first ranks smashed into the defenders could almost be felt. Apprehensively he glanced across to Guebral and the Dead Boys. They were knelt in a little group, their eyes closed, their faces set in rigid lines of concentration. Tarl knew how important they were. He could still sense the Power of Shikara's spell hovering, ready to seep into the minds of the allied army and fill them with doubt. It was vital that the Dead Boys counteract this, or the battle was lost. He wished he could help them, but he knew that his Power wasn't up to it. He was better off acting as a soldier, using his magic as a weapon. Unfortunately, this meant that he was going to have to get uncomfortably close to the action.

Tarl swallowed, desperately trying to keep control of the contents of his stomach. Not for the last time, he wished that he had never left that nice, safe, comfortable job in Orcville's Blue Balrog club . . .

The main body of orcs smashed into the Cydorians like a hammer-blow, and yet somehow the line held. Desperately the men fought, for orc blades seemed to be coming at them from all angles and the viciously barbed points of the long Ferder lances jabbed through the enemy ranks at them from other orcs behind. Steel clashed with steel, blade sliced through flesh, the agonised screams of the wounded filled the air, and the ground became slippery with red and black blood. But at the centre of it all stood Issimo, his voice ringing out above the sounds of battle as he called encouragement to his men. Above him flew the Standard of Cydor, a white *taboghee* flower on a green background, and beside him fought Ronan and Tyson. Ronan's vast sword wrought havoc, his mighty two-handed blows capable of slicing an orc clean in two, and Tyson's arm struck faster than a snake as her blade flickered in and out. No orc could come near them, and the pile of bodies in front of them grew. But for every orc that fell, another took its place, and slowly, gradually, the Cydorians began to be driven backwards.

The left wing of the orc army attacked the Dwarves with slightly less enthusiasm, for orcs and Dwarves are old enemies. There has always been something about the squat, powerful figures with their forked beards, glittering eyes and whirling, razor-edged battle-axes that orcs find distinctly unsettling. Even so, they pressed home their attack with ardour. Grimly, silently the Dwarves defended, and though they were outnumbered two to one, yet still they held their positions on the hill, and the orcs could make no progress against them. But though the Dwarves held, they too could make no forward progress, and on the Fields below they could see their Cydorian allies being pushed backwards by sheer weight of numbers.

For a moment the orc attack faltered, and as Rokanwrolin regrouped his men the thought of counter-attacking was in his mind. But then another large section of the main orc army wheeled leftwards to join the attack on the Dwarves, and from their blood-red banners Rokanwrolin could tell that they were Easterlings, not orcs, men with no in-built fear of his people to overcome. Sighing, he ordered his army to stand firm against the next attack, and they waited grimly as the second wave began to roll inexorably up the hill towards them.

The orcs' right wing attacked the Vagens on a broad front. The dyke, however, was steep and high, and the orcs found it difficult to climb. Some scaled it further north and tried to attack along the top, but the Vagens had barricaded it here, driving sharpened stakes into the earth and down the beach to the sea's edge, and the northernmost end of Marten's force defended this with ease. Many orcs managed to scale the slope and attacked his troops, but they were easily held. The majority, however, slanted south-wards along the foot of the dyke and smashed home into Krage's waiting section. The fighting here was fierce and bloody, far worse than anything the Vagens had ever known, yet their training and self-belief held good. Though many fell, their stylish leather jerkins ripped and torn, their linen shirts soaked with blood, the flashing Orcbane blades of their colleagues took ample revenge. And at their centre, Krage's whirling battle-axe was a barrier that no orc could pass.

In the centre, the Cydorians still gave ground. This was usually a good tactic, as the attackers were hindered by the slippy, blood-soaked ground and the mass of bodies, but such was the weight of attack and the carnage amongst the defenders that the gradual retreat was in danger of becoming a rout. And yet somehow Issimo, his voice hoarse and cracking, managed to rally his troops. Still the standard flew above his head, and Ronan and Tyson fought beside him. Vast numbers of orcs had died, yet still they pressed forwards. And then all at once it seemed to Ronan as though the weight of attack on their segment of the front had slackened, although the Cydorians to the left were as hard-pressed as ever. For a moment he leaned upon his sword, thinking that they might be prevailing. But then the orc attackers parted, leaving a gap that pointed like an arrow straight at the centre of the Cydorian line, and through this gap came charging a great mass of Southrons mounted on the fearsome Freaks.

For an instant there was a deathly silence within the Cydorians' ranks, as every soldier saw the horror that approached, and then the cavalry smashed into the line in a welter of ripping teeth, slashing hooves and hacking scimitars. Still Issimo stood firm, as did those men beside him, but elsewhere the line crumbled as Cydorians turned to flee, and the gloating Southrons pursued them, hacking them down as they fled.

Along the dyke the orc attack had become fiercer, but Marten's men were managing to hold the top, though many had fallen. To the rear, Klaer was watching carefully, trying to gauge the moment when her reserve force would need to be thrown into the struggle, when beside her Dene suddenly grabbed her arm.

'Look!' he yelled. 'Down by the ships!'

A platoon of some fifty Easterlings had swum unseen around the end of the barricade, and had come ashore by the ships. One had even managed to bring a lighted torch with him, and others were unwrapping waterproofed torches and lighting them from his. The threat to the ships was obvious. Klaer knew that if the battle was lost, not a Vagen would escape alive without the fleet to aid their escape. Reacting instantly, she yelled the order to attack and charged down the beach with the rest of the reserve at her heels.

The instant that the Southrons appeared through the heart of the orc army, the commander of the Cydorians' reserve grabbed his war-horn and sounded the order to charge. One moment Tarl was sitting placidly on horseback, watching the battle from comparative safety, the next moment he found himself part of a hurtling, pell-mell charge towards the enemy. He looked about him to see where Ravannon and her friends were, but they seemed to have vanished. Suddenly the butterflies were fluttering away in his stomach, and the old familiar sparks were skittering out from the ends of his fingers. This time, he thought, keep control of the Power. Don't let it all out in one big explosion. Keep control. And then they were threading their way through fleeing guardsmen, and a red-eyed, slavering Freak was charging straight at him.

The shingle clutched at the Vagens' running feet like mud, slowing them down badly. Two hundred yards ahead, the Easterlings' torches blazed into life. Dene realised that they were going to be too late. By the time Klaer and the others had managed to cut down the enemy, several of the longships would be well ablaze. With the way they were beached right next to each other, the blaze could spread right along the line of ships in minutes. But he had learned something from his time with Marten. Quickly he muttered a desperate invocation to Arfebraun, the Vagen God of Fire, praying that the torches would burn long and hard with a fierce, unquenchable fire. Instantly, every single one went out as though doused with cold water. And then Klaer's troops reached the Easterlings, and the slaughter began.

The Southron rider screamed a terrifying war-cry, his fearsomely painted face creased in a rictus of hate, his raised scimitar ready to carve through flesh and bone, but somehow Tarl's control held. He flung his hand up, pointing at the charging Freak, but instead of letting the Power flood out of him in one vast release, he squeezed one tiny fraction out, and then bit down on the rest. As a result, a single small red fireball burst out of his fingers and blew the Freak's head clean off. The beast crashed to the floor, sending its rider flying beneath Tarl's pounding hooves, and Tarl reined in his horse and stared round frantically.

In front of him, the entire reserve were fighting hand to hand with the main body of Southrons, but all around him other Southrons were freely chasing after fleeing Guards. Aiming carefully he squeezed off another fireball, again blowing the head off a Freak, but this time the Cydorian it was pursuing saw what had happened and, as the rider came crashing to the ground, he turned back with an expression of cold fury on his face and hewed the Southron's head clean off. The same thing happened when Tarl blew up a third Freak, but this time the struggling rider was hacked to pieces by two Guards.

That was more like it! With a smile on his face, Tarl began to ride round the rear of the Cydorian line, methodically destroying every pursuing Southron mount that came in sight, and leaving their riders to the vengeance of the Cydorian infantry. Gradually, the hunting Southron cossacks became the hunted, and the fleeing Cydorians regrouped.

On the hill-side, the weight of advancing Easterlings pressed home against the Dwarves, yet still they stood firm. Bit by bit the struggle fragmented, and man, orc and dwarf hunted each other about the broken rocks and hummocks. The dead bodies mounted, but somehow the dwarves held firm. Their axes hummed and sang through the air, and imperceptibly, gradually, they began to push their enemies back down the hill.

To the rear of the battle, the Dead Boys knelt on the ground, their eyes still tightly closed, their faces strained and tense. Shikara's Power was almost too much for them, even working together, yet still they strove to stop her spreading her dark mage-spell of despair over the allied army. Their minds were engrossed in this to the exclusion of everything else, and all their other senses were shut down. And so they were completely unaware of the squadron of twenty Southron cavalry that burst through the Cydorian line and bore down on them with scimitars raised.

The battle raged on along the length of the dyke. At its foot the bodies were piled three or four high now, and the attacking orcs could hardly gain a foothold on the blood-soaked slopes, yet still they pressed forwards. At the north end they had managed to dislodge most of the barricade of stakes, and here Harald Silverbeard stood with his followers, grimly but determinedly defending the flank. But as the pressure on the dyke slowly eased, so it increased on the Vagens in Krage's section. Vast numbers of orcs were slowly pushing them backwards, and their line was being stretched to breaking point.

From his vantage-point on the dyke Marten could see that Krage was in imminent danger of being swamped. Where the *klat* was the reserve? He turned to gesture to Klaer, but she and her entire section had disappeared. Marten stared to the south, baffled, unaware of the struggle on the beach behind him, and then turned back to the battle. Something had to be done! If Krage's men were pushed further back and the line broke, the orcs would be up on the dyke south of Marten, and he and his men would be cut to pieces. There was only one thing for it.

'Vagens! To me! Charge!' he roared, striving to lift his voice above the sounds of battle. Only a hundred or so of the nearest warriors heard him, but as he leapt forward and slithered down the slope they followed him, yelling his name. Their momentum took them straight through the orcs trying to scale the slope and, leaping over the heaped bodies, they burst upon the flank of the enemy like a thunderclap. For a while the surprise of their attack carried them forwards, but then the orcs turned to face them, and the struggle turned into a confused mass of hacking, slicing, screaming fighters.

Marten's arm was aching now, and his shield was riven and useless. Throwing it aside, he used both hands to wield his sword. His head ached with the noise and the clamour, and the sweat rolled down his brow into his eyes, nearly blinding him. Back and forth his sword hacked, and orc after orc fell before it, but still more pressed forwards to take their place, and he began to realise that soon, sheer exhaustion would defeat him and one of their countless blades would find a way past his defence. And then his foot slipped from under him, and three howling orcs leapt forward with raised swords.

In the centre, too, the battle had lost its shape, deteriorating into a series of individual struggles. Issimo still stood beneath the banner with Ronan and Tyson beside him as the fighting flowed about them. At one point, although the battle raged all around, no orcs faced them, and they were able to draw breath for a moment. Ronan heard the sound of a horse cantering up to their rear, and turned in time to see Tarl slipping out of the saddle to join them. He looked tired and spent, but was just about able to dredge up enough Power to generate a rather soggy and slow-moving fireball that was still strong enough to blow the head off a charging Freak, and Tyson stepped swiftly forwards to dispatch its rider with one clean stroke. But then another mass of orcs charged them, and once again they found themselves fighting for their lives.

When the cavalry reserve had attacked the Southrons, Tarl had been unable to find Ravannon and her four friends for the simple reason that they had not joined the charge. Tarl had told her about the Dead Boys, and she had immediately grasped their importance to the allies. She had a feeling that they needed to be protected, and so when the twenty cossacks burst through the lines and sped towards them, she and her four friends were ready. Urging their mounts into a gallop, they raced to intercept the Southrons, who turned to face them, grinning confidently.

But although they were only five against twenty, Ravannon and the others had dedicated their lives to fighting on horseback. Their thoroughbred mounts with their sharp, metal-shod hooves were the equal of the Freaks, and fought as one unit with their riders. Five of the Southrons had fallen before a scimitar-blow from behind neatly decapitated Blue Sonjë. Six more died before one of the Freaks fastened its teeth into Bathsuke's leg, and she was dragged from the saddle to be trampled under the hooves. But still the other Southrons fought on.

Then one Freak broke free of the skirmish and rode furiously towards the motionless Dead Boys. Ravannon and Judge were still fighting for their lives, but Kaz the Knife managed to drag

Slingshot round and rode after him. The Southron's Freak reared as he hauled on its reins, and his lethal scimitar rose and fell twice in succession. Two of the still figures sank to the ground in lifeless heaps, but as he raised his weapon a third time Kaz's arm whipped forwards, and her foot-long knife sank up to its hilt in his exposed armpit. Wordlessly he toppled out of the saddle, and she twitched Slingshot sideways to trample him underfoot before dragging the great horse round and charging back into the fray. Three more of the Southrons fell, and then the rest were fleeing back towards the enemy lines.

Ravannon wiped her dripping sword and sheathed it, and then leaving Kaz to bandage the gaping slash that a scimitar had left down the length of Judge's arm, she rode across to the Dead Boys. One of them, a man whose skin seemed to be covered in tattoos, lay face-down, his head almost cloven in two. Another lay on his back, his neck nearly severed, his metal hands stained crimson with his own blood. But six of them knelt there unharmed, their eyes closed, their faces twisted with the strain as they strove to keep Shikara's spells at bay.

On his knees, Marten plunged his sword forwards, skewering one of the orcs, and then desperately hauled it free to parry the blows of the other two. But the muscles of his arms were aching so much now that they shook, and one of the orcs, a large powerful *Uttuk*, brushed his sword aside with ease. The other drew back its blade with a grin, but then a battle-axe hummed past Marten's head to slam into its throat, and black blood fountained high into the air. Krage stepped past Marten, hauled his axe back, and slammed it deep into the *Uttuk*'s side. But in his haste, the Vagen Warleader had exposed his flank. An orc stabbed forwards, and the red-smeared tip of its sword burst out through Krage's side in front of Marten's horrified eyes. The battle-axe fell from Krage's hands, and he sagged backwards. A roar of triumph went up from the attacking orcs and they surged forwards, scenting victory. But then a red mist seemed to envelop Marten. Roaring with anger he grabbed the fallen axe and struck Krage's slayer so hard a blow in the chest that the axe burst clean through in a spray of blood, almost severing the top third of its body. He turned just in time to see Krage's smile of satisfaction as he was avenged, and then the

Vagen leader's eyes rolled up in his head and he slumped to the ground.

Then Marten went berserk, hewing, slicing, hacking with the axe, and no enemy could stand in his path. He was dimly aware of Klaer and her troops surging over the dyke and slamming into the orcs' flank, but the next thing he knew was that everywhere the enemy were running, fleeing, streaming from the battlefield in front of him. He saw Dene striding towards him, a red-tipped sword in his hand, a look of triumph on his face, but then his head began to spin, and he knew no more.

On the hill-side too, orcs and Easterlings were running. The Dwarves had held, although it had been a close-run thing, and many of their number lay dead or injured. But those that could still fight streamed down towards the Fields, for they could see that the Cydorians and their enemies were still locked together, and the battle could yet go either way.

Issimo and the others seemed to be fighting in a sea of enemies. Few of his men were left now, and those that still stood were desperately tired. One by one they dropped, until only Ronan, Tyson, Tarl and five others stood by the General, and still the orcs came at them. And though the others tired, still Ronan wielded his sword in lethal, two-handed blows, and no enemy could withstand him. But then an onslaught fiercer than all the rest began. Three of the Guards died, and then a fourth, and then a lance stabbed through the throng of enemies, piercing Issimo's chest. Gasping, he sagged backwards, and the standard-bearer behind him dropped the banner to cradle the dying General in his arms. Beside them Tarl grabbed the standard and waved it defiantly, but an arrow came from nowhere and buried itself in his left shoulder. Crying out in agony he fell to the ground, and as his eyes closed the last sight he had was of Ronan and Tyson fighting back to back, surrounded by orcs.

Guebral's eyes flew open, and she stared around, dazed. Although she had needed total concentration to fight against Shikara's Power, she had kept one last vestige of her mental senses attuned to Tarl, and she had heard his wounded cry. Wincing at the sight of Image and Shiftfister lying dead on the grass, she got shakily to her feet, and then looked at the others. They were going to have to do without her for a while. She had a man to save.

With the last of her strength Tyson drove her sword home in the throat of the massive *Uttuk* to the left of her, but not before it had caught Ronan a glancing blow on the head with its war-club. Dazed, he sank to his knees, and Tyson stood over him, ready to defend him if necessary, but suddenly there didn't seem to be any orcs left.

There was a soft *pop* behind her, and Guebral materialised right beside the wounded Tarl. Tyson gave her a tired smile, but when she turned her head back to the front she saw that Shikara was striding through the ranks of dead bodies towards them, her face a mask of frustrated rage. Exhaustedly Tyson tried to raise her sword, but found to her horror that she seemed to be frozen in position. Shikara must have placed some sort of mage-spell on her, and she was helpless. Try as she might, she could not get her trapped muscles to respond.

But then Shikara stopped a few feet away, her face rigid with concentration. Out of the corner of one eye, Tyson could see Guebral kneeling beside Tarl with one arm raised, and the ring on her finger was pulsing with a green glow. There seemed to be some mental battle going on, some sort of Power struggle between the two of them. Tyson realised that Guebral was holding Shikara at bay, but from the strained expression on her face it was obvious that she could not do so for long, and a triumphant smile began to play around the sorceress's lips.

Desperately Tyson strove to break free from the hold that Shikara had put on her, but in vain. And then the odds shifted even more against her. A single orc archer suddenly rose from amongst the bodies and stood there, its mouth curved in a snarl, an arrow fitted to its bow. Shikara grinned openly.

'Shoot her,' she commanded. 'Not the warrior woman. The little scrawny one kneeling down, with the ring on her finger. Shoot *her*.'

Tyson watched helplessly as the orc grinned mirthlessly, and then raising its bow it fired the arrow unerringly straight between Shikara's shoulder-blades. With a startled shriek she slumped forwards to her knees, and Tyson could almost physically feel Guebral's mind-power wresting control from the wounded sorceress. Suddenly she found that she had control of her body again, and summoning one last effort she staggered forwards and thrust the point of her sword into Shikara's throat. For an instant the sorceress stared up into her eyes, and she could feel the woman's Power struggling to spring free of Guebral's grip, but then Shikara's eyes rolled upwards and her lifeless body slumped to the ground.

For a few moments Tyson leant tiredly on her sword and dragged air into her labouring lungs, and then she looked round. At her feet, Ronan had sat up and was dazedly shaking his head. Behind her, Guebral was hugging the wounded Tarl, but Tyson could see that he was still breathing, and having witnessed what the girl could do for sick donkeys, she didn't think he was in too much danger.

A few paces away, the orc archer had slumped to the ground amidst the bodies and was snivelling to itself. Sword at the ready, Tyson strode threateningly across.

'Why did you do that?' she demanded. 'Why did you shoot your commander?'

Chigger looked up at the terrifying woman warrior and shrugged his shoulders tiredly.

'That mad bitch has dragged us half-way across Midworld,' he said, 'and quite frankly, I've had enough! I just want to go home to the wife and kids!'

And the homesick orc buried his head in his hands and started quietly weeping.

Beside the dyke, Marten staggered to his feet and shook his head to clear it. Next to him, Dene was leaping about excitedly, yelling, 'We did it, we did it!' Dazedly he looked around. There were bodies everywhere, but the only living people on this part of the battlefield were Vagen. By the Gods, Dene was right! They had done it!

And then Klaer came striding apprehensively through the bodies, with Fjonë at her side. The worried look on her face was instantly transformed into one of relief when she saw him standing upright.

'You're OK!' she gasped, and Marten drew breath to tell her that yes, he was fine, save for one or two cuts and bruises. But he couldn't, because she grabbed him and started kissing him so fiercely that for one wonderful moment he thought he was going to pass out again. Then he returned her kiss with interest.

Dene watched them avidly. Wonderful, he thought. That's the way to treat a battle-comrade. Happily he turned to Fjonë.

'You're OK!' he gasped, in much the same manner as Klaer, and then he grabbed the startled woman and kissed her. Fjonë too responded, but in a rather different way to Marten.

And so Dene became the last allied casualty of the Battle of Grey Sea Fields. He was also the only one who had to be treated for badly bruised testicles.

ENDINGS

Don't overlook Yai'El's canal architecture. Sure, the Night-fire is spectacular, and everyone knows about the Bird Market, but you'll be amazed at the sheer beauty of the waterside structures. Check out the exquisitely carved wooden lock-gates and the wonderful marble quaysides. Yai'El locks and quays are renowned the world over.

The Rough Chronicle to Cydor

Tyson sat on the bench of the open-air restaurant feeling happier than she had ever thought possible. The table in front of her was littered with used plates and nearly empty glasses and bottles. Ronan was next to her with his massive arm draped around her shoulders, and Tarl and Guebral were sat on the other side of the table. Tarl's shoulder was bandaged and supported by a sling, but he was on the mend. The fully recovered Puss was flat-out on the ground beside them with its muzzle buried in a huge plate of *mulampos*, and Tarl had been cracking them all up with descriptions of the after-effects the last time that the little donkey had eaten the fiery dish.

'And of course trumpet-bum was underneath the restaurant table, hidden by the table-cloth,' finished Tarl. 'No one knew he was there. Every single diner in the place was holding their nose and staring at me with a disgusted look on their face. Except for one guy, who owned a cabaret bar. He came across and asked me if I'd ever thought of going into show business.'

He finished his story and grinned happily at Guebral. Tyson watched the two of them, fascinated. A change had come over Tarl. The furtiveness had gone, to be replaced by an open friendliness. He no longer looked like someone who would deal cards off the bottom of the pack the minute your back was turned. He looked like someone who would deal cards off the bottom of the pack to your face, in an honest and friendly way, and then would probably buy you a drink with your own money after you'd lost it all.

He and Guebral were a good match, though. Tyson listened as they began a discussion on the merits of the various poker games in town. Tarl was in favour of heading off to the regular Cydorian Sweat school in the back room at Gondilla's Heartburn Café, whereas Guebral was keen on playing her usual game of Stud at the North Star tavern. Having discovered what the other wanted to do, each of them began to argue that this was what they would rather do as well, really. Tyson grimaced. It was so touching it almost made you sick.

She knocked back the last of her wine and looked up at Ronan. He was staring across the canal, but his eyes were far away and there was a set look on his face, a look she recognised. The look of a man who knows that he has serious wrongs to right and is wondering how to go about doing so. She dug him in the ribs with one finger.

'Not yet, we don't,' she said to him.

'Hmph? Eh? What?' he said, a little guiltily. 'We don't what?'

'You're thinking about going after the board of the Orcbane Sword Corporation, aren't you, babe?'

'Damn right. We can't let those immoral creeps get away with it. We'll have to do something about them.'

'But first we need a holiday, right?'

'Right.' Ronan nodded, and then clicked his fingers. 'Oh, I meant to tell you – Tarl fixed it up with Dene. He and Marten are calling in here for a few days on their way home. Then they're going to sail us down to Perplec, and we can laze around there for a while.'

Tyson smiled and leant back against his arm. Perplec was reputedly one of the most beautiful cities in Midworld. Built at the mouth of the river Errone, it also had the best fish restaurants in Iduin, a thriving wine industry, and stretching away to the south, miles of unspoilt beaches lapped by the warm waters of the Maelvanta Sea. The biggest worry there would be whether she should go and have some lunch, lie on the beach a bit longer, or drag her man back to their room for a little love-making.

She sighed happily. It was good to be part of a team, instead of being on her own. And it would be nice to see Marten and Dene again. She wondered how they were doing, and if they had managed to organise Krage's traditional Vagen funeral all right. She would quite like to have been there for that.

Marten and Dene stood on the hill overlooking the beach with the twenty other Vagens who had volunteered to stay behind for the funeral, watching proudly as the burning longship that bore Krage's body sailed out into the bay. It was a solemn, sad moment, and strangely moving, but Marten felt almost elated. It had been years since anyone had been accorded the honour of a traditional funeral, but when Marten had suggested it, the rest of the tribe had been all in favour. But it was strange how unpopular Krage had turned out to be after his death. Hardly anyone had wanted to hang about to see him sent off to Valhalla with full honours. Even Klaer and Kamila had gone back home.

Marten thought this was a shame, because they had really done Krage proud. They had laid his corpse at the front of the longship on an elevated platform of silver birch (symbolic of riches to come in the afterlife). At his feet they had laid a golden eagle (symbolic of yet more riches). Beside him, so that he could be fully prepared for the next world, they had placed his weapons, his appointments notebook, a tub of hair-gel and a tube of breath-freshener. To his lapel they had affixed a name-tag that read 'Hi, my name is Krage', to avoid the need for formal introductions in Valhalla.

Then they had piled kindling and dry brushwood about the platform. Marten had held a lighted torch aloft, and had said a few words about what a good sort of bloke Krage had been, how they would miss him, and how the Vagen tribe wouldn't be the same without him. Then he had laid the inscribed silver letter-opener in the corpse's folded hands (it said 'To Krage, from all the tribe, wishing you good luck in your new life'), and had plunged the torch deep into the brushwood before leaping ashore.

They had loosed the mooring-ropes, and the off-shore breeze had filled the single sail. Now the longship was heading out to sea, and the roaring flames were licking about the corpse that was its only passenger. It truly was a stirring sight.

Marten squinted sideways at the others as they stood watching the ship and awaiting his orders, and smiled to himself. There wasn't much to this leadership business, really. From the moment after the battle when Klaer had proposed him as the new Warleader, he'd taken to it like a goat to . . . no, like a duck to water. All you had to do was plan ahead and issue a few confident-sounding orders, and other people took care of the details for you. In just three days he had liaised with the other allied armies, taken care of all the dead, and had worked out and signed a non-aggression pact with the new leader of the Cydorians, Rord Stryk. Now Krage's funeral had gone like clockwork, and they could sail home. And when they got there, he had one or two little plans that he could start putting into practice.

Marten grinned openly. Lobbo had been right! He was a born leader! Beside him, Dene shifted uneasily and then coughed a little anxiously.

'Marten?'

Marten watched the longship for a few more seconds. It was a stirring sight, right enough.

'What?' he answered out of the corner of his mouth.

There was a moment's pause.

'That's our only boat. How are we going to get home?'

Suddenly there was a yawning chasm where Marten's stomach had been, as the slow realisation of what a spectacularly stupid thing he had done crept over him.

'*Klat!* We've got to get it back!'

Quickly he yelled out orders to the others. Unfortunately, this time they didn't go down too well.

It would have been an interesting lesson in Vagen culture for any spectators who might have been watching. They would have gone home with the impression that, at funerals, the Vagens burnt the corpse on a boat and then chased two of their number round the countryside, throwing large rocks at them. And it was a very interesting lesson for Marten. It taught him in no uncertain terms that this leadership thing wasn't going to be quite such a smooth ride as he had imagined.

APPENDIX ONE

Unfamiliar words or concepts that are not covered below may be found in the appendix to *Ronan the Barbarian*.

ANTHIA – A fern with distinctive reddish fronds that grows in Iduin and Nevin. Dried and powdered it is used in Atrovian cookery, and provides both the distinctive taste and the unpleasant after-effects of this cuisine. It is a powerful purgative, and according to elven herbalists a small rolled-up portion of the frond makes an excellent and remarkably quick-acting laxative when inserted anally. Hence the old Iduinian saying, 'With fronds like that, who needs enemas'.

BARROT – A small and incredibly friendly furry animal which just *loves* humans. Young *barrots* tend to attach themselves to the first person they see after their eyes open, and they remain firmly devoted to that person for the rest of their life. There are numerous stories of *barrots* that have been left behind when families move house, only to turn up months later after tracking their owners over hundreds of miles. In fact, they would make the perfect pet if it wasn't for one slight drawback – their dietary habits.

Barrots are extremely greedy and will eat anything. However, their stomach is adapted to digest only their natural food – the leaves of the *gulada* plant. It is unable to cope with anything else, and immediately regurgitates it. This means that your sweet little *barrot* will spend half its time eating your shoes, clothes, ornaments or furniture, and the rest of its time blowing chunks all over the carpet. This has given rise to the rumour that when people move, many *barrots* have been left behind accidentally on purpose. As we have seen, this is a strategy that doesn't work too well. A *barrot* really is for life.

Incidentally, there is a flourishing and unusually honest building firm in Welbug that has named its houses *Barrots*, on the grounds that once you've acquired one, you may not find it too easy to get rid of.

BEWILDEBEEST – A migratory antelope-like ungulate that roams the plains of Cydor and Behan. *Bewildebeests* have the shortest memory retention span of any large animal (usually no longer than four seconds), and are frequently found milling about in large herds in the middle of the plains, trying to remember just why it was that they migrated there in the first place.

BRAAL – The Goddess of Atheists, which is probably the most unrewarding job in the whole pantheon. Braal hasn't received a single prayer for nearly two centuries, and after sitting around for one hundred and ninety-seven years filing her nails, doing the crossword in the *Valhalla Times* and drinking endless cups of nectar she would like it to be known that *any* prayer from *any* person, no matter how weird, would be ever so welcome.

BULLOW – A wild-flower with aggressively sharp, spiky leaves, rather like a thistle with attitude.

DRAIN-WORM – An aquatic snake found in the canals of the city of Yai'El. They are extremely slimy and highly venomous, and are often employed by tabloid newspapers as gossip columnists.

FALANA – A parasitic marine worm, distantly related to the *maremma-leech* [q.v.], which attaches itself to whales or large fish and sucks their blood. *Falanas* are lethal to humans, as they are about eight feet long and have a suck like an industrial vacuum cleaner. Once attached they have been known to turn a full-grown man completely inside out in seconds.

FREAKS – Mutated horses bred by Southron cossacks, and noted for their ferocity. They are carnivorous, and have six-inch long fangs and taloned fetlocks. Their meat, however, is a great orc delicacy, being both extremely tasty and remarkably filling. Hence the old orc saying, 'I'm as full as if I'd just had a freak-horse meal'.

HAPPY-ONIONS – Grown mainly in the elven realm of Nevin, *happy-onions* are similar in most ways to the normal variety of onion. However, when sliced they give off fumes that contain nitrous oxide (or laughing gas), as well as a mild narcotic, and so instead of crying, people tend to burst into fits of uncontrollable giggles. As regards taste, they are no better than normal onions, but they are certainly much more fun to cook with.

HARI THE SHIPWRIGHT – Probably the most reviled and despised Vagen of all time. Hari was a skilled and clever shipwright, but something of a traditionalist. When the Vagens decided they wished to build a huge new vessel, capable of mounting raids as far away as the Northern Mountains, Hari was put in charge. There were many rumours at the time of strange new vessels being built by the dwarves of western Frundor, vessels clad in iron that were all but unsinkable in battle. Most Vagens wanted their new boat to be so built, but Hari would have none of this, and averred that it would be made solely from wood, in the traditional way.

And so it was. The keel was of oak, the masts of ash, and the deck was of finest blackwood, stolen from the timber-yards of Perplec in the largest Vagen raid ever mounted. Even the massive anchor was of wood, hewn from the bole of a single yew tree by Hari himself. But this was his undoing.

When the ship was launched, Vagens from every village in the Maelvanta Islands gathered and watched in awe. The *Mithril Storm* was bigger than six longships put together, yet slid through the water as lightly and as quickly as a pleasure yacht. But as they watched a squall blew up, driving the ship northwards. Her captain sought shelter in a bay on the south coast of Scawdror, but when he let down the massive wooden anchor, it floated. The *Mithril Storm* was driven on to the rocks and pounded to pieces. Nine Vagens lost their lives.

Unsurprisingly, Hari was blamed for this disaster. He found himself ostracised by the rest of the Vagens, and everywhere he went, people would shout scorn and abuse at him, reminding him of the stupidity of making an anchor out of wood. These cat-calls have slipped into their language as a term of abuse, and to this day Vagens still greet those whom they despise with cries of 'yew anchor'.

KLAT – The inclusion of this orcish swear-word in the Chronicles of Ronan has produced a deluge of enquiries from intrigued readers who wish to know its exact meaning. Once again we are prevented from elaborating by the bounds of good taste. However, the following hint may be of use.

Imagine a small and rather cute hamster sitting on the table in front of you, minding its own business. Imagine that you are holding a large lump-hammer in your right hand. Smash this down as hard as you can on to the hamster. Right? OK. That hamster is now well and truly *klatted*.

We hope this is of some help.

LENKAT – A swift and savage predator with sleek hair and masses of gleaming, razor-sharp teeth, rather like a cross between a large cheetah and the entire Osmond family, but even more unpleasant to meet.

MAREMMA-LEECH – Otherwise known as the human-leech, this is an unpleasant worm-like parasite found in marshy areas, which attaches itself firmly to a host and sucks its blood. It is one of two species of leech found in Midworld, the other being the orc-leech, which has adapted over the years to tolerate the high alcohol content of orc blood. They are quite easy to tell apart, as the orc-leech spends a lot of time mumbling to itself (occasionally pausing to sing very out-of-tune songs), and throwing up in corners. The best way to get rid of a maremma-leech is to soak it in alcohol, which kills it. The best way to get rid of an orc-leech is to give up alcohol. After a couple of days of sobriety the orc-leech usually gets fed up, and drops off to go and find a host who is a bit more fun.

MASTIC – A style of decorative wood-carving developed by Rikko the Dubious, the elven craftsman of Clorton. Owing to an unfortunate fixation, he had the habit of decorating most of the wonderful pieces of furniture he made with carvings that bore a distinct resemblance to the female breast, and, as he got older, these carvings became more and more extreme. Nowadays his furniture is in great demand for the more up-market brothels and bordellos. Rikko himself is, alas, currently incarcerated in the

Welbug Home for Sad Old Pervs. He still practises his talents, however, and the banisters there are said to be a most remarkable sight.

MEGOCERI – Vast, lizard-like creatures that were prevalent in Iduin during the First Age. They were characterised by two main features: a rapacious and continuous hunger, and a complete lack of even the slightest vestige of intelligence. Highly dangerous, they would literally eat anything that moved. People, animals, falling trees, a landslide, anything. However, by the Second Age the species had been all but wiped out by chronic indigestion, and the few that still prowled the depths of the Great Desert were comparatively safe, being restricted to a diet of antacid tablets and rice pudding. In recent years, semi-domesticated *megoceri* have been bred for racing in the Terrordrome at Velos.

PASARONI – A Behanian sausage made from pork, garlic, chopped ham, garlic, pepper, garlic, herbs, salt, and garlic. Extra garlic is often added, just to spice it up a bit. *Pasaroni* is particularly useful during decorating as you will find that, after eating it, your breath will strip off the old wallpaper in seconds.

SALEMON THE SHITE – An incredibly inept wizard who toured the clubs of the Northern Mountains for a while with his conjuring act. His speciality tricks included Getting a Rabbit Irretrievably Stuck in a Top Hat, and Sawing an Assistant in Half and Killing Them. He eventually switched to a sword-swallowing act, but died on stage after being so moved by the first round of applause he had ever received that he took a bow while the sword was still inside his throat.

SKARRADS – Large primitive fish, remnants of prehistoric times. They are gentle vegetarians, living entirely on a diet of kelps and sea-weed. The fact that they kill hundreds of people every year is due entirely to their extremely rudimentary sensory perception apparatus and their vestigial brain. They tend to swim along with their mouths open, grabbing whatever they happen to come across, in the vague expectation that it must be some variety of seaweed. Unfortunately for the many bathers that get grabbed, by the time your average *skarrad* has figured out that seaweed hasn't got any legs and doesn't usually thrash about screaming when you pull it underwater, it is too late.

SPAV – An extremely obscene orc word. In the more unenlightened countries of the world we would probably not be allowed to print a translation of its meaning, but this is modern-day Britain, so here goes. A *spav* is a ██ or an ██, although the word is often used to refer to a ███ with moist ██s. However, coarse elements frequently use the term when referring to ██ing the █████ with a ██ (which is, of course, illegal).

SWING-BALL – An orcish ball-game that is highly popular during raucous orc parties. It is best played when extremely drunk. The rules of the game are as follows. One player attempts to hit his opponent's balls as hard as possible with a heavy wooden bat. His opponent then in turn attempts to hit the first player's balls as hard as possible. The loser is the first one to pass out from the pain.

TOAD-WAX – A jet-black substance used in the manufacture of cheap candles by Gloïn Brothers Inc., a family firm of Dwarves based in the Chrome Mountains. The exact method of production of toad-wax is, mercifully, a closely guarded secret, but it is rumoured to include the slow boiling of large numbers of toads in vast metal cauldrons. A few courageous animal rights protesters from the city of Mel did once attempt to gain access to the underground factory of Gloïn Brothers, but nothing has ever been heard of them since. However, there was a very strong rumour that, a few weeks afterwards, Gloïn Brothers were selling a new range of animal-rights-campaigner-wax candles. The only conclusion that can safely be drawn from this is that you don't *klat* about with dwarves.

TERRORDROME – The vast amphitheatre in the city of Velos, in Iduin. Originally, the large oval track was used for horse or chariot races, but over the years public demand for newer, more spectacular forms of entertainment led eventually to events such as the hugely dangerous *megoceri* races of today. Even domesticated *megoceri* are rapaciously savage, and as a result their jockeys lead a short but extremely exciting life. Betting is heavy, and the public are able to wager on who will win the race, how many will finish, how many jockeys will be killed, and whether the crowd will be attacked, pursued, trampled, or even eaten. Champion jockey last season was Ligger Pottes, who managed to win three races before being torn into bloody fragments in the finishing straight by Crusp, his mount in the Velos Gold Cup.

VENDAI STRIP – That part of the Street of Night in Atro which is occupied exclusively by inns, taverns, elf-weed bars, cafés, gambling dens and night-clubs, and which is named after the folk that first settled there. The Vendai were a tribe of extremely intelligent elves who traditionally placed the utmost importance on the enjoyment of life. The most highly venerated members of their society were musicians, actors, brewers, comedians, chefs and publicans. Under Vendai law it was an offence punishable by imprisonment to hinder or prevent anyone from having a good time, and anyone who was found guilty of being a mime artist, clown, kazoo-player or theatre critic was summarily executed – and preferably as painfully as possible.

WEGGING – Don't ask. It's to do with personal hygiene and it's horrible. Believe me, you don't want to know.

YUMBLE – A breed of lap-dog engineered during the First Age by the Dark Dwarves in their necromantic laboratories deep beneath the Irridic Mountains. Yumbles have large appealing eyes, a small sweetly scented tongue, vestigial legs (so they have to be carried everywhere), and gorgeously soft long fur which automatically changes colour to match whatever outfit their owner is wearing. They live solely on chocolate, and their digestive system is so efficient that they excrete no solid matter whatsoever. They are extremely popular with the sort of elderly madwoman who writes appalling romantic fiction and wears half a ton of make-up in the mistaken belief that this in some way improves her looks.

APPENDIX TWO

MULAMPOS

There have been numerous enquiries from interested readers about this fiery Southern dish. For those who like to live dangerously (or are tired of living), here is the recipe. It is taken from Theo Dikfly's definitive *Through the Eye of a Needle – Atrovian Cookery for Beginners*, available from Succubi Publications (Ilex) Ltd, priced at 8 *tablons*.

ATROVIAN SPICE MIX
You will need:

4 tablespoons cumin seeds
12 dried *anthia* fronds
3 teaspoons black peppercorns
3 teaspoons cardamon seeds
7.5cm cinnamon stick, crushed
4 teaspoons black mustard seeds
3 teaspoons *valdian poppy* seeds

(Note – if *anthia* is unavailable, use 12 dried red chillies, and fenugreek seeds can be used in place of *valdian poppy* seeds.)

Put spices in a heavy-based frying pan and fry over a medium heat for 5–10 minutes, stirring, until browned. Cool, then grind to a fine powder with mortar and pestle. Store for up to two months.

(Warning – like chillies, *anthia* should be handled with care. After handling, wash your hands immediately, and be careful not to touch your eyes, lips or private bits until you have. Or anyone else's private bits, for that matter.)

MULAMPOS – *Serves 4*
You will need:

750g boneless *alaxl* leg
6 tablespoons vegetable oil

2 *happy-onions*, finely sliced
10 teaspoons Atrovian spice mix (see above)
60ml white wine vinegar
1 teaspoon soft brown sugar
2.5cm fresh *taboghee* root, grated
6 cloves garlic, crushed
1 teaspoon turmeric
1 teaspoon paprika
1 teaspoon ground coriander
1 *taboghee* flower, to garnish

(Note – if you have difficulty in obtaining fresh *alaxl* meat, pork can be used instead, and root ginger makes an acceptable substitute for *taboghee* root. If *happy-onions* are unavailable or illegal, normal onions can be used, but they aren't anything like as much fun to cut up.)

Wipe the *alaxl* leg and cut into 2.5cm cubes. Heat half the oil in a heavy-based pan, add onions and cook for 10 minutes or until brown and crisp, stirring constantly. Remove with slotted spoon and set aside.

Mix together vinegar, sugar, *taboghee* root, Atrovian spice mix, garlic, turmeric, paprika and coriander, blending to a smooth paste. Add remaining oil to pan and fry *alaxl* meat until slightly browned, then remove with slotted spoon and set aside.

Add spice mixture to pan and cook, stirring, for 2–3 minutes. Return meat and any juices to pan. Stir in 250ml water and bring to the boil, then simmer, covered, for 45 minutes. Stir in three-quarters of the onion and cook for a further 15–30 minutes, until *alaxl* meat is tender and cooked through.

Serve hot, garnished with remaining onions and the *taboghee* flower.

Next Day – You will need:

Two toilets
Eight rolls of toilet paper
Two industrial-strength room deodoriser sprays
Very tolerant neighbours